I had forgotten to close my curtain, which I usually did.

As a result, when the full, bright moon came to shine directly through my window, I awakened. I opened my eyes to see the silver-white disk gazing at me. However beautiful it was, it disturbed my sleep. I half rose and put my hand out to draw the curtain.

Good God! What a cry!

The silence of the night was ripped in half by a savage, shrill scream that echoed from one end of Thornfield to the other.

My pulse stopped; my heart stood still; my outstretched arm was paralyzed. The cry died away, but now over me—yes, in the room just above mine—I heard a struggle. A half-smothered voice shouted, "Help! help! help! Rochester! For God's sake, come!"

A Note about *Jane Eyre*

The action in *Jane Eyre* takes place in England, in the early 1800s. At that time, it made a great deal of difference what social class a person was born into. As *Jane Eyre* begins, little Jane is an orphan being brought up in her late uncle's home. Her uncle's family is considered upper-class, but Jane, whose father was a poor minister, is of a lower social class than her cousins.

Jane will later find work as a governess (a kind of live-in tutor for a child) in the home of an upper-class gentleman, Mr. Rochester. As a governess, Jane is considered higher in class than an ordinary servant. But even though she is intelligent and well-educated, she is not considered an equal to Mr. Rochester or his friends (many of whom have inherited titles such as Lord and Lady). Even though Jane and Mr. Rochester soon become good friends, the people around them do not expect them to have a relationship other than that of a master and servant. Much of the drama in *Jane Eyre* has to do with Jane's determination to earn the respect of the "higher-born" people around her.

CHARLOTTE BRONTË

JANE EYRE

**Edited, with an Afterword,
by Beth Johnson**

TP THE TOWNSEND LIBRARY

JANE EYRE

TP THE TOWNSEND LIBRARY

For more titles in the Townsend Library,
visit our website: **www.townsendpress.com**

All new material in this edition is
copyright © 2003 by Townsend Press.
Printed in the United States of America

0 9 8 7 6 5 4 3 2

Illustrations © 2003 by Hal Taylor

Townsend Press, Inc.
439 Kelley Drive
West Berlin, New Jersey 08091
cs@townsendpress.com

ISBN-13: 978-1-59194-009-8
ISBN-10: 1-59194-009-5

Library of Congress Control Number:
2003100037

Chapter 1

It wasn't possible to take a walk that day. We had been outside for an hour in the morning, but now the cold winter wind was blowing and a hard rain was falling. Going outdoors again was out of the question.

I was glad that it was raining. I never liked long walks, especially on chilly afternoons. I hated coming home with cold hands and feet. I hated being scolded by Bessie, the nanny. And I hated feeling worthless compared to the other children: Eliza, John, and Georgiana Reed.

Eliza, John, and Georgiana now were gathered around their mother in the living room. Mrs. Reed lay on a sofa by the fireplace. For once, her darlings were not arguing or crying, and she looked perfectly happy.

Mrs. Reed had sent me away from the group. "I'm sorry to have to send you away," she had said, "but until Bessie tells me that you are trying to become a more pleasant child, you don't deserve to join us."

"What does Bessie say I have done?" I had asked.

"Jane, I don't like complainers or questioners. Besides, a child should not talk back to an adult like

1

that. Go sit somewhere, and until you can speak pleasantly, be quiet."

I slipped into the dining room, which was next to the living room. It contained a bookcase, so I helped myself to a book, being careful to choose one with pictures. I climbed onto the window seat and sat there cross-legged. Once I closed the curtain that hid the window seat, I was nearly invisible.

I couldn't see anything on my right except the red curtain. But to my left were clear panes of glass, protecting me from the dreary November day. Sometimes, instead of looking at my book, I stared out into the wintry afternoon. In the distance I could see nothing but mist and cloud. Nearby, heavy rain swept over the lawn and bushes.

I returned to my book, a history of British birds. I was not interested in the subject. But there were some illustrations that fascinated me. They showed far-off places that stirred my imagination:

Norway's coast, Lapland's cold shores, Siberia, the Arctic. The illustrations mixed with strange, shadowy pictures that formed in my childish mind. I saw a haunted churchyard; ships attacked by sea monsters; a terrible, black-horned thing that was too scary to think about. These thoughts were as interesting as the stories that Bessie sometimes told us on winter evenings. When she was in a good mood, she would let us sit around her as she did her ironing, and she would tell us tales of love and adventure.

With the book on my knee, I was happy—as happy, at least, as I ever was. I hoped that I would not be interrupted. But then the dining-room door opened.

"Boo! Madam Mope!" John Reed cried. Then he paused. He thought that the room was empty. "Where the dickens is she?" he continued. "Lizzy! Georgy!" he called to his sisters. "Jane is not here. Tell Mother that she has run out into the rain, the bad animal!"

"It is good that I closed the curtain," I thought. I hoped very much that he wouldn't find me. And he wouldn't have found me (because he was not very bright) if Eliza hadn't poked her head into the doorway and said, "She is in the window seat, John."

I came out immediately because I did not like the idea of being dragged out by John. "What do you want?" I asked.

"Say, 'What do you want, Master Reed?'" John

answered. "I want you to come here." Seating himself in an armchair, he waited for me to come stand before him.

John Reed was fourteen years old, and I was only ten. He was tall and heavy for his age, with a nasty, pasty complexion. He stuffed himself at every meal, which made him feel sick and gave him dull eyes and flabby cheeks. He should have been away at boarding school, but his mother had taken him out. She had said that he needed to rest for a month or two "on account of his delicate health." The school principal had told her that what John needed was less cake and candy. But Mrs. Reed didn't believe it. According to her, John looked unhealthy because he had studied too much and had been homesick.

John did not like his mother or sisters much, and he absolutely hated me. He bullied and punished me, not just two or three times a week but constantly. I was terrified of him, and there was no one I could turn to for help. The servants did not like to offend their young master by speaking up for me. Mrs. Reed was blind and deaf on the subject. She seemed to never see him hit me or hear him abuse me, even though he did it right in front of her. He did it even more often behind her back.

I always obeyed John. I came up to his chair, and he stuck out his tongue at me so far that I thought it might fall out. I knew he soon would hit me. While waiting for the blow, I thought about how disgusting and ugly he looked. Maybe he could tell what I was thinking because all at once, without speaking, he struck me hard. I nearly fell. Once I regained my balance, I stepped away from his chair. "That is for speaking so rudely to Mother," he said, "and for sneaking behind curtains, and for the look in your eyes just now, you rat!" I was so used to John's abuse that I never thought of saying anything back to him. I only worried about when he would hit me again. "What were you doing behind the curtain?" he asked.

"I was reading."

"Show me the book." I returned to the window seat and got it. "You have no business taking our books," he said. "You are a charity case, Mother says. You have no money; your father didn't leave you any. You shouldn't be allowed to live here with a gentleman's children and eat the same meals that we do, and wear clothes our mother has to pay for. I'll teach you to take my books. They are mine. The whole house belongs to me, or it will in a few years. Go and stand by the door, away from the mirror and windows."

I did what he told me, not understanding what he was going to do. But when I saw him lift the book to throw it at me, I tried to jump out of the way. I was not quick enough. The book hit me and I fell, striking my head against the door and cutting it. The cut bled; the pain was sharp. Suddenly I was not afraid anymore. My anger was too strong. "You wicked, cruel boy!" I cried. "You are like a murderer! You are like a slave driver! You are like the

Roman emperors!" I had read a book about Rome and its cruel, evil emperors. I had thought then that they sounded like John, but I never had expected to say such a thing out loud.

"What? What?" he cried. "Did she say that to me? Did you hear her, Eliza and Georgiana? I'll tell Mother! But first . . ." He ran straight at me. I felt him grab my hair and my shoulder. In that moment I really saw him as a tyrant, a murderer. I felt a drop or two of blood from my head trickle down my neck, and my pain overcame my fear of him. I fought back as never before. I don't remember exactly what I did with my hands, but he called me "Rat! Rat!" and bellowed.

Help arrived quickly. Eliza and Georgiana had run for Mrs. Reed, who now came upon the scene, followed by Bessie and Mrs. Reed's maid, Miss Abbot. We were pulled apart. I heard the words "Dear, dear! What an awful girl to fly at Master John! Did anybody ever see such a temper!" Then Mrs. Reed ordered, "Take her away to the red room, and lock her in there." Four hands immediately seized me, and I was forced upstairs.

Chapter 2

I struggled all the way up the stairs. I never had resisted before, so Bessie and Miss Abbot were shocked. I think I was almost out of my mind. I knew that I was in deep trouble for striking back at John. I already was doomed; so, like any other rebel slave, I was going to fight for all I was worth.

"Hold her arms, Miss Abbot. She's like a mad cat."

"For shame! For shame!" Miss Abbot cried. "What shocking behavior, Miss Eyre, to strike a young gentleman, Mrs. Reed's son! He is your young master."

"Master? How is he my master? Am I a servant?" I cried.

"No, you are less than a servant because you do nothing to earn your keep. There, sit down, and think over your wickedness."

By this time they had gotten me into the red room, as Mrs. Reed had ordered. They forced me to sit down on a stool. I shot back up like a spring, but their two pairs of hands stopped me at once. "If you don't sit still, you'll have to be tied down," Bessie said. "Miss Abbot, lend me your belt; she would break mine." Miss Abbot began to take off the requested belt.

The shameful idea of being strapped down took the fight out of me. "Don't take it off!" I cried. "I won't move." To show that I meant it, I grabbed the stool with both my hands.

"Be sure that you don't," Bessie said. When she saw that I really was calming down, she let me go. Then she and Miss Abbot stood with folded arms, looking at me doubtfully. They seemed to be wondering if I'd gone crazy. "She never acted like this before," Bessie finally said, turning to Miss Abbot.

"I'm not surprised, though," Miss Abbot replied. "I've often told the missis my opinion about the child, and the missis has agreed with me. She's an underhanded little thing. I never saw a girl of her age with such a sneaky expression."

Bessie didn't answer, but then she spoke to me. "You have to remember, Miss, that you owe a lot to Mrs. Reed. She lets you live here. If she sent you away, you would have to go to the poorhouse." I had nothing to say in reply. Bessie's remarks were not new to me. For as long as I could remember, people had been reminding me that I was an orphan living on charity. The words hurt, but after all this time, I only half listened to them.

Now Miss Abbot joined in. "And you shouldn't think that you're equal to the Misses Reed and Master Reed just because their mother kindly allows you to be brought up with them. They will have a great deal of money, and you will have none. You should be humble and try to get along with them."

"We're telling you this for your own good," Bessie added, more gently. "You really should try to be useful and pleasant. Then, perhaps, you'll be allowed to stay here. But if you become bad-tempered and rude, the missis will send you away, I am sure."

"Besides," Miss Abbot said to Bessie, "God will punish her. He might strike her dead in the middle of a tantrum, and then where would she go? Come, Bessie, let's go. I wouldn't be her for anything. Say your prayers, Miss Eyre, when we are gone. If you don't ask for forgiveness, God might let something bad come down the chimney and take you away."

They went, shutting the door and locking it behind them. I was in a large bedroom. It hardly ever was slept in, except when there were so many visitors at Gateshead Hall that it had to be used. Yet it was one of the largest and most impressive bedrooms in the mansion. There was a huge bed made of dark mahogany, with red curtains all around it. The two large windows also were hung with red draperies. The carpet was red, the table at the foot of the bed was covered with a crimson cloth, and the walls were painted a soft pink. The tables and chairs were mahogany, like the bed. In the middle of all this deep, dark color, the white sheets, bedspread, and piled-up pillows made the bed stand out vividly. Also very noticeable was a roomy white easy chair with a footstool in front of it. I thought that it looked like a throne.

This room was chilly because it seldom had a fire. It was silent because it was far from the playroom and kitchen. It was solemn because people rarely entered it. Its only visitors were a housemaid who came in on Saturdays to dust and Mrs. Reed herself. Mrs. Reed sometimes came in to look into a certain dresser drawer where she kept some papers, her jewel box, and a small picture of her dead husband. In that picture lay the secret of the red room, why it was rarely used even though it was so handsome: Mr. Reed had died in this room nine years before. From that day, the room had been off limits.

I wondered if Bessie and Miss Abbot truly had locked the door. When I finally dared to move, I checked to see. They had. I was locked in as tightly as any prisoner. Returning to my seat, I passed a mirror and glanced at my reflection. Against all the cold darkness of the room, the little white-faced figure that stared back at me seemed ghostly and strange. I thought it looked like one of the imps or fairies that sometimes appeared in Bessie's stories. I shivered and sat down again.

As I sat, I thought about my situation. I remembered all of John Reed's cruelty, the way his sisters ignored me, and how Mrs. Reed disliked me. "Why?" I asked myself. Why did they all hate me? They didn't hate Eliza, even though she was stubborn and selfish. Georgiana was spoiled and cruel, but everyone loved her. She was a beauty, and her golden curls and pink cheeks seemed to make up for all her faults. No one ever criticized or punished John, even though he killed the pigeons and peacock chicks, let the dogs chase the sheep, and deliberately ruined many plants in the garden. He called his mother "old girl" and made fun of her. He never obeyed her, yet she called him "my own darling." I didn't do anything bad. I did everything that I was told, yet I was the one called naughty, rude, and sneaky.

My head still ached and bled from John's attack, but nobody had scolded him. When I had turned on him to keep him from hurting me more, everyone had called me a wicked girl. "Unfair! Unfair!" I thought. I searched my mind for a solution. Perhaps I would run away. If I couldn't do that, maybe I would refuse to eat or drink and let myself die.

How upset I was that afternoon! As long as I thought, I could not see any answer to the question, "Why am I so disliked?" Today, many years later, I see the reason clearly: I was an intruder at Gateshead Hall. I was completely different from anyone else who lived there; I had nothing in common with Mrs. Reed or her children. They didn't love me, and I didn't love them. Why would they even like me? I was unlike them, and I was useless to them. There was nothing about me that made me welcome. I know now that if I had been a clever, cheerful, playful child, they would have been happier to have me around, even if I was poor and dependent on them.

Daylight was fading. The rain still was beating on the windows, and the wind howled. As the room grew darker and colder, I grew more depressed. Everyone said that I was wicked. Maybe I was. Hadn't I just been thinking about starving myself to death? Surely that was a bad thing to do. Did I really think that the cemetery at Gateshead Church would be a pleasant home? Mr. Reed was buried in that cemetery. I could not remember him, but I knew that he had been my uncle, my mother's brother. He had brought me, as an orphaned baby, to the house. In his final hours he had made Mrs. Reed promise to bring me up as one of her own children. Mrs. Reed probably thought that she had kept her promise. I had to admit that she had, in a way. It must have been hard for her to have this strange, unwanted child suddenly and permanently attached to her family.

Just then a strange thought came to me. I believed that if Mr. Reed had been alive, he would have been kind to me. Now, as I sat looking at the red room's dark, shadowy walls, I began to remember things I had heard about the dead. Didn't they say that when a man's last wishes are not obeyed, he cannot rest easy in his grave? Didn't such ghosts sometimes rise to make things right? What if Mr. Reed's spirit appeared before me, here in this room? I dried my tears and tried to sob more quietly, terrified that Mr. Reed would hear and come to comfort me. Although his intentions would be kind, I was horrified at the idea of such a visit.

I tried to get control of myself, to shake off my fear. I looked around the dark room to assure myself that no ghostly visitor had arrived. At that moment a gleam of light appeared on the wall. Was it, I wondered, moonlight coming through the curtains? No; moonlight didn't move, and this did. While I watched, it glided up the wall and across the ceiling, where it quivered above my head. Now I realize that it probably was the light from a lantern someone was carrying across the yard, but in my emotional, nervous condition, I was sure that it was a sign from another world. My heart beat so loudly that it filled my ears with sound, which I thought was the rushing of wings. Something seemed to be near me. I could not stand it any longer. I rushed to the door and shook the handle with all my might.

Steps came running down the hall, the key turned, and Bessie and Miss Abbot came in. "Miss Eyre, are you ill?" Bessie asked.

"What a dreadful noise! It went quite through me!" Miss Abbot exclaimed.

"Take me out! Take me out!" I shrieked.

"Why? Are you hurt? Have you seen something?" Bessie demanded.

"I saw a light, and I thought that a ghost would come," I sobbed. I now had taken hold of Bessie's hand; she did not snatch it from me.

"She screamed on purpose," Miss Abbot declared in some disgust. "And what a scream! If she had been in great pain, I would excuse it, but she only wanted to bring us here. I know her naughty tricks."

"What is all this?" another voice demanded. Mrs. Reed came along the hallway, her cap flying and her gown rustling. "Abbot and Bessie, I believe I gave orders that Jane Eyre should be left in the red room until I let her out myself."

"Miss Jane screamed so loud, ma'am," Bessie pleaded.

"Let go of Bessie's hand, child," Mrs. Reed said. "You cannot get out so easily, I promise you. I cannot bear insincerity, particularly in children. It is my duty to show you that tricks will do you no good. You now will stay here an extra hour, and I will let you out then only if you are perfectly obedient and quiet."

"Oh, Aunt, have pity!" I cried. "Forgive me! I cannot bear it. Let me be punished some other way! I will be killed if . . ."

"Silence! All this emotion is disgusting," she said. And I'm sure she truly was disgusted with me. She thought that I was a mere actress. To her, I was a mixture of bad temper, mean spirit, and dangerous two-facedness.

Bessie and Miss Abbot had left us. Without another word, Mrs. Reed, impatient with my wails and wild sobs, pushed me back into the room and locked the door. I heard her walk away. Soon after she was gone, I must have had some sort of fit. I became unconscious.

Chapter 3

The next thing that I remember is waking up and feeling as if I'd had a nightmare. In front of me was something glowing and red. I heard voices, but I couldn't understand what they were saying. Someone's gentle hands were helping me to sit up in bed. My confusion began to clear. I found that I was in my own bed and that the red glare was only the fire in the fireplace. It was nighttime. Bessie stood at the foot of my bed, and a man sat in a chair beside me. I recognized the man as Dr. Lloyd, a physician who sometimes came to the house.

"Well, who am I?" he asked me. I answered with his name and held out my hand to him. He took my hand, smiled, and told me that I would feel better soon. Then he told Bessie to watch me carefully and not let anyone bother me. He added that he would come again the next day, and he left.

I felt sad once he was gone. Something about him made me feel safe and protected, but that feeling left with him.

"Do you think that you can sleep now, Miss?" Bessie asked softly.

I was afraid to answer her because I thought that she soon would begin to scold me. But I said, "I will try."

"Would you like something to drink, or could you eat something?"

"No, thank you, Bessie."

"Then I think that I will go to bed because it is past midnight. But you may call me if you want anything during the night," she said.

She was so polite! Her kindness made me feel brave enough to ask, "Bessie, what is the matter with me? Am I ill?"

"You became sick in the red room, probably from crying so hard," she said. "I'm sure you'll be better soon."

Bessie went into the maid's room next door. I heard her say, "Sarah, come and sleep in Miss Jane's room with me tonight. I don't want to be alone with the poor child. She might die. I wonder what she saw in there! The missis really was too hard on her."

Sarah came back with her. They both went to bed, but they whispered together for half an hour before they went to sleep. I overheard scraps of their conversation, and I realized that they were talking about me. "Something passed her, all dressed in white, and vanished." . . . "There was a great black dog behind him." . . . "She saw a light in the churchyard just above his grave." And so on. At last Bessie and Sarah slept, and then the fire died out. I lay awake, nervous and afraid, for much of that awful night.

The next day, by noon, I was up and dressed and sat wrapped in a blanket. I felt weak and tired, but worse than that was my overwhelming sadness. I kept crying silently. I should have been happy because none of the Reeds were at home, Miss Abbot was sewing in another room, and Bessie, as she tidied up around me, spoke to me more kindly than ever before. All of these things should have added up to a paradise of peace, compared to the usual scolding and abuse. But it was no use; nothing could make me feel happy.

Bessie had been down to the kitchen, and now she brought up a piece of pie on a pretty china plate painted with birds and rosebuds. I always had loved that plate. I often had asked to be allowed to touch it, but I had been told that I didn't deserve such a privilege. Today, though, the plate was placed on my lap, and I was invited to eat the luscious slice of pie. It was too late; I was not hungry, and the painted pictures seemed strangely faded.

Bessie then asked if I wanted a book. Books always had been my favorite pastime, and I automatically asked for *Gulliver's Travels*, a story that I had read again and again. How I loved the descriptions of the foreign lands that Gulliver visited! One was filled with little people and their tiny cows, sheep, and houses; another was filled with giants and their huge dogs and cats. Yet, when Bessie placed the book into my hand, I found the story full of eerie dread and evil. I closed the book and put it on the table, beside the untouched piece of pie.

Bessie now had finished dusting and tidying the room. She took out a basket of silk and satin scraps and began making a new hat for Georgiana's doll. Meanwhile she sang a song that began, "In the days when we went gypsying, a long time ago." I had often heard the song and always had enjoyed it because Bessie had a sweet voice. But now, although her voice was sweet, I found the melody indescribably sad. To me, it sounded like a funeral song. "Oh, Miss Jane, don't cry," Bessie said when she had finished. She might as well have said to the fire, "Don't burn!" But how could she know how deeply depressed I was?

Then Dr. Lloyd came again. "Well, you're already up!" he said as he walked in. "How is she, Bessie?"

Bessie answered that I was doing very well.

"Then she should look more cheerful. Come here, Miss Jane. Your name is Jane, is it not?"

"Yes, sir. Jane Eyre."

"Well, you have been crying, Miss Jane Eyre. Can you tell me why? Are you in pain?"

"No, sir."

"She's probably crying because she could not go out with the others in the carriage," Bessie said.

"Surely not!" Dr. Lloyd said. "She is too old to cry about such a silly thing."

I thought so too, and I was insulted by Bessie's suggestion. I answered, "I never cried about such a thing in my life. I hate going out in the carriage. I cry because I am miserable."

"Oh, for shame, Miss!" Bessie said.

The good doctor seemed a little puzzled. He

looked at me very steadily. His face was not handsome, but there was something pleasant and wise about it. Finally, he asked, "What made you ill yesterday?"

"She had a fall," Bessie said.

"She fell? That's like a baby again!" he said. "Can't she manage to walk at her age? She must be eight or nine years old."

"I was knocked down," I blurted out, my pride hurt again. "But that did not make me ill."

Dr. Lloyd reached into his pocket for his pipe. He took a long time filling it with tobacco and finally lighting it. As he finished, a loud bell rang for the servants' dinner. He knew what it was. "That's for you, Bessie," he said. "You go along. I'll give Miss Jane a lecture until you come back."

Bessie didn't want to go, but she knew that she did not have a choice.

"All right now. The fall did not make you ill. What really happened?" Dr. Lloyd asked as soon as Bessie was out of hearing.

"I was shut up in a room where there is a ghost," I said.

Dr. Lloyd smiled and frowned at the same time. "Ghost! You are a baby after all! You are afraid of ghosts?"

"Of Mr. Reed's ghost. He died in that room. Neither Bessie nor anyone else will go into it at night if they can help it. It was cruel to shut me up alone without even a candle, so cruel that I think I never will forget it."

"And that's all that is making you so miserable?" Dr. Lloyd asked. "Are you afraid now, in the daylight?"

"No, but night will come again before long," I answered. "Besides, I am very unhappy about other things."

"What other things? Can you tell me some of them?" he asked.

I wanted very much to answer him, but it was difficult. Even when children feel something deeply, they often find it hard to put their feelings into words. After a long pause, I began to try. "For one thing, I have no father or mother, brothers or sisters," I began.

"You have a kind aunt and cousins," he answered.

Again I paused, then clumsily continued, "John Reed knocked me down, and my aunt shut me up in the red room."

Dr. Lloyd puffed on his pipe for a few moments. "Don't you think that Gateshead Hall is a very beautiful house?" he asked. "Aren't you thankful to have such a fine place to live?"

"It is not my house, sir," I said. "And people say that I don't have any right to be here."

"But surely you can't be silly enough to wish to leave such a splendid place?" he asked.

"If I had anywhere else to go, I would be glad to leave," I said. "But I can't leave Gateshead until I am grown up."

"Well, perhaps you could leave. Who knows?"

he said. "Don't you have any relatives besides Mrs. Reed?"

"I don't think so, sir."

"None on your father's side?"

"I don't know," I answered. "I asked my aunt once, and she said that I might have some Eyre relatives, but she didn't know anything about them."

"If you did have some, would you like to go live with them?" he asked.

I thought about that, but being poor seemed terrible to me. I didn't know then that there were hard-working, respectable people who didn't have much money. To me, being poor meant being dirty, cold, and hungry. "No, I wouldn't want to live with poor people," I finally said.

"Not even if they were kind to you?" he asked.

I shook my head. I could not imagine poor people being kind. Living with them, I thought, would mean asking for pennies on the street. As much as I hated Gateshead, I would not trade it for a life like that.

"But are your relatives so very poor? Aren't they working people?" Dr. Lloyd asked.

"I don't know. My aunt says that if I have any relatives, they must all be beggars. I do not want to be a beggar."

"Would you like to go to school?"

This was something new to think about. I hardly knew what school was. I knew that John Reed hated his school, but I was nothing like John. Bessie sometimes talked about the family she had lived with before coming to Gateshead. The young ladies of that family went to school. They spoke French, sang, played the piano, and painted beautiful pictures. I envied them. Besides, school would be a complete change, and it would take me away from Gateshead. "Yes, I would like to go to school," I announced.

"Well, well! Who knows what might happen?" Dr. Lloyd said as he got up. "A change would do you good, certainly."

Just then Bessie returned. At the same moment, we heard a carriage rolling up the driveway. "Is that Mrs. Reed coming home?" Dr. Lloyd asked. "I would like to speak to her before I go." He and Bessie left the room.

I heard later that Dr. Lloyd recommended to Mrs. Reed that she send me away to school. Apparently she liked the idea because I heard Miss Abbot tell Bessie later, when she thought I was asleep, "The missis will be glad to get rid of such a tiresome, sneaky child."

During that overheard conversation, I learned more. Miss Abbot told Bessie that my father had been a poor preacher and that my mother's wealthy family had not wanted my mother to marry him. My mother's father, my grandfather Reed, had been so angry that he had cut my mother off without a penny. Then, only a year after my parents' wedding, my father caught a fever while he was visiting some poor members of his congregation. My mother caught it from him, and within a month they both were dead.

Bessie sighed when she heard this sad story. "Poor Miss Jane. I pity her, Abbot."

"Yes," Miss Abbot responded. "If she were a nice, pretty child, I might feel sorry for her too. But you really can't care about a little toad like that."

"Not very much, it's true," Bessie agreed. "Just imagine how pitiful a beauty like Miss Georgiana would be in the same situation."

"Yes, I am crazy about Miss Georgiana!" Abbot cried. "That little darling! With her long curls, and her blue eyes, and her cheeks so pink, she looks like a little painted doll. Bessie, I am hungry. Isn't supper ready?"

"I believe so, and I'm hungry too. Come, we'll go down." And they went.

Chapter 4

From my conversation with Dr. Lloyd, and from what I'd overheard Bessie and Miss Abbot say, I thought that I would be leaving Gateshead soon. That idea gave me hope, and I began to get better. But days and weeks went by, and no one said a word about my going to school.

Mrs. Reed was colder than ever. She hardly ever spoke to me, and she did everything she could to keep me away from her children. I ate my meals alone and spent my days in the bedroom while her children were with her in the living room. Still, I believed that she would send me away. Why would she keep me in her house when she clearly disliked me so?

Following their mother's orders, Eliza and Georgiana spoke to me as little as possible. John stuck out his tongue whenever he saw me. Once, he tried to hit me, but I instantly turned on him with all the hatred that I had felt during our last encounter. He ran away, screaming that I had broken his nose. I had hit him pretty hard, and I had wanted to hit him again, but in no time he had gone to his mother. I heard him blubbering how "that nasty Jane Eyre" had attacked him like a mad cat. But his mother stopped him rather harshly.

"Don't talk to me about her, John. I told you not to go near her," she said. "Don't pay any attention to her. I don't want either you or your sisters associating with her."

When I heard that, I leaned over the banister and shouted, without thinking, "They don't deserve to associate with me!"

Mrs. Reed was a heavy woman, but when she heard my words, she ran up the stairs and, like a whirlwind, swept me into my tiny bedroom. Forcing me down onto the bed, she ordered me to stay there and not say a single word for the rest of the day.

Again, words burst out of me without my permission. "What would Uncle Reed say to you if he were alive?" I demanded.

"What?" Mrs. Reed asked in great surprise. Her usually cold, calm gray eyes took on a fearful look. She snatched her hand from my arm, and she stared at me as if she really did not know whether I was a child or a devil.

I knew I was in for it now, but I went on. "My Uncle Reed is in heaven, and he can see everything that you do and think," I said. "So can my papa and mama. They know how you shut me up all day and how you wish I were dead."

That was enough to get Mrs. Reed over her shock. She shook me and slapped my face, then left me without a word.

Then Bessie supplied all the words that Mrs. Reed hadn't said. She lectured me for a full hour, telling me that I was a wicked and ungrateful child. I half believed her because the only feelings in my heart right then were bad ones.

November, December, and half of January passed. Christmas and the New Year had been celebrated at Gateshead with the usual presents and parties. Of course, I had not taken part in the holiday celebrations. All I had been allowed to do was watch Eliza and Georgiana put on their party dresses and have their hair curled and arranged. During a party I would sit at the top of the stairs, where I could hear the piano or harp being played, the hurrying of the servants, the jingle of glass and china, and the broken hum of conversation as the living room door opened and closed. Whenever I got tired of this, I would go to my silent room, where I felt sad but not miserable.

To tell the truth, I didn't want to attend the Reeds' parties, where I would have been ignored. If Bessie had kept me company, I would have liked to spend party evenings quietly with her. But as soon as she had dressed the other girls, Bessie would go to the kitchen to gossip with the other servants, and she usually took the room's only candle with her. I then would sit playing with my doll until the fire burned low, glancing around nervously to make sure that no ghosts were coming to join me. When the fire burned out, I would quickly get undressed and jump into bed, hiding under the covers from the cold and dark. I always took my doll with me. I think that people need something to love, and I cared deeply for the little doll, although it was as shabby as a scarecrow. I pretended that it was alive and had feelings. When I wrapped it carefully in my nightgown, I imagined that it was happy, and I felt happier because of this.

The hours that I would lie there waiting for the guests to go home were long ones. I would listen anxiously for the sound of Bessie coming up the stairs. Sometimes she would come in to look for her thimble or scissors, and sometimes she would bring me a snack. Then she would sit on the bed while I ate it, and when I had finished, she would tuck me in and say goodnight. Twice she kissed me. When Bessie was gentle like this, I thought she was the best, prettiest, kindest person in the world.

When I remember Bessie Lee now, I remember her as an intelligent, capable young woman who had a gift for storytelling. She was pretty, too: slim, with black hair, dark eyes, and a lovely complexion. Certainly she had a quick temper and was not always fair, but she was by far my favorite person at Gateshead Hall.

It was January fifteenth, about nine o'clock in the morning. Bessie had gone down to breakfast, and my cousins had not yet been called to join their mama. Eliza was putting on her hat and warm coat to go and feed her chickens. She enjoyed that task because she was allowed to sell the eggs that she gathered. Eliza liked money; she would have sold the hair off her head if anyone had wanted to buy it. Georgiana sat in front of the mirror, tying into her hair some artificial flowers and feathers that she had found in the attic.

I was dusting the room and making my bed because Bessie had ordered me to have the room straightened up before she returned. When I finished that job, I went to the window seat to tidy up some books and doll's furniture scattered there. But Georgiana ordered me not to touch her playthings. Having nothing else to do, I started breathing on the frost-covered window to clear a space to see through. As I looked across the yard, the gates opened and a carriage drove through. I didn't care; visitors to Gateshead had nothing to do with me. I was more interested in a hungry little robin hopping about on the twigs of a bare tree near the window. I crumbled the last of my breakfast toast and was trying to open the window to put the crumbs onto the windowsill when Bessie hurried into the room.

"Miss Jane, take off your apron. What are you doing there? Have you washed your hands and face yet?" I gave another tug before I answered because I wanted the bird to have the bread. The window opened, and I threw out the crumbs. Closing the window, I replied, "No, Bessie; I have just finished dusting."

"You troublesome, careless child! Why were you opening the window?" Bessie was in too much of a hurry to wait for an answer. She hauled me to the washstand, scrubbed my hands and face, hastily brushed my hair, took off my apron, and told me to rush downstairs because Mrs. Reed wanted me in the breakfast room. I would have asked why, but Bessie already was gone.

I slowly walked downstairs. It had been nearly three months since Mrs. Reed had asked me to come see her for any reason. Now I felt afraid to go. I stood in the empty hall outside the breakfast room for ten minutes, too scared to enter. But when I heard Mrs. Reed impatiently ringing the bell that she kept with her, I knew I had to go in.

As I hesitantly walked into the room, a black pillar rose in front of me. At first it looked like a black pillar. In fact, it was a very tall man, dressed entirely in black, with a grim face like a carved mask. Mrs. Reed was sitting in her usual chair by the fireplace. She pointed in my direction and said to the solemn stranger, "This is the little girl I was telling you about."

The man turned to look at me. He spoke in a deep bass voice. "She is small. How old is she?"

"Ten," Mrs. Reed answered.

"That old?" he said in surprise. Then he spoke to me. "What is your name, little girl?"

"Jane Eyre, sir."

"Well, Jane Eyre," he said, "are you a good child?"

There was no way to answer this question. Everyone in my little world said that I was not. Mrs. Reed answered for me by shaking her head and saying, "Perhaps the less said about that, the better, Mr. Brocklehurst."

"Indeed! I am sorry to hear this," Mr. Brocklehurst said. "Then she and I must have a little talk." He sat in the armchair near Mrs. Reed's. "Come here," he told me. I stepped nearer to him and gazed into his face, marveling at his enormous nose and large, prominent teeth. "There is no sight as sad as a naughty child," he began, "especially a naughty little girl. Do you know where wicked people go after they die?"

"They go to hell," I answered promptly.

"And what is hell? Can you tell me that?" Mr. Brocklehurst asked.

"It is a pit full of fire," I said.

"Quite right," Mr. Brocklehurst said. "Would you like to fall into that pit and burn there forever?"

"No, sir," I said.

"What must you do to make sure that does not happen?" he asked.

I thought for a moment and then gave this answer: "I must stay healthy and not die."

Mr. Brocklehurst's eyebrows shot up. "How can you keep healthy and never die?" he thundered. "Children younger than you die every day. Only two days ago I was at the funeral of a good little child who was only five years old. Her soul is now in heaven. I am afraid you would not go to heaven if you were to die now." I stared down at his large feet, not knowing what to say. "Do you say your prayers each morning and night?" he continued.

"Yes, sir."

"Do you read the Bible?"

"Sometimes."

"Do you read it with pleasure? Are you fond of it?"

"I like Revelation, and the book of Daniel, and Genesis and Samuel, and a little bit of Exodus, and some parts of Kings and Chronicles, and Job and Jonah," I explained.

"And the Psalms? I hope you like them?" he asked.

"No, sir," I answered honestly.

"No? Oh, that is shocking! I know a little boy, younger than you, who can say six psalms by heart. When you ask him which he would rather have, a cookie to eat or a verse of a psalm to learn, he says,

'Oh! The verse of a psalm! Angels sing psalms. I want to be a little angel here below.' Then I give him two cookies for being so good."

"Psalms are not interesting," I remarked.

"That proves you have a wicked heart," Mr. Brocklehurst announced. "You must pray to God to take away your heart of stone and give you a heart of flesh."

I was about to ask him just how God might go about that operation when Mrs. Reed interrupted, telling me to sit down. "Mr. Brocklehurst, as I told you in my letter, this little girl has a bad character and temper. If you accept her at Lowood Institution, you and the teachers must keep a very strict eye on her. Her worst fault is a tendency to tell lies. I'm telling Mr. Brocklehurst this in front of you, Jane, so that you know he has been warned."

Of all the unkind things that Mrs. Reed ever had done to me, this was the cruelest. I knew that her words would go with me to my new home, destroying the possibility of my being happy there. Mr. Brocklehurst already saw me as a deceitful, poisonous child. And what could I do to change his mind? Nothing. Anything I said would be taken as a lie. I wiped away some tears.

"That is a terrible fault in a child," Mr. Brocklehurst agreed. "All liars will be condemned to the lake of fire and brimstone. She will be watched, Mrs. Reed. I will speak to Miss Temple and to her teachers."

"And as she grows up, I don't want her given

any unrealistic ideas about her future," Mrs. Reed continued. "She should be taught to be useful and humble. And I want her to spend all her vacations at Lowood."

"That makes perfect sense, Mrs. Reed," Mr. Brocklehurst replied. "At Lowood we take special care that our students never develop the sin of pride. Only the other day my daughter Augusta happened to visit the school with her mother; later she said, 'Oh, Daddy, how quiet and plain all the girls at Lowood look! They are almost like poor people's children. They stared at my dress as if they never had seen nice clothes before.'"

"That sounds ideal," Mrs. Reed said. "If I had searched all over England, I don't think I could have found a school that is better suited to a child like Jane Eyre. I will send her to Lowood as soon as possible. As you can imagine, I am anxious to see her leave here."

"No doubt, Mrs. Reed. And now I must leave you. I will inform Miss Temple that a new student is coming."

"Goodbye, Mr. Brocklehurst. Do remember me to your dear wife and children."

"I certainly will. Little girl, here is a book called *The Child's Guide*," he said, turning to me and putting a thin book into my hand. "Be sure to read the story about Martha G., a naughty, lying child who died quite suddenly." With these words, he left.

Mrs. Reed and I were left alone. She went back

to her sewing, and I watched her silently. Every word she had said to Mr. Brocklehurst echoed in my memory. I could hardly contain the resentment that I felt. Eventually she looked up and caught my eye. Something about my look must have offended her because she said irritably, "Go back to your room now."

I got up and went to the door, but then I turned and walked back to her. I would be silent no more. "I am not a liar," I blurted out. "If I were a liar, I could say that I love you. But I do not love you. I hate you more than anyone in the world except your son John. And you should give this book about a lying child to Georgiana because she tells lies, but I don't."

She stared at me icily. "Do you have anything else to say?" she asked, more as one would speak to an adult enemy than to a child.

Her cold look made me all the more determined to have my say. I continued, "I am glad that you are not really related to me. I never again will call you Aunt as long as I live. I never will come to see you when I am grown up. And if anyone asks me how I liked you and how you treated me, I will say that the very thought of you makes me sick and that you treated me with miserable cruelty."

"How dare you say that, Jane Eyre?"

"How dare I, Mrs. Reed? Because it is the truth. You think that I don't have any feelings and that I don't need any love or kindness, but I do. You have no pity. I will remember, to my dying day, how you threw me into the red room and locked me up there. And you were punishing me because your wicked boy hit me—knocked me down for nothing. I will tell anybody who asks me exactly what happened. People think that you are a good woman, but you are bad, hard-hearted. You are the liar!" As I spoke these words, I suddenly felt the strongest sense of freedom and triumph that I ever had experienced. It was as if invisible chains around me had broken.

My words had been effective. Mrs. Reed looked frightened. Her sewing had slipped from her lap, and her face twisted as if she was going to cry. "Jane, you are mistaken. What is the matter with you? Why are you shaking so? Do you want a drink of water?" she asked.

"No, Mrs. Reed."

"Is there anything else you need, Jane? I promise you, I want to be your friend."

"You do not want to be my friend. You told Mr. Brocklehurst that I have a bad character and that I lie. I will tell everyone at Lowood what you are and what you have done."

"Jane, you don't understand," she said. "It is for your own good. Children must be corrected for their faults."

"Dishonesty is not my fault!" I cried in a savage voice.

"But you are hot-tempered, Jane. That you must admit. Now, go back to your room, my dear, and lie down a little."

"I am not your dear. I cannot lie down. Send me to school soon, Mrs. Reed, because I hate living here," I said.

"I will indeed send her to school soon," Mrs. Reed murmured as if to herself. Gathering up her sewing, she walked quickly out of the room.

I was left there alone, aware that I had won the battle. At first I felt overjoyed, but soon I began to feel sorry that I had spoken so harshly. I was only a child, and I did not know what to do with the fierce emotions that I felt. I picked up a book and tried to distract myself with it, but I could not pay attention to the words. Finally I laid the book down and walked outdoors into the cold, gray day. I leaned against a gate, feeling miserably confused.

All at once I heard a clear voice call, "Miss Jane! Where are you? Come to lunch!" It was Bessie's voice, but I did not move. After a moment she came to find me. "You naughty little thing!" she said. "Why don't you come when you are called?"

Compared with my dark thoughts, even Bessie's frowning face was a relief. After my fight with Mrs. Reed, Bessie's scolding didn't seem important. To her surprise, I put my arms around her and said, "Oh, come on, Bessie; don't scold me."

Somehow my action pleased her. "You are a strange child, Miss Jane," she said as she looked down at me. "Is it true that you are going to school?"

I nodded.

"And won't you be sorry to leave poor Bessie?" she asked.

"What does Bessie care for me? She is always scolding me," I answered.

"Well, it's because you're such a queer, frightened, shy little thing. You should be braver."

"If I were braver, I just would get more knocks," I said.

"Oh, don't be silly. But you've had a rough time of it here, it's true. When my mother came to see me last week, she said that she wouldn't want to trade places with you. But come in now. I've got some good news for you. Mrs. Reed, Master John, and the young ladies are going out this afternoon, and you and I will have tea together. I'll ask the cook to bake you a little cake, and then we'll pack your suitcase. Mrs. Reed wants you to leave Gateshead in a day or two, and you can choose which toys you want to take along."

"All right, Bessie, but you must promise not to scold me anymore until I go."

"Well, I'll try, but you must be a good girl, too. Please don't jump when I happen to speak sharply to you. It's so irritating."

"I don't think that I'll ever be afraid of you again, Bessie, because I have gotten used to you. Soon I'll have another group of people to be afraid of."

"If you're afraid of them, they'll dislike you," Bessie warned.

"As you dislike me, Bessie?"

"I don't dislike you, Miss. I think I like you better than any of the other children," she said.

"You don't show it."

"You sharp little thing! What makes you so brave today?" she asked.

"Well, soon I won't be with you anymore. Besides, . . . " I was going to say something about my scene with Mrs. Reed, but on second thought I decided it might be better to stay silent about that.

"And so, you're glad to leave me?"

"Not at all, Bessie. Actually, just now I'm rather sorry."

"'Just now I'm rather sorry!' Listen to you, sounding so cool and collected! I suppose if I asked you for a hug, you'd say, 'Just now I'd rather not.'"

"I'd like to give you a hug," I answered. Bessie bent down, and we hugged each other warmly. I followed her into the house feeling much comforted.

That afternoon was a sweet and peaceful one, and in the evening Bessie sang some of my favorite songs. Even for me, life had its sunny moments.

Chapter 5

It was four days later. Long before sunrise Bessie came to my room and found me already up and nearly dressed. I was to leave Gateshead that day by a horse-drawn coach that would pass by at 6 a.m.

Bessie was the only other person already awake. She had lit a fire, and now she made me some breakfast. But like most children when they are excited, I could not eat, even though Bessie begged me to swallow a few mouthfuls. So she wrapped up some biscuits and put them into my bag, then helped me on with my coat and hat and wrapped herself in a shawl. As she and I passed Mrs. Reed's bedroom on our way downstairs, she said, "Aren't you going to go in and say goodbye to Mrs. Reed?"

"No, I'm not," I answered. "She came to my room last night and said that I shouldn't disturb her in the morning, or my cousins either. Then she told me to remember that she always had been my best friend and to say nice things about her and be grateful to her."

"What did you say, Miss?"

"Nothing. I covered my face with the blanket and turned from her to the wall."

"That was wrong, Miss Jane."

"It was quite right, Bessie. Mrs. Reed has not

been my friend; she has been my enemy."

"Oh, Miss Jane! Don't talk like that!" she said.

"Goodbye to Gateshead!" I cried as we passed through the hall and out the front door.

The moon had set, and it was very dark. Bessie carried a lantern whose light showed the wet path underfoot. It was so raw and chilly that my teeth chattered as we hurried down the drive. It was almost six, and I heard the distant noise of the coach's wheels. Then it pulled into sight, drawn by four horses. "Hurry aboard!" the driver said. I clung to Bessie, kissing her with all my might. But my suitcase was thrown aboard, and I had to climb in after it. "Isn't anyone going with her? It's fifty miles!" the driver said.

Bessie shook her head. "Take good care of her!" she called to him.

"Yes, yes," he answered, and the door was slammed shut. With that I was separated from Bessie and Gateshead and whirled away to unknown and mysterious places.

I don't remember much about the journey. I know only that the day seemed to last forever and that we seemed to travel hundreds and hundreds of miles. We stopped in a large town and went into a restaurant for dinner. I still could not eat, though, so I was left to wait outside the dining room. The afternoon stretched into evening, and I began to feel that we were getting very far from Gateshead. We were not driving through towns anymore but passing through valleys and woods. The sound of wind and rain outside the coach finally lulled me to sleep.

I had not slept long when I awoke, aware that the coach had stopped moving. The door was open, and a woman dressed like a servant peered in at us. "Is there a little girl called Jane Eyre here?" she asked. I answered, "Yes," and was lifted out. My suitcase was handed down, and the coach instantly drove away.

I was stiff after the long trip and bewildered by the strangeness of everything around me. I followed the servant through a door and into a room with a fire. She left me there, alone. I stood warming my numb hands at the fire and looking around at the room. It was not as big or luxurious as the rooms at Gateshead, but it was nice enough.

Before I could explore further, the door opened and two women entered. The first one was a tall lady with dark hair, dark eyes, and a pale face. She looked at me carefully for a moment. "The child is very young to be sent here alone," she said. Kindly laying her hand on my shoulder, she added, "Are you tired?"

"A little, ma'am," I answered.

"She'd better be put to bed soon, Miss Miller," she said. "But give her something to eat first. Is this the first time you have left your parents to come to school, my dear?"

I explained that I had no parents. She asked me a few more questions: how old I was, how well I could read and write and sew. Then she touched my cheek gently, said she hoped that I would be a good child, and left me with Miss Miller.

Something about the first lady's appearance and voice had made me like her. The other lady, Miss Miller, seemed more ordinary. She looked overworked and as though she were always in a hurry. She was, I found out later, a teacher's assistant.

I followed Miss Miller from room to room of the large building we were in until I began to hear many voices. We entered a wide, long room filled with tables. Seated around them was a great congregation of girls, ranging in age from about nine to twenty. They seemed countless to me, although I later learned that there were about eighty of them. They were studying their schoolbooks.

Miss Miller sat me on a bench near the door and then announced, "Hall monitors, collect the books and put them away!" Four of the oldest girls rose and did as Miss Miller had told them. "Hall monitors, bring in the supper trays!" she said next. The girls went out and soon returned, carrying trays topped with a plate of biscuits, a pitcher of water, and a mug. Those who were thirsty took a drink from the mug (the girls all shared the same one). I still was too tired and excited to eat.

After the meal there were prayers. Then it was time for bed. I was too exhausted to notice what the bedroom was like, except that it was very large and filled with long rows of beds. The night passed rapidly. I was too tired even to dream. I woke up only once to hear the wind howl and the rain fall in torrents.

When I next opened my eyes, a loud bell was ringing, and the girls were up and dressing. It still was dark outside. I reluctantly climbed out of bed in the bitter cold and dressed myself, shivering. I had to wait a long time to wash because six girls shared each washstand.

The bell rang again. The girls formed a line and marched downstairs into a cold schoolroom. Miss Miller was there. She said a prayer and then called out, "Form classes!" The girls made a lot of noise as they scurried about, while Miss Miller repeatedly shouted "Silence!" and "Order!" When the noise died down, the girls had arranged themselves in four semicircles. At the head of each semicircle were a table and a chair. Another bell tinkled, and three ladies entered the room. Each walked to a table and took her seat. Miss Miller took the fourth chair, which was nearest to the door, and the youngest children sat around her. I was told to sit with this group.

Now the activities began. We started with yet more prayer, then said some verses from the Scriptures. Then there was reading of Bible chapters, which lasted a full hour.

That tiresome bell now rang for the fourth time. This time we marched into another room for breakfast. How glad I was at the prospect of getting something to eat! I was nearly sick from hunger, having eaten almost nothing the day before. The dining room was large, with a low ceiling. On two long tables were steaming pots. To my dismay, a horrible odor rose from them. I saw looks of disgust on the other students' faces. As the tall girls in the first class went to get their portions, I heard more than one of them whisper, "Disgusting! The porridge is burned again!"

"Silence!" one of the teachers barked. A long grace was said, and a hymn was sung. Then a servant brought in some tea for the teachers, and the meal began. Because I was ravenous, nearly fainting with hunger, I gulped down a spoonful or two of my portion without noticing its taste. But as my first hunger passed, I realized what a nauseating mess was in my bowl. Burned porridge is almost as bad as rotten potatoes; it's nearly impossible to be hungry enough to eat it. The spoons moved slowly. I saw each girl taste her food and try to swallow it, but in most cases the effort soon was given up. Breakfast was over, and no one's hunger was satisfied. We gave thanks for what we had not received, sang a second hymn, and returned to the schoolroom.

The teachers resumed their posts, but everyone seemed to be waiting for something. The eighty girls sat straight-backed and motionless. They looked like paper dolls, all made alike, with their hair pulled tightly back from their faces. They wore identical high-necked brown dresses, each with a removable white collar. Tied to the front of each dress was a little work-bag. Each girl wore high wool stockings and plain shoes, fastened with brass buckles. About twenty of the students were full-grown girls—actually, young women. Even the prettiest of them looked odd in this plain, childish costume.

Suddenly the whole school rose, as if moved by a common spring. Because everyone was looking in one direction, I looked too. There I saw the person who had welcomed me the previous night. She stood at the bottom of the long room, near the fireplace. The lady walked slowly up the room. Even now I remember the admiration that I felt that day. Here, in broad daylight, I saw that she was tall, fair, and shapely. Her brown eyes were filled with kindly light, and her long lashes softened her gaze. She wore her dark-brown hair in the fashion of the day, clustered in curls. Her dress also was fashionable, made of purple cloth trimmed with black velvet. Although watches were not as common then, she wore a gold one pinned to the front of her dress. To complete the picture, imagine fine, regular features; a pale, clear complexion; and a calm, dignified bearing. You will then have an idea of Miss Temple, the superintendent of Lowood.

Miss Temple took her seat before a pair of globes placed on one of the tables. She called the first class around her and began giving a geography lesson. Meanwhile, the other teachers gave history and grammar lessons for an hour. Then it was time for writing and arithmetic, and Miss Temple gave music lessons to some of the older girls.

When the clock struck twelve, Miss Temple stood and said, "I have a word to say to all of the pupils." Lessons were ended, and the girls had begun to chatter, but the noise immediately stopped. She went on. "This morning you had a breakfast that you could not eat. You must be hungry. I have ordered that a lunch of bread and cheese be served to everyone." The teachers looked at her with surprise. "I will take the responsibility," she said to them, and she left the room.

Presently the bread and cheese was brought in and handed out, to the delight of the whole hungry school. The next order was, "To the garden!" Each girl put on a straw bonnet and a gray cloak. I was given the same hat and cloak, and I followed the crowd outside.

The wide garden was surrounded by walls so high that it was impossible to look beyond them. A covered veranda ran down one side of the garden, and a middle space was divided into dozens of little flower beds. These beds were gardens for the pupils to tend; each bed had an owner. Doubtless, they would look pretty when full of flowers, but now, at the end of January, all was wintry blight and brown decay. I shuddered as I stood and looked around me. It was dark and foggy, a nasty day for outdoor exercise. The ground still was soaked from yesterday's rains. Some of the stronger girls ran about and played games. But many pale, thin ones gathered together on the veranda, for shelter and warmth; as I stood among them, our thin clothes penetrated by the cold mist, I heard frequent coughing.

I hadn't spoken to anyone yet, and no one seemed to notice me. But I was used to loneliness, so that did not bother me much. I leaned against a pillar of the veranda and drew my cloak tight around me. Trying to forget the cold that nipped me, and my still-unsatisfied hunger, I watched and thought. Then a cough behind me made me look around. I saw a girl sitting on a stone bench near me. She was bent over a book. From where I stood, I could see the title, Rasselas. The name seemed strange. Feeling my gaze, the girl looked up, and I said, "Is your book interesting?" I already had decided to ask her to lend it to me some time.

"I like it," she answered.

"What is it about?" I continued. I don't know where I found the courage to start a conversation with a stranger. It wasn't like me to do that, but seeing that she was a reader, like me, made me think that she might be friendly.

"You may look at it," the girl replied, handing me the book.

I did look and quickly decided that I liked the title better than the book itself. Rasselas looked dull to my childish taste; I saw nothing about fairies or genies, and the type was very small. I returned it to her, and she was about to start reading when I interrupted again, pointing to the writing over the door nearest to us. "Can you tell me what the name on that stone over the door means? What is Lowood Institution?"

"Here. This house where you have come to live," she answered.

"But why do they call it 'Institution'? Is it different from other schools?"

"It is partly a charity school. You and I, and all the rest of us, are charity children. Isn't your father or your mother dead?"

"Both died before I can remember," I replied.

"Well," she explained, "all the girls here have lost either one or both parents, and this is an institution for educating orphans."

"Do we pay no money? Do they keep us for nothing?"

"We pay, or our friends pay, fifteen pounds a year."

"If someone pays, why do they call us charity children?"

"Because fifteen pounds is not enough for board and teaching, so other people contribute the rest."

"What other people?" I demanded.

"Different charitable ladies and gentlemen in this neighborhood and in London."

"Does this house belong to that tall lady who said that we were to have some bread and cheese?" I asked.

"To Miss Temple? Oh, no! I wish it did. She works for Mr. Brocklehurst. He buys all of our food and supplies."

"Does he live here?"

"No. Two miles off, in a large house."

"Is he a good man?" I asked.

"He is a minister. People say that he does good works."

"Did you say that tall lady was called Miss Temple?"

"Yes."

"What are the other teachers called?"

"The one with red cheeks is Miss Smith. She supervises our sewing; we make all our own clothes. The little one with black hair is Miss Scatcherd. She teaches history and grammar. The one who wears a shawl is Madame Pierrot. She teaches French."

"Do you like the teachers?"

"Well enough. Miss Scatcherd is quick-tempered, so you must be careful with her.

Madame Pierrot is not a bad sort of person."

"But Miss Temple is the best, isn't she?"

The girl nodded. "Miss Temple is very good and very clever. She is better than all the rest."

"Have you been here long?"

"Two years."

"Are you an orphan?"

"My mother is dead."

"Are you happy here?"

"You ask too many questions. I have given you enough answers for now. I want to get back to my reading."

But at that moment the bell rang for dinner, and we re-entered the house. The odor that now filled the dining hall was only slightly more appetizing than the one that had accompanied breakfast. Dinner was served in two huge pots, from which rose a strong smell of rancid fat. The mess consisted of mushy potatoes and strange shreds of rusty meat, mixed and cooked together. A fairly large portion of this was given to each pupil. I ate what I could and wondered whether every day's meals would be like this.

After dinner we returned to the schoolroom and our lessons, which continued until five o'clock. The only thing of real interest that happened was this: the girl with whom I had been talking was sent out of history class in disgrace, by Miss Scatcherd. As her punishment for something, she had to stand alone in the middle of the large schoolroom. I thought that it was a shameful punishment, especially for such a big girl (she looked at least thirteen). I expected her to be very embarrassed, but she didn't cry or even blush. On the contrary, she seemed completely calm, even as everyone in the room stared at her. "How can she bear it so quietly?" I asked myself. "If I were in her place, I would want the earth to open and swallow me up. She is looking at the floor, but I'm sure that she does not see it. It is as if her sight has turned inward and gone down into her own heart. I wonder what sort of girl she is."

Soon after 5 p.m. we had a small mug of coffee and half a slice of brown bread. I devoured my bread and drank my coffee gratefully, but I gladly could have eaten twice as much. Then there was another thirty minutes of recreation, then study time, then a glass of water and a piece of oat cake. Finally there were prayers and then bed. Such was my first day at Lowood.

Chapter 6

The next day began as the previous one had, with getting up and dressing by candlelight. But this morning we were unable to wash because the water in the pitchers was frozen. All night a keen northeast wind had whistled through the crevices of our bedroom windows, making us shiver in our beds.

Before the long hour and a half of prayers and Bible reading ended, I felt ready to perish with cold. Breakfast came at last. This morning the porridge was not burned; it was edible, but the quantity was small. How tiny my portion seemed! I wished that it were twice as much.

During the day I was assigned to the fourth class and given regular tasks. I wasn't used to school, and the lessons seemed long and difficult. I was confused, too, by the frequent changes from one subject to another. So I was glad when Miss Smith gave me a piece of cloth, together with a needle and thread and a thimble. She sent me to sit in a quiet corner of the schoolroom, with directions to hem the cloth.

Most of the others were sewing as well, but one class still stood around Miss Scatcherd's chair reading aloud. Because the room was so quiet, it was easy to hear every girl's performance as well as

Miss Scatcherd's compliments or complaints. The subject was English history. One of the readers was the girl to whom I had talked the previous day. At first she did very well. But then she made some mistake in pronunciation. After that, Miss Scatcherd kept criticizing her: "Burns, . . ." (That, it seems, was her name. At Lowood girls were called by their last names, as boys are elsewhere.) "Burns, you are standing on the side of your shoe; straighten up immediately." "Burns, you poke your chin most unpleasantly; pull it in." "Burns, I insist that you hold your head up; I will not have you stand there like that." And so on.

The girls read through their chapter twice, then closed the books. Miss Scatcherd began to question them. The lesson had been about the reign of King Charles I, and there were many difficult questions about that time's economy and shipping. Many of the girls stumbled, but Burns answered every question perfectly. I kept expecting Miss Scatcherd to praise her. Instead she suddenly cried, "You dirty, disagreeable girl! You have not cleaned your nails this morning!" Burns did not answer. I wondered why she was silent. "Why doesn't she explain that she couldn't clean her nails or wash her face because the water was frozen?" I thought.

Just then Miss Smith asked me to help her for a few moments. As she worked, she asked me if I had been to school before and how much experience I had in sewing and knitting. I lost track of

what was going on between Burns and Miss
Scatcherd.

When I returned to my seat, Burns was leaving
the class. She returned in half a minute, carrying a
bundle of twigs tied together at one end. With a
respectful curtsey, she presented this ominous tool
to Miss Scatcherd. Then she quietly turned her back
and loosened her collar. The teacher instantly began
to strike Burns on the neck, six times, with the
bunch of twigs. Not a tear rose to Burns's eyes; her
peaceful expression did not change. But I paused in
my sewing because my fingers trembled with my
anger at this sight. "Stubborn girl!" Miss Scatcherd
exclaimed. "Nothing can correct your sloppy habits.
Put the rod away." Burns obeyed. I looked at her
hard as she returned to the room. She was just putting her handkerchief back into her pocket, and the
trace of a tear glistened on her thin cheek.

The evening recreation hour was the most
pleasant time of day at Lowood. The bit of bread
and cup of coffee that we consumed provided a little energy, even if it didn't satisfy our hunger. The
schoolroom felt warmer than in the morning, and
the girls' chatter made the world seem more cheerful. During that time I would wander alone, without feeling lonely, among the laughing groups.
Now and then, when I passed the windows, I
would lift the blind and look out. Sometimes it
would be snowing so hard that a drift would form
against the lower panes. Putting my ear close to the
window, I would hear the wind moaning outside.

If I had recently left a good home and kind parents, this probably would have been the hour when I felt most homesick. The sound of the wind would have made me sad. But as it was, the noise and strangeness of it all excited me. I wanted the wind to howl more wildly and the twilight to deepen to darkness.

I made my way to one of the fireplaces. There I found Burns, silent and absorbed in her book, which she read by the flames' dim light. "Is it still Rasselas?" I asked.

"Yes," she said. "I am just finishing it."

Five minutes later she shut the book. I was glad of this. "Now," I thought, "maybe I can get her to talk." I sat down by her on the floor. "What is your name besides Burns?"

"Helen."

"Do you come from somewhere far from here?"

"I come from a place farther north, nearly on Scotland's border."

"Will you ever go home?"

"I hope so, but nobody can be sure of the future."

"You must want to leave Lowood," I remarked.

"Why should I? I was sent to Lowood to get an education. It would be no use if I left before I did that."

I objected, "But that teacher, Miss Scatcherd, is so cruel to you!"

"Not cruel," she answered. "She is strict, though, and she dislikes my faults."

"If I were in your place, I would hate her," I said indignantly. "I would resist her. If she struck me with that rod, I would take it and break it under her nose."

"Probably you would do nothing of the sort. If you did, Mr. Brocklehurst would expel you from the school, and that would make your family unhappy. It is better to patiently endure pain than to do something that will hurt others. Besides, the Bible tells us to return good for evil."

"But it is disgraceful to be whipped and to be sent to stand in the middle of a room full of people," I said. "I could not bear it."

"But it would be your duty to bear it if you could not avoid it," she answered. "It is silly to say that you cannot bear what it is your fate to bear."

I listened to her with amazement. I could not understand this talk of endurance and forgiveness. Clearly, Helen Burns saw things differently than I did. I suspected that she might be right, but I would think about that later. "You say that you have faults, Helen. What are they? To me you seem very good."

"Then you should learn not to judge by appearances," she said. "I am, as Miss Scatcherd said, very sloppy. I don't keep my things in order. I am careless. I forget rules. I read when I should be studying. My thoughts wander during lectures. This is all very provoking to Miss Scatcherd, who is naturally very neat and punctual."

"And cross and cruel," I added. But Helen kept silent. I went on. "Is Miss Temple as strict with you as Miss Scatcherd?"

At Miss Temple's name, a soft smile crossed Helen's serious face. "Miss Temple is full of goodness. It hurts her to scold anyone, even the worst girl in the school. She sees my errors and tells me about them gently. If I do anything good, she praises me generously. But I am so full of faults that even her gentle reminders aren't enough to cure me. I still forget things and am very careless."

"When Miss Temple teaches you, do your thoughts wander?"

"No, not often. Miss Temple is generally so interesting and teaches so clearly."

"Well, then, with Miss Temple you are good!"

"In a way. I don't actually do anything; I just follow her easily. I shouldn't get credit for that kind of goodness."

"You should get credit," I argued back. "You are good to people who are good to you, and that is all that you should be. If people were kind and obedient to those who are cruel and unjust, the wicked people would have it all their own way. They never would feel afraid, so they never would change. In fact, they would grow worse and worse. When we are struck without a reason, we should strike back very hard, hard enough to teach the person who struck us never to do it again."

"You will change your mind, I hope, when you

grow older," she said. "You are only a little girl. You should read the New Testament and notice what Christ says and how he reacts. Follow his example."

"What does he say?"

"Love your enemies. Bless those who curse you. Do good to those who hate you and abuse you."

"Then, I should love Mrs. Reed, which I cannot do," I said. "I should bless her son, John, which is impossible." Helen asked me to explain, and I poured out my own tale of suffering and resentment. I spoke with great bitterness and anger, without holding anything back. Helen listened patiently until I stopped. I thought she then would say something, but she did not. "Well?" I asked impatiently. "Isn't Mrs. Reed a hard-hearted, bad woman?"

"She has been unkind to you—because she dislikes your character, as Miss Scatcherd dislikes mine. But how well you remember every little thing that she has done and said to you! Wouldn't you be happier if you tried to forget her actions? To me, life is too short to spend it holding grudges. There is hope for everyone to be forgiven and live happily in our eternal home. When I think about this, I easily can forgive the sinner, even while I hate the sin. So I never have to worry myself thinking about revenge. I can live calmly, looking joyfully ahead to the end."

I saw from Helen's dreamy look that she didn't

want to talk to me anymore. She wanted to be alone with her thoughts. But she was not allowed much time for meditation. A monitor, a great rough girl, came up exclaiming, "Helen Burns, if you don't go and put your drawer in order, I'll tell Miss Scatcherd to come and look at it!" Helen sighed as she got up, obeying the monitor without a word.

Chapter 7

My first term at Lowood seemed an age, and not a golden age either. It was a struggle to get used to the new rules and tasks. My fear of failure bothered me more than my physical hardships, although those hardships were no small thing.

During January, February, and part of March, deep snows and, later, flooded roads prevented us from going beyond the garden walls except to go to church. Even so, we had to spend an hour outside every day. Our clothing did not protect us from the severe cold. We had no boots, and the snow got into our shoes and melted there. Our ungloved hands and our feet became numb and frostbitten. I remember the torture that I suffered every morning as I thrust my raw, swollen toes into my shoes.

The supply of food continued to be scant. Although we had the hearty appetites of growing children, we received scarcely enough food to keep an invalid alive. Much abuse grew out of this shortage. When the biggest and hungriest girls had a chance, they would coax or bully the little ones into giving up their portion. Many times I was forced to share with two older girls the precious morsel of brown bread given out at teatime. After surrendering half the coffee in my mug to a third girl, I often swallowed the remainder in tears forced from me by hunger pangs.

I have not yet said anything about Mr. Brocklehurst's visits. That gentleman was away from home during most of my first month at Lowood. His absence was a relief to me. I dreaded his coming. But at last, he did come.

One afternoon (I had been at Lowood three weeks), I was puzzling over a problem in long division when I caught sight of a figure passing the outer window. I recognized its gaunt outline. Two minutes later, when all of the students and teachers rose to their feet, I did not have to look up to know who had entered the room. A long stride crossed the schoolroom; presently the same black column that had frowned on me so ominously at Gateshead was standing beside Miss Temple. I now glanced sideways at this piece of architecture. Yes, I was right; it was Mr. Brocklehurst, looking longer, narrower, and more rigid than ever.

I felt frozen with horror. I remembered all too well what Mrs. Reed had said about my disposition, and I remembered Mr. Brocklehurst's promise to warn Miss Temple and the other teachers about my vicious nature. I had been dreading the fulfillment of his promise, and now here he was. He stood at Miss Temple's side; he was speaking low in her ear. I believed he was telling her about my villainy, and I watched her with painful anxiety, expecting every moment to see her glance at me with disgust. I listened, too. Because I happened to be seated quite near, I caught most of what he said.

What I heard relieved me: "You may tell Miss Smith that I forgot the darning needles she asked for, but I will bring some next week. She should not give out more than one at a time to each pupil. If they have more, they are apt to be careless and lose them. And, oh, ma'am, I wish that the wool stockings were better looked after. The last time I was here, I went into the kitchen garden and examined them drying on the line. From the size of the holes in them, I am sure that they have not been well mended." He paused.

"Your directions will be attended to, sir," Miss Temple said.

"And, ma'am," he continued, "the laundress tells me that some of the girls have two clean collars per week. That is too many; the rules limit them to one."

"I think I can explain that, sir. Agnes and Catherine Johnstone were invited to have tea with some friends in town last Thursday, and I gave them permission to put on clean collars for the occasion."

Mr. Brocklehurst nodded. "Well, for once it may pass, but do not let it happen too often. There is another thing that surprised me. In looking over the housekeeper's accounts, I found that a lunch of bread and cheese has been served to the girls twice during the past two weeks. Who introduced this new practice and by what authority?"

"I am responsible, sir," Miss Temple replied. "The breakfast was so poorly prepared that the pupils could not possibly eat it, and I dared not let them go hungry until dinnertime."

"Madam, listen to me an instant. You know that I do not wish these girls to get accustomed to luxury. We intend to make them hardy, patient, and self-denying. When some little disappointment of the appetite occurs, such as the spoiling of a meal, do not replace the meal with something more tasty than what was lost. This is pampering the body. Temporary hunger should be seen as an opportunity to strengthen the spirit. At such a time, Miss Temple, a wise teacher would remind the girls of the sufferings of the early Christians or of Christ's warning that man does not live by bread alone. Madam, only think about it! When you put bread and cheese into the mouths of these children, you may indeed feed their vile bodies, but think how you starve their immortal souls!"

As he spoke, Mr. Brocklehurst had been standing on the hearth with his hands behind his back, majestically surveying the whole school. Suddenly he blinked as if he had seen something that either dazzled or shocked him. Turning, he said excitedly, "Miss Temple! Miss Temple! What is that girl with curled hair? Red hair, ma'am—curled, curled all over!" Extending his cane, his hand shaking, he pointed to the awful object.

"It is Julia Severn," Miss Temple answered very quietly.

"Julia Severn, ma'am? And why does she have curled hair? Why, in defiance of every rule of this house, does she wear her hair in a mass of curls?"

"Julia's hair curls naturally," Miss Temple replied, even more quietly.

"Naturally? We are not to conform to nature. I want these girls to be the children of Grace! I have said again and again that I want the girls' hair to be arranged modestly and plainly. Miss Temple, that girl's hair must be cut off. I will send a barber tomorrow. And I see others who are almost equally offensive. Tell everyone in the first form to rise and face the wall."

Miss Temple gave the order, and the first class obeyed. Leaning back a little on my bench, I could see the faces that they made in response to this unusual request. It was a pity that Mr. Brocklehurst could not see them too. Maybe he would have realized that, whatever he might do with the students' outside, the inside was beyond his control. He examined the backs of the students' heads, then pronounced his sentence: "Cut all the girls' hair short."

Miss Temple objected.

"Madam," he said, "I have a Master to serve whose kingdom is not of this world. My mission is to cure these girls of the lusts of the flesh. I will teach them to clothe themselves with modesty, not with braided hair and costly apparel. Each of the young persons has a mane of hair twisted in braids that vanity itself might have woven. These, I repeat, must be cut off. Think of the time wasted, of . . ."

Mr. Brocklehurst was interrupted by three other visitors who entered the room. It was a shame that they had not arrived a little earlier and heard his lecture on fashion because they were splendidly dressed in velvet, silk, and furs. The two youngest of the trio, girls of sixteen and seventeen, wore gray fur hats trimmed with ostrich feathers. Under their hat brims fell a profusion of blond hair, elaborately curled. The older lady was wrapped in a costly velvet shawl trimmed with fur, and she wore a wig of French curls. These ladies were Mr. Brocklehurst's wife and two daughters. They were respectfully greeted by Miss Temple and shown to seats of honor. Apparently, they had come with Mr. Brocklehurst to help him inspect the school. They now proceeded to give a list of complaints and suggestions to Miss Smith, who was in charge of the dormitories.

But I had no time to listen to what they said; other matters attracted my attention. While I had been listening to Mr. Brocklehurst and Miss Temple's conversation, I had been hiding my face by holding my slate up high. My trick might have worked if my treacherous slate had not somehow slipped from my hand. Falling with a tremendous crash, it drew every eye to me. As I stooped to pick up the two fragments of slate, I prepared myself for the worst. It came.

"A careless girl!" Mr. Brocklehurst said. "I see it is the new pupil." He continued loudly, "Let the child who broke her slate come forward!"

I could not have moved on my own; I was paralyzed with fear. But two big girls pulled me to my feet and pushed me toward the dreaded judge. Miss Temple came to meet me, whispering, "Don't be afraid, Jane; I saw that it was an accident. You will not be punished." The kind whisper went to my heart like a dagger. "Another minute and she will despise me," I thought. My pulse raced with hatred against Reed, Brocklehurst & Co. I was no Helen Burns.

"Fetch that stool," Mr. Brocklehurst said, pointing to a very high one. It was brought. "Place the child on it." I was placed there, by whom I don't know. I was in no condition to notice details. I was aware only that they had hoisted me to the height of Mr. Brocklehurst's nose, that he was within a yard of me, and that the silk dresses of his wife and daughters extended below me.

"Ladies," Mr. Brocklehurst said, turning to his family, "Miss Temple, teachers, and children, do all of you see this girl?" Of course they did; I felt their eyes like flames against my scorched skin. "You see that she still is young," Mr. Brocklehurst said. "You observe that she looks like an ordinary child. God graciously has given her the shape that He has given to all of us. No obvious deformity marks her. Who would think that the Evil One already had found a servant in her? Yet this, I grieve to say, is the case. My dear children," he continued in tragic tones, "this is a sad, melancholy occasion. It is my duty to warn you that this girl, who could be one of God's own lambs, is instead an intruder and an alien. You must be on your guard against her. Shun her example! Avoid her company. Exclude her from your games. Shut her out from your conversation. Teachers, you must watch her carefully. Weigh her words well. Study her actions. Punish her body to save her soul if, indeed, her salvation is possible. This girl—I hate to say it—this child, the native of a Christian land, is worse than many a little heathen who prays to false gods. This little girl is a liar!"

At these words the female Brocklehursts produced their pocket handkerchiefs and dried their tearful eyes. The older lady shook her head sorrowfully while the two younger ones whispered, "How shocking!"

Mr. Brocklehurst resumed his lecture. "All this I learned from her guardian, a generous lady who adopted this orphan and raised her as her own daughter. This good lady's kindness was repaid by such dreadful ingratitude that she finally was forced to separate this girl from her own young children, so that her vicious example would not contaminate their purity. She has sent the girl here to be healed." With this conclusion, Mr. Brocklehurst buttoned his coat. He muttered something to his family and bowed to Miss Temple. Then all the great people sailed from the room. Turning at the door, my judge said, "Let her stand half an hour longer on that stool. Let no one speak to her for the rest of the day."

There I was, mounted on the high stool—I, who had said that I could not bear the shame of standing on my own feet in the middle of the room. I can't begin to describe what I felt. Just as my throat was closing and I felt that I could not take another breath, Helen Burns rose from her seat and passed me. She smiled at me as she went by. What a smile! It lit up her thin face and weary gray eyes like the reflection from an angel's face. Yet, at that moment Helen wore an arm badge calling her "Untidy." An hour before, I had heard Miss Scatcherd sentence her to a dinner of bread and water because she had made an ink blot on her writing exercise. Such is people's imperfect nature. There are spots on the surfaces of the clearest planets. Eyes like Miss Scatcherd's can see only those tiny defects and are blind to the stars' brightness.

Chapter 8

Before the half-hour ended, five o'clock struck. School was dismissed, and everyone went into the dining hall for tea. I now dared to climb down from my stool. It was deep dusk. I crept into a corner and sat on the floor. The courage that Helen had lent me began to dissolve. I sank and, with my face to the floor, wept. I had meant to be so good at Lowood, to make so many friends, to earn respect and win affection. And I had been making progress. That very morning I had reached the head of my class. Miss Miller had praised me warmly. Miss Temple had smiled at me; she had promised to teach me drawing and to let me start French lessons if I continued to make progress for two more months. The other pupils had received me well enough. But now, here I lay crushed and stepped on. Could I ever rise again? "Never," I thought. I wished that I could die.

While sobbing, I heard someone coming. I looked up and saw Helen Burns. The fading fires showed her coming up the long, vacant room. She was carrying my bread and coffee. "Come, eat something," she said. But I pushed away both the bread and the coffee; I felt as if a crumb or drop would choke me. I could not stop crying, although

I tried. Helen sat down on the ground near me, wrapped her arms around her knees, and rested her head on them.

I was the first to speak. "Helen, why do you stay with a girl whom everybody believes to be a liar?"

"Everybody, Jane? Why, there are only eighty people who have heard you called a liar. The world contains hundreds of millions."

"But I don't have anything to do with the millions. Those eighty people whom I do know despise me."

"Jane, you are mistaken. Probably not one person in the school dislikes you. I am sure that many of them pity you."

"How can they pity me after what Mr. Brocklehurst said?"

"Mr. Brocklehurst is not a god. He is not even a great and admired man. He is not liked here. If he had treated you as a favorite, that would have made enemies for you. As it is, most of us would offer you sympathy if we dared. Teachers and pupils may act cold for a day or two, but there are friendly feelings hidden in their hearts. If you keep doing well, they will show these feelings. Besides, Jane, . . ." She paused.

"Well, Helen?" I asked, putting my hand into hers.

She rubbed my fingers gently to warm them, and went on. "Even if all the world hated you and believed that you were wicked, as long as your own conscience was clear, you would not be without friends."

I shook my head. "No, it isn't enough for me to think well of myself. If others don't love me, I would rather die than live. I cannot bear to be alone and hated, Helen. To gain some real affection from you, or Miss Temple, or any other whom I love, I would willingly have my arm broken, or let a bull toss me, or stand behind a kicking horse and let it dash its hoof at my chest, or . . ."

"Hush, Jane! You place too much value on people's love. Your Creator has provided you with better helpers than your feeble self or than people as feeble as you. All around us is an invisible world, a kingdom of spirits. Those spirits watch and guard us. If we were dying in pain and shame, and hatred crushed us, angels would see our tortures. If we were innocent, they would recognize our innocence. I know that you are innocent of Mr. Brocklehurst's charge because I see the honesty in your eyes. Why should we feel overwhelmed with distress? Life soon is over, and death is the entrance to happiness and glory."

I was silent. Helen had calmed me, but as she finished speaking, she breathed a little fast and began to cough. For the moment, I forgot my own sorrows and felt concern for her. Resting my head on her shoulder, I put my arms around her waist. She cuddled me, and we sat in silence.

Soon another person came in. It was Miss Temple. "I came to find you, Jane Eyre," she said.

"I want you in my room; because Helen is with you, she may come too." We followed her to her apartment. It contained a good fire and looked cheerful. Miss Temple told Helen to sit in a low armchair on one side of the hearth. Sitting in another, she called me to her side. "Is it all over?" she asked, looking at my face. "Have you cried your grief away?"

"I am afraid that I never will do that."

"Why?"

"Because I have been wrongly accused, and you, ma'am, and everybody else will now think me wicked."

"We will think you what you show yourself to be, my child. Continue to be a good girl, and you will satisfy us. Now tell me: who is the lady whom Mr. Brocklehurst called your guardian?"

"Mrs. Reed, my uncle's wife. My uncle is dead, and he left me in her care."

"She didn't adopt you, then?"

"No, ma'am. She was sorry to have to take me in. The servants told me that before my uncle died, he got her to promise that she always would keep me."

"Well now, Jane, you know that when criminals are accused, they are allowed to speak in their own defense. You have been charged with being a liar. Defend yourself to me as well as you can. Say whatever you remember, but be careful not to exaggerate."

After thinking for a few moments, to arrange

what I wanted to say, I told her the story of my sad childhood. Exhausted by emotion, I was less excited and more subdued than I generally was when speaking on that subject. I spoke calmly and simply, and I felt that Miss Temple fully believed me. As I told my story, I mentioned that Dr. Lloyd had come to see me after the fit. I had not forgotten the frightening episode of the red room. In my memory, nothing could soften the agony that had clutched my heart when Mrs. Reed had ignored my begging and locked me in the dark and haunted chamber a second time.

I finished. For a few minutes Miss Temple looked at me in silence. Then she said, "I know Dr. Lloyd a little. I will write to him. If his memory agrees with your statements, I will publicly clear you of Mr. Brocklehurst's accusation. To me, Jane, you are clear now." She kissed me and kept me at her side, where I was most content.

Then she turned her attention to my friend. "How are you tonight, Helen? Have you coughed much today?"

"Not quite as much, I think, ma'am."

"And the pain in your chest?"

"It is a little better."

Miss Temple got up, took Helen's hand, and felt her pulse. Then she returned to her own seat. As she did so, I heard her sigh sadly. Then she roused herself and said cheerfully, "But you two are my visitors tonight; I must treat you as such." She rang her bell. "Barbara," she said to the servant who answered it, "I have not had tea yet. Bring the tray and cups for these two young ladies." A tray soon was brought. How pretty the china cups and bright teapot looked, placed on the little round table near the fire! How fragrant the toast and steaming tea were! Unfortunately (I was beginning to be hungry), I noticed that the bread was a very small portion. Miss Temple noticed it too. "Barbara," she said, "can't you bring a little more bread and butter? There is not enough for three."

Barbara went out. She soon returned, saying, "Madam, Mrs. Harden says that she has sent up the usual quantity." Mrs. Harden, I should mention, was the housekeeper. She was a woman after Mr. Brocklehurst's own heart, composed of equal parts of whalebone and iron. "Oh, very well!" Miss Temple said, "we must make do, I suppose." Smiling, she added, "Fortunately, it is within my power to remedy this problem." She invited Helen and me to the table and placed before each of us a cup of tea with one delicious but thin morsel of toast. She then got up, unlocked a drawer, and took out a large poppy-seed cake. "I meant to give each of you some of this to take with you," she said, "but because there is so little toast, you must have it now." She proceeded to cut generous slices. We feasted that evening as if on nectar and ambrosia. The most delightful part of the evening was the smile on Miss Temple's face as she saw us satisfy our famished appetites on the food that she so generously supplied.

When tea was over, she again invited us to sit by the fire. A conversation followed between Helen and her that was a privilege to hear. I already had been in awe of Miss Temple, but now my wonder at Helen Burns increased beyond measure. The good meal, the warm fire, and the presence of our beloved teacher seemed to unleash some brilliance within her. It glowed in the bright color of her cheek, which until now always had been pale. It shone in her eyes, which suddenly were even more beautiful than Miss Temple's. Her speech seemed to flow from deep within, from her very soul. It amazed me to hear such eloquence from a girl of only fourteen. They spoke of things that I never had heard about: nature's secrets, far-away countries, former nations and times. They spoke of books. How many they had read! What stores of knowledge they possessed! Much too soon the bell announced bedtime. Miss Temple hugged us both, saying, "God bless you, my children!" She held Helen a little longer than me and let her go more reluctantly. Her eyes followed Helen as she reached the door. For the second time that evening, she breathed a sad sigh. She even wiped a tear from her cheek.

About a week after this happened, Miss Temple received a reply to the letter that she had written to Dr. Lloyd. Apparently he backed up my entire account of what had happened at Gateshead. Miss Temple called the whole school together and announced that she had looked into the charges made against me and was happy to say that I was free of blame. The teachers then shook hands with me and kissed me, and a murmur of pleasure ran through the other students.

Much relieved, I set to work with new enthusiasm, determined to overcome every difficulty. I worked hard, and I was successful. My memory improved. Mental exercise sharpened my wits. In a few weeks I was promoted to a higher class. In less than two months I was allowed to begin studying French. I sketched my first cottage (whose walls sloped as much as those of the leaning tower of Pisa) on the same day.

That night, when I went to bed, I forgot to imagine a meal of hot mashed potatoes, roast beef, and jam pudding, as I usually did to satisfy my hunger. Instead I feasted by imagining the beautiful artwork that someday would come from my own hands. I envisioned pencil drawings of picturesque houses and trees, rocks and ruins, and groups of cattle, as well as paintings of butterflies hovering over perfect roses, birds picking at ripe cherries, and wrens' nests enclosing pearl-like eggs. I had fantasies of being able to translate a little French story that Madame Pierrot had shown me that day. I still was busy with my happy imaginings when I fell sweetly asleep.

Chapter 9

Lowood's hardships lessened. Spring was here. The snows had melted; the cutting winds had turned mild. My wretched feet began to heal. Now we could endure our hour of recess in the garden. Sometimes, on a sunny day, it even began to be pleasant. A greenness grew over the brown flower beds. Flowers peeped out among the leaves: snow-drops, crocuses, and golden-eyed pansies. On Thursday afternoons (which were half-holidays) we now took walks and found even sweeter flowers opening under the hedges.

April gave way to bright, serene May. The days were filled with blue sky, placid sunshine, and soft southern breezes. All around me Lowood came to life. It became green and flowery; the bare skeletons of its great trees were restored to majestic life. Woodland plants sprang up everywhere. Countless varieties of moss filled its hollows, and the ground was sunny with wild primrose plants. All this I enjoyed fully, freely, unwatched, and almost alone. This unusual freedom had a cause, which I now must tell you.

The forest in which Lowood sat was beautiful. Whether it was healthy was another question. The fog often lay heavy around us, and as the fog crept

into the orphan asylum, so did the germs of a terrible disease: typhus. By the time May arrived, the
school was a hospital. Semi-starvation and neglect
had weakened many of the pupils. Forty-five of the
eighty girls were ill at one time. Classes were can-
celed, rules relaxed. The few who continued to be
healthy were allowed almost unlimited freedom.
The doctors caring for the sick girls insisted that
outdoor exercise would help keep us free of disease.
Even if they had not, there was no one to supervise
us. Miss Temple's attention was absorbed by the
patients. She lived in the sickroom, never leaving it
except to snatch a few hours' rest at night. The
teachers were busy preparing for the departure of
those girls lucky enough to have friends and relatives willing to remove them from Lowood. Many,
already ill, went home only to die. Others died at
the school and were buried quietly and quickly.

But I, and the other girls who stayed healthy,
fully enjoyed the beautiful season. We were allowed
to ramble in the woods, like gypsies, from morning
until night. We did whatever we liked, went wherever we liked. We lived better, too. Mr.
Brocklehurst and his family never came near
Lowood now, and the cross housekeeper was gone,
driven away by the fear of infection. The woman
who replaced her was more generous. Besides,
there were fewer to feed. The sick could eat little,
so our plates were better filled. When there was no
time to prepare a regular dinner (as often happened), she would give us a large piece of cold pie

or a thick slice of bread and cheese, and this we carried away with us to the woods, where we each chose the spot we liked best and dined happily.

My favorite seat was a smooth, broad stone that rose white and dry from the middle of the brook and could be reached only by wading through the water. I accomplished this feat barefoot. The stone was just broad enough to accommodate another girl and me. That girl was usually my chosen comrade, Mary Ann Wilson. Mary Ann was a clever, observant person whose society I enjoyed. She was older than I, knew more of the world, and could tell me many things that I liked to hear. We got along swimmingly.

Where, meanwhile, was Helen Burns? Why did I not spend these sweet days of liberty with her? Had I forgotten her? Surely Mary Ann was not Helen's equal. Mary Ann could only tell me amusing stories and exchange gossip with me. Helen gave those who enjoyed the privilege of her conversation a taste of far higher things. I never tired of her; I never ceased to love her as much as anyone else I ever have known. But Helen was ill. For some weeks she had been out of my sight, resting in a room upstairs. She did not have typhus; instead, she had a disease called consumption. In my ignorance I believed that consumption was something mild that time and care would cure. This idea of mine was strengthened by the fact that once or twice, on very warm afternoons, Helen was brought downstairs and taken by Miss Temple into the garden. Even on these occasions, I was not allowed to go and speak to her. I only saw her from the schoolroom window, and then not clearly because she was wrapped in blankets.

One evening in early June, Mary Ann and I stayed out very late in the woods. As usual, we had separated ourselves from the others. This time, however, we had wandered so far that we had lost our way. We needed to ask for directions at a lonely cottage, where a man and woman lived and tended a herd of half-wild pigs.

When we got back, it was after moonrise. A pony, which we knew to be the doctor's, was standing at the garden door. Mary Ann commented that someone must be very ill for Dr. Bates to be there so late. She went into the house, but I stayed behind a few minutes to plant in my garden a handful of roots that I had dug up in the forest. When I was done, I lingered a little longer. The flowers smelled so sweet; it was such a pleasant evening, so serene, so warm. I was enjoying these things when a thought entered my mind as it never had before: "How sad to be lying in bed now, in danger of dying! This world is pleasant. How dreary to be called from it and have to go who knows where." I believe this was my first serious attempt to understand the mystery of death. I shuddered at the thought of tottering and plunging over the cliff into the darkness beyond. While I was thinking over this new idea, I heard the front door open. Dr. Bates came out; a nurse was with him.

After Dr. Bates rode away, I ran up to the nurse. "How is Helen Burns?" I asked.

"Very poorly," she answered.

"Has Dr. Bates been to see her?"

"Yes."

"What does he say about her?"

"He says that she won't be here long."

If I had heard this phrase the previous day, I would have thought it meant that Helen soon would be leaving for her home up north. I would not have suspected it meant that she was dying. But I knew instantly now! I realized that Helen Burns was in her last days in this world. I experienced a shock of horror, then a strong surge of grief. I had to see her, and I asked what room she lay in.

"She is in Miss Temple's room," the nurse said.

"May I go up and speak to her?"

"Oh no, child! It is time for you to come in. You'll catch the typhus if you stay out in the evening damp." The nurse closed the front door, and I entered by the side entrance that led to the schoolroom. I was just in time. It was nine o'clock, and Miss Miller was calling the pupils to go to bed.

Two hours later I still was wide awake. From the dormitory's silence, I knew that all my companions were asleep. I rose softly, put on my dress, and crept barefoot in search of Miss Temple's room. It was at the house's other end, but I knew my way, and the light of the unclouded summer moon enabled me to find it easily. An odor of medicine and vinegar warned me when I came near the fever room, and I passed its door quickly, fearful that the nurse who sat up all night would hear me. I dreaded being discovered and sent back, because I felt that I must see Helen. I needed to hug her before she died. I needed to exchange one last word with her.

Finally I reached the door of Miss Temple's room. A light shone through the keyhole and under the door. Everything was profoundly still. Coming near, I found the door slightly ajar. I gave it a gentle push and looked in. Close by Miss Temple's bed stood a cot partially surrounded by curtains. I saw the outline of a body under the blankets, but the hangings hid the face. The nurse to whom I had spoken in the garden sat, asleep, in an easy chair, and a candle burned dimly on the table. Miss Temple was not to be seen. I learned afterwards that she had been with a delirious patient in the fever room. I paused by the bed. My hand was on the curtain, but I preferred speaking before I pulled it back. I dreaded seeing a corpse. "Helen," I whispered, "are you awake?"

She stirred and pulled back the curtain. I saw her face, pale and thin, but otherwise unchanged. My fear disappeared. "Is it you, Jane?" she asked in her gentle voice.

"Oh!" I thought, "She is not going to die; they are mistaken. She could not speak so calmly if she were." I sat on the bed and kissed her cheek. I touched her forehead, cheek, hand, and wrist. All were deathly cold, but she smiled in her usual way.

"Why are you here, Jane? It is past eleven o'clock. I heard it strike some minutes ago."

"I came to see you, Helen. I heard that you were very ill, and I could not sleep until I had spoken to you."

"You came to say goodbye, then. I think you are just in time."

"Are you going somewhere, Helen? Are you going home?"

"Yes. To my long home, my last home."

"No! No, Helen!" I said, distressed.

While I tried to stop my tears, a coughing fit seized Helen. When it was over, she lay exhausted for some minutes. Then she whispered, "Jane, your little feet are bare. Lie down and cover yourself with my quilt." I did. Helen put her arm over me, and I nestled close to her. After a long silence, she whispered, "I am very happy, Jane. When you hear that I am dead, you must not grieve. There is nothing to grieve about. We all must die one day, and my illness is not painful; it is gentle and gradual. My mind is at rest. By dying young, I will escape a lot of suffering. I didn't have qualities or talents that would have enabled me to make my way very well in the world. I would have constantly made mistakes."

"But where are you going, Helen? Can you see? Do you know?"

"I believe. I have faith. I am going to God."

"Where is God? What is God?"

"My Maker and yours, who never will destroy

what He created. I believe that God is good. I can put my soul in His care without any fear. God is my father. God is my friend. I love Him. I believe that He loves me."

"Will I see you again, Helen, when I die?"

"Yes, dear Jane. You will come to the same place of happiness and be received by the same mighty universal parent." I hugged Helen more tightly. She seemed dearer to me than ever. I felt as if I could not let her go. Presently she said, in the sweetest tone, "How comfortable I am! That last coughing fit has tired me a little. I feel as if I could sleep. But don't leave me, Jane. I like having you near me."

"I'll stay with you, Helen. No one will take me away."

"Are you warm, dear?"

"Yes."

"Goodnight, Jane."

"Goodnight, Helen."

She kissed me, and we both slept.

When I awoke, it was day, and I somehow was moving. I realized that I was in someone's arms. The nurse held me, and she was carrying me through the hall back to the dormitory. I was not scolded for leaving my bed because people had other things to think about. No answers were given to my many questions. But a day or two later, I learned that Miss Temple had found me in the little bed, my face against Helen Burns' shoulder, my arms around her neck. I was asleep, and Helen was dead.

Her grave is in the churchyard near Lowood.
For fifteen years it was covered only by a grassy
mound, but now a gray marble tablet marks the
spot. It is inscribed with her name and the words "I
will rise again."

Chapter 10

Up to this point I have recorded the events of my life in detail. I have given almost ten chapters to my first ten years. But this is not a regular autobiography. I am recording only those events that might interest others. Therefore, I now skip over eight years almost in silence. Only a few lines are necessary.

The typhus fever swept through Lowood and gradually disappeared. However, the number of victims had drawn attention to the school. People in authority looked into the disease's origin, and bit by bit various facts emerged that caused considerable public anger. The site's unhealthy nature, the quantity and quality of the children's food, the unwholesome water used in its preparation, the pupils' wretched clothing and accommodations— all these things were discovered, and the discovery produced results that embarrassed Mr. Brocklehurst but benefited the school.

Several wealthy people in the county made large donations so that a more suitable building could be constructed in a better location. New rules were introduced. Diet and clothing were improved. Management of the school's funds was entrusted to a committee. Because of Mr.

Brocklehurst's wealth and family connections, he could not be dismissed, but his duties now were shared by kinder and more tolerant gentlemen. With these improvements, the school became in time a truly useful institution. I remained a Lowood resident for eight more years: six as a pupil and two as a teacher.

During these eight years my life was busy and not unhappy. I had an excellent education placed within my reach. A fondness for some of my studies, together with a delight in pleasing my teachers (especially the ones I loved), urged me on. I took full advantage of all that was offered, and in time I rose to be the first class's top student. Then I was offered a teaching position, a job that I performed energetically for two years. But at the end of that time, something changed.

Throughout my years at Lowood, Miss Temple had continued as its superintendent. I owed the best part of my education to her instruction. Her company had been my greatest comfort. She had been to me a substitute mother and governess and eventually a friend. But then she married and moved with her new husband (a minister, an excellent man, almost worthy of such a wife) to a distant county. As a result she was lost to me. From the day that she left, I was not the same. With her went everything that had made Lowood feel like home to me.

On her wedding day I saw her, dressed in traveling clothes, step into a carriage. I then returned to my own room and spent alone the half-holiday that had been granted in honor of the occasion. I walked about my apartment most of the afternoon. At first I thought that I was only missing Miss Temple, but then a discovery dawned on me. Thanks in large part to Miss Temple, I had been content for years to allow Lowood to be my whole world. Now I remembered that the real world was wide and that varied sensations and excitements awaited those who had the courage to go forth into it. I wanted to seek real knowledge of life amid its dangers. I went to my window, opened it, and looked out. There were the building's two wings; there was the garden; there was the hilly horizon. My eyes passed all other things to rest on the farthest objects, the hills' blue peaks. I wanted to go beyond them.

An age seemed to have passed since the day I had come to Lowood. I had not left it since. All of my vacations had been spent at school. Mrs. Reed never had sent for me. Neither she nor any member of her family ever had visited me. Not a single letter or message ever had come for me. School rules, school duties, school habits and notions, and voices, and faces, and phrases, and costumes, and preferences, and dislikes—this was all I knew of existence. Suddenly that was not enough. In one afternoon I grew tired of the routine of eight years. I desired liberty. If liberty was too much to ask for, I at least wanted change and stimulation. "If not that," I cried, half desperate, "at least give me a new way of serving!"

Now the supper bell rang, calling me down-stairs. I was not free to resume my interrupted train of thought until bedtime. Even then the teacher who shared my room kept me from thinking, with her flood of small talk. How I wished that sleep would silence her! It seemed to me that if I could return to the idea that had entered my mind as I stood at the window, I would get some idea of what I should do.

Miss Gryce began snoring at last. Until now her nightly noise had annoyed me, but tonight I welcomed those first deep snores. At last I was alone with my thoughts. "A new way to serve! There is something in that," I thought. "I have served here for eight years. Now all I want is to serve elsewhere. Can't I do at least that? Is it not possible? Yes, yes. But how?"

A kind fairy seemed to drop the answer onto my pillow; as I lay down, it came quietly to my mind: "People who want new situations advertise. You must advertise in the local newspaper."

"How?" I asked the fairy who seemed to be whispering into my ear. "I know nothing about advertising."

Her reply was smooth and prompt: "You must send the advertisement and the money for it to the editor of the *Herald*. In it, say that replies should be addressed to J. E. and sent to the Lowton post office. About a week after you send your letter, go to the post office and see if there are any responses.

If there are, act accordingly." This seemed practical advice.

The next morning I was up with the sun, and before classes began I had composed the following advertisement: "A young lady accustomed to teaching wishes to find a situation in a private family where the children are under fourteen." (I thought that, because I was barely eighteen, I should not teach pupils nearer to my own age.) "She is qualified to teach the usual branches of a good English education, including French, drawing, and music. Address replies to J.E., care of the post office, Lowton."

This document remained locked in my drawer all day. After tea I asked the new superintendent for permission to go to Lowton, in order to do some errands. It was a walk of two miles and the evening was wet, but the days still were long. I visited a shop or two, mailed the letter at the post office, and came back through heavy rain, with dripping garments but a relieved heart.

The following week seemed long, but it ended at last. Once more, at the close of a pleasant autumn day, I found myself walking to Lowton. This time my excuse for going to town was to get measured for a pair of shoes, so I took care of that business first. When it was done, I stepped into the post office. It was run by an elderly woman who wore spectacles on her nose and black mittens on her hands. "Are there any letters for J.E.?" I asked. The woman peered at me over her spectacles. Then she opened a drawer and fumbled among its contents for such a long time that I began to lose hope. At last, having held a letter in front of her spectacles for nearly five minutes, she handed it to me with a distrustful glance. It was addressed to J.E. "Is there only one?" I asked.

"There are no more," she said.

I put the letter into my pocket and started home. I didn't have time to open it. I was required to be back by eight, and it already was seven-thirty.

Various duties awaited me when I arrived home. I had to sit with the girls during their hour of study; then it was my turn to read prayers and see the girls to bed. Afterwards I had my supper with the other teachers. Even when we finally retired for the night, Miss Gryce still was my companion. We had only a short piece of candle in our candlestick, and I dreaded that she would talk until it burned out. Fortunately, the heavy supper she had eaten made her sleepy, and she was snoring before I finished undressing. I now took out my letter and opened it.

The message was brief: "If J.E., who advertised in the *Herald* last Thursday, possesses the qualifications that she has mentioned, and if she can provide satisfactory references, a situation teaching one little girl can be offered to her. The salary is thirty pounds per year. J.E. is requested to send references and further details to Mrs. Fairfax of Thornfield, near Millcote."

I examined the document for a long time. The

writing was old-fashioned and rather uncertain, like that of an elderly lady. This reassured me. I had been haunted by the fear of getting into some sort of trouble, and I had hoped that the results of my advertisement would be something very proper and respectable. An elderly lady seemed exactly right to me. Mrs. Fairfax. I imagined her in a black gown and widow's cap: chilly, perhaps, but not unpleasant, a model of elderly English respectability. Thornfield. That must be the name of her house. Millcote. I brushed up my memory of the map of England. Yes, I remembered it. The town was seventy miles closer to London than Lowood was. That pleased me very much. I wanted to go somewhere full of life and movement, and Millcote was a large manufacturing town. Not that I enjoyed the idea of long chimneys and smoke clouds. "But," I told myself, "Thornfield probably will be a good distance out of town." At this point my final inch of candle sputtered and went out.

The next day steps had to be taken. I no longer could keep my plans to myself. I met with the superintendent and told her that I had been offered a situation in which the salary would be double what I now received (at Lowood I got only fifteen pounds per year). I asked her to inform the governing committee and ask them whether they would let me mention them as references.

The next day the superintendent laid the affair before Mr. Brocklehurst, who said that Mrs. Reed must be written to because she was my guardian.

Accordingly, a note was sent to that lady. This was her reply: "Jane Eyre may do as she pleases. Long ago I stopped interfering in her affairs."

After what seemed to me an endless delay, the committee gave me formal permission to accept the new job. In addition, because I always had conducted myself well as both a teacher and a pupil at Lowood, they would provide me with a letter attesting to my good character and abilities. I forwarded a copy of this letter to Mrs. Fairfax and soon received that lady's reply. She stated that she was satisfied, and she asked me to report in two weeks to assume the post of governess in her house.

I now was busy preparing to go, and the two weeks passed rapidly. I did not have a large wardrobe, so the last day gave me plenty of time to pack my trunk, the same one that I had brought with me from Gateshead eight years before. The box was tied shut. In half an hour the baggage cart was to call for it, and the next morning I would follow in a carriage. I had brushed my black traveling dress; prepared my bonnet, gloves, and muff; and searched through my drawers to make sure that nothing was left behind. Now, having nothing more to do, I sat down and tried to rest. I could not; I was too excited. One phase of my life was closing tonight; a new one was opening tomorrow. It was impossible to relax during the interval.

"Miss," said a servant who met me in the lobby, where I was wandering like a troubled spirit, "a person below wishes to see you."

"No doubt, the driver of the baggage cart," I thought, and ran downstairs. I was passing the teachers' sitting room when someone ran out, crying, "It's her! I am sure. I would know her anywhere!" She stopped me, taking my hand. I looked at her and saw a woman dressed like an upper-class servant. She looked motherly yet still young and very good-looking, with black hair and eyes and a fresh complexion. "Well?" she asked in a voice and with a smile that I half recognized. "You haven't forgotten me, have you, Miss Jane?"

In another second I was hugging and kissing her happily. "Bessie! Bessie! Bessie!" That was all I said. She half laughed, half cried, and we went into the parlor. By the fire stood a little three-year-old fellow. "That is my little boy," Bessie said.

"Then you are married, Bessie?"

"Yes. Nearly five years. To Robert Leaven, the coachman. I have a little girl besides Bobby there, and I've named her Jane."

"And how do they all get on at Gateshead? Tell me everything about them, Bessie. But sit down first. Bobby, come and sit on my lap, won't you?" But Bobby preferred to stay at his mother's side.

"You're still not very tall, Miss Jane, nor very stout," Bessie continued. "I dare say they haven't fed you too well at school. Miss Eliza is head and shoulders taller than you, and Miss Georgiana would make two of you in width."

"Georgiana is handsome, I suppose, Bessie?"

"Very. She went up to London last winter with

her mama, and everybody admired her, and a young lord fell in love with her. His relatives were against the marriage, and—what do you think?—he and Miss Georgiana planned to elope. But they were found out and stopped. It was Miss Eliza who reported on them. I believe she was jealous. Oh, she and her sister lead a cat-and-dog life together. They always are quarrelling."

"Well, and what of John Reed?"

"Oh, he is not doing as well as his mama would like. He went to college, but he was expelled. Then his uncles wanted him to study law, but he is such an undisciplined young man, they never will make much of him, I think."

"And Mrs. Reed?"

"The missis looks well enough, but I think she's not quite easy in her mind. Mr. John's conduct does not please her. He spends a great deal of money."

"Did she send you here, Bessie?"

"No, indeed, but I have long wanted to see you. When I heard that there had been a letter from you, and that you were going to another part of the country, I thought that I'd just come and get a look at you before you were quite out of my reach."

"I am afraid you are disappointed in me, Bessie," I said, laughing. Bessie's glance, although affectionate, did not seem admiring.

"No, Miss Jane, not exactly. You look like a lady, and it is as much as I expected of you. You were no beauty as a child." I smiled at Bessie's frank answer, even though it did not make me entirely happy. At eighteen most people would like to think that they please in appearance as well as character. "I dare say that you are clever, though," Bessie continued, meaning to comfort me. "What can you do? Can you play the piano?"

"A little."

There was a piano in the room. Bessie went and opened it. Then she asked me to sit down and give her a tune. I played a waltz or two, and she was charmed. "The Miss Reeds cannot play nearly as well!" she said happily. "I always said that you were cleverer than they. And can you draw?"

"That is one of my paintings over the fireplace." It was a landscape in watercolors. I had given it to the superintendent as a gift, in gratitude for her help with the committee, and she had had it framed.

"Well, that is beautiful, Miss Jane! It is as fine a picture as any that Miss Reed's drawing teacher could paint, and the young ladies could not come near it. And have you learned French?"

"Yes, Bessie. I can read it and speak it."

"Oh, you are quite a lady, Miss Jane! I knew that you would be. You will get on whether your relatives help you or not. There was something that I wanted to ask you. Have you ever heard anything from your father's kinfolk, the Eyres?"

"Never in my life."

"Well, you know the missis always said that

they were poor and quite despicable. They may be poor, but I believe that they are quite as respectable as the Reeds because one day, nearly seven years ago, a Mr. Eyre came to Gateshead and wanted to see you. The missis said that you were at school fifty miles away. He seemed very disappointed because he could not stay. He was going on a voyage to a foreign country, and the ship was to sail from London in a day or two. He looked like a real gentleman, and I believe that he was your father's brother."

"What foreign country was he going to, Bessie?"

"An island thousands of miles away, where they make wine. The butler did tell me . . ."

"Madeira?" I suggested.

"Yes, that is it. That was the very place."

"So he went?"

"Yes. He did not stay in the house many minutes. The missis was very high-handed with him. Afterwards she called him a 'sneaking tradesman.' My Robert believes that he was a wine merchant."

"Very likely," I answered, "or perhaps a clerk or agent to a wine merchant."

Bessie and I talked about old times an hour longer. Then she had to leave me. The next morning I saw her again for a few minutes at Lowton, while I was waiting for the coach. We then parted for our different locations: she for my old home of Gateshead, I for new duties and a new life in the unknown area of Millcote.

Chapter 11

I arrived at Millcote's George Inn after a sixteen-hour trip through the chill of an October day. No one appeared to be waiting for me there, so I sat somewhat uncomfortably for a while, all kinds of doubts and fears troubling my mind. Finally I spoke to a waiter: "Is there a place in this neighborhood called Thornfield?"

"Thornfield? I don't know, ma'am. I'll inquire at the bar." He vanished but instantly reappeared. "Is your name Eyre, Miss?"

"Yes."

"Person here waiting for you."

I jumped up, took my muff and umbrella, and hurried to meet a man standing by the open door. I dimly saw a one-horse carriage in the lamp-lit street. "This will be your luggage, I suppose?" the man said rather abruptly when he saw me, pointing to my trunk.

"Yes." He hoisted it onto the vehicle, and I got in. Before he shut the door, I asked him how far it was to Thornfield.

"A matter of six miles."

"How long will it take to get there?"

"An hour and a half." He fastened the door and climbed to his own seat outside. And we set off.

Our progress was slow and gave me plenty of time to think. I was content to be so near my journey's end. As I leaned back in the comfortable cart, I felt at peace. "Judging from the plainness of the servant and carriage," I thought, "Mrs. Fairfax is not a very fancy person. That's good. The only time that I lived among fashionable people was at Gateshead, and I was miserable with them. I wonder if she lives alone with the little girl. I will try my best to make friends with her. But who knows if I will succeed? At Lowood I was able to please people, but with Mrs. Reed my best never was good enough. I pray that Mrs. Fairfax won't turn out to be a second Mrs. Reed! But if she does, I do not have to stay with her. I always can advertise again. I wonder how much farther we need to go."

The driver let his horse walk all the way, and I believe that at least two hours had passed when he finally turned in his seat and said, "You're not far from Thornfield now." I looked out and saw that we were passing a church. About ten minutes later, the driver got down and opened a pair of gates. We passed through, and they clanged shut behind us. We slowly ascended a drive and came upon the long front of a house. Candlelight gleamed from one curtained window, but all the rest was dark. We stopped at the front door, which was opened by a maid, and I walked in.

"Will you come this way, ma'am?" the girl said. I followed her across a hall lined with high doors. She showed me into a room whose double illumination

of fire and candle at first dazzled me, contrasting as it did with the darkness that I had experienced for the past two hours. When I could see, I was presented with a cozy and agreeable picture. I saw a snug, small room; a round table by a cheerful fire; an old-fashioned, high-backed armchair; and in that chair the neatest imaginable little elderly lady. She wore a widow's cap, black silk gown, and snowy white apron. She was exactly as I had imagined Mrs. Fairfax, only less dignified and more kindly-looking. She was knitting, and a large cat sat peace-fully at her feet. In short, it was a perfect picture of domestic comfort. There could not have been a more reassuring sight for a new governess. As I entered, the old lady got up and kindly came forward to meet me.

"How do you do, my dear? I am afraid you have had a long ride. John drives so slowly. You must be cold. Come to the fire."

"Mrs. Fairfax, I suppose?" I said.

"Yes, you are right. Do sit down." She showed me to her own chair and then began to remove my shawl and untie my bonnet-strings. I told her not to trouble herself, but she said, "Oh, it is no trouble. I dare say your hands are numb with cold. Leah, make a little hot cocoa and cut a sandwich or two for Miss Eyre."

"Now, then, come up closer to the fire," she continued. "You've brought your luggage with you, haven't you, my dear?"

"Yes, ma'am."

"I'll see that it is taken to your room," she said, and bustled out.

"She treats me like a guest!" I thought. "I didn't expect anything like this. I don't believe that governesses always are treated so kindly. But I must not celebrate too soon."

Mrs. Fairfax returned and cleared her knitting and a book or two from the table, to make room for the tray that Leah now brought. She then handed me my cup and plate. This was more attention than I ever had received. It surprised me to be treated like this by my employer. But I tried to act casual.

"Will I have the pleasure of seeing Miss Fairfax tonight?" I asked after I had enjoyed my cocoa and sandwich.

"What did you say, my dear? I am a little deaf," the good lady answered.

I repeated the question more distinctly.

"Miss Fairfax? Oh, you mean your pupil. She is named Miss Varens."

"Oh! Then, she is not your daughter?"

"No. I have no family."

I wanted to ask how Miss Varens was related to Mrs. Fairfax, but I thought that it would not be polite to ask too many questions. Besides, I was sure to learn eventually.

Mrs. Fairfax sat down opposite me and took the cat onto her lap. "I am so glad that you have come," she said. "It will be quite pleasant living here now with a companion. To be sure, Thornfield is a fine old house, but in the winter it is dreary to be alone, even in the nicest surroundings. Of course, I am not really alone. Leah is a nice girl, and John and his wife are very decent people. But they are only servants, and if I talked to them as equals, I would lose my authority. Last winter— it was a very severe one, if you remember; when it did not snow, it rained and blew—not a creature except the butcher and mailman came to the house from November until February. I got quite melancholy sitting alone night after night. Sometimes I asked Leah to read aloud to me, but I don't think that the poor girl liked the task much. In spring and summer I get on better. Sunshine and long days make such a difference, you know. Then, at the beginning of this autumn, little Adele Varens and her nurse came, and you know how a child livens up a house. Now that you also are here, I will be quite cheerful."

My heart really warmed to this good lady as I heard her talk. I drew my chair a little nearer to her and told her that I hoped we would be good friends. "But I won't keep you sitting up late tonight," she said. "It is midnight now, and you have been traveling all day. You must feel tired. If you have gotten your feet warmed, I'll show you your bedroom. I've had the room next to mine prepared for you. It is only a small room, but I thought that you would like it better than one of the large front bedrooms. It is true that they have finer furniture, but they are so dreary and solitary, I wouldn't like to stay in them myself." I thanked her for her thoughtfulness. I truly was fatigued and ready to sleep. I went to bed feeling both weary and content.

When I awoke, it was broad daylight. My bedroom seemed a bright little place as the sun shone in between the blue curtains onto the flowered walls and a carpeted floor. It was so unlike Lowood's bare wood and stained plaster that my spirits immediately rose. I thought that a happier time of life was beginning for me, one that was to have flowers and pleasures as well as thorns and toils.

I got up and dressed myself with care. I had to be plain because I had only the simplest clothing and jewelry, but it was my nature to be neat and clean. I sometimes regretted that I was not better-looking. I wished that I had rosy cheeks, a straight nose, and a small cherry mouth. It seemed a misfortune that I was so little, pale, and plain-looking. However, when I had brushed my hair very smooth and put on my black dress, which at least fit nicely, I thought that I looked good enough to please Mrs. Fairfax and not horrify my new pupil. I ventured forth to begin my first full day at Thornfield.

The hall door stood open, so I stepped outside. It was a fine autumn morning. I looked up and examined the front of the mansion. It was a fine house, three stories high. In the near distance were hills that seemed to embrace Thornfield. The location was quieter and more secluded than anything that I had expected to find so near to Millcote's noise and bustle. I stood enjoying the view and pleasant fresh air, and listening with delight to the crows' cawing.

I was just thinking what a large place it was for one lonely little woman like Mrs. Fairfax to inhabit, when that lady appeared at the door. "What! Out already?" she said. "I see that you are an early riser." I went up to her and received a friendly kiss on the cheek. "How do you like Thornfield?" she asked. I told her that I liked it very much. "Yes," she said, "it is a pretty place. But I fear that it will get out of order unless Mr. Rochester decides to live here permanently or, at least, visit it more often. Great houses and grounds need attention."

"Mr. Rochester?" I asked. "Who is he?"

"Thornfield's owner," she responded. "Didn't you know that he was called Rochester?"

Of course I did not. I never had heard of him before. But the old lady seemed to regard his existence as a fact with which everyone must be acquainted. "I thought that Thornfield belonged to you," I continued.

"To me? Bless you, child. What an idea! To me! I am only the housekeeper, the manager. It's true that I am distantly related to the Rochesters. At least, my husband was. He was a clergyman. That church near the gates was his. The present Mr. Rochester's mother was a Fairfax and my husband's second cousin. But that means nothing to me. I consider myself only an ordinary housekeeper. Mr. Rochester always is polite to me, and I expect nothing more."

"And the little girl, my pupil?"

"Mr. Rochester is her guardian. He asked me to find a governess for her. Here she comes with her 'bonne,' as she calls her nurse."

The mystery, then, was explained. This friendly little widow was no great lady but an employee like myself. This did not disappoint me. On the contrary, I felt more pleased than ever. The equality between her and me was real, not just the result of kindness on her part. As I was thinking all of this over, a little girl came running up the lawn, followed by her nurse. I looked at my pupil, who did not notice me at first. She was only seven or eight years old, petite and delicate, with a pale, small-featured face and a great tumble of hair falling in curls to her waist.

"Good morning, Miss Adele," Mrs. Fairfax said. "Come and meet the lady who is going to teach you and make you a clever woman some day."

The little girl turned to me. "Is that my governess?" she asked her nurse, in French, while pointing to me.

"Yes, indeed," that lady answered, also in French.

"Are they foreigners?" I asked Mrs. Fairfax, amazed at hearing the French language.

"Yes. Adele was born in France and, I believe, never left it until six months ago. When she first came here, she couldn't speak any English. Now she can talk a little, but I don't understand her; she mixes it so with French. But you will understand her better, I believe."

Fortunately, I had been taught French by a French lady, and I always had made a point of talking with Madame Pierrot as often as I could. Adele came and shook hands with me when she understood that I was her governess. As we walked in to breakfast, I made a few comments to her in French. She replied briefly at first, but after we were seated at the table and she had examined me for some ten minutes with her large hazel eyes, she suddenly began chattering fluently. "Ah! You speak my language as well as Mr. Rochester does," she said in French. "I can talk to you, and so can Sophie. She will be glad because nobody here understands her. Madam Fairfax is all English. Sophie is my nurse. She came over the sea with me in a great ship with a chimney that smoked—how it did smoke!—and I was sick, and so was Sophie, and so was Mr. Rochester. Mr. Rochester lay down on a sofa in a pretty room called the salon, and Sophie and I had little beds in another place. I nearly fell out of mine; it was like a shelf. And, Mademoiselle, what is your name?"

"Eyre. Jane Eyre."

"Aire? Bah! I cannot say it. Well, our ship stopped in the morning, before it was daylight, at a great city—a huge city with very dark houses and all smoky, not at all like the pretty, clean town that I came from. Mr. Rochester carried me to the land, and we all got into a coach, which took us to a beautiful large house, larger than this and finer, called a hotel. We stayed there nearly a week. Every day, Sophie and I walked in a great green place full of trees, called the park, where there were many children besides me and a pond with beautiful birds that I fed with crumbs."

"Can you understand her when she runs on so fast?" Mrs. Fairfax asked. I understood her very well because Madame Pierrot, too, had been quite a talker. "I wish," the good lady continued, "that you would ask her a question or two about her parents. I wonder if she remembers them."

"Adele," I inquired, "with whom did you live when you were in that pretty, clean town you spoke of?"

"Long ago I lived with Mama, but she has gone to live with the Holy Virgin. Mama used to teach me to dance and sing and to say poetry. A great many gentlemen and ladies came to see Mama, and I used to dance for them or sing to them. I liked it. Shall I sing now?"

She had finished her breakfast, so I gave her permission to sing. Climbing down from her chair, she placed herself on my lap. Then, folding her little hands before her, shaking back her curls, and lifting her eyes to the ceiling, she began to sing. It was an opera tune. Adele was singing the part of a deserted lady bewailing her lover's faithlessness. This lady told her maid to dress her in her brightest jewels and richest robes, and she promised to meet the false lover that night at a ball and prove to him, by the cheerfulness of her behavior, that his desertion had not bothered her. The song seemed a strange choice for a little girl. My guess was that the point was to amuse the audience by having them hear notes of love and jealousy warbled by an innocent child—a point that I thought was in very bad taste. But Adele sang prettily. When she was done, she jumped from my knee and said, "Now, Mademoiselle, I will recite some poetry." She began an old French fable, reciting the little piece with great expression, which was very unusual at her age. It was clear that she had been carefully

trained.

"Was it your mama who taught you that piece?" I asked.

"Yes, and we practiced so many times. She made me lift my hand—this way—when I recited a question, so that I would remember to raise my voice. Now shall I dance for you?"

"No, that is enough for now. But after your mama went to the Holy Virgin, as you say, with whom did you live then?"

"With Madame Frederic and her husband. She

took care of me, but she is not related to me. I think that she is poor because her house is not as fine as Mama's. I was not there long. Mr. Rochester asked me if I would like to go and live with him in England. I said yes because I knew Mr. Rochester before I knew Madame Frederic, and he always was kind to me and gave me pretty dresses and toys. But he has not kept his word because he has brought me to England and now he has gone away, and I never see him."

After breakfast we went to the library that Mr. Rochester had indicated should be used as a schoolroom. I found Adele obedient but not particularly studious. She was not used to schoolwork. I felt that it would be unwise to try too much too quickly, so after we had gotten through a few easy lessons, I let her return to her nurse.

I then decided to busy myself until dinnertime by drawing some little sketches for Adele's use. As I was going upstairs to fetch my drawing supplies, Mrs. Fairfax called to me. "Your morning school hours are over now, I suppose," she said. The door to the room in which she was standing was open, so I went in to find her. The room was large and stately, with purple chairs and curtains, a Turkish carpet, walnut-paneled walls, one vast window, and a high, decorated ceiling. Mrs. Fairfax was dusting some vases that stood on a sideboard. "What a beautiful room!" I exclaimed as I looked around. I never had seen a room half as gorgeous.

"Yes. This is the dining room. I have just

opened the window to let in a little air and sunshine. Everything gets so damp in rooms that seldom are used. The drawing room over there feels like a tomb."

"How beautifully you keep these rooms, Mrs. Fairfax!" I said. "There is not a speck of dust, and none of the furniture is covered. Except that the air feels chilly, you would think that people were using them every day."

"Well, Miss Eyre, I never know when Mr. Rochester is going to arrive for one of his rare visits. I've noticed that it annoys him to arrive and find everything covered up and then to have a bustle of arranging begin, so I like to keep the rooms ready."

"Is Mr. Rochester a very particular, fussy man?" I asked.

"I wouldn't say so, but he has his tastes, and he expects to have things here done in accordance with them."

"Do you like him? Is he generally liked?"

"Oh, yes. The family always has been respected here. Almost all of the land in this neighborhood has belonged to the Rochesters for longer than anyone can remember."

"Well, but leaving his land out of the question, do you like him? Is he a likable man?"

"I have no reason not to like him. I believe that his tenants consider him a fair and generous landlord."

"What sort of character does he have?"

"He has a very good character, I suppose. He is rather peculiar perhaps. He has traveled a great deal and seen much of the world. I dare say he is clever, but I've never had much conversation with him."

"In what way is he peculiar?"

"I don't know. It isn't easy to describe. But when he speaks to you, you do not always know whether he is joking or serious, whether he is pleased or displeased. You don't thoroughly understand him—at least, I don't. But it doesn't matter. He is a very good master."

This was the only description of our employer that I got from Mrs. Fairfax. There are people who have no gift for sketching a character or observing and describing important points, either in persons or things. The good lady evidently belonged to this class. In her eyes Mr. Rochester was Mr. Rochester—a gentleman, our employer—and that was that. She clearly was puzzled by my wish to know more about him.

When we left the dining room, she offered to show me the rest of the house. I followed her upstairs and downstairs, admiring as I went, because everything was very handsome. As we reached the third floor, I was struck by how old-fashioned the furnishings were, as though the house were a shrine to another age. Here in the daylight I liked the rooms' hush and gloom, but I would not have wanted to spend the night in one of those wide, heavy beds, where everything would have looked strange in the pale gleam of moon-light. "Do the servants sleep in these rooms?" I asked.

"No. They use smaller rooms in the back. If there were a ghost at Thornfield Hall, this would be its haunt."

"I can see why. You have no ghost, then?"

"None that I ever heard of," Mrs. Fairfax replied, smiling. "Would you like to see the rest of the house?"

I followed her up a very narrow staircase to the attic, and from there up a ladder and through a trap door to the house's roof. Leaning over the banister and looking far down, I surveyed the grounds laid out like a map. I saw the bright velvet lawn; the field, wide as a park and dotted with ancient trees; the church at the gates; the road; the tranquil hills; and the horizon bounded by a sky promising good weather. Nothing in the scene was particularly remarkable, but it was all very pleasing. When I turned from it and re-entered the trap door, I could scarcely see my way down the ladder. The attic seemed as black as a tomb compared with that sunlit scene of grove, pasture, and green hill.

Mrs. Fairfax stayed behind a moment to fasten the trap door while I groped my way to the attic's exit and descended the narrow staircase. The stair-case led to a long hallway that separated the third story's front and back rooms, and I lingered in this hallway. Narrow, low, and dim, its two rows of small black doors all shut, the hallway looked like a corridor in Bluebeard's castle. While I stopped there, I heard the last sound that I would have expected in such a still, solemn place: a laugh. It was a strange laugh, somehow formal, without humor. I listened harder. The sound ceased but then began again, louder. It rose until it seemed to awaken an echo in every lonely room, although it clearly had originated in only one. I could have pointed out the door to the room from which it came. "Mrs. Fairfax!" I called because I now heard her descending the stairs. "Did you hear that loud laugh? Who is it?"

"Some of the servants, probably," she answered. "Perhaps Grace Poole."

"Did you hear it?" I inquired again.

"Yes, plainly. I often hear her. She sews in one of these rooms. Sometimes Leah is with her, and they frequently are noisy together." The laugh was repeated, this time ending in an odd murmur. "Grace!" Mrs. Fairfax called. I really did not expect any Grace to answer because the laugh was as tragic, as odd a laugh as any I had ever heard. If it had not been high noon, I would have felt superstitiously afraid. However, I quickly realized that my thoughts were foolish. The door nearest to me opened, and a servant came out. She was a woman in her thirties, with a square figure, red hair, and a hard, plain face. I hardly could imagine anyone less ghostly in appearance. "Too much noise, Grace," Mrs. Fairfax said. "Remember your instructions." Grace curtseyed silently and returned to the room.

"Grace does some sewing and helps Leah with her housemaid's work," Mrs. Fairfax explained. "She is a little odd sometimes, but she does her work well. By the way, how have you gotten on with your new pupil this morning?"

The conversation turned to Adele and continued until we reached the light and cheerful downstairs region. Adele came running to meet us in the hall, exclaiming that she was hungry. We found dinner ready and waiting for us in Mrs. Fairfax's room.

Chapter 12

My first pleasant impression of Thornfield Hall turned out to be justified. Mrs. Fairfax was just what she had appeared: an even-tempered, kindly woman. My pupil was a lively child who had been somewhat spoiled, and she therefore was sometimes wild and careless. But once she was put entirely in my care, she soon forgot her bad habits and became obedient and teachable. She made reasonable progress and seemed to become fond of me. In turn, her high spirits and cheerful chatter made me fond of her, and we were happy together.

So was I completely content? No. I suppose I will be criticized by people who think that a woman's every need should be satisfied by caring for a pleasant child and living in friendly surroundings. But peace and quiet are not enough to satisfy people, women as well as men. Women need mental exercise as much as men do. It is narrow-minded to say that they should confine themselves to making puddings and knitting stockings, playing the piano and embroidering. It is thoughtless to condemn them, or laugh at them, if they want to do more or learn more than custom has said is necessary.

When I wandered the house in my restless

moments, I frequently heard Grace Poole's laugh. It was the same low, slow "Ha! Ha!" that first had frightened me. I also heard her eccentric murmurs, which were stranger than her laugh. Sometimes I saw her. She would come out of her room with a basin, plate, or tray in her hand; go down to the kitchen; and shortly return, generally carrying a glass of beer. Her appearance certainly did not fit with the odd noises that she made. She was hard-featured and very serious. Several times I tried to talk with her, but she was a person of few words. She cut me short each time with a brief reply.

The other members of the household—John and his wife; Leah the housemaid; and Sophie the French nurse—were decent people but not particularly interesting. With Sophie I would speak French. Sometimes I asked her questions about her native country, but her answers were rather dull and did not encourage me to continue.

October, November, and December passed. One January afternoon, Mrs. Fairfax asked me to give Adele the day off because she had a cold. When Adele eagerly seconded the request, it reminded me how precious occasional holidays had been to me in my own childhood, and I agreed. It was a fine, calm day but very cold, and I was tired of sitting in the library. Mrs. Fairfax just had written a letter that was waiting to be mailed, so I put on my bonnet and cloak and volunteered to take it to the post office in Hay. The two-mile journey would be a pleasant afternoon walk. I settled Adele comfortably in her little chair by the fireside and gave her a storybook and her best doll (which I usually kept in a drawer). Then I kissed her and set out.

The ground was hard, the air was still, and my road was lonely. I walked quickly until I got warm; then I walked slowly to enjoy myself. It was three o'clock, and the short winter day already was becoming dim. I was a mile from Thornfield. In summer the lane where I walked was lovely with wild roses; in autumn, with nuts and blackberries. Now, in winter, its delight lay in its utter solitude and quiet. If there was a breeze, it made no sound here because there were no leaves to rustle. The bare bushes and trees were as still as the white, worn stones that dotted the path. The little brown birds that occasionally stirred in the hedge looked like single reddish leaves that had forgotten to drop. The lane ran uphill all the way to Hay. When I was halfway to the top, I stopped to rest on a stone gate. Gathering my cloak around me, I did not feel cold, although the brook running alongside the path was frozen solid. From my seat I could look down on Thornfield. On the hilltop above me sat the rising moon, pale as a cloud but growing brighter by the moment.

A rude noise broke on this fine, silent scene. It was a tramp, tramp sound, backed up with a metallic clatter, A horse was coming, although I still could not see it because of the lane's windings. I had been just about to continue my journey;

instead, because the path was narrow, I sat still to let the horse go by. It was very near but not yet in sight. Then, in addition to the tramp, tramp, I heard a rushing noise, and a great dog bounded into view. It was a black and white creature, lion-like, with long hair and a huge head. For a moment I was alarmed, but it passed me quietly enough, only glancing in my direction. It was followed by a tall horse with a rider. Horse and rider passed, and I rose to walk on.

But then there was a sliding sound, an excla-mation, and a clattering tumble. The man and horse were down! They had slipped on the sheet of ice that glazed the path. The dog came bounding back and, seeing his master in a predicament, barked until the hills echoed. He sniffed around the fallen man and horse and then ran up to me, obviously begging for assistance. I obeyed him and walked down to the traveler, who was struggling free of his horse.

His efforts were so vigorous that I thought he could not be badly hurt, but I asked him, "Are you injured, sir?" I think that he was swearing, but I am not certain. Whatever he was muttering, he did not answer me directly. "Can I do anything?" I asked.

"Just stand out of the way," he answered as he rose, first to his knees and then to his feet. I did, and then began a heaving, stamping, clattering process, accompanied by a barking and neighing that drove me further away, but I was not going to leave until I saw that all was well. Finally the horse was on its feet again, and the dog was silenced with a "Down, Pilot!" The traveler stooped to feel his foot and leg, hobbled to the gate where I had been resting, and sat down.

I drew near him again. "If you are hurt, I can fetch someone either from Thornfield Hall or from Hay."

"Thank you, but I will be all right. It's just a sprain." Again he stood up and tried his foot, but the effort made him groan with pain.

There was still enough light for me to see him plainly. He was of medium height and seemed very broad-chested, although his riding cloak partly hid his figure. He had a dark face with stern features, and his eyes looked angry just now. He was not very young but was not yet middle-aged; he looked about thirty-five. I felt no fear of him or even much shyness. If he had been a handsome young man, I would not have dared to keep questioning him against his will. I had a natural admiration for beauty, elegance, and gallantry, but if I had met a man who possessed those qualities, I would have known that they were not meant for me. I would have shunned them as one does fire, lightning, or anything else that is bright but foreign. If this stranger had smiled and been good-humored with me, I would have gone on my way without bothering him further. But his frown and rough manner somehow made me more comfortable. When he waved to me to go, I ignored him and announced, "Sir, I can't leave you alone here at such a late hour until I see that you are able to mount your horse."

He looked at me when I said this. Before, he hardly had turned his eyes in my direction. "You ought to be at home yourself," he said, "if you have a home in this neighborhood. Where do you come from?"

"Just down there. I am not afraid of being out late when there is moonlight, and I will be glad to go on to Hay to fetch you some help if you need it. I am going there anyway to mail a letter."

"You live just down there? Do you mean at that house?" he said, pointing to Thornfield Hall.

"Yes, sir."

"Whose house is it?"

"Mr. Rochester's."

"Do you know Mr. Rochester?"

"No, I never have seen him."

"He is not at home, then?"

"No."

"Can you tell me where he is?"

"I cannot."

"You are not a servant at Thornfield, surely. You are . . ." He stopped and ran his eye over my clothing, which, as usual, was quite simple. I was wearing a black wool cloak and a black bonnet. Neither of them was fine enough for a lady's maid. He seemed unable to decide what I was, so I helped him.

"I am the governess."

"Ah, the governess!" he repeated. "The devil take me if I hadn't forgotten! The governess."

Again he examined me. In two minutes he rose from the gate. Pain crossed his face as he tried to move. "I won't send you to fetch help," he said, "but you may help me a little yourself if you will be so kind."

"Yes, sir."

"Try to take hold of my horse's bridle and lead him to me. Are you afraid to do that?" I was afraid, but I put my muff down on the gate and went up to the tall horse. I tried to catch the bridle, but the horse was spirited and would not let me come near its head. I tried again and again, always unsuccessfully, and I was very afraid of its stamping feet. The traveler waited and watched for some time. At last he laughed. "I see," he said. "The mountain will not be brought to Mohammed, so all you can do is help Mohammed go to the mountain. I must ask you to come here." I came. "Excuse me," he continued. "It is necessary that I make you useful." He laid a heavy hand on my shoulder and, leaning on me, limped to his horse. He caught its bridle and sprang to his saddle, grimacing as he made the effort because it wrenched his sprain. "Now," he said, "just hand me my whip. It lies there under the hedge." I found it. "Thank you," he said. "Now hurry on your errand, and get home as soon as you can."

With the touch of a spur, he and his horse rushed away, the dog bounding along behind them. All three vanished into the deepening twilight. I picked up my muff and walked on. The incident was

over. It was of no importance, yet it was a change in my monotonous life. My help had been needed, I had given it, and I was pleased to have done something, even an unimportant thing. I was tired of my passive existence; I wanted to act. Also, this stranger's face made an interesting addition to my memory's portrait gallery. It was different from the other portraits hanging there: first of all, it was masculine; secondly, it was dark, strong, and stern.

I still was thinking about that face when I entered Hay and mailed the letter at the post office; I saw it as I walked quickly downhill all the way home. When I came to the gate, I stopped a minute, looking around and listening, thinking that a horse's hooves might ring on the path again and that a cloaked rider and a Newfoundland dog might reappear. But I saw only the hedge and a willow tree rising still and straight to meet the moonbeams. Then I remembered that I was late, and I hurried on.

I did not like re-entering Thornfield. To walk through its door was to return to stillness and inactivity. I thought with dissatisfaction of my lonely little room, of tranquil Mrs. Fairfax, of spending the long winter evening alone with her. These thoughts snuffed out the faint excitement awakened by my walk. But there was nothing else to do, so I went in.

The hall was unlit, but a warm glow came from the great dining room, whose door stood open to show a cheerful fire in the grate. Its flames reflected pleasantly on the marble hearth and brass fire-irons, the purple draperies and polished furniture. I had just become aware of a cheerful mingling of voices, including Adele's, when the door closed.

I hurried to Mrs. Fairfax's room. There was a fire there, too, but no candle and no Mrs. Fairfax. Instead, all alone, sitting on the rug and gazing solemnly at the blaze, was a great black and white dog just like the one I'd seen in the lane. "Pilot?" I asked. The dog rose and walked over to sniff me. I petted him, and he wagged his great tail. I rang the bell, and Leah entered. "What dog is this?"

"He came with Master."

"With whom?"

"With Master. Mr. Rochester. He has just arrived."

"Indeed! Is Mrs. Fairfax with him?"

"Yes, and Miss Adele. They are in the dining room. John has gone for a doctor because Master has had an accident. His horse fell, and his ankle is sprained."

"Did the horse fall in Hay Lane?"

"Yes. Coming down the hill, it slipped on some ice."

"Ah! Bring me a candle, will you, Leah?"

Leah brought the candle. She was followed by Mrs. Fairfax, who repeated the news, adding that Dr. Carter now was with Mr. Rochester. Then Mrs. Fairfax hurried out to give orders about tea, and I went upstairs to take off my things.

Chapter 13

On his doctor's orders, Mr. Rochester went to bed early that night, and he slept late the next morning. When he did come down, it was to take care of business matters.

Adele and I now had to find a new schoolroom because Mr. Rochester was using the library to receive his visitors. I carried our books and other materials to a room upstairs. This morning Thornfield Hall was a changed place, no longer silent as a church. It echoed with knocks at the door and clangs of the bell. Steps rang in the hall, and new voices spoke downstairs. I liked the change.

Adele was not easy to teach that day. She could not concentrate but instead kept running to the door and looking over the banisters to see if she could glimpse Mr. Rochester. She made up excuses to run downstairs and visit the library, where I knew she was not wanted. When I got a little angry and made her sit still, she talked continuously of Mr. Rochester and the presents he had brought her. He had hinted the night before that when his luggage arrived, there would be a box that would interest her. "That must mean that there is a gift for me and perhaps one for you, too. Mr. Rochester asked me my governess's name. He asked if you were a little person, rather thin and pale. I said yes because that is true, isn't it, Miss?"

Adele and I ate lunch together in Mrs. Fairfax's parlor. The afternoon was wild and snowy, and we spent it in the schoolroom. At dark I let Adele put her work away and run downstairs. Because it was quieter now and the doorbell had stopped ringing, I guessed that Mr. Rochester was free to see her. Left alone, I walked to the window, but nothing was to be seen there. Twilight and snowflakes thickened the air and hid even the nearby shrubs. I let the curtain down and returned to the fireside, where I sat until Mrs. Fairfax came bustling in.

"Mr. Rochester would like you and Adele to have tea with him in the drawing room," she said. "He has been so busy all day that he could not see you before. You should change your dress."

"Must I?"

"Yes, you'd better. When Mr. Rochester is here, I always dress more formally in the evening." To me, this seemed unnecessary. However, I went to my room and replaced my ordinary black dress with one of black silk. "You should add a pin," Mrs. Fairfax said. I had a little pearl ornament that Miss Temple had given me as a goodbye gift. I put it on, and we went downstairs to the dining room.

Pilot lay basking in the heat of a superb fire; Adele was kneeling near him. And there was Mr. Rochester half lying on a couch, his foot propped on a cushion. He was looking at Adele and Pilot.

The fire shone on his face, and I recognized my traveler by his broad, black eyebrows; square forehead; and strong nose. His mouth, chin, and jaw all were grim-looking—yes, very grim. His figure was strong and athletic, although not tall or particularly beautiful. Mr. Rochester must have heard us come in, but it seemed that he was not in the mood to notice us because he didn't lift his head as we approached.

"Here is Miss Eyre, sir," Mrs. Fairfax said.

He nodded, still not taking his eyes from the dog and child. "Let Miss Eyre be seated," he said. It seemed to me that what he really meant was, "Why the devil should I care whether Miss Eyre is here or not?" I felt no embarrassment. If he had met me with a show of fine manners, I would have been confused because I could not be graceful and elegant in return. His behavior suited me; it meant that I owed him nothing. Besides, I was enjoying the situation's strangeness and wondering what he would do next. He continued imitating a statue; he neither spoke nor moved.

Mrs. Fairfax seemed to think that someone should be friendly, so she began to talk. She said sympathetic things about the pressure he had been under all day and the annoyance of his sprain. Then she praised his patience in putting up with all of it.

"Madam, I would like some tea," he replied. Mrs. Fairfax rang the bell. When the tray came, Adele and I went to the table, but the master did not leave his couch.

"Will you give Mr. Rochester his cup?" Mrs. Fairfax asked me. "Adele might spill it."

I did as she asked. As Mr. Rochester took the cup from my hand, Adele cried out, "Isn't it true that you have a present in your suitcase for Miss Eyre?"

"Who talks of presents?" he said gruffly. "Did you expect a present, Miss Eyre? Are you fond of presents?"

"I hardly know, sir," I said. "I don't have much experience with them, but most people think they are pleasant things."

"Miss Eyre, you should learn a lesson from Adele. The moment that she sees me, she loudly demands a present. You beat around the bush."

"Adele can make such demands," I answered lightly. "She and you are old friends, and she says that you are in the habit of giving her gifts. But I am a stranger and have done nothing to deserve one."

"Oh, don't fall back on false modesty! I have talked with Adele and find that you have taught her well. In a short time she has improved a great deal."

"Sir, you now have given me my present, and I thank you. A teacher's favorite gift is praise of her pupil's progress."

"Humph!" Mr. Rochester said, and he drank his tea in silence. "Come to the fire," he said when the tray had been taken away and Mrs. Fairfax had settled into a corner with her knitting. Adele wanted to sit on my lap, but she was ordered to amuse herself with Pilot. "You have been living in my house three months?"

"Yes, sir."

"And you came from?"

"Lowood school."

"Ah! A charitable institution. How long were you there?"

"Eight years."

"Eight years! You must have a strong will to live. Half that time in such a place could kill anyone. No wonder you have an otherworldly look about you. I wondered where you had gotten that face. When you appeared in Hay Lane last night, I thought of fairy tales and thought that perhaps you had bewitched my horse. I am not sure yet. Who are your parents?"

"I have none."

"I thought not. And so, you were waiting for your people when you sat on that gate?"

"My people? Who do you mean?"

"The men in green—the leprechauns—or whatever type of fairy you spring from. It was a proper moonlit evening for them. Did I interfere with one of your ceremonies, and so you spread that damned ice over the path?"

I shook my head. "The men in green all left England a hundred years ago," I said, speaking as seriously as he had done. "And not even in Hay Lane can you find a trace of them. I don't think they ever will come back."

Mrs. Fairfax had dropped her knitting and seemed to be wondering what sort of talk this was.

"Well," Mr. Rochester resumed, "if you have no parents, you must have some other relatives. Uncles and aunts?"

"No. None whom I ever saw."

"And your home?"

"I have none."

"Where do your brothers and sisters live?"

"I have no brothers or sisters."

"Who recommended you to come here?"

"I advertised, and Mrs. Fairfax answered my advertisement."

"And I am daily thankful that I did," Mrs. Fairfax put in. "Miss Eyre has been a fine companion to me and a kind, careful teacher to Adele."

"Don't trouble yourself to tell me what Miss Eyre is like," Mr. Rochester answered. "I will judge for myself. She began by making my horse fall."

"She what?" Mrs. Fairfax asked in amazement.

"I have her to thank for this sprain." The housekeeper shook her head in bewilderment. "Miss Eyre, have you ever lived in a town?" Mr. Rochester continued.

"No, sir."

"Have you seen much of the world?"

"Nothing but Lowood's pupils and teachers, and now Thornfield's residents."

"Have you read much?"

"Whatever books came my way, but they have not been numerous."

"I see you have lived a nun's life. No doubt, you have been taught all about religion. Brocklehurst, who I understand directs Lowood, is a parson, is he not?"

"Yes, sir."

"And you girls probably worshipped him."

"Oh, no."

"No? You say that very coldly."

"I disliked Mr. Brocklehurst, and most of the pupils felt the same way. He is a harsh man. He cut off our hair, and to save money he bought us bad needles and thread, with which we hardly could sew."

"That was very false economy," remarked Mrs. Fairfax, who once again understood the conversation's drift.

"That was why you disliked him?" Mr. Rochester demanded.

"When he was completely in charge of the school, he starved us. He bored us with long lectures once a week, and in the evening he read to us from horrible books about sudden deaths and God's judgment, which made us afraid to go to bed."

"What age were you when you went to Lowood?"

"Ten."

"And you stayed there eight years. You are now eighteen, then?"

"Yes."

"Arithmetic, you see, is useful. With a face like

yours, I would not have been able to guess your age. And what did you learn at Lowood? Can you play?"

"A little."

"Of course. That is what all young ladies say. Go sit at the piano and play a tune." I obeyed. "Enough!" he called out in a few minutes. "You play 'a little,' I see, like any other English school-girl. Better than some but not well." I closed the piano and returned.

Mr. Rochester continued. "Adele showed me some sketches this morning, which she said were yours. Probably a teacher helped you?"

"No, indeed!" I objected.

"Ah! Your pride didn't like that, eh? Well, bring me your drawings, but don't tell me something is original if it isn't. I can recognize patch-work."

"Then, I will say nothing, and you will judge for yourself, sir."

I brought the portfolio of my pictures, and he examined them carefully. He laid three in front of him and pushed the rest away. "I see that these were indeed done by one person. Was it you?"

"Yes, sir."

"When did you find time to do them? They must have taken much time and some thought."

"I did them during the last two vacations that I spent at Lowood, when I had nothing else to do."

"Where did you get the models for the pictures?"

"Out of my head."

"That head I see now on your shoulders?"

"Yes, sir."

"Is there other furniture of the same kind within?"

"I believe so. Perhaps some is better."

He spread the pictures before him and again stared at them. "Were you happy when you painted these pictures?" Mr. Rochester finally asked.

"I was completely absorbed in them. Yes, I was as happy as I ever have been."

"That is not saying much. I believe your pleasures have been few. But enough. Put them away."

I barely had put them back into the portfolio when he looked at his watch and suddenly said, "It is nine o'clock, Miss Eyre. What are you doing, letting Adele stay up so late? Take her to bed." Adele went to kiss him goodnight. He accepted the kiss but didn't seem to like it any more than Pilot would have. "Goodnight to you all," he said, waving his hand toward the door to dismiss us. Mrs. Fairfax folded up her knitting, I took my portfolio, and we left.

After I put Adele to bed, I joined Mrs. Fairfax. "You said that Mr. Rochester is not very peculiar," I commented.

"Well, is he?"

"I think so. He is very changeful and abrupt."

"He may seem that way to a stranger, but I am so used to him that I never think about it. And then, if he acts oddly, we must excuse him."

"Why?"

"Partly because it is his nature (none of us can help our nature), and partly because he no doubt has painful thoughts that bother him and make his spirits low."

"Thoughts about what?"

"Family troubles, for one thing."

"But he has no family."

"Not now, but he had a family. His older brother died nine years ago."

"Nine years is a long time. Was he so fond of his brother that he still has not gotten over it?"

"Why, no, I wouldn't say that. There were some misunderstandings between them. His brother, Rowland Rochester, was not quite fair to Mr. Edward. Perhaps he turned their father against him. The old gentleman did not want to divide the family property, but he wanted Mr. Edward to have some wealth, too, to keep up the family name. So, as soon as Mr. Edward was of legal age, old Mr. Rochester and Mr. Rowland took some steps that were not quite fair. What they did put Mr. Edward in a painful position, for the sake of making his fortune. I don't know exactly what happened, but he never got over it. He is not very forgiving. He broke off relations with his family, and now for many years he has led an unsettled life. I don't think that he ever has stayed at Thornfield for two weeks at a time, even after his brother's death left him master of the place. Indeed, it's no wonder that he avoids the old place."

"Why should he avoid it?"

"Perhaps he thinks it is gloomy."

I would have liked a clearer explanation, but Mrs. Fairfax either could not or would not give me more information about what had happened to hurt Mr. Rochester so much. It was obvious that she wanted me to drop the subject, so I did.

Chapter 14

The next few days I saw little of Mr. Rochester. Gentlemen from the neighborhood were constantly stopping in and often staying for dinner. When his leg was better, he often went out on horseback, not returning until late at night. My only contact with him was passing him in the hall or on the stairway. Sometimes he would act very cold, barely nodding at me. Sometimes he was warm and friendly. His mood changes did not offend me because I knew that they had nothing to do with me. Something else was affecting him.

One day he had company to dinner and sent for my drawings, apparently to show them to his guests. After the visitors left, I received the message that Adele and I should join him downstairs. I brushed Adele's hair and made her neat while she chattered on about whether her present had arrived. Sure enough, a little carton was waiting on the table when we entered the dining room. "My present! My present!" she exclaimed, running towards it.

"Yes, there is your present at last. Take it into a corner, you genuine daughter of Paris, and amuse yourself with it," said Mr. Rochester's deep and rather sarcastic voice. He was sitting in an immense easy chair at the fireside. "Just don't bother me with your conversation about it, do you understand?"

Adele raced to a sofa with her treasure and was busy untying the cord that secured the lid. Lifting several toys and other objects out of the silvery layers of tissue paper, she exclaimed, "Oh, heavens! How beautiful!" and then was happily silent.

"Is Miss Eyre there?" Mr. Rochester now demanded, half rising from his seat to look around to the door. "Ah! Well, come forward. Sit down here." He drew a chair near to his own. "I am an old bachelor, and I am not fond of children's prattle," he continued. "No, don't pull the chair farther off, Miss Eyre. Sit down exactly where I placed it—if you please, that is. Confound these good manners! I continually forget them. Nor do I particularly enjoy the company of simple-minded old ladies. But now that I think of it, I mustn't ignore Mrs. Fairfax. She is a relative, at least by marriage, and they say that blood is thicker than water."

He sent for Mrs. Fairfax, who soon arrived, knitting basket in hand. "Good evening, madam," he said to her. "I need you to do me a favor. I have forbidden Adele to talk to me about her presents, and she is bursting with things to say. Please listen to her. It will be one of the most charitable acts you ever have performed." When Mrs. Fairfax joined Adele on the sofa, the child quickly filled her lap with her carton's contents, pouring out in broken English her delight with it all.

"Now that I have made sure that my guests are amused, I am free to attend to my own pleasure. Miss Eyre, pull your chair a little further forward. I cannot see you without disturbing my position in this comfortable chair, and I don't intend to do that."

As he sat in his easy chair, Mr. Rochester looked different than I had seen him before. He was not so stern or nearly so gloomy. There was a smile on his lips, and his great, dark eyes sparkled, probably with the wine from dinner. I noticed those eyes for the first time. There was something in them that may not have been softness but at least reminded me of softness. He had been looking into the fire, and I had been looking at him, when he suddenly turned and caught my gaze. "You are studying me, Miss Eyre," he said. "Do you think I am handsome?"

If I had had time to think, I would have come up with some polite, vague answer, but the words slipped from my tongue too quickly. "No, sir."

"My word, there is something unusual about you!" he exclaimed. "You look like a little nun, sitting there with your hands folded, so quiet and grave. Yet, when I ask you a question, you fire back an answer as blunt as you please. What do you mean by it?"

"Sir, please excuse me. I should have said that beauty is in the eye of the beholder, or that outer beauty does not matter, or something of that sort."

"You should have said no such thing," he

scoffed. "Beauty does not matter, indeed! Under the pretense of apologizing, you stick the knife farther in! Go on, tell me what faults you find with me. I suppose that I have all my arms and legs, two eyes, and a nose like any other man?"

"Mr. Rochester, I wish I had said nothing. It was a blunder."

"No, you will not get off so easily. Go ahead. For instance, is there anything wrong with my forehead?"

"Indeed not. It shows that you are a man of considerable intelligence, although perhaps not very charitable toward others."

"There again! Another stick of the knife, because I said that I do not like the company of children and old women. No, young lady, I am not 'very charitable,' but I do have a conscience. Besides, I was not always as I am now. When I was your age, I had plenty of feeling for other people. But Fortune has knocked me around since then. She has kneaded me with her knuckles, and now I am as hard and tough as a rubber ball. Maybe there is still a soft spot or two hidden in that ball. Do you think that leaves hope for me?"

"Hope of what, sir?"

"Hope of my turning from rubber back into human flesh."

"He certainly has drunk too much wine," I thought. I did not know how to answer his strange question. How could I tell whether he was capable of changing?

"You looked very puzzled, Miss Eyre. Although you are not pretty any more than I am handsome, a puzzled air becomes you. Besides, it is convenient because it keeps those searching eyes of yours away from my face and busies them with the flowers on the rug. Young lady, I feel quite talkative tonight."

With this announcement he rose from his chair and stood, leaning his arm on the marble mantelpiece. When he was in that pose, I was able to notice his broad-chested body as well as his face. I am sure that most people would have thought him an ugly man. Yet he had a proud, dignified way about him. It was clear that he did not worry about his lack of beauty and was confident that he had inner qualities that made up for it. I found myself thinking that he probably was right.

"I am in a talkative mood tonight," he repeated. "That is why I sent for you. The fire was not enough company for me. Pilot wasn't, either. Adele is a little better but still far below the mark, and the same for Mrs. Fairfax. I am convinced that you can do better. I would like to learn more about you. So—speak." Instead of speaking, I smiled, and not in a very humble way. "Speak," he urged again.

"What about, sir?"

"Whatever you like. I leave it up to you."

I continued to sit, saying nothing. "If he expects me to talk for the mere sake of talking and showing off, he has tried the wrong person," I thought.

"You are silent, Miss Eyre."

I still was silent. He glanced at me, and I felt that he was reading my thoughts. "You are stubborn . . . and annoyed," he said. "I understand. My request was ridiculous, even rude. Miss Eyre, I beg your pardon. I don't mean to act superior to you. That is," he said, correcting himself, "I am superior only in the sense that I am twenty years older than you and a hundred years more experienced. It is because of this that I want you, please, to talk to me a little now. I need you to distract my thoughts, which are stuck on a painful subject."

"I am very willing to amuse you if I can, sir," I replied. "But I don't know what will interest you. Ask me questions, and I will do my best to answer them."

"Very well. Do you agree that I have a right to be a little bossy because I am old enough to be your father, have fought through many experiences, and have roamed half the world while you have lived quietly with one set of people in one house?"

"Do as you please, sir."

"That is no answer. You are being evasive. Tell me what you think."

"I don't think, sir, that you have a right to command me merely because you are older than I or because you have seen more of the world. If you are superior, it is because you have made good use of that time and experience."

"Very well said, but I won't accept it because it

doesn't suit my case. Forget about whether or not I am superior, then. Will you agree to receive my orders now and then without being annoyed or hurt by my tone?"

I smiled, thinking to myself, "Mr. Rochester is peculiar. He seems to forget that he pays me thirty pounds a year to receive his orders."

"The smile is very well," he said, noticing my expression, "but speak."

"I was thinking, sir, that very few employers would care whether or not their employees were annoyed by their orders."

"Employees! Oh yes, I had forgotten the salary! Well then, considering the money, will you agree to let me boss you a little?"

"Not considering the money, sir, but because you forgot the money and because you care whether an employee is comfortable, I heartily agree."

"And will you agree to give up all those polite forms and phrases that I'm supposed to say, without thinking that I am deliberately being rude?"

"I will not mistake informality for rudeness, sir. I like informality, but no free person will submit to rudeness, even for a salary."

"Rot! Most free people will submit to anything for a salary. However, I thank you for your answer and the manner in which it was given. You are frank and sincere. But I don't mean to flatter you. If you are different than the majority of young schoolgirl governesses, it is because nature made you that way. And for all I know, you may be no better than the rest. You may have unbearable faults that make up for your few good points."

"So may you," I thought. Our eyes met as the thought crossed my mind.

He seemed to read the glance and answered as though I had spoken. "Yes, yes, you are right," he said. "I have plenty of faults of my own. God knows, I can't be too critical of others. I was pushed onto the wrong path at the age of twenty-one, and I never have recovered my way. I might have been very different. I might have been as good as you. I envy you your peace of mind, clean conscience, unpolluted memory. A memory without stain must be an exquisite treasure. Is it not?"

"How was your memory when you were eighteen, sir?"

"Clean. Healthful. No gush of sewer water had turned it into a stinking puddle. Nature meant me to be a good man, Miss Eyre, yet you see that I am not. You don't see? You must take my word for it. If you knew my past, you would say that I should have done better. You would be right. When fate wronged me, I did not have the wisdom to remain cool. I turned desperate, and then I became a worse and worse man. I wish I had been stronger— God knows, I do! Before you do wrong, Miss Eyre, think of the remorse that you will feel. Remorse is the poison of life."

"Repentance is said to be its cure, sir."

"It is not its cure. To reform may be its cure. I

could reform—I still have the strength for that—but what is the use of thinking about that, cursed as I am? Besides, because happiness is forever denied me, I have a right to get pleasure out of life. And I will get it, whatever it costs."

"Then you will grow worse and worse, sir."

"Possibly. Yet, why should I grow worse if the pleasure that I get is sweet and fresh? I may get it as sweet and fresh as the wild honey that the bee gathers on the hillside."

"Such pleasure will sting. It will taste bitter, sir."

"How do you know? You have never tried it. How very serious you look, yet you are as ignorant of the world as this vase! You have no right to preach to me, you youngster. You know nothing of life and its mysteries."

"I am only reminding you of your own words, sir. You said that error brought remorse, and you said that remorse was the poison of life."

"Who is talking about error? The notion that flitted across my brain was not an error. I believe it was an inspiration rather than a temptation. Here it comes again! It is no devil, I assure you. Or if it is, it has put on the robes of an angel of light. I think that when such a guest asks to enter my heart, I must let it in."

"Distrust it, sir. It is not a true angel."

"How do you know? How can you distinguish between a fallen angel of darkness and a messenger from God?"

"I am judging by your face, sir. It was troubled when you said that the thought had returned to you. I feel certain that it will bring you more misery if you listen to it."

"Not at all. It brings the most gracious message in the world. At any rate, you are not my conscience-keeper, so don't worry about it. Here, come in, lovely wanderer!" He seemed to speak to a vision, and he extended his arms as though to embrace it.

"Sir, I don't understand you at all," I said. "This conversation has gotten out of my depth. I know only one thing: you said that you are not as good as you would like to be and that you regret your imperfection. You suggested that your bad memories are poison to you. It seems to me that if you tried hard, you could eventually become the man you want to be. In a few years you would have a new, clean store of memories, which would give you pleasure instead of pain."

"Very good, Miss Eyre. And I am forming good intentions. My actions and the people with whom I associate will be different than before."

"Better?"

"Better."

"May it all go well with you, then," I said as I rose. I thought it was useless to continue a conversation that I could not understand.

"Where are you going?"

"To take Adele upstairs. It is past her bedtime."

"You are afraid of me because I talk in riddles."

"Your language is puzzling, sir, but although I am bewildered, I certainly am not afraid. It is past nine, sir."

"Never mind. Wait a minute. Adele is not ready to go to bed. I have been watching her as well as you. About ten minutes ago she pulled a little pink silk dress out of her box. Joy lit her face as she unfolded it. Flirtation runs in her blood. 'I'll put it on now!' she cried, and she rushed out of the room. In a few minutes she will return, and I know what I will see: a miniature version of her mother, Celine Varens, as she used to appear on the stage. But never mind that. Stay now, to see whether I am right."

Before long, Adele's step was heard in the hall. She entered, transformed as her guardian had predicted. Her brown dress had been replaced with a dress of pink silk, very short and as full in the skirt as it could be gathered. A wreath of rosebuds encircled her forehead. On her feet were silk stockings and white satin sandals. "How do you like my dress?" she cried, bounding forward. "And my stockings and my shoes? Watch me dance!" Spreading out her dress, she crossed the room in graceful steps. When she reached Mr. Rochester, she dropped onto one knee at his feet, exclaiming, "Monsieur, thank you a thousand times. It is just like something my mama would have worn, no?"

"Precisely!" he answered. "Her mama charmed the gold out of my pockets, Miss Eyre. I have been green, grass green. My springtime is gone, but it has left this French blossom on my hands. In some moods I gladly would be rid of her. I don't value the plant from which she grew because I found it was a plant that could be fertilized only with gold. I have only half a liking for the blossom, especially when it looks as artificial as it does now. I keep her in the hopes that I can be forgiven for my sins, great and small, through such a good deed. I'll explain all of this some day. Goodnight."

Chapter 15

Not long after, Mr. Rochester did explain it. One afternoon he happened to meet Adele and me walking outdoors. While she played with Pilot, he asked me to walk along a long beech-lined avenue within sight of her. He then said that Adele was the daughter of a French opera dancer, Celine Varens, for whom he had felt what he called a "grand passion." Celine had said that she returned his passion, even more strongly. She had called him her idol, saying that she preferred his "athletic type" to more elegant, handsome men.

"Miss Eyre," he continued, "I was so flattered by this that I gave her an apartment in a hotel, complete with servants, a carriage, furs, diamonds, and so on. In other words, I began the process of ruining myself like any other stupid man. I got what I deserved. One night I happened to stop by Celine's apartment when she did not expect me. She was not home. But it was a warm night, and I was tired of strolling through Paris, so I went out onto her balcony to enjoy a cigar. I'll have one now, if you don't mind." He paused to take out and light the cigar. "I sat lazily on the balcony overlooking the street when I saw the elegant carriage and two beautiful horses that I had given to Celine. She was returning, and my heart thumped with impatience. The carriage stopped at the hotel door, and Celine's little foot emerged. I was about to call down, 'My angel!' when a second figure jumped from the carriage and, with Celine, entered the hotel.

"You never have felt jealousy, have you, Miss Eyre? Of course not, because you have not been in love. Your soul sleeps peacefully, but I tell you, someday wild currents, foam, and noise will break the stream of your life. Either you will be dashed to pieces on the rocks or lifted up and carried into calmer waters, as I am now.

"I like this day. I like its steel sky. I like the sternness and stillness of the world under this frost. I like Thornfield, yet how long have I hated the very thought of it, shunned it like the plague? How I do still hate . . ." He stopped and was silent, striking his boot against the hard ground. Some awful thought seemed to grip him so tightly that he could not go on. I never had seen an expression like the one that crossed his face. Pain, shame, anger, impatience, disgust, hatred—all seemed to be battling for the upper hand. Finally, with an effort that was painful to see, he continued walking.

"Did you leave the balcony, sir," I asked, "when Miss Varens entered?"

I almost expected him to be angry at my question. To the contrary, his face cleared. "Oh, I had forgotten Celine! Well, to go on. When I saw my charmer come in accompanied by her young man,

I seemed to hear a hiss, and the green snake of jealousy glided into my coat and ate its way to my heart's core. "Isn't it strange that I should be telling you this?" he said, again interrupting himself. "As if men usually talk about their mistresses to an inexperienced girl like you! But I know what sort of mind yours is. It will not be infected. I do not mean to harm it, but if I did, I could not. The more you and I converse, the better, because while I cannot hurt you, you may improve me."

Finally he proceeded. "I remained on the balcony. 'Let me prepare an ambush,' I thought. So I closed the curtain between her bedroom and the balcony, leaving an opening only big enough for me to see through. As I sat back down, the pair entered the bedroom. I then saw the couple clearly. There was Celine, shining in satin and jewels—my gifts—and there was her companion, an army officer. I knew him. He was a nobleman and as brainless a youth as I ever had met. The moment that I recognized him, my jealousy vanished and my love for Celine turned to ashes. A woman who could betray me for such a rival was not worth fighting for. She deserved only scorn. Of course, I deserved more scorn for having believed in her. They began to talk. Their conversation was frivolous, greedy, heartless, and senseless. My name was mentioned. Neither of them possessed enough wit to do me much damage, but they insulted me as coarsely as they could in their little way. Celine laughed about my personal defects—'deformities' she called them—although she always had praised what she had called my 'masculine beauty.' In this she was very different from you, who told me point-blank that you did not think me handsome. The contrast struck me at the time, and . . ."

Adele came running up at this point. "Monsieur, John has just come to say that your lawyer is waiting to see you."

"Ah! In that case I must be brief. Opening the curtain, I walked in on them. I told Celine that she was free. I told her to move out of the hotel and gave her some money for her immediate needs. I ignored her screams, hysterics, and prayers and made an appointment with the officer for a duel the next morning. The following day I had the pleasure of putting a bullet into one of his weak arms. I then thought that I was done with everything associated with Celine. Unluckily, however, Celine gave birth to a child, Adele, and claimed that she was my daughter. That is possible but unlikely. Pilot is more like me than Adele is. A few years after I broke with Celine, she abandoned Adele and ran away to Italy with a musician. I did not, and still do not, believe that Adele is my daughter, but when I heard that she was living in poverty, I took the poor thing out of the slime and mud of Paris and transplanted it here, to grow up clean in the soil of an English country garden. Mrs. Fairfax found you to teach her, but now that you know that she is the illegitimate child of a French opera-girl, you might think of your job differently. Will you soon tell me that you have found another job and that I should find a new governess?"

"No," I replied. "Adele is not responsible for either her mother's faults or yours. I am fond of her. Now that I know she is parentless—forsaken by her mother and disowned by you, sir—I will love her more than before. How could I prefer some wealthy family's spoiled child, who would hate her governess as a nuisance, to a lonely little orphan who sees her as a friend?"

"Oh, that is how you see it! Well, I must go in now, and you must too. It is getting dark."

But I stayed out a few minutes longer with Adele and Pilot. Adele and I ran a race and played a game of badminton. When we went in, I took her onto my lap and kept her there for an hour, letting her chatter as much as she liked. As we talked, I studied her face, looking for some likeness to Mr. Rochester. I found none. It was a pity; if she had resembled him, he would have cared for her more.

When I was alone in my room, I thought over the tale that Mr. Rochester had told me. As he had said, there was nothing extraordinary in the story itself. A wealthy Englishman had an affair with a French dancer, and she betrayed him. But there was something decidedly strange in the fit of emotion that had seized him as he spoke of his present happiness and his newly revived pleasure in Thornfield.

I was growing fond of Mr. Rochester. Indeed, I sometimes felt that he was more like family than an employer. I listened to his conversation with great enjoyment because he opened my mind to the world, with all its novel scenes and ways. Was Mr. Rochester ugly in my eyes? No, reader. My gratitude, and our many friendly moments together, made his face the object I most liked to see. His presence in a room was more cheering than the brightest fire. I had not forgotten his faults; indeed, I could not because he showed them frequently. He was proud, sarcastic, and sometimes harsh. He was moody, too. More than once, when he sent for me to read to him, I found him sitting in his library with his head resting on his folded arms. When he looked up, his scowl was a fearsome thing to see. But I believed that his moodiness and harshness were the result of some cruel trick of fate and that he was naturally a better man. I thought that there were excellent materials in him, although for now they were somewhat spoiled and tangled. I grieved for his grief, whatever it was, and would have given much to remove it from him.

As I put out my candle and tried to sleep, I thought again about his strange relationship with Thornfield. "What is it that alienates him from the house?" I asked myself. "Will he leave it again soon? Mrs. Fairfax said that he seldom stays longer than two weeks at a time, and he has been here for eight weeks. If he does go, the change will be a sad one. Suppose he is gone during spring, summer, and autumn. How joyless the sunshine and fine weather will seem!"

I do not know if I fell asleep after that. At any rate, I became wide awake when I heard a vague murmuring. It seemed just above me. I rose and sat up in bed, listening. All was silent. I tried again to sleep, but my heart beat anxiously. The clock struck two. Just then it seemed that my bedroom door was touched, as if fingers had swept it as they groped along the dark hallway outside. I asked, "Who is there?" Nothing answered. Fear chilled me. Then I remembered that it might be Pilot. When the kitchen door was left open, he often wandered to the door of Mr. Rochester's room. I had seen him lying there in the mornings. The idea calmed me, and I lay down. I began to feel drowsy again. But I was not fated to sleep that night. I scarcely had begun to dream, when a laugh—low, suppressed, and deep—sounded at my door's keyhole. I stood up and looked around, but I could see nothing. While I stared, the goblin laugh was repeated, and I knew that it came from outside my door. My first impulse was to rise and lock the door, and the next was to call out, "Who is there?"

Something gurgled and moaned. I heard steps moving toward the third-story staircase. A door opened and closed, and all was still. "Was that Grace Poole? Is she possessed by the devil?" I thought. It was impossible to stay by myself. I would go to Mrs. Fairfax. I threw on a robe, unlocked the door, and opened it with a trembling hand. There was a burning candle resting on the floor. I was surprised to see this, then horrified to realize that the air was dim with smoke.

Something creaked. It was a door standing ajar, and that door was Mr. Rochester's. Smoke poured from his room in a blue cloud. I thought no more of Mrs. Fairfax, Grace Poole, or the laugh. In an instant I was in his room. Tongues of flame darted around the bed. In the midst of the blaze, Mr. Rochester lay in a deep sleep. "Wake up! Wake up!" I cried. I shook him, but he only murmured and turned. The smoke had stupefied him. I could not waste a moment; a tongue of flame had touched the sheets. I rushed to his washstand and found a tall pitcher filled with water. I dashed this over the bed and the sleeper, flew back to my own room, brought my own water jug, baptized the bed again, and, by God's aid, managed to extinguish the flames.

The hiss of the quenched fire, the breaking of a pitcher that I flung away when I had emptied it, and, above all, my splashing him with water woke Mr. Rochester at last. Although it now was dark, I knew that he was awake because I heard him exclaiming at finding himself lying in a pool of water. "Is there a flood?" he cried.

"No, sir," I answered. "There has been a fire. Get up. You are thoroughly soaked. I will fetch you a candle."

"Is that Jane Eyre?" he demanded. "What have you done with me, you witch? Who is in the room besides you? Have you plotted to drown me?"

"I will fetch you a candle, sir. In heaven's

name, get up. Someone has plotted something. You must find out who and what it is."

"There! I am up now. Where is my dressing gown? Run. Bring a candle." I did run. I brought the candle that still remained in the hallway. He took it from my hand, held it up, and surveyed the bed, all blackened and scorched, the sheets drenched, the carpet swimming in water. "What is it? And who did it?" he asked.

I quickly told him what had happened: the strange laugh in the hallway, the footsteps going up to the third story, the smoke, the smell of fire that had brought me to his room, and how I had soaked him with all the water that I could lay hands on. He listened gravely. As I went on, his face expressed more concern than surprise. He did not immediately speak when I concluded. "Shall I call Mrs. Fairfax?" I asked.

"Mrs. Fairfax? No. What can she do? Let her sleep."

"Then I will fetch Leah and wake John and his wife."

"Not at all. Be still. You have a shawl on. If you are not warm enough, take my cloak. Sit in the armchair there, and I will wrap you in it. Place your feet on the stool to keep them out of the wet. I am going to leave you for a few minutes. I will take the candle. Remain where you are until I return. Be as still as a mouse. I must pay a visit upstairs. Don't move or call anyone."

I watched the light withdraw as he left. He walked silently up the hallway, opened the staircase door as quietly as possible, and shut it after him, and the last ray vanished. I was left in darkness. I listened for some noise but heard nothing. A long time passed. I grew weary. It was cold, despite the cloak, and I saw no point in staying. I was about to risk Mr. Rochester's anger by disobeying him when the light once more gleamed dimly in the hallway, and I heard the sound of bare feet. "I hope it is he," I thought, "and not something worse."

He re-entered, pale and gloomy. "I have figured it all out," he said, setting his candle down on the washstand. "It is as I thought."

"How, sir?"

He did not answer but stood staring at the ground for a moment. Then he said in a rather peculiar tone, "I forget whether you said you saw anything when you opened your bedroom door."

"No, sir. Only the candlestick on the ground."

"But you heard an odd laugh? You have heard that laugh before, or something like it?"

"Yes, sir. There is a woman called Grace Poole who sews here. She laughs in that way. She is a strange person."

"Exactly. Grace Poole. You have guessed it. She is, as you say, very strange. Well, I will think about this. Meanwhile, I am glad that you are the only person, besides me, who knows what happened tonight. You are no talking fool. Please say nothing about it. I will explain this state of affairs to the others," he said, pointing to the ruined bed. "Now, return to your room. I will sleep on the sofa in the library for the rest of the night. It is nearly four. In two hours the servants will be up."

"Goodnight, then, sir," I said, turning to leave.

He seemed surprised—oddly so, since he just had told me to go.

"What!" he exclaimed. "Are you leaving me already?"

"You said that I could go, sir."

"But not like that! Not without a word or two of thanks. Why, you have saved my life! Snatched me from a horrible and excruciating death! And you walk past me as if we were strangers! At least shake hands." He held out his hand, and I gave him mine. He took it first in one, then both of his. "You have saved my life. I have the pleasure of owing you an immense debt. I cannot say more. To owe my life to anyone else would feel intolerable to me, but with you, it is different. To be in your debt is no burden, Jane." He paused, gazing at me. More words seemed to tremble on his lips, but he choked them back.

"Goodnight again, sir. You owe me no debt."

But he continued. "When I first saw you, I knew that you would do me good in some way at some time. The expression in your eyes did not..." He stopped, then proceeded hastily, "did not delight my innermost heart for nothing. People talk about soul mates. I have heard of fairy godmothers. There are grains of truth in the wildest fables. My cherished preserver, goodnight!" Strange energy was in his voice, strange fire in his look.

"I am glad that I happened to be awake," I said, trying to turn away.

"What! You are going?"

"I am cold, sir."

"Cold? Yes, you are standing in a pool of water. Go, then, Jane. Go."

But he still held my hand, and I could not free it. I thought of a solution. "I think I hear Mrs. Fairfax coming, sir," I said.

"Well, go then."

He relaxed his grip at last, and I could go. I returned to my bed but didn't even try to sleep. Until morning dawned I was tossed on a wild ocean where waves of trouble rolled under surges of joy. Too unsettled to rest, I rose as soon as day dawned.

Chapter 16

The day after this sleepless night, I both wanted to see Mr. Rochester and was afraid to see him. I needed to hear his voice again, but I dreaded looking him in the eye. I kept expecting him during the early part of the morning. He sometimes stopped in to see Adele in the schoolroom, and I felt sure that he would come.

But the morning passed as usual; nothing happened to interrupt Adele's studies. A bit later I heard some bustle in Mr. Rochester's bedroom. There was Mrs. Fairfax's voice, and Leah's, and the cook's, and John's. I could make out some of their exclamations: "What a mercy that Master was not burned in his bed!" "It is always dangerous to keep a candle lit at night." "How fortunate that he thought to use the water jug!" "It's a wonder that no one else woke up." Along with this talk were the sounds of scrubbing and moving things around. When I passed the room, I saw through the open door that everything was back in order. Leah stood in the window seat, cleaning the smoke-stained panes of glass. I was about to speak to her because I wondered how Mr. Rochester had explained what had happened. But as I entered the room, I saw a second person there—a woman sitting on a chair and sewing rings onto new curtains. The woman was none other than Grace Poole.

There she sat, solemn as usual, absorbed in her work. Nothing in that ordinary face suggested that this was a woman who had attempted murder the previous night and whose intended victim had confronted her with her crime. I was amazed and bewildered. She looked up while I stared. "Good morning, Miss," she said in her usual brief manner, then picked up another ring and went on with her sewing.

"Good morning, Grace," I said. "Has anything happened here? I thought that I heard the servants talking together a while ago."

"Master was reading in his bed last night, and he fell asleep with his candle lit. The curtains caught fire, but fortunately he awoke and put out the fire with a jug of water."

"How very strange!" I said, still looking at her hard. "Didn't Mr. Rochester wake anybody? Didn't anyone hear him?"

She again raised her eyes to me. This time there was something different—careful—in her expression. "The servants sleep so far away, Miss, that they would not be likely to hear. Mrs. Fairfax's room and yours are the nearest to Master's, but Mrs. Fairfax said she heard nothing. She is rather deaf, you know." She paused and then added, "But you are not deaf, Miss. Perhaps you heard something?"

"I did," I said, dropping my voice so that Leah, who was still polishing the panes, could not hear me. "At first I thought it was Pilot, but Pilot cannot laugh. I am certain that I heard a laugh, a strange one."

She threaded her needle with a steady hand, then said very calmly, "It doesn't seem likely that Master would laugh, Miss, when he was in such danger. You must have been dreaming."

"I was not dreaming," I said a little heatedly because her coolness irritated me.

"Have you told Master that you heard a laugh?" she asked.

"I have not had the chance to speak to him this morning."

"You did not think to open your door and look out into the hallway?" she asked.

She seemed to be cross-examining me, attempting to learn new information. The idea struck me that if she thought I suspected her, she would play some of her evil tricks on me. I should be on my guard. "On the contrary," I said, "I locked my door."

"Don't you lock your door every night before you get into bed?"

"What a devil!" I thought. "She wants to know my habits, so that she can plan accordingly." Then I replied sharply, "Up until now, I have not locked my door. I didn't think it was necessary. I was not aware of any danger at Thornfield Hall. But in the future I certainly will lock it every night."

"It would be wise to do so," she answered. "This neighborhood is as quiet as any that I know, and I never have heard of a robbery attempt here. Still, there are thousands of pounds' worth of silver and other goods here. I always think it's best to be on the safe side. It's an easy thing to lock a door, and then you have a barrier between you and any trouble that may be about. People say, 'God will take care of me,' but I say that we can help God out by using our common sense."

I stood still, absolutely dumbfounded by her hypocrisy, when the cook entered. "Mrs. Poole," she said, addressing Grace, "the servants' dinner will soon be ready. Will you come down?"

"No. Just put my glass of beer, a bit of meat and cheese, and some pudding on a tray, and I'll carry it upstairs."

The cook then told me that Mrs. Fairfax was waiting to eat with me, so I left. During dinner I hardly heard Mrs. Fairfax's conversation about the fire. I was busy puzzling over the mystery of Grace Poole. What was her position at Thornfield? Why hadn't she been handed over to the police or, at the very least, sent away from the house? Mr. Rochester almost had called her a criminal last night. Why didn't he accuse her openly? And why had he told me to keep silent? It was very strange. This bold, haughty gentleman seemed to be in the power of one of his servants—so much in her power that when she tried to kill him, he did nothing. If Grace had been young and pretty, I would have been tempted to think that he had some special feeling for her. But as hard-faced and middle-aged as she was, that idea seemed impossible. "Yet," I reflected, "she has lived here many years, and she and Mr. Rochester were young together. Is it possible that some foolish action of his, years ago, has given her power over him? Is she blackmailing him?" But again I thought of Mrs. Poole's square, flat figure and dry, unlovely face. "No, surely that cannot be it," I told myself again. "And yet," continued the secret voice that talks to us in our own hearts, "you are not beautiful either, and perhaps Mr. Rochester likes you. At any rate, you often have felt as if he did. And last night—remember his words; remember his look; remember his voice!" I remembered it all. The whole scene came before me again, vivid and alive.

By now I was in the schoolroom, bending over Adele and helping her with her drawing. She looked up with a start. "What is it, Mademoiselle?" she asked. "Your hand is trembling like a leaf, and your cheeks are as red as cherries!"

"I am hot, Adele, from bending down." She went on sketching; I went on thinking.

When darkness fell and Adele left me to go play in the nursery with Sophie, I wildly desired to see Mr. Rochester. I waited for the bell to ring below. I listened for Leah coming up with a message. I sometimes imagined that I heard Mr. Rochester's step, and I turned to the door, expecting to see him. The door remained shut. Still, it was only six o'clock, and he often sent for me at seven or eight.

At last I heard a step on the stairs, but it was only Leah, telling me that tea was ready in Mrs.

Fairfax's room. I was glad at least to go downstairs because that brought me nearer to Mr. Rochester. "You must want your tea," Mrs. Fairfax said kindly as I joined her. "You ate so little at dinner. I am afraid you are not well today. You look flushed and feverish."

"Oh, I'm quite well."

"Then you must prove it by showing me a good appetite. Will you fill the teapot while I finish this bit of knitting?" After she completed her task, she rose to close the curtain. "It is clear tonight," she said, looking through the window. "Mr. Rochester had a pleasant day for his journey."

"Journey! Has Mr. Rochester gone somewhere? I did not know that he was out."

"Yes. He left the moment that he finished breakfast. He has gone to Mr. Eshton's place, ten miles on the other side of Millcote. I believe that there is quite a party gathered there: Lord Ingram, Sir George Lynn, Colonel Dent, and others."

"Do you expect him back tonight?"

"No, and not tomorrow either. He likely will stay a week or more. When these fine, fashionable people get together, they are so surrounded by elegance and entertainment that they are in no hurry to separate. Gentlemen are especially in demand on such occasions, and Mr. Rochester is such lively company that I believe he is a general favorite. The ladies are very fond of him, although you could not call him a handsome man. I suppose his talents and abilities, and perhaps his wealth and good family, make up for any little fault of that kind."

"Are there ladies at the party?"

"Oh, yes. There are Mrs. Eshton and her three daughters, very elegant young ladies. And there are Blanche and Mary Ingram, who are very beautiful women. I will never forget seeing Blanche here, six or seven years ago, when she was a girl of eighteen. She came for a Christmas ball that Mr. Rochester gave. You should have seen the dining room that day—how richly it was decorated, how brilliantly lit! At least fifty ladies and gentlemen were present, and Miss Ingram was considered the belle of the evening."

"What was she like?"

"She is tall, with a fine figure and a long, graceful neck. She has a beautiful olive complexion, dark and clear, and eyes rather like Mr. Rochester's: large and black, and as brilliant as her jewels. And what a head of hair! It is raven black, and it was so beautifully arranged. She wore a crown of thick braids and, in front, the longest, glossiest curls that I ever saw. She was dressed in pure white, with an amber-colored scarf over one shoulder."

"She was greatly admired?"

"I should say so, and not only for her beauty but also for her talents. She sang while a gentleman accompanied her on the piano. Then she and Mr. Rochester sang a duet."

"Mr. Rochester? I did not know he could sing."

"Oh! He has a fine bass voice and excellent

taste in music."

"And this beautiful and talented lady is not yet married?"

"No, she is not. I gather that neither she nor her sister has a very large fortune. Old Lord Ingram's estates were not well managed, and the oldest son received almost everything."

"But I wonder that a wealthy gentleman hasn't fallen in love with her. Mr. Rochester, for instance. He is rich, is he not?"

"Oh, yes. But you see, there is a considerable difference in age: Mr. Rochester is nearly forty, and she is only twenty-five."

"What of that? More unequal matches are made every day."

"True, but I can't imagine that Mr. Rochester

would do such a thing. But you are eating nothing!"

"I am too thirsty to eat. Will you give me another cup of tea?"

When I was alone again, I reviewed the information that I had received. I looked into my heart, examined its thoughts and feelings, and tried my best to pull them into the realm of common sense, where they belonged. "You," I said, "Mr. Rochester's favorite? You have the power of pleasing him? You are important to him in any way? You fool! This morning you repeated last night's scene to yourself, did you? Hide your face, and be ashamed! He said something in praise of your eyes, did he? You blind puppy! Open them wide and look on your own stupidity! It does a woman no good to be flattered by a man who cannot possibly intend to marry her. It is madness for a woman to let a secret love kindle within her when it must remain unreturned and unknown. Listen, then, Jane Eyre. This is your sentence. Tomorrow place the mirror before you and faithfully draw your own likeness in chalk, without softening one defect. Then write under it, 'Portrait of a governess, without family, poor and plain.' Afterwards, mix your freshest, finest, clearest tints. Choose your most delicate camel-hair brushes. Create the loveliest face that you can imagine, according to Mrs. Fairfax's description of Blanche Ingram. Then title it 'Blanche, a talented lady of the upper class.' Whenever you imagine that Mr. Rochester thinks well of you, take out these two pictures and compare them. Say, 'Mr. Rochester probably could win that lady's love if he wished to. Is it likely that he would waste a serious thought on a poor and insignificant employee?'

"I'll do it," I promised myself, then fell asleep.

I kept my word. An hour or two was enough to sketch my own portrait in chalk. In about two weeks I had completed a portrait of an imaginary Blanche Ingram. It was a lovely face, and, when compared with my chalk portrait, the contrast was as great as anyone could have asked. The task did me good. It kept my head and hands busy, and it drove home a warning to my heart. Before long, I had reason to be glad that I had done such a thing. Thanks to it, I was able to meet what happened later with reasonable calm.

Chapter 17

A week passed, and there was no news of Mr. Rochester. Ten days, and still he did not come. Mrs. Fairfax said that she would not be surprised if he went straight from the Eshtons' to London, and then on to France, and didn't show his face again at Thornfield for a year. He often left like this, quite unexpectedly, she said. When I heard this, I began to feel a strange chill at my heart. I actually was permitting myself to experience a sickening sense of disappointment. But I quickly pulled myself together, reminding myself that Mr. Rochester's movements were not my concern. I went on with my day's business calmly enough, but I must confess that I kept thinking of reasons why I should leave Thornfield. In my mind I wrote several advertisements and wondered about new situations.

Mr. Rochester had been absent about two weeks when the mailman delivered a letter to Mrs. Fairfax. "It is from the master," she said as she looked at the return address. "Now I suppose we will know whether or not we should expect his return." While she opened the letter and read it, I went on drinking my coffee (we were at breakfast). It was hot and would serve to explain the fiery glow that suddenly rose to my face. Why my hand shook, and why I spilled half of my cup's contents into my saucer, I did not choose to think about. "Well, I sometimes think that Thornfield is too quiet, but it sounds as though we'll be busy enough now, at least for a little while," Mrs. Fairfax said, still holding the note in front of her eyeglasses.

Before I allowed myself to ask any questions, I tied the string of Adele's apron, which happened to be loose. After helping her to another bun and refilling her mug with milk, I said casually, "Mr. Rochester is not likely to return soon, I suppose?"

"Indeed, he is. In three days, he says. That will be next Thursday. And not alone either. I don't know how many fine people are coming with him. He said that all the best bedrooms should be prepared, and the library and drawing rooms should be cleaned. I am to hire more kitchen help from wherever I can. The ladies and gentlemen will bring their own servants, so we will have a full house." Mrs. Fairfax finished her breakfast and hurried away to begin the preparations.

The three days were as busy as she had predicted. I had thought that the rooms at Thornfield already were beautifully clean and well-arranged, but it appears that I was mistaken. Three women were hired to help. Such scrubbing, brushing, washing of paint, and beating of carpets, such taking down and putting up of pictures, polishing of mirrors and windows, lighting of fires in bedrooms, and airing of sheets I never saw before or since.

Adele was wildly excited at the thought of the coming guests. She was excused from school because Mrs. Fairfax had asked me to help her. I was in the kitchen all day, learning to make custards and cheesecakes and French pastry. The guests were expected to arrive Thursday afternoon, in time for dinner at six. During these days I had no time to think over my fantasies about Mr. Rochester, and I believe that I was as active and cheerful as anyone except Adele.

The only times that my thoughts turned dark were when I would see the third-story staircase door open slowly and Grace Poole come out. I would see her glide along, occasionally looking into the bustling, topsy-turvy bedrooms. She would say a quiet word to the hired women about the proper way to polish a grate, or clean a marble mantelpiece, or remove wallpaper stains, and then pass on. Twice a day she would come down to the kitchen, eat her meal, and smoke a pipe at the hearth. Then she would return to her gloomy upper room, carrying her pint of beer with her. Only one hour in twenty-four did she spend below with the other servants. She spent all the rest of her time in some upstairs room. There she sat and sewed—and laughed drearily to herself—as lonely as a prisoner in a dungeon. The strangest thing of all was that no one in the house except me seemed to find anything peculiar in all of this. In fact, I overheard part of a conversation about Grace between Leah and one of the hired women. Leah had been saying something I had not heard, and the woman remarked, "She gets good wages, I guess?"

"Yes," Leah said. "I wish I had as good. Mine aren't anything to complain about, but they're not one-fifth what Mrs. Poole receives. She is saving, too. I wouldn't be surprised if she had enough now to live independently if she wanted to leave. But she isn't forty yet, and she's strong and able. It's too soon for her to retire."

"She is a good hand, I expect," the other said.

"Oh, yes. She understands what she has to do," Leah answered. "There aren't many people who could replace her, not for any amount of money."

"That's the truth!" was the reply. "I wonder whether the master . . ." The woman was going to continue, but Leah turned, saw me, and nudged her companion. "Doesn't she know?" I heard the woman whisper. Leah shook her head, and the conversation was dropped. All I had learned from it was this: there was a mystery at Thornfield, and it was a mystery from which I was purposely shut out.

Thursday came. All the work had been completed the previous evening. The carpets were laid down, snowy-white quilts spread, dressing tables arranged, furniture polished, flowers piled in vases. Everything looked fresh and bright.

Afternoon arrived. Mrs. Fairfax put on her best black satin gown, her gloves, and her gold watch because it was her task to greet the company and show the ladies to their rooms. I had no need to make any change because I would not be called on to leave my own cozy room.

It had been a mild, serene spring day. It was drawing to an end now, but the evening was warm, and I sat at work in the schoolroom with the window open. "It is getting late," Mrs. Fairfax said, rustling in her satin. "I am glad that I planned dinner for an hour later than Mr. Rochester mentioned because it is past six now. I have sent John down to the gates to see if there is anything on the road. Here he is!" she said, leaning out the window. "Well, John, any news?"

"They're coming, ma'am," John answered. "They'll be here in ten minutes."

Adele flew to the window. I followed, standing where I could see without being seen. The ten minutes seemed very long, but at last we heard wheels. Four riders galloped up the drive. After them came two open carriages. Fluttering veils and waving feathers filled the vehicles. Two of the riders were young, dashing gentlemen. The third was Mr. Rochester, on his black horse, with Pilot bounding before him. At his side rode a lady. Her purple riding coat almost swept the ground. Her veil streamed on the breeze; gleaming through it was rich raven hair. "Miss Ingram!" Mrs. Fairfax exclaimed, and she hurried downstairs.

A joyous babble now echoed from the hall. There were gentlemen's deep tones and ladies' silvery laughter. I could distinguish the voice of Thornfield's master, welcoming his guests to his home. Then light steps ascended the stairs; there was a tripping through the hallway, soft laughs, the opening and closing of doors, and, for a time, a hush.

"They are changing their dresses," Adele said. Listening attentively, she had followed every movement. She sighed.

"Aren't you hungry, Adele?"

"Yes. It's been five or six hours since I ate anything."

"Well now, while the ladies are in their rooms, I will go down and get you something to eat."

I cautiously descended the back stairs that brought me directly to the kitchen. There I discovered a cold chicken, a loaf of bread, some tarts, and two plates. With this I fled back upstairs. I had reached the hallway, and was just shutting the door behind me, when the ladies began to exit their rooms. I could not continue to the schoolroom without passing some of their doors, and I did not like the idea of being surprised with my cargo of food. So I stood still and waited. My end of the hall was dark and windowless, and I was unlikely to be seen. As the doors opened, the fair ladies poured out, with dresses that gleamed richly in the twilight. They descended the staircase as noiselessly as a bright mist rolls down a hill. Their appearance left me with an impression of highborn elegance such as I never had seen before.

I found Adele peeping through the schoolroom door. "What beautiful ladies!" she cried.

"Oh, I wish I could go with them! Do you think Mr. Rochester will send for us after dinner?"

"No, I do not. Mr. Rochester has other things to think about. Never mind the ladies tonight; perhaps you will see them tomorrow. Here is your dinner."

Adele was quite hungry, so the chicken and tarts kept her attention for a while. It was a good thing that I had gotten this food. Otherwise, Adele, Sophie (with whom we shared our meal), and I would not have had any dinner. Everyone downstairs was too engaged to think of us. Dessert was not served until after nine, and at ten o'clock footmen still were running to and fro with trays and coffee cups.

I allowed Adele to sit up much later than usual. It amused her to look over the banister and watch the servants passing by. At eleven, her eyes were drooping heavily, so I carried her to bed. It was nearly one o'clock before the gentlemen and ladies returned to their rooms.

The next day brought fine weather, and the group set out to explore the neighborhood. They left just after noon, some on horseback, the rest in carriages. I witnessed both the departure and the return. As before, Miss Ingram was the only lady rider, and, as before, Mr. Rochester galloped at her side. The two rode a little apart from the rest. I pointed this out to Mrs. Fairfax, who was standing at the window with me. "You said they were not likely to be married," I said, "but you see that Mr. Rochester evidently likes her best of all the ladies."

"Yes, no doubt he admires her."

"And she must admire him," I added. "Look how she leans toward him as they speak. I wish I could see her face. I have not had a glimpse of it yet."

"You will see her this evening," Mrs. Fairfax answered. "I mentioned to Mr. Rochester how much Adele wished to be introduced to the ladies, and he said, 'Let her come into the drawing room after dinner. Ask Miss Eyre to come, too.'"

"Oh, he was only being polite," I protested. "Surely I don't really need to go."

"Well, I said to him that I did not think you would be comfortable with a group of strangers, but he replied, 'Nonsense! If she objects, tell her that I particularly want her. If she resists, I will come and fetch her myself.'"

"I will not give him that trouble," I answered. "I will go if I must, although I don't want to. Will you be there, Mrs. Fairfax?"

"No. I begged off, and he excused me. I'll tell you how to manage it so that you won't have to make a formal entrance, which is the most embarrassing part of the business. You must go into the drawing room while it is empty, before the ladies leave the dinner table, and choose a seat in a quiet corner. You don't need to stay long. Just let Mr. Rochester see that you are there. Then slip away. Nobody will notice."

"Will these people stay here long, do you think?"

"Perhaps two or three weeks. After Easter, Sir George Lynn will have to go to London on business, and I daresay Mr. Rochester will go with him. It surprises me that he already has stayed so long at Thornfield."

I felt considerably nervous about joining the party. Adele had been ecstatic all day after hearing that she was to be presented to the ladies in the evening. It was not until Sophie began to dress her that she calmed down. By the time she had her curls arranged, her pink silk frock put on, her long sash tied, and her lace mittens adjusted, she looked as grave as any judge. As for me, I put on my best dress (a silver-gray one purchased for Miss Temple's wedding and never worn since), smoothed my hair, and put on my pearl pin. We went downstairs.

We found the drawing room empty. A large fire burned silently on the marble hearth, and candles shone amid the exquisite flowers that covered the tables. Without a word, Adele sat down on the footstool that I pointed out to her. I retired to a window seat and, taking a book from a nearby table, tried to read.

Soon I heard the soft sound of sweeping dresses; a band of eight ladies entered the room, all wearing magnificent gowns. I rose and curtseyed to them. One or two nodded in return. The others only glanced at me. The ladies scattered about the room, reminding me of a flock of white plumy birds. Some of them lay casually on the sofas. Some bent over the tables and examined the flowers and books. The rest gathered in a group around the fire.

I learned their names afterwards and will mention them now. First, there were Mrs. Eshton and two of her daughters. Mrs. Eshton evidently had been pretty when younger and still was good-looking. Her oldest daughter, Amy, was small and childlike in face and manner. The second, Louisa, was taller and more elegant, with a very pretty face. Lady Lynn was a large, heavy woman of about forty, very erect and haughty-looking. She wore a gown of a rich purple fabric that seemed to change color in the firelight. Mrs. Dent was less showy but, I thought, more ladylike. She was slender, with a pale, gentle face and fair hair. Her black satin dress, lace scarf, and simple pearl jewelry pleased me better than the other lady's rainbow radiance.

But the three most striking women were Lady Ingram and her daughters, Blanche and Mary. All three were tall and shapely. The mother was around fifty. Her figure still was fine, her hair still black, her teeth still perfect. Most people would have called her splendid-looking for her age, and that was true, physically speaking. But there was an expression of extreme haughtiness about her. Her eyes were fierce and hard; they reminded me of Mrs. Reed's. Her speaking voice was unbearably pompous. Blanche and Mary were of equal height, straight and tall as poplars. Mary was too slender, but Blanche had a beautiful figure. I studied her, of course, with special interest. First, I wished to see whether Mrs. Fairfax had described her accurately. Second, I wanted to know if she resembled the miniature that I had painted of her. Finally, I wanted to know (I must admit) if she was likely to suit Mr. Rochester's taste. In many ways, she was much like both my picture and Mrs. Fairfax's description. The fine figure, the beautiful shoulders, the graceful neck, the dark eyes and black ringlets all were there. But her face? Her face was a youthful version of her mother's—hard and proud—except that the pride in Blanche's face was not as solemn. Blanche continually laughed while her lip curled with scorn.

I listened as Blanche began talking about botany with gentle Mrs. Dent. It seemed that Mrs. Dent had not studied that science, although she said that she liked flowers. Miss Ingram, it was clear, had studied botany. As she talked, making much use of her greater vocabulary, it became obvious to me that she was making fun of Mrs. Dent's ignorance. What she was doing might be clever, but it decidedly was not good-natured.

Did I now think that Miss Ingram was a woman whom Mr. Rochester would choose? I could not tell; I did not know his taste in female beauty. She certainly was majestic. Most gentlemen would admire her, I thought, and I had seen evidence that Mr. Rochester admired her. To remove my last doubts, I would have to see them together.

Do not think, reader, that Adele had been sitting motionless on the stool at my feet all this time.

No. When the ladies had entered, she had risen, gone to meet them, curtsied, and gravely said, "Good evening, ladies." Miss Ingram had looked down at her mockingly and exclaimed, "What a little puppet!" Lady Lynn had said, "It is Mr. Rochester's ward, I suppose—the little French girl he was speaking of." Mrs. Dent had kindly taken Adele's hand and given her a kiss. Amy and Louisa Eshton had cried out together, "What a love of a child!" Then they had invited her to join them on a sofa, where she now sat between them, chattering alternately in French and broken English. Adele held the attention not only of the young ladies but also of Mrs. Eshton and Lady Lynn, and they all spoiled her to her heart's content.

At last, coffee was brought in, and the gentlemen joined us. Henry and Frederick Lynn were dashing young men, and Colonel Dent was a fine soldierly gentleman. Mr. Eshton, a judge, had a theatrical kind of good looks. His hair was white, while his eyebrows and whiskers still were dark. Lord Ingram was tall and handsome, like his sisters.

And Mr. Rochester? He came in last. I tried to concentrate on the embroidery that I had brought along to keep my hands busy. When I saw him, I instantly recalled the last moment we had met. I again saw his face, bent close to mine, looking at me with eyes that showed a full and overflowing heart. How close we had been at that moment! What had happened since to make us now so distant? I felt the change so strongly that I was not surprised when, without looking at me, he took a seat in the other side of the room and began talking with some of the ladies. His attention soon was fastened on them, and I knew that I could look at him as much as I liked. I could not help myself. I was like a man dying of thirst who knows that the well before him is poisoned yet drinks as deeply as he can. It is true that beauty is in the eye of the beholder. My master's face was not beautiful according to any standards of beauty, but it was more than beautiful to me. I had not intended to love him. I had tried hard to eliminate from my soul the seeds of love that I detected there. But now, at the first renewed sight of him, they sprouted, green and strong. Without even looking at me, he made me love him.

Coffee was served. Since the gentlemen had entered, the ladies had become as lively as larks. Frederick Lynn had taken a seat beside Mary Ingram and was showing her the illustrations in a splendid book. She looked, smiled now and then, but said little. Tall Lord Ingram leaned on the back of the chair in which lively little Amy Eshton was sitting. She glanced up at him and chattered like a wren. Henry Lynn was sitting on a footstool beside Louisa; Adele shared it with him. He was trying to speak French with Adele, and Louisa was laughing at his blunders.

With whom would Blanche Ingram pair? She was standing alone at the table, gracefully bending over an album. She seemed to be waiting to be sought. But instead of waiting long, she selected a mate. Mr. Rochester stood alone near the fire. Taking a place on the opposite side of the mantelpiece, she confronted him, "Mr. Rochester, I thought you were not fond of children."

"I am not."

"Then why did you take charge of such a little doll as that?" She pointed to Adele. "Where did you pick her up?"

"I did not pick her up. She was left on my hands."

"You should have sent her to boarding school."

"I could not afford it."

"But you have a governess for her. I saw a person with her just now. Is she gone? No. There she is. You pay her, of course. It must be as expensive as boarding school, or even more expensive, because you have to feed both of them."

I feared—hoped?—that the reference to me would make Mr. Rochester glance my way. But he never turned his eyes. "I have not considered the subject," he said indifferently, looking straight in front of him.

"No. You men never do consider economy and common sense. You should hear Mama on the subject of governesses. Mary and I had at least a dozen in our day. Half of them were hateful; the rest were ridiculous. Weren't they, Mama?"

"Did you speak, my own?" her mother said. Blanche repeated her question, and Lady Ingram responded with great feeling. "My dearest, don't mention governesses. The very word irritates me. No one knows what I have suffered from their stupidity. I thank heaven that I am finished with them now!" At this point Mrs. Dent bent over and whispered something into her ear. I suppose it was a reminder that one of the dreadful creatures was present in the room. "Too bad!" her Ladyship said. "I hope it may do her good." Then, in a lower tone but still loud enough for me to hear, she said, "I noticed her. I am a great judge of faces, and in hers I see all the faults of her class."

"What are they, madam?" Mr. Rochester inquired.

"I will tell you in private," she replied.

"But my curiosity needs satisfaction now."

"Ask Blanche. She is nearer to you than I am."

"No, Mama! I have just one word to say of the whole tribe: they are a nuisance. What tricks Theodore and I used to play on our governesses Miss Wilson, Mrs. Grey, and Madame Joubert! The best fun was with Madame Joubert. Miss Wilson was a poor sickly thing and not worth the trouble. Mrs. Grey was so thick-skinned that she didn't notice anything. But poor Madame Joubert! I still can see her having hysterics when we spilled our tea, crumbled our bread and butter, tossed our books up to the ceiling, or drummed the desks with our rulers."

Amy Eshton joined in with her soft, childish voice. "Louisa and I used to tease our governess, too. But she was such a good creature that she would bear anything. Nothing made her angry. She never was cross with us, was she, Louisa?"

"Oh dear," Miss Ingram said, curling her lip sarcastically, "I suppose we now will have to listen to all of the guests' memories of their governesses. In order to avoid such a boring conversation, I suggest that we introduce a new topic. Mr. Rochester, do you second my motion?"

"Madam, I support you on this point as on every other."

"Then let's sing together," she said, and she settled herself on the piano bench.

"Now I can slip away," I thought. But the sounds that filled the air halted me. Mrs. Fairfax had said that Mr. Rochester possessed a fine voice. He did. It was a mellow, powerful bass into which he poured great feeling; it touched my heart. I waited until the last note had ended and the chatter of conversation, which had quieted, resumed. Then I slipped out through a side door.

As I hurried toward the staircase, I noticed that my shoe was untied and knelt to tie it. When I heard the dining room door open, I rose hastily and found myself face to face with Mr. Rochester.

"How are you?" he asked.

"I am very well, sir."

"Why didn't you come and speak to me in the room?"

I thought that I could have asked him the same thing, but I said only, "I did not wish to disturb you. You seemed busy, sir."

"What have you been doing during my absence?"

"Nothing in particular. Teaching Adele as usual."

"And getting a good deal paler than you were. What is the matter?"

"Nothing, sir."

"Did you catch a cold that night you half drowned me?"

"Not in the least."

"Come back to the drawing room. You are deserting too early."

"I am tired, sir."

He looked at me for a minute. "And a little depressed," he said. "What about? Tell me."

"Nothing. Nothing, sir. I am not depressed."

"I think that you are. You are so sad that a few more words would bring tears to your eyes. Indeed, there are tears now, shining and swimming. Now one has fallen from your lashes to the floor. If I had time and was not in mortal dread of some gossiping nuisance of a servant passing, I would find out what all this means. Well, tonight I will excuse you. But understand that as long as my visitors stay, I expect you to appear in the drawing room every evening. Now go, and send Sophie to fetch Adele. Goodnight, my . . ." He stopped, bit his lip, and abruptly left me.

Chapter 18

These were merry, busy days at Thornfield Hall. How different they were from the first three months of stillness and monotony that I had passed beneath its roof! Now there was life everywhere, movement all day long. You hardly could cross a hallway without running into a fashionable lady's maid or a handsome young servant. Even when the fine weather ended and rain set in for days, the guests' enjoyment never ceased. Their indoor amusements only became more varied.

One evening they played charades. The servants emptied closets and wardrobes to supply shawls, dresses, draperies, hooped petticoats, bonnets, and every sort of antique costume for the players to choose from as they disguised themselves. "Will you play?" Mr. Rochester asked as the teams were being organized. I shook my head, and he did not insist as I had feared. A little later Mr. Eshton repeated the invitation, but Lady Ingram instantly vetoed it. "No," I heard her say, "she looks too stupid for any such game."

The guests acted out scenes from history and literature, Biblical stories, and famous episodes from the theater. In one Mr. Rochester was wrapped in colorful shawls, a turban on his head.

With his dark eyes and swarthy skin, he looked the image of an Arabian sheik. He soon was joined by Miss Ingram, who also was dressed in Arabian fashion. A crimson scarf was tied sash-like around her waist; an embroidered handkerchief was knotted about her forehead; her beautiful arms were bare, and one of them gracefully balanced a pitcher on her head. After giving the "sheik" a drink of water, she stared in astonishment as he produced a jewel box, then laid magnificent jewels at her feet. As he fastened the bracelets onto her arms and rings into her ears, she glowed with delight.

My memory of the rest of the evening is vague, but I still can see the consultation that followed each scene. I see Mr. Rochester turn to Miss Ingram, and Miss Ingram to him. I see her lean her head toward him, until her jet-black curls almost brush against his cheek. I hear their whisperings. I recall their exchanged glances. Even today the feelings aroused by what I saw burn in my memory. I had learned to love Mr. Rochester. I could not unlove him now, even though he had ceased to notice me. I could pass hours in his presence, and he never once would turn his eyes in my direction. A highborn lady absorbed all of his attentions. If this lady ever glanced at me by chance, she instantly looked away, as though I were too insignificant for her to notice. I could not unlove him, although I felt sure that he soon would marry this very lady. I could see her proud confidence in that fact.

These facts did not cool my love, although

they caused me great unhappiness. You may think that jealousy, too, bothered me, but I was not jealous. Miss Ingram was not worth my jealousy. For a governess to say that about such a lady might seem ridiculous, but it was true. I did not admire Miss Ingram. She was very showy, but she was not genuine. She was splendid-looking and talented, but her heart was cold and poor. She would repeat clever ideas that she had read in books, but she had no real opinions of her own. There was no tenderness, pity, or truth in her, as was clear from her attitude toward little Adele. If the child approached her, she would push her away with a snarl, always treating her with coldness. I was not the only one to notice her behavior. Mr. Rochester himself saw all of this and seemed untouched by it. This lack of feeling, as much as anything else, gave me pain.

He was going to marry her, I assumed, because her rank and connections pleased him. I saw that he did not love her. If he had sincerely cared for her, I would have died inside but wished them both well. If Miss Ingram had been a good and kindly woman, I would have been caught between the two tigers of jealousy and despair. Then, my heart torn out and devoured, I would have admired her and been quiet for the rest of my days. I have not criticized Mr. Rochester's plan of marrying a woman he did not love. It surprised me when I first realized that was his intention. But the longer I thought about it, the less I felt justified in judging either him or Miss Ingram. I supposed that they were acting according to principles that they had been taught since their childhoods. I assumed that many people in their class acted like this, although I could not understand why. It seemed to me that if I were a gentleman like Mr. Rochester, I would marry only a wife whom I could love. This seemed such an obvious point, however, that I decided there must be good arguments against it that I did not understand. Otherwise, all the world would act as I thought it should.

My thoughts were very much caught up in my master and his future bride. I saw only them, heard only their voices. Indeed, Mr. Rochester was the life and soul of the party. If he was absent from the room an hour, a dullness seemed to steal over his guests. His re-entrance gave everyone fresh life.

His absence was particularly felt one day when he had been called to Millcote on business and was not expected back until late. The afternoon was wet, so the guests had postponed their planned visit to a nearby gypsy camp. Some of the gentlemen had gone to the stables. The younger ones, together with the younger ladies, were playing pool while the older ladies played cards. Blanche Ingram had fetched a novel from the library and flung herself onto a sofa.

It was nearly dusk when little Adele, who was kneeling in the window seat, exclaimed, "Here comes Mr. Rochester!" I turned, and Miss Ingram darted forward from her sofa. The others, too, looked up from their occupations because we all heard the crunching of wheels and the splashing of horse hooves on the wet gravel. "Why is he in a carriage?" Miss Ingram asked. "He left on horseback, didn't he? And Pilot was with him. What has he done with the animals?" The carriage stopped, and a gentleman emerged. But it was not Mr. Rochester. It was a tall, fashionable stranger. "How annoying!" Miss Ingram exclaimed. "You tiresome monkey," she scolded Adele. "What are you doing, giving out wrong information?" She glared at me too, as though I shared Adele's fault.

Some conversation was heard in the hall, and the newcomer entered. He greeted us and said, "It appears that I come at an inconvenient time, when my friend Mr. Rochester is not at home. But I have had a very long journey; with your kind permission I will wait here until he returns." His manner was polite. His accent was somewhat unusual, not exactly foreign but not altogether English. He was about Mr. Rochester's age and at first glance was a fine-looking man. On closer examination, though, there was something in his face that was less pleasant. It was a silly, lazy face, too used to easy living.

I saw the visitor again at dinner, where he seemed relaxed and comfortable, even among a party of strangers. I liked his looks even less than before. His eyes had an odd, blank look, and there was nothing strong, firm, or thoughtful about his appearance. In my mind I compared him to Mr. Rochester. The comparison was like that between a farm goose and a fierce falcon. He had spoken of

Mr. Rochester as an old friend, but I could not imagine what the two men had in common.

After dinner, sitting quietly in my corner, I could hear the stranger's conversation. I learned that he was Mr. Mason and that he had just arrived from Jamaica. I was greatly surprised to learn that he had first met Mr. Rochester there. I knew that Mr. Rochester had traveled a good deal, but I had thought that his wanderings had been confined to Europe.

Just then an unexpected thing happened. A servant stopped by Mr. Eshton's chair and said something to him in a low voice, of which I heard only the words "old woman . . . quite troublesome."

"Tell her that she will be arrested if she makes a nuisance of herself," the judge said.

"No, stop!" Colonel Dent interrupted. "Don't send her away, Eshton. We should consult the ladies." Speaking more loudly, he continued, "Ladies, you talked of visiting the gypsy camp. Sam here says that one of the old women is in the servants' hall at this moment and insists on coming in to tell fortunes. Would you like to see her?"

"I cannot possibly allow such a person to enter here," Lady Ingram announced.

"Indeed, Mama, you can and you will," Blanche haughtily declared as she turned around on the piano stool. "I want to hear my fortune. Sam, bring her in."

"Yes! Yes!" all the young ladies and gentlemen

cried. "Let her come. It will be great fun!"

The servant hesitated. "She's a rough-looking old thing," he said.

"Go!" Miss Ingram ordered.

The man went but returned in a moment. "She won't come now," he said. "She says it's not her mission to appear before the 'vulgar herd' (them's her words). I have to show her into a room by herself; then those who wish to consult her have to go to her one by one."

"You see now, Blanche," Lady Ingram began. "She is very rude. Now just think, my angel girl, and . . ."

"Show her into the library," the "angel girl" cut in. "Do what I say, blockhead!"

Sam vanished again. "She's ready now," he said as he reappeared. "She wishes to know who her first visitor will be."

"I think I'd better look in on her before any of the ladies go," Colonel Dent said.

"Tell her, Sam, that a gentleman is coming."

Sam went and returned. "She says, sir, that she will speak only with ladies who are young and single."

"By Jove, she has taste!" Henry Lynn exclaimed.

Miss Ingram rose solemnly. "I'll go first," she said, and she swept from the room.

The minutes passed very slowly. Fifteen went by before the library door again opened and Miss Ingram returned to us. Would she laugh? Would she take it as a joke? Everyone looked at her with eager curiosity, but she stared back coldly. She walked stiffly to her seat and took it in silence.

"Well, Blanche?" Lord Ingram said.

"What did she say, Sister?" Mary asked.

"What did you think? Is she a real for- tuneteller?" Miss Eshton demanded.

"Don't be silly," Miss Ingram replied. "Really, you are too easily taken in. She performed the usual tricks and said the things that all such people say. My curiosity is gratified, and I think that Mr. Eshton would do well to have the old hag arrested, as he threatened." With that, Miss Ingram took a book, leaned back in her chair, and refused to speak further. I watched her for nearly half an hour. During all that time she never turned a page. Instead, her face grew darker and more dissatisfied. She obviously had heard something that greatly displeased her.

Meanwhile, Mary Ingram, Amy Eshton, and Louisa Eshton declared that they did not dare to go alone, and they visited the old woman as a group. Their visit was not as quiet as Miss Ingram's had been. We heard hysterical giggling and little shrieks proceeding from the library. After about twenty minutes, they burst through the door and came running across the hall as if they were scared half out of their wits. "How strange she is!" they all cried. "She told us such things! She knows all about us!" They sank, breathless, into their seats. They declared that the gypsy had told them things they had said and done when they were mere children; she also had described books and ornaments that they kept at home as well as presents that relatives had given them. They said that she even had guessed their thoughts and had whispered in the ear of each the name of the person she liked best in the world. All this they told with much blushing, giggling, and exclaiming.

In the midst of this confusion, I heard a cough at my elbow. I turned and saw Sam. "If you please, Miss, the gypsy declares that there is another young lady in the room who has not been to her yet. She swears that she will not go until she has seen her. I thought it must be you. What should I tell her?"

"Oh, I will go by all means," I answered. I was glad of the chance to satisfy my curiosity. I slipped out of the room without anyone's noticing.

"If you like, Miss," Sam said, "I'll wait in the hall for you. If she frightens you, just call and I'll come in."

"No, Sam, you can go back to the kitchen. I am not afraid." I was very interested and excited.

Chapter 19

The library looked peaceful as I entered it. The fortuneteller was seated in an easy chair near the fireplace. She wore a red cloak and a broad-brimmed hat tied, with a striped handkerchief, under her chin. She was bending over the fire and seemed to be reading in a little black book. She muttered words to herself as she read. She continued reading for several moments after I entered. I stood on the rug and warmed my hands, waiting until she shut her book and slowly looked up. Her hat-brim shaded her face, but I could see, as she raised it, that it was a strange one. It looked all brown and black, and her jaw was wrapped in a white bandage.

"Well, do you want your fortune told?" she said in a voice as harsh as her features.

"I don't care. You may please yourself, but I should warn you that I have no faith."

"You are an impudent girl. I could tell it from the way you stepped as you entered the room."

"Could you? You have a quick ear."

"I have, and a quick eye and a quick brain."

"You need them all in your trade."

"I do, especially when I have customers like you to deal with." The old woman snickered under

her hat and bandage. She then took out a short black pipe and began to smoke. After gazing at the fire a few moments, she said very deliberately, "You are cold, sick, and silly."

"Prove it," I responded.

"I will. You are cold because you are alone. You are sick because the sweetest feelings that anyone can have stay far away from you. You are silly because, although you suffer, you will not invite those feelings to approach, or even go to meet them where they await you." She again put her pipe to her lips and smoked with vigor.

"You could say all of that to almost anyone who lives as a single employee in a great house."

"I might say it to almost anyone, but would it

be true of almost anyone? You are very close to happiness—yes, within reach of it—but you need to move toward it."

"I don't understand riddles."

"If you wish me to speak more plainly, show me your palm."

"And I must cross yours with silver, I suppose?"

"To be sure." I gave her a shilling. She put it into an old stocking that she took out of her pocket. She took my hand in hers, bent her face over it, and examined it closely. "It is too fine," she said. "I can make nothing of such a hand. It is almost without lines. Besides, what is in a palm? The future is not written there."

"I believe that," I said.

"No," she continued, "it is in the face: on the forehead, around the eyes, in the lines of the mouth. Kneel, and lift up your head." I knelt within half a yard of her. She stirred the fire, so that a light broke from the disturbed coal. The glare threw her face into deeper shadow while it illuminated mine. "I wonder what feelings you brought with you tonight," she said. "I wonder what you think during all the hours you sit in that room, with those fine people flitting around you. You have nothing in common with them, no sympathy, no communication."

"I often feel tired, sometimes sleepy, but seldom sad," I answered.

"Then you have some secret hope to lift you

and please you with whispers of the future?"

"No. My greatest hope is to save enough money to rent a little house and set up a school in it."

"That is little food for a spirit like yours—that and sitting in the window seat (you see, I know your habits)."

"You have learned them from the servants."

"Ah! You think you are clever. Well, perhaps I have. To be truthful, I am acquainted with one of them—Mrs. Poole."

I was startled when I heard that name. "You are?" I thought. "Then you are involved in the devil's work after all!"

"Don't be alarmed," the strange being continued. "Mrs. Poole is quiet and trustworthy. Anyone may confide in her. But, as I was saying . . . Sitting in the window seat, do you think of nothing but your future school? Have you no interest in any of the people around you? Is there not one face you study? One figure whose movements you watch with curiosity?"

"I like to observe all the faces and figures."

"But do you never single out one from the rest, or maybe two?"

"I frequently do, when a pair's gestures or looks seem to be telling a tale. It amuses me to watch them."

"What tale do you most like to hear?"

"Oh, I don't have much choice. Generally they run on the same theme—courtship—and promise to end in the same catastrophe: marriage."

"And do you like that monotonous theme?"

"I don't care about it. It means nothing to me."

"Nothing to you? When a lady, young and full of life and health, charming with beauty and the gifts of rank and fortune, sits and smiles into the eyes of a gentleman whom you . . ."

"Whom I what?"

"Whom you know and perhaps think well of."

"I don't know the gentlemen here. I scarcely have exchanged a syllable with any of them. As to thinking well of them, some of them seem respectable and middle-aged; others are young, dashing, and handsome. All of them are free to enjoy the smiles of anyone they please."

"You don't know the gentlemen here? You scarcely have exchanged a syllable with any of them? Does that include the master of the house?"

"He is not at home."

"Oh, how you quibble! He went to Millcote this morning and will be back tonight or tomorrow. Does that little absence blot him out of existence?"

"No, but I cannot see what Mr. Rochester has to do with what you are talking about."

"I was talking of ladies smiling into gentlemen's eyes. Lately so many smiles have been poured into Mr. Rochester's eyes that they overflow like two cups filled above the brim. Haven't you noticed that?"

"Mr. Rochester has a right to enjoy his guests' company."

"No question about his right. I am asking about your observations. Have you noticed Mr. Rochester being willing to receive those smiles and grateful for them?"

"Grateful? I have not detected gratitude in his face."

"Detected! You have analyzed, then. And what did you detect, if not gratitude?"

I said nothing.

"Haven't you seen love? And, looking forward, haven't you seen him married and his bride happy?"

"Not exactly. Your witch's skill is failing you."

"What the devil have you seen, then?" she demanded.

"Never mind. I came here to receive information, not to give it. Can you see, then, that Mr. Rochester is to be married?"

"Yes. To the beautiful Miss Ingram."

"Soon?"

"Appearances would say so. No doubt, they will be an extremely happy pair. He must love such a handsome, witty, accomplished lady. And she probably loves him or, if not him, at least his wallet. I know that she considers the Rochester estate very desirable, although (God pardon me!) I told her something on that subject about an hour ago that made her look very upset. The corners of her mouth fell half an inch. I would advise her suitor to look out. If another comes, with a fatter bankroll, he'll be out with the garbage."

"But I did not come to hear Mr. Rochester's fortune. I came to hear my own, and you have told me nothing of it."

"Your fortune is yet doubtful. When I examined your face, one trait contradicted another. Chance has offered you a measure of happiness. She has laid it carefully on one side for you. It is up to you to stretch out your hand and take it. Whether you will do so is the problem I study. Kneel on the rug again." Once again she stared into my face for a long time. "I see no enemy to happiness except in the forehead. That brow says, 'I can live alone if self-respect requires me to. I will not sell my soul to buy happiness.' Now," the old witch continued, "I would like to prolong this moment forever, but I dare not. So far I have controlled myself thoroughly. I have acted as I swore to myself that I would act, but to try further is beyond my strength. Rise, Miss Eyre. Leave me. The play is over."

Where was I? Did I wake or sleep? Had I been dreaming? Did I still dream? The old woman's voice had changed. Her accent and gesture were as familiar to me as my own face in a mirror. I got up but did not go. I looked, stirred the fire, and looked again. She pulled her hat and bandage more tightly around her face and again waved at me to leave. The firelight shone on her hand as it stretched out, and I at once noticed that hand. It was no older or more withered than my own. It was round and smooth, and a broad ring flashed on the little finger—a ring I had seen a hundred times. Again I looked at the face, which no longer was turned from me. The hat and bandage had been removed.

"Well, Jane?" the familiar voice asked. And Mr. Rochester stepped out of his disguise.

"Now, sir, what a strange idea!"

"But well carried out, eh? Don't you think so?"

"You must have managed well with the ladies."

"But not with you?"

"You did not act like a gypsy with me."

"How did I act? Like myself?"

"No, like something I cannot explain. I believe you have been trying to draw me out. You have been talking nonsense to make me talk nonsense. It is scarcely fair, sir."

"Do you forgive me, Jane?"

"I cannot tell until I have thought about it. If I find that I have not said anything too silly, I will try to forgive you, but it was not right."

"Oh, you have been very careful, very sensible."

"May I leave now, sir?"

"No. Stay a moment, and tell me what the people in the drawing room are doing."

"Discussing the gypsy, I suppose."

"Sit down. Let me hear what they said about me."

"I'd better not stay long, sir. It must be near to eleven o'clock. Oh, are you aware, Mr. Rochester, that a stranger arrived here this evening?"

"A stranger? No. Who can it be? Is he gone?"

"No. He said that he had known you a long time and that he was sure you wouldn't mind if he waited here until you returned."

"The devil he did! Did he give his name?"

"His name is Mason, sir, and he comes from the West Indies. From Jamaica, I think."

Mr. Rochester was standing near me. He had taken my hand as if to lead me to a chair. As I spoke, he gave my wrist a violent squeeze, and the smile froze on his lips. "Mason! The West Indies!" he said, growing whiter than ashes. He hardly seemed to know what he was doing.

"Do you feel ill, sir?" I asked.

"Jane, I've had a shock. I've had a shock."

"Oh, lean on me, sir."

"Jane, you offered me your shoulder once before. Let me have it now."

"Yes, sir. Yes. Take my arm."

He sat down and made me sit beside him. He held and stroked my hand and looked at me with a troubled expression. "My little friend," he said. "I wish that I were on a quiet island with only you and that all trouble, danger, and hideous memories were gone from me."

"Can I help you, sir? I'd give my life to serve you."

"Jane, if I need help, you are the one I will ask. I promise you that."

"Thank you, sir. Tell me what to do. I'll try to do it."

"Fetch me a glass of wine from the dining room. They will be having supper there. Tell me if Mason is with them and what he is doing."

I went. I found all the guests at supper, as Mr. Rochester had said. Everyone seemed very cheerful, laughing and talking loudly. Mr. Mason stood near the fire, talking to Colonel and Mrs. Dent, and appeared as merry as any of them. I filled a wine glass and returned to the library.

Mr. Rochester looked less pale, and he took the glass from my hand. "Here's to your health, my guardian angel!" he said. He swallowed the contents and returned the glass to me. "What are they doing, Jane?"

"Laughing and talking, sir."

"They don't look grave and mysterious, as if they had heard something strange?"

"Not at all. They are full of jokes."

"And Mason?"

"He was laughing, too."

"If all these people came and spat at me, what would you do, Jane?"

"Show them out of the room, sir, if I could."

He half smiled. "But if I were to go to them, and they looked at me coldly and whispered among themselves and then left me one by one, what then? Would you go with them?"

"No, sir. I would stay with you."

"To comfort me?"

"Yes, sir, to comfort you as well as I could."

"And if they shunned you, too, for staying with

me?"

"I would care nothing about their shunning."

"Go back into the room now. Quietly step up to Mason, and whisper into his ear that I am here and wish to see him. Show him in here; then leave us."

"Yes, sir."

I did as he asked. The guests all stared at me as I walked through them. I found Mr. Mason, delivered the message, and led him to the library. Then I went to my room.

Late that night, after I had been in bed some time, I heard the visitors go to their rooms. I heard Mr. Rochester saying, "This way, Mason. This is your room." He spoke cheerfully. His voice set my heart at ease. I soon was asleep.

Chapter 20

I had forgotten to close my curtain, which I usually did. As a result, when the full, bright moon came to shine directly through my window, I awakened. I opened my eyes to see the silver-white disk gazing at me. It was beautiful but disturbed my sleep. I half rose and put my hand out to draw the curtain.

Good God! What a cry! The night's silence was ripped in half by a savage, shrill scream that echoed from one end of Thornfield Hall to the other. My pulse stopped. My heart stood still. My outstretched arm was paralyzed. The cry died away, but now over me—yes, in the room just above mine—I heard a struggle. A half-smothered voice shouted, "Help! Help! Rochester! For God's sake, come!" A door opened, and I heard someone rushing along the hallway. Another step stomped on the flooring above me. Something fell. Then there was silence.

I put on some clothes and hurried from my room. Terrified murmurs were sounding in every room. Door after door opened. One guest after another looked out. Eventually the hallway filled with people. "Oh! What is it?" . . . "Who is hurt?" . . . "What has happened?" . . . "Fetch a light!" . . .

"Is it a fire?" . . . "Are there robbers?" the guests exclaimed. "Where the devil is Rochester?" Colonel Dent cried. "He is not in his room."

"Here!" was shouted in reply. "Be calm, all of you. I'm coming." The door at the end of the hall opened, and Mr. Rochester advanced with a candle. He had just descended from the upper story.

Miss Ingram ran to him and seized his arm. "Tell us what has happened!" she demanded.

"Please, don't pull me down or strangle me," he replied because both the Eshton girls were clinging to him now, and the two oldest ladies, in vast white bathrobes, were bearing down on him like ships in full sail. "It's all right! Everything is all right!" he cried. "A servant has had a nightmare; that is all. She's an excitable, nervous person, and she ended up having a fit of hysterics. Please go back to your rooms, so that the house will be quiet and she can be looked after properly. Ladies, you will catch cold if you stay in this drafty hallway any longer." And so, alternately coaxing and commanding, he managed to get them all back into their rooms.

I did not wait to be ordered back into mine but retreated to it unnoticed—not, however, to go to bed. Instead I dressed myself carefully. I probably had been the only person to hear the sounds that had followed the scream because they had come from the room above mine. I was certain that they were not the result of a servant's dream, and I decided to be ready for any emergency. Once I was dressed, I sat a long time by the window looking out over the silent grounds and fields, waiting for . . . I did not know what I was waiting for. It seemed to me that some event must follow the strange cry, struggle, and call.

But quiet returned to the house. In about an hour Thornfield Hall was again as hushed as a desert. Not liking to sit in the cold and dark, I thought I would lie down on my bed, even though I was fully dressed. Just as I stooped to take off my shoes, there was a quiet tap at my door. "Am I needed?" I asked.

"Are you up?" my master's voice—the one that I had expected to hear—replied.

"Yes, sir."

"And dressed?"

"Yes."

"Do you have a sponge in your room? And some smelling salts? Bring them both, and come with me very quietly."

My slippers were thin; I could walk over the carpeted floor as softly as a cat. Mr. Rochester glided down the hall and up the stairs. He stopped in the third story's dark, low corridor. I had followed and stood at his side. Holding a key, he began to unlock one of the small black doors. He paused, and spoke to me again. "You don't get sick at the sight of blood?"

"I don't think so, sir."

"Give me your hand," he said. "It won't do to risk fainting." I put my fingers into his. "Warm and steady," he remarked, then turned the key and opened the door.

I saw a room that I remembered seeing the day Mrs. Fairfax first showed me around the house. The walls were hung with tapestries, but one tapestry now was looped up to reveal a door that usually was concealed. This door was open, and a light shone out of the room within. I heard within it a snarling sound, almost like a dog growling over a bone.

"Wait a moment," Mr. Rochester said, and he went forward to the inner apartment. A shout of laughter greeted his entrance, noisy at first and ending in Grace Poole's goblin "Ha! Ha!" I heard low voices.

Then Mr. Rochester emerged, shutting the door behind him. "Here, Jane," he said. I walked around to the other side of a large bed. An easy chair was near the bed, and a man sat in it. His head leaned back, and his eyes were closed. As Mr. Rochester held the candle over him, I recognized Mr. Mason, whose face now was pale and lifeless-looking. I saw, too, that one of his arms and one side of his body were soaked in blood. Mr. Rochester fetched a basin of water from the washstand. "Hold that," he said. While I obeyed, he took the sponge, dipped it in, and moistened the corpse-like face. He then asked for my smelling salts and waved them under Mr. Mason's nose. Soon the man opened his eyes and groaned. Mr. Rochester opened the shirt of the wounded man, whose arm and shoulder were bandaged, and began sponging away the blood that was trickling down.

"Am I dying?" Mr. Mason murmured.

"Pooh! No. A mere scratch. Have courage, man. I'll fetch a doctor for you now. You'll be able to leave here by morning, I hope. Jane," he continued.

"Sir?"

"I have to leave you here with this gentleman, for an hour or perhaps two. Clean away the blood as I am doing. If he feels faint, give him a sip of water and put the smelling salts under his nose. Do not talk with him. Richard, if you speak with her, it will be at the risk of your life." The poor man groaned again. He looked as if he dared not move. Fear, either of death or of something else, seemed to almost paralyze him. Mr. Rochester put the sponge into my hand, and I began to use it as he had. He watched me a second, then said, "Remember; no conversation," and left the room.

It gave me a strange feeling to hear the key turn in the lock and Mr. Rochester's step retreat down the stairs. Here I was in the mysterious third story, locked into one of its rooms, night all around me, a pale and bloody man under my hands, and a murderess separated from me by a single door. Yes, that was terrifying. I could bear the rest, but I shuddered at the thought of Grace Poole bursting in on me.

I was determined to do as I had promised. I must watch this ghastly face, its eyes now shut, now

open, now wandering around the room, now staring at me. I must dip my hand again and again into the basin of reddened water and wipe away the trickling blood.

As I kept to my task, I wondered what terrible mystery resided in Thornfield Hall that its owner could not remove. What horror had caused fire and now blood at night's deadest hours? This man whom I bent over—this commonplace stranger— how had he become entangled in the web of horror? Why had he been attacked? What had made him come to this part of the house when he should have been asleep in bed? Why was he so tame about the violence done to him? Why did he quietly obey Mr. Rochester's command to be silent? And why had this passive man's mere name horrified my strong, proud master? I could not forget Mr.

Rochester's look as he had whispered, "Jane, I've had a shock. I've had a shock." I could not forget how the arm that he had rested on my shoulder had trembled.

Finally, as dawn's gray light began to streak the horizon, I heard Pilot bark in the yard far below. Five minutes later I heard the key grating in the lock and knew that my watch was over. It could not have lasted more than two hours, but many a week has seemed shorter. Mr. Rochester entered with the doctor. "Now, Carter, be quick," he said to the medical man. "You have only half an hour in which to dress the wound and get the patient out of here."

"But is he well enough to move, sir?"

"No doubt of it. It is nothing serious. He is mostly frightened. Come, set to work."

The doctor bent over Mason. "Now, my good fellow, how are you?" he asked.

"She's finished me off, I think," Mason faintly replied.

"Oh, you've lost a little blood; that's all," Mr. Rochester scoffed. "Carter, tell him there's no danger."

"I can do that honestly," said Carter, who now had undone the bandages. "I only wish that I had gotten here sooner, so that he would not have lost so much blood. What is this? The flesh on his shoulder is torn, not cut. This wound wasn't made with a knife but with teeth!"

"She bit me," Mason murmured. "After Rochester took the knife from her, she went after me like a tigress."

"You should have fought her off immediately," Mr. Rochester said.

"What could I do? It was frightful!" Mason added, shuddering. "And I did not expect it. She looked so quiet at first."

"I warned you," Mr. Rochester responded. "I said, 'Be on your guard when you go near her.' You could have waited until tomorrow, when I would have been with you. It was madness to try to talk to her at night, and alone."

"I thought that I could do some good."

"You thought! You thought! It makes me impatient to hear you. But you have suffered enough, so I will say no more. Carter, hurry! The sun will rise soon, and I want him out of here."

"In a moment, sir. The shoulder is bandaged. I must look at this other wound in the arm. She has had her teeth here, too, I think."

"She sucked the blood. She said she'd drain my heart," Mason said.

At this, Mr. Rochester shuddered and an expression of horror and hatred crossed his face. But he said only, "Be quiet, Richard. Never mind her gibberish. Don't repeat it."

"I wish I could forget it," Mr. Mason answered.

"You will when you are out of the country. When you get back to Jamaica, you can think of her as dead and buried, or you needn't think of her at all."

"Impossible to forget this night!"

"It is not impossible. Have some energy, man. Two hours ago you thought that you were as dead as a herring, and here you are alive and talking. There! Carter is done with you, or nearly so. I'll make you decent in no time. Jane," he said, turning to me for the first time since his re-entrance, "take this key. Go to my bedroom and fetch a clean shirt."

I went and returned, then waited while Mr. Rochester dressed and tidied his guest. "Was anybody awake below when you went down, Jane?" Mr. Rochester asked.

"No, sir. All was still."

"We will get you safely out of here, Dick. That will be better for both you and the poor creature in that room. I have worked very hard to avoid exposure, and I would not like it to come like this. Where did you leave your cloak? You can't travel a mile without it in this damned cold climate. Ah, here it is. Now, Jane, go down the back stairs and tell the carriage driver, whom you will find in the yard, to be ready. And, Jane, if anyone is up, come to the foot of the stairs and let me know, very quietly."

It was now half past five, and the sun was on the point of rising, but I found the kitchen still dark and silent. The carriage was waiting as Mr. Rochester had said, and he and the doctor managed to guide Mr. Mason to his seat without too much trouble. Dr. Carter climbed in beside him. "Take care of him," Mr. Rochester said to the doctor, "and keep him at your house until he is well. I will ride over in a day or two to see how he is getting on. Richard, how are you feeling?"

"The fresh air makes me feel better, Edward. And, Edward . . ."

"Well, what is it?"

"Take good care of her. Let her be treated as tenderly as possible. Let her . . ." But here he stopped and burst into tears.

"I will do my best, as I have been doing," Mr. Rochester answered. He shut the carriage door, and the vehicle drove away. "But I wish to God there was an end to it!" he added to himself.

I supposed that he was finished with me, and I began to return to the house. However, I heard him call, "Jane!" and went to where he was waiting for me. "Stay out here where the air is fresh for a few moments," he said. "The house is a dungeon, don't you think?"

"It seems to me a splendid mansion, sir."

"It is slime and dust," he said. "Here everything is sweet and pure." We were walking down a path edged with apple, pear, and cherry trees on one side and all sorts of flowers on the other. The flowers were as fresh as a lovely spring morning could make them. "Jane, would you like a flower?" He picked a half-open rose, wet with dew, and handed it to me. "You have passed a strange night, and it has left you pale. Were you afraid when I left you alone with Mason?"

"Yes. I was afraid that someone might come

out of the inner room."

"But I had locked the door. I had the key in my pocket. I would have been a careless shepherd if I had left a lamb—my pet lamb—unguarded so near a wolf's den. You were safe."

"Will Grace Poole still live here, sir?"

"Oh, yes. Don't trouble your head about her. Put the thing out of your thoughts."

"It seems to me that your life is in danger as long as she stays."

"Never fear. I will take care of myself."

"Is the danger that you spoke of last night gone now, sir?"

"Not until Mason is out of England, and maybe not even then. I live, Jane, as though I were standing on a fault line in the earth. Any day, it may crack open and spit fire."

"But Mr. Mason appears to be such a harmless man, and you seem to have influence over him. It is hard to believe that he would deliberately injure you."

"Oh, no! Mason will not knowingly hurt me. But unintentionally, by one careless word, he might deprive me of happiness forever."

"Tell him to be cautious, sir. Let him know what you fear, and show him how to avoid the danger."

He laughed harshly, hastily took my hand, and as hastily let it go again. "Ever since I have known Mason, I have only had to say to him, 'Do this,' and he has obeyed me. But I cannot give him orders in this case. I cannot say, 'Beware of harming me, Richard,' because I must not let him know that he is capable of harming me. Now you look puzzled; I will puzzle you further. You are my little friend, are you not?"

"I like to serve you, sir, and to obey you in all that is right."

"Precisely. I see that you do. I see genuine happiness in your eyes when you are helping me and pleasing me—working for me, as you say, 'in all that is right.' But if I asked you to do something that you thought was wrong, there would be no light-footed running, no quickness, no lively glance and bright eyes. My friend would turn to me, quiet and pale, and say, 'No, sir, that is impossible. I cannot do it because it is wrong.' Well, you too have power over me and may hurt me, yet I do not dare show where I am vulnerable. As faithful and friendly as you are, I fear that you would stab me at once."

"If you have no more to fear from Mr. Mason than you have to fear from me, you are very safe."

"God grant that may be so! Here is a bench, Jane. Sit down." The bench was set in an arch in the ivy-lined wall. Mr. Rochester sat, leaving room for me, but I kept standing. "Sit," he repeated. "The bench is long enough for two. You don't hesitate to sit beside me, do you? Is that wrong, Jane?" I answered him by sitting. "Now, my little friend, while this spring morning awakens, I will tell you a story that you must try to pretend is your own. But first, look at me and tell me that you don't mind staying here and that I am not holding you against your will."

"No, sir. I am content."

"Well then, Jane, try to imagine this. Suppose you are not a well-disciplined girl but a wild boy who has been spoiled all of his life. Imagine that you are in a foreign land and that you have committed a great mistake there—a mistake that will follow you all of your life and stain your existence. Mind you, I don't say a crime. I am not speaking of the shedding of blood or any other unlawful act. My word is 'mistake.' The results of what you have done become unbearable. You do what you can to obtain relief—careless things, but not unlawful. Still, you are miserable because you have no hope and expect to have none until your dying day. You wander here and there, seeking happiness in pleasure, the kind of heartless sensual pleasure that dulls the mind. Sick in your heart and soul, you come home after years of banishment. There you make a new acquaintance. How or where doesn't matter. You find in this stranger the good and bright qualities that you have sought for twenty years and never found before. Here they are, fresh and healthy. This person's company revives and refreshes you. You feel that better days are coming. You want to begin your life again and spend your remaining days in worthier ways. To accomplish this, are you justified in jumping over an obstacle, a mere custom? Can you be forgiven for ignoring convention?" He paused for an answer.

What was I to say? Oh, for some good spirit to suggest a wise response! The west wind whispered in the ivy around me, but no spirit whispered into my ear.

Mr. Rochester continued, "Can this sinful wanderer, now seeking forgiveness and rest, risk the world's opinion in order to have this gentle, gracious stranger with him forever?"

"Sir," I answered, "a sinner's forgiveness never should depend on another person. Men and women die. They do wrong. If this person has suffered and made mistakes, let him look higher than other people for the strength to change and heal."

"But the instrument, the instrument of that healing!" Mr. Rochester exclaimed. "God, who does the work, creates the instrument. I will tell you directly that I am this worldly, wicked man, and I believe that I have found the instrument for my cure in . . ." He paused. The birds went on singing, the leaves lightly rustling. I thought they should stop their songs and whispers to wait and listen, as I did, but they would have had to wait many minutes. The silence went on and on.

At last I looked up at Mr. Rochester. He was looking at me. "No doubt, you have noticed my special attentions toward Miss Ingram," he said in quite a different tone. His face had changed, too. It had lost all of its softness and had become harsh and sarcastic. "Don't you think that if I married her, she would thoroughly redeem me?" He got up, went to the other end of the walk, and then came back humming a tune. "Jane, Jane," he said, stopping before me, "you are quite pale. Don't you curse me for disturbing your rest?"

"Curse you? No, sir."

"Shake hands to prove it. What cold fingers! They were warmer last night when I touched them at the door of the mysterious room. Jane, when will you again stay awake with me while others sleep?"

"Whenever I can be useful, sir."

"For instance, the night before I am married! I am sure that I will not be able to sleep. Will you promise to sit up with me to keep me company? I can talk to you of my lovely bride because now you have seen her and know her."

"Yes, sir."

"She's a rare one, isn't she, Jane?"

"Yes, sir."

"A strapping figure of a woman, isn't she? Big and robust, just as ancient Roman ladies must have been. Bless me! There are Dent and Lynn in the stables! Go in through that hedge, so they won't see you."

As I went one way and he went another, I heard him in the yard, saying cheerfully, "Good morning, gentlemen! Mason was up earlier than any of us. I rose at four to see him off."

Chapter 21

The day after the incident with Mr. Mason, I was asked to go downstairs because a visitor wished to see me. When I entered the room where the visitor was waiting, he rose. He looked like a gentleman's servant, and he was dressed all in black, as if he were in mourning. "I'm sure you don't remember me, Miss," he said. "My name is Leaven. I was Mrs. Reed's coachman when you were at Gateshead eight or nine years ago, and I still live there."

"Oh, Robert, how good to see you!" I responded. "I remember you very well. You used to give me a ride sometimes on Miss Georgiana's pony. Bessie told me that you and she had married. How is she?"

"My wife is very well, thank you. She gave me another little one about two months ago. We have three children now, and she and the baby are both thriving."

"And are the Reeds well, Robert?"

"I am sorry to say no, Miss. They are very badly at present—in great trouble. You see, Mr. John died a week ago at his home in London."

"Oh, dear. How is his mother bearing up?"

"Very poorly, Miss. Mr. John was very wild. He ruined his health and wasted all of his money

among the worst men and women he could find.
He got into debt and went to jail. His mother
helped him out twice, but as soon as he was free, he
went back to his old habits. He came down to
Gateshead about three weeks ago, demanding that
his mother give him more money. The missis
refused, and he went away. The next news was that
he was dead. The fact is, he killed himself, Miss."

I was silent. There seemed nothing to say.

Robert went on. "The missis hasn't been well
for a long time. The loss of money and fear of
poverty wore on her. Then she heard the news
about Mr. John's death, and she had a stroke. For
three days she didn't speak at all, but last Tuesday
she seemed a little better. She seemed to want to
say something, and she kept making signs to my
wife and mumbling. However, it was only yesterday
morning that Bessie understood that she was saying
your name. She keeps saying, 'Bring Jane. Fetch
Jane Eyre. I want to speak to her.' Bessie is not sure
whether she is in her right mind or means anything
by the words, but she told Miss Eliza and Miss
Georgiana and suggested that they send for you.
The young ladies didn't want to, but their mother
grew so restless and said, 'Jane, Jane,' so many
times that they finally agreed. If you can get ready,
Miss, I would like to take you back with me early
tomorrow morning."

"Yes, Robert, I will be ready. It seems to me
that I should go."

With that, I went in search of Mr. Rochester. I

found him playing pool with Miss Ingram and the two Eshton girls. I approached the master where he stood at Miss Ingram's side. She turned as I drew near and looked at me haughtily. Her eyes seemed to demand, "What can the creeping creature want now?" I remember her appearance at that moment. It was very graceful and striking. She wore a simple sky-blue dress, and a brilliant blue scarf was twisted in her hair. "Does that person want you?" she asked Mr. Rochester.

Mr. Rochester turned to see who "that person" was. He threw down his cue and followed me from the room. "Well, Jane?" he asked, when we were out of the others' hearing.

"If you please, sir, I want permission to leave for a week or two."

"To do what? To go where?"

"To see a sick lady who has sent for me."

"What sick lady? Where does she live?"

"At Gateshead. It is about a hundred miles from here."

"Who is she that she sends for people from so far away?"

"Her name is Reed, sir. Mrs. Reed."

"Reed of Gateshead? I knew of someone of that name. He was a judge."

"It is his widow, sir."

"What have you to do with her? How do you know her?"

"Mr. Reed was my uncle, my mother's brother."

"The devil he was! You never told me that

before. You always said you had no relatives."

"None who would own me, sir. Mr. Reed is dead, and his wife sent me away."

"Why?"

"Because I was poor and burdensome and she disliked me."

"But Reed had children, didn't he? And so, you have cousins? Just yesterday Sir George Lynn was speaking of a Reed of Gateshead; he said that Reed was one of the worst rascals in London. And Ingram mentioned a Georgiana Reed, who was much admired for her beauty a season or two ago."

"John Reed is dead, sir. He ruined himself and half ruined his family. He has committed suicide. The news so shocked his mother that it brought on a stroke."

"What good can you do her? Nonsense, Jane! Don't go running a hundred miles to see an old lady who probably will be dead before you reach her. Besides, you say that she cast you off."

"Yes, sir, but that was long ago and when her circumstances were very different. I would not feel right about refusing her now."

"How long will you stay?"

"As short a time as possible, sir."

"Promise me to stay only a week."

"I'd better not make that promise. I might have to break it."

"In any case, you will come back. You will not be persuaded to live with her again?"

"Oh, no! I certainly will return."

Mr. Rochester meditated. "When do you wish to go?"

"Early tomorrow morning, sir."

"Well, you must have some money. You can't travel without money, and I imagine you do not have much. I haven't paid you your salary yet. How much do you have in the world, Jane?" he asked.

I drew out my purse, counted, and said, "Five shillings, sir." He took the purse, poured the coins into his palm, and chuckled as if the amount amused him. He pulled out his own wallet and offered me a fifty-pound note.

"But you owe me only fifteen, and I don't have change," I said.

"I don't want change. You know that. Take your wages." I refused to accept more than he owed me. He scowled at first but then said, "Right! I'd better not give you all of it. If you had fifty pounds, you could stay away for months. Here is ten. Isn't that plenty?"

"Yes, sir, but now you owe me five."

"Come back for it, then."

"Mr. Rochester, I might as well mention another matter of business while I have the chance."

"Matter of business? I am curious to hear it."

"You have told me, sir, that you are going to be married."

"Yes. What of it?"

"In that case, sir, Adele should go away to school. I am sure you will agree."

"To get her out of the way of my bride, who might otherwise walk over her a bit too harshly? You're right. Adele, as you say, must go to school. But what about you?"

"I must look for another position."

"And old Madam Reed, or her daughters, will help you find a place, I suppose?"

"No, sir. We are not on good terms. I will advertise."

"You will walk up the pyramids of Egypt!" he growled. "Don't you dare advertise! I wish that I had offered you only ten shillings instead of ten pounds. Give me back nine pounds, Jane. I need it."

"So do I, sir," I returned, putting my hands and my purse behind me.

"You miser!" he said. "Refusing me a request! Give me five pounds, Jane."

"Not five shillings, sir, nor five pennies."

"Just let me look at the money."

"No, sir. You are not to be trusted."

"Jane!"

"Sir?"

"Promise me one thing."

"I'll promise you anything I can, sir."

"Just this: don't advertise. Trust me to find a situation for you."

"I will be glad to do so, sir, if you promise that Adele and I will both be safely out of the house before your bride enters it."

"Very well! Very well! I give my word. You go

tomorrow, then?"

"Yes, sir. Early."

"Will you come down to the drawing room after dinner?"

"No, sir. I must prepare for the journey."

"Then, you and I must say goodbye for a little while?"

"I suppose so, sir."

"How do people perform that ceremony of parting, Jane? Teach me. I'm not quite up to it."

"They say 'Farewell' or use any other form that they prefer."

"Then say it."

"Farewell, Mr. Rochester, for the present."

"What must I say?"

"The same, if you like, sir."

"Farewell, Miss Eyre, for the present. Is that all?"

"Yes."

"It seems a little dry to me, and unfriendly. I would like something else—shaking hands, for instance—but no, that would not satisfy me either."

"How long is he going to stand with his back against that door?" I asked myself. "I want to start packing."

The dinner bell rang, and he bolted away without another syllable. I saw him no more during the day, and I left before he had risen in the morning.

I reached Gateshead about five o'clock in the afternoon on the first of May. First I went to

Bessie's cottage. I found Bessie sitting by the fire with her newborn. Little Robert and his sister played quietly in a corner.

"Bless you! I knew you would come!" Mrs. Leaven exclaimed as I entered.

"Yes, Bessie," I said after I had kissed her. "Am I too late? How is Mrs. Reed?"

"She is alive and more right in the head than she was. The doctor says she may linger a week or two yet, but he does not think she will recover."

"Has she mentioned me lately?"

"She was talking about you only this morning and wishing you would come. But she is sleeping now; at least, she was ten minutes ago when I was up at the house. She usually lies in a kind of stupor all afternoon and wakes up about six or seven. Why don't you rest yourself here an hour, Miss, and then I will go to the house with you?"

Robert entered, and Bessie laid her sleeping child in the cradle and went to welcome him. Afterwards she insisted that I take off my bonnet and have some tea. She said that I looked pale and tired. Memories of old times crowded back on me as I watched her bustling about, setting out the tea tray with her best china, cutting bread and butter, toasting a tea cake, and giving little Robert or Jane an occasional tap or push, just as she used to give me. Bessie still had her quick temper as well as her good looks.

Over our tea she asked if I was happy at Thornfield Hall and what sort of person the mistress was. I told her that there was only a master, and she asked whether he was a nice gentleman and if I liked him. I told her that he was a rather ugly man but that he treated me kindly and I was content. Then I described the fashionable guests who had been staying at the house lately. Bessie listened to these details with great interest.

Our hour together passed quickly. Bessie gave me my bonnet and cloak, and we walked from her little cottage to the great house. It was with Bessie that I had last walked down that path, nearly nine years ago. On a dark, misty, raw morning in January, I had left an unfriendly home feeling desperate and bitter. That same unfriendly house now rose before me. Strangely, the sight of it made my heart ache. The old flames of my resentment were put out, and I felt far greater confidence in my own worth.

Bessie led me into the old breakfast room, which looked precisely as it had on the morning that I was introduced to Mr. Brocklehurst. Glancing at the bookcases, I could see *Gulliver's Travels* and *The Arabian Nights* in their old positions. The room's inanimate objects had not changed, but the living things had, almost beyond recognition.

Two young ladies appeared before me. One was tall, almost as tall as Miss Ingram. She was very thin, with a pasty face and severe look. Her dress was so plain that it was nun-like; indeed, her only ornament was a string of ebony beads and a crucifix. This, I felt sure, was Eliza. The other certainly was Georgiana, but not the Georgiana I remembered (the slim, fairy-like girl of eleven). This was a full-blown, very plump young woman, fair as a doll, with handsome features, melting blue eyes, and curling yellow hair. Her dress was black, too, but it was as stylish as her sister's was plain.

The two greeted me coldly and soon returned to their reading. Sitting between them, ignored, I was surprised to find how little I cared about their rudeness. "How is Mrs. Reed?" I asked, looking calmly at Georgiana.

"Mrs. Reed? Oh, you mean Mama. She is extremely poorly. I doubt if you can see her tonight."

"If you would just step upstairs and tell her that I am here, I would appreciate it," I said. Georgiana opened her blue eyes in astonishment at my boldness. "She particularly asked to see me," I added, "and I do not want to make her wait any longer than necessary."

"Mama does not like being disturbed in the evening," Eliza remarked.

I rose, took off my bonnet and gloves, and said that I would ask Bessie if she would go see Mrs. Reed on my behalf. I found Bessie and sent her on my errand. In the past, people's rudeness always had intimidated me. Only a year before, if I had been received as I was that day at Gateshead, I would have turned around and left the very next morning. Now I saw how foolish that would be. I had traveled a hundred miles to see my aunt. Her daughters' bad behavior was no concern of mine. So I asked the housekeeper to show me to a room, telling her that I probably would stay a week or two. I had my suitcase taken to that room and then met Bessie on the stairs. "The missis is awake," she said. "I have told her you are here. Come. Let's see if she recognizes you."

I did not need to be guided to the well-known room, to which I often had been summoned for a scolding. I softly opened the door and approached the bed. I remembered Mrs. Reed's face well, and I eagerly looked at the invalid on the piled-up pillows. Although I had left this woman in bitterness and hatred, I now felt no emotion other than some sympathy for her sufferings. I felt a strong desire to forget and forgive all injuries and to be friends. I stooped down and kissed her face, and she turned to me.

"Is this Jane Eyre?" she asked.

"Yes, Aunt Reed. How are you, dear Aunt?" I once had promised that I never would call her Aunt again. I thought it was no sin to break that promise now. I had taken her hand, and it would have pleased me if she had squeezed mine kindly in return. But hatred such as Mrs. Reed's is not easily erased. She pulled her hand away, turned her face from me, and remarked that the night was warm. From her icy expression, I saw that she was determined to think badly of me until the end. "You sent for me," I said, "and I am here. I intend to stay until you are better."

"Oh, of course! You have seen my daughters?"

"Yes."

"Well, tell them that I want you to stay until I can talk some things over with you. Tonight it is too late, and I can't remember what they are. But there was something I wished to say. Let me see. . . ." Turning restlessly, she pulled the bedclothes around her. My elbow rested on a corner of the quilt and held it down. At once, she was irritated. "Sit up!" she said. "Don't pull at my quilt. Are you Jane Eyre?"

"I am."

"I had more trouble with that child than anyone would believe. She was such a burden! She annoyed me so much, with her sudden bursts of temper and the unnatural way that she continually watched me! I declare, she talked to me once as if she were mad. No child ever spoke or looked as she did. I was glad to get her away from the house. What did they do with her at Lowood? The fever broke out there, and many of the pupils died. She did not die, but I said that she did. I wish she had died!"

"A strange wish, Mrs. Reed," I said. "Why do you hate her so much?"

"I always disliked her mother. She was my husband's only sister and a great favorite with him. He objected when his family disowned her for making her low marriage, and when news came of her death, he wept like a simpleton. He insisted on taking in the baby, although I begged him to send it to a foster home. I hated it the first time I set eyes on it—a sickly, whining thing! It would wail in its cradle all night long—not screaming heartily like any other child, but whimpering and moaning. Reed pitied it, and he paid far more attention to it than to his own children. He would try to make my children friendly to the little beggar, but the darlings could not bear it, and he was angry with them when they showed their dislike. An hour before he died, he made me promise to keep the brat. He was a weak man, naturally weak. John is not at all like his father, and I am glad of it. John is like me and like my brothers. Oh, but I wish he would stop tormenting me with letters for money! I have no more money to give him. We are getting poor. I must send away half the servants and shut up part of the house. Two-thirds of my income already goes to paying the interest on the mortgages. John gambles dreadfully and always loses, poor boy! I feel ashamed for him when I see him." She was getting very excited.

"I think I'd better leave her now," I said to Bessie, who stood on the other side of the bed.

"Perhaps, Miss, but she often talks this way at night. In the morning she is calmer."

I rose. "Stop!" Mrs. Reed exclaimed. "There is something else I want to say. He threatens me. He threatens me with his own death or mine. I dream sometimes that I see him lying with a great wound in his throat. I have such heavy troubles. What is to be done? How am I to get the money?"

Bessie managed to give her a sedative drink, and Mrs. Reed began to doze. I then left her.

For ten days I had no further conversation with her. She was either delirious or in a stupor, and the doctor forbade everything that might excite her. Meanwhile, I got on as well as I could with Georgiana and Eliza. They were very cold at first. Eliza would sit half the day sewing, reading, or writing and scarcely utter a word to either her sister or me. Georgiana would chatter nonsense to her canary by the hour and take no notice of me.

I kept busy with my drawing. I would take a seat away from Georgiana and Eliza, near the window, and sketch any idea that came into my head. It might be a glimpse of the sea between two rocks, a ship crossing in front of a rising moon, or an elf sitting in a sparrow's nest. One morning I began sketching a face with, I thought, no one particular in mind. I took a soft black pencil and worked away. Soon I had traced a broad forehead and square lower jaw. That outline pleased me, and I quickly filled the face with features. I gave it strong horizontal eyebrows, a well-defined nose with a straight ridge and full nostrils, a flexible-looking mouth with tolerably full lips, and a firm chin with a cleft down its middle. I added some black whiskers and wavy hair. Now for the eyes. I had left them for last because they required the most careful working. I drew them large. I shaped them well. I traced the eyelashes long and dark. There. I had a friend's face to look at. What did it matter that these young ladies turned their backs on me? I looked at the portrait and smiled at it.

"Is that a portrait of someone you know?" asked Eliza, who had approached me unnoticed. I said that it was only an imaginary person and hid it beneath my other papers. Of course, I lied. It was, in fact, a faithful portrait of Mr. Rochester. But what business was that of hers? Georgiana also came to look. My other drawings pleased her, but she called my portrait "an ugly man." They both seemed surprised by my skill. I offered to sketch their portraits, and each eagerly agreed.

Over the next days, both sisters began to seek me out for conversation. Georgiana loved to describe the brilliant social success that she had enjoyed in London. Her conversation always ran on the same theme: herself, her loves, her woes. She never once spoke of either her mother's illness or her brother's death. Each day she spent about five minutes, no more, in her mother's sickroom. Eliza still spoke very little; she had no time to talk. I never saw a busier person than she seemed to be. She woke up very early and divided her day into portions, with each portion having its assigned task. Three times a day she studied a little book of prayers. For three hours she sewed a gold border onto a huge square of crimson cloth, which she told me would cover the altar of a new church near Gateshead. Two hours she spent writing in her diary, two working by herself in the kitchen garden, and one doing bookkeeping. She seemed to want no company and no conversation, and I believe she was happy in her way.

One evening Eliza told me that John's behavior, and her family's troubles, had worried her very much in the past. But now she was peaceful because she had made her own plans. When her mother died, she would retire to a place of peace and religious works. I asked if Georgiana would go with her. "Of course not," she answered, speaking so that her sister would hear her. "Georgiana and I have nothing in common. We never have had anything in common. She is a fat, weak, puffy, useless thing that does nothing but complain. From the moment that our mother's coffin is carried to Gateshead Church, Georgiana, you and I will be as separate as if we never had known each other. Do not think that because we happened to be born of the same parents, I will let you weigh me down in any way."

"You didn't need to tell me any of that," Georgiana retorted. "Everybody knows that you are the most selfish, heartless creature in existence. I know how you hate me. I witnessed it in the trick you played on me with regard to Lord Edwin Vere. You could not bear to see me raised above you, so you were a spy and informer and ruined my prospects forever." Georgiana took out her handkerchief and blew her nose for an hour afterwards while Eliza sat cold and industrious.

It was a wet and windy afternoon. Georgiana had fallen asleep on the sofa while reading a novel;

Eliza was attending a service at the new church. I decided to go upstairs and see the dying woman. She lay there nearly ignored. The servants paid her little attention. The hired nurse slipped out of the room whenever she could. Bessie was faithful, but she had her own family to care for and could come to the house only occasionally. I found the sick-room unwatched, as I had expected. No nurse was there. The patient lay still, her head sunk in the pillows, and the fire was dying. I put more wood onto the fire, rearranged the bedding, gazed awhile at the woman who no longer could gaze on me, and then moved to the window to watch the storm beat down. I was thinking of Helen Burns and of her dying words, so strong in faith, and wondering about the fate of the spirit lying in the bed behind me. Then a feeble voice murmured, "Who is that?"

Mrs. Reed hadn't spoken for days. Surprised, I went up to her. "It is I, Aunt Reed."

"Who? Who are you?" she asked, looking at me with surprise and some alarm. "Where is Bessie?"

"She is at her cottage, Aunt."

"Aunt," she repeated. "Who calls me Aunt? You are not a member of my family, but I know you. Why, you are like Jane Eyre! I wanted to see Jane!" I gently assured her that I was the person she wanted to see. "I am very ill, I know," she said before long. "I was trying to turn myself a few minutes ago, and I find that I cannot move. I want to ease my mind before I die. Is the nurse here? Is there no one in the room but you?" I assured her that we were alone. "Well, I have twice done you a wrong that I now regret. One time was in breaking my promise, to my husband, to bring you up as my own child. The other . . ." She stopped, then made an effort and continued. "Well, I must get it over with. Eternity is before me. I had better tell you. Go to my dresser, open the top drawer, and take out the letter you will see there." I obeyed. "Read the letter," she said.

It was short: "Madam, Will you have the goodness to send me the address of my niece, Jane Eyre, and to tell me how she is? I want to invite her to join me in Madeira. I have been fortunate in my business dealings, and, because I am unmarried and childless, I wish to adopt her and leave her at my death whatever I may have to give. Yours, John Eyre, Madeira." The letter was three years old. "Why did I never hear of this?" I asked.

"Because I disliked you too much to help you. I could not forget your conduct toward me, Jane— the fury with which you once turned on me, the tone in which you declared that I had treated you with miserable cruelty. Bring me some water! Hurry!"

"Dear Mrs. Reed," I said as I helped her drink, "do not think about this anymore. Let it pass from your mind. Forgive me for speaking to you like that. I was a child then. Nine years have passed since that day."

She paid no attention to what I said, but when

she had tasted the water and rested a moment, she went on. "I tell you I could not forget it, and I took my revenge. For you to be adopted by your uncle, and live in ease and comfort, was more than I could bear. I wrote to him. I said that I was sorry but that Jane Eyre had died of typhus fever at Lowood. Now act as you please. Write and tell him that I lied. I think you were born to be my torment. My last hour is tortured by the memory of a deed that, except for you, I never would have been tempted to commit."

"I wish you would forget it, Aunt, and think of me with kindness and forgiveness."

"You have a very bad disposition," she said. "To this day it is impossible to understand how, for nine years, you patiently bore any treatment but then, in the tenth year, you lashed out all fire and violence. I never will comprehend it."

"My disposition is not as bad as you think," I answered. "I am passionate but not cruel. When I was a child, I would have been glad to love you if you had let me. Let's finally be friends. Won't you kiss me?" I bent my cheek down to her, but she would not touch it. She said that I irritated her by leaning over the bed, and she again demanded water. As I laid her down (I had raised her and supported her on my arm while she drank), I covered her ice-cold hand with mine. The feeble fingers shrank from my touch. "Love me, then, or hate me as you like," I said. "You have my full forgiveness. Ask now for God's, and be at peace." Poor, suffering woman! It was too late for her to change her frame of mind. She always had hated me, and she hated me still.

The nurse now entered, and Bessie followed. I lingered another half-hour, hoping to see some sign of warmth or friendship, but Mrs. Reed gave none. At midnight she died. I was not present to close her eyes, nor was either of her daughters.

The next morning the nurse came to tell us that it was over. Eliza and I went to look at her; Georgiana, who had burst into loud weeping, said that she could not. Eliza surveyed her mother calmly. After a silence of some minutes, she observed, "With her constitution she should have lived to a good old age. Troubles shortened her life." Then her mouth trembled for a moment. She turned and left the room, and so did I. Neither of us had shed a tear.

Chapter 22

Mr. Rochester had given me only one week's leave of absence, but a month passed before I left Gateshead. I wanted to go immediately after the funeral, but Georgiana begged me to stay until she could leave for London. She had been invited to live there with her uncle's family. Georgiana dreaded being left alone with Eliza, so I put up with her feeble-minded wailings and selfish complaints as well as I could, and did my best in sewing for her and packing her dresses. While I worked, she was idle, and I thought to myself, "If you and I were living together permanently, we would do things differently. You would do your share of work, or else it would remain undone. It is only because I know that we will part soon, and because your mother has just died, that I am being patient."

At last I saw Georgiana off, but now it was Eliza's turn to ask me to stay another week. She said her own plans required all her time and attention because she was about to depart for some unknown place. All day long she stayed in her own room, filling trunks, emptying drawers, burning papers, and speaking with no one. She asked me to look after the house, to see visitors, and to answer the notes of sympathy that came to the house.

One morning she told me that I was free to go. "I am grateful to you for your valuable service," she said. "What a difference between living with someone like you and living with Georgiana! You perform your part in life and burden no one. Tomorrow," she continued, "I am leaving for France, where I will live a quiet religious life in a convent. I plan to become a nun."

With these words we went our separate ways. Because I will not have any reason to mention Georgiana or Eliza again, I may as well tell you that Georgiana married a wealthy, worn-out man of fashion and that Eliza now is the mother superior of the convent to which she moved.

My journey back to Thornfield was tedious: fifty miles one day, a night spent at an inn, and fifty more miles the next day. I was going back, but how long was I to stay there? Not long; of that I was sure. I had heard from Mrs. Fairfax. Mr. Rochester had left for London three weeks before, but he was expected back before my return. Mrs. Fairfax guessed that he had gone to make arrangements for his wedding because he had talked of purchasing a new carriage. She said the idea of his marrying Miss Ingram still seemed strange to her, but from what everybody said, the event would take place soon. My next question was, "Where will I go?" I dreamed of Miss Ingram during my night at the inn: I saw her closing Thornfield's gates in front of me and pointing to the road. I saw Mr. Rochester watching us both, his arms folded, smiling scornfully.

I had not told Mrs. Fairfax the exact date of my return because I did not want a carriage to meet me at Millcote. I preferred to walk the remaining distance from there to Thornfield. Leaving my luggage to be shipped later, I slipped away from a Millcote inn at about six o'clock on a June evening to walk to Thornfield. I felt glad as my steps approached the great house, so glad that I stopped to ask myself why. "Mrs. Fairfax will be pleased to see you," I told myself, "and little Adele will clap her hands and jump with joy, but you know very well that you are thinking of another and that he is not thinking of you." Still, my heart answered, "Walk more quickly! Be with him while you can; in a few more days or weeks, you will be parted from him forever!"

In Thornfield's meadows, haymakers were just quitting their work and returning home with their rakes on their shoulders. I had only another field or two to cross; then I would reach the gates. How full of roses the hedges were! But I had no time to gather any. I wanted to be at the house. I passed a tall bush, partially blocking the path, and then I saw Mr. Rochester sitting on the wall, a book and pencil in his hand. He was writing.

He was not a ghost, yet every nerve I had was unstrung. I did not think that I would tremble this way when I saw him, or lose my voice. I began to turn away. I knew another path to the house; I would use it rather than make a fool of myself. But it did not matter if I knew twenty other ways; he had seen me.

"Hello!" he cried, and he put away his book and pencil. "There you are! Come here, if you please." I did come, although I do not know how. I barely was aware that I was moving. I concentrated on appearing calm. "Here she is: Jane Eyre coming on foot from Millcote. It's one of your tricks not to send for a carriage and come clattering noisily home like a mortal being, but to steal along with the twilight as if you were a dream or ghost. What the devil have you done with yourself this last month?"

"I have been with my aunt, sir, who is dead."

"A true Janian reply! Good angels, protect me! She comes from the other world, from the realm of the dead, and tells me so when she meets me alone here in the twilight! If I dared, I'd touch you to see if you are real or a shadow, but I don't have the courage. You truant!" he added. "Gone from home a whole month! You probably forgot all about me!"

I knew there would be pleasure in meeting him again, but I had not anticipated the rush of joy that swept over me at the sight of him. And his last words were sweet to me. They implied that it mattered to him whether or not I forgot him. And he had spoken of Thornfield as my home! He did not leave his seat, so I asked if he had been to London.

"Yes. I suppose you found that out through your psychic power."

"Mrs. Fairfax told me in a letter."

"And did she inform you what I went to do?"

"Oh yes, sir! Everybody knew your errand."

"You must see the carriage, Jane, and tell me if you don't think it will suit Mrs. Rochester very well. She will look like one of history's wicked queens, leaning back against those purple cushions. I wish, Jane, I were a physically better match for her. Tell me now, you fairy creature, can't you give me a charm, or a spell, or something to make me a handsome man?"

"That would be past magic's power, sir," I said. In my thoughts, I added, "A loving eye is all the charm that is needed. To my eyes you are handsome enough."

Mr. Rochester sometimes had the power to read my unspoken thoughts. Now he ignored my spoken response, but he smiled at me with a certain smile that he used only rarely. It contained the real sunshine of feeling, and he shed it over me now. "You may go, Jane," he said, making room for me to pass. "Go on home, and rest your weary little wandering feet at a friend's fireside."

All I had to do now was obey him in silence. I passed him without a word and meant to leave him calmly. But something turned me around. I said— or something in me said, in spite of me—"Thank you, Mr. Rochester, for your great kindness. I am strangely glad to get back to you. Wherever you are is my home, my only home."

I walked on as fast as I could. Little Adele was half wild with delight when she saw me. Mrs. Fairfax received me with her usual plain friendliness. Leah smiled, and even Sophie greeted me with glee. This was very pleasant. There is no happiness like that of being loved by other people and feeling that they welcome your company.

That evening I tried with all my strength to shut out thoughts of the future and to ignore the voice that warned me of coming grief and separation. When tea was over and Mrs. Fairfax had taken up her knitting, and I had taken a seat near her and Adele had nestled close to me, a sense of mutual affection seemed to surround us with a ring of golden peace. I uttered a silent prayer that we wouldn't part soon or be far from one another.

When Mr. Rochester entered unannounced and looked at us, he seemed to enjoy the sight of such a friendly group. He said he supposed Mrs. Fairfax was happy now that she had gotten her adopted daughter back and that he saw Adele was content with her "English mama." I half hoped that, even after his marriage, he might find a way to keep the three of us together.

Two calm weeks followed my return to Thornfield Hall, although it was a calm broken by some questions. Nothing was said of the master's coming marriage, and I saw no preparations for such an event. Almost every day I asked Mrs. Fairfax if she had heard anything yet, but her answer always was in the negative. Once she said she had asked Mr. Rochester when he was going to bring his bride home, but he had answered her with a joke, and she did not know what to make of it.

One thing particularly surprised me: there was

no traveling back and forth to Miss Ingram's home. To be sure, it was twenty miles away, but what is twenty miles to an eager lover? To a horseman like Mr. Rochester, it would be an easy ride. I began to wonder, hopefully, if the engagement had been broken, if the rumor had been mistaken, or if one or both parties had changed their minds. I would look at my master's face to see if it were sad or fierce, but I could not remember a time when it had been so happy and content. Never had he called me more frequently to his presence. Never had he been kinder to me. And, alas, never had I loved him so well.

Chapter 23

The midsummer weather was spectacular. The skies were pure and the sun radiant, as if a band of Italian days had come from the south, like a flock of glorious migrating birds that had alighted to rest awhile in England.

One evening Adele, weary from gathering wild strawberries in Hay Lane half the day, went to bed at twilight. I watched her fall asleep. When I left her, I went to the garden. It was the day's sweetest hour. Cool dew had fallen on the scorched earth, and the setting sun had left the sky a glorious purple streaked with the light of red jewels. I walked awhile on the pavement, but a subtle, well-known scent—the scent of Mr. Rochester's cigar—warned me that I was not alone. I saw him standing with his back to me, gazing at some flower beds.

Not wanting to disturb his solitude, I turned to leave. But he spoke without turning around. "Jane, come and look at this fellow." I had made no noise, and he had not looked in my direction. How had he known that I was there? Wondering, I approached him and saw that his attention was captured by a huge moth dancing above the flowers. "Look at his wings," he said. "He reminds me of a West Indian moth. One does not often see so large and colorful a night rover in England. There! He is flying away."

The moth roamed on, and I also was retreating, but Mr. Rochester followed me. "Do come back, Jane," he said. "On such a lovely night it is a shame to sit in the house. Surely no one can want to go to bed while a moonrise like this is about to occur." It is one of my faults that I sometimes cannot think of an excuse when I need one. I did not want to walk alone with Mr. Rochester in the shadowy orchard at this hour, but I could not find an excuse for leaving him. "Jane," he went on, as we strayed in the direction of the horse chestnut tree, "Thornfield is a pleasant place in summer, is it not?"

"Yes, sir."

"You must have become somewhat attached to the house. You have an appreciation for natural beauty."

"I am attached to it, indeed."

"And although I don't understand how, I perceive that you have become fond of that foolish little child Adele, too, and even of simple Mrs. Fairfax."

"Yes, sir; in different ways, I have an affection for both."

"And would be sorry to part with them?"

"Yes."

"Pity!" he said, and sighed. "Life always goes that way. No sooner have you gotten settled in a pleasant resting place, than it is time to move on."

"Must I move on, sir?" I asked. "Must I leave Thornfield?"

"I believe you must, Jane. I am sorry, but I believe you must."

This was a blow, but I did not let it show. "Well, sir, I will be ready when the order to march comes."

"It has come now. I must give it tonight."

"Then, you are going to be married, sir?"

"Exactly. Precisely. With your usual sharpness, you have hit the nail on the head."

"Soon, sir?"

"Very soon, my—that is, Miss Eyre. You'll remember, Jane, the first time I hinted to you that I intended to put my old bachelor's neck into the sacred noose and take Miss Ingram to my bosom. (She's an extensive armful, but that's not the point; one can't have too much of such an excellent thing as my beautiful Blanche.) Well, as I was saying, . . . Listen to me, Jane! You're not turning your head to look for more moths, are you? I wish to remind you that it was you who first said to me that if I married Miss Ingram, both you and little Adele had better trot out of here. I am ignoring the insult you pass on my beloved's character; I notice only its wisdom. Adele must go to school, and you, Miss Eyre, must get a new situation."

"Yes, sir. I will advertise immediately. Meanwhile, I suppose . . ." I was going to say, "I suppose I may stay here until I find somewhere else to go," but I stopped, not sure that I could speak the words calmly.

"In about a month I hope to be a bride-groom," Mr. Rochester continued. "In the mean-time, I myself will look for a new position for you."

"Thank you, sir. I am sorry to give you the trouble."

"No need to apologize! I consider that when an employee does her duty as well as you have done yours, she has a claim upon her employer for any assistance that he can conveniently give her. Indeed, my future mother-in-law already has suggested a position that I think will suit you. It is to oversee the education of the five daughters of Mrs. Dionysius O'Gall of Bitternutt Lodge, Connaught, Ireland. You'll like Ireland, I think. They say the Irish are warm-hearted."

"It is a long way off, sir."

"No matter. A girl of your good sense will not object to a voyage."

"Not the voyage, but the distance. And the sea is a barrier . . ."

"From what, Jane?"

"From England and from Thornfield."

"Well?"

"From you, sir." I said this almost involuntari-ly. Also against my will, tears gushed. I did manage to cry quietly, however. The thought of Mrs. O'Gall and Bitternutt Lodge struck dread in my heart. Worse yet was the thought of all the ocean water that would separate me from the man at whose side I now walked. I thought, too, that an even wider ocean divided us—the ocean of wealth, social class, and custom. "It is a long way," I said again.

"It is, to be sure. When you get to Bitternutt Lodge, I never will see you again. I never go to Ireland, not having much of a liking for that country. We have been good friends, Jane, have we not?"

"Yes, sir."

"And when friends are about to separate, they like to spend their remaining time with each other. Come! We'll talk about your voyage for half an hour or so. Let's sit here in peace tonight for one last time." We sat on the bench. "It is a long way to Ireland, Jane, and I am sorry to send my little friend on such a trip. But how is it to be helped? Are you related to me in some way, Jane?" By this time, I could not say a word in response. My heart barely was beating. "Because," he said, "I sometimes have a strange feeling with regard to you—especially when you are near me, as now. It is as if I had a string somehow tied under my left ribs, tightly knotted to a similar string tied to you. And if that ocean, and two hundred miles or so of land comes between us, I am afraid that string will snap, and I have the nervous feeling that I will begin bleeding inside. As for you, you'd forget me."

"I never would, sir. . . . " I could not go on.

"Jane, do you hear that nightingale singing in the wood? Listen!"

As I listened, I began sobbing uncontrollably,

unable to repress my feelings any longer. When I could speak, it was only to gasp out, "I wish I never had been born, or at least never had come to Thornfield."

"Because you are sorry to leave it?" Mr. Rochester asked.

"I grieve to leave Thornfield," I finally managed to say. "I love Thornfield. I love it because I have lived a full and delightful life here. I have not been trampled on. I have not been petrified. I have talked, face to face, with someone whom I respect, in whom I delight. I have known you, Mr. Rochester, and it fills me with terror and anguish to know that I must be torn from you forever. I see the necessity of departure, and it is like looking at the necessity of death."

"Where do you see the necessity?" he asked suddenly.

"Where? You, sir, have placed it before me."

"In what shape?"

"In the shape of Miss Ingram, a noble and beautiful woman. Your bride."

"My bride! What bride? I have no bride!"

"But you will have."

"Yes, I will! I will!" he said with grim determination.

"Then I must go. You have said it yourself."

"No. You must stay! I swear it, and I will keep my word."

"I tell you I must go!" I retorted. Anger mixed with my grief. "Do you think I can stay here to become nothing to you? Do you think that I am a machine, without feelings? Can I bear to have my morsel of bread snatched from my lips, my drop of water dashed from my cup? Do you think that because I am poor, plain, and little, I have no heart or soul? You think wrong! I have as much soul as you and as much heart! And if God had given me beauty and wealth, I would make it as hard for you to leave me as it now is for me to leave you. I am not talking to you in polite, conventional ways. It is my spirit that speaks to your spirit, just as if we both had passed through the grave and stood at God's feet as equals. We are equal!"

"We are!" Mr. Rochester repeated. "So," he added, taking me in his arms. Pulling me to him, he pressed his lips to mine. "So, Jane!"

"Yes. So, sir," I answered. "And yet not so. Because you are a married man—or as good as a married man—and married to a woman who is inferior to you. She is someone with whom you have no sympathy, whom I do not believe you truly love because I have heard you sneer at her. I would be ashamed of such a marriage. Therefore, I am better than you. Let me go!"

"Where, Jane? To Ireland?"

"Yes, to Ireland. I have spoken my mind and can go anywhere now."

"Jane, be still. Don't struggle so, like a frantic bird that is tearing its own feathers in its desperation."

"I am no bird. I am a free person with an independent will, and I am leaving you." I pulled away at last and stood erect before him.

"Your destiny will be decided by your will," he said. "I offer you my hand, my heart, and a share of all my possessions."

"You joke, and I laugh at you."

"I am asking you to pass through life at my side—to be my second self and my best earthly companion."

"You have already made the choice of your earthly companion, and you must abide by it."

"Jane, be still a few moments. You are overexcited. I will be still, too."

The only voice was that of a singing nightingale. Listening to it, I wept again. Mr. Rochester sat quietly, looking at me gently and seriously. Some time passed before he said, "Come to my side, Jane. Let us understand each other."

"I never again will come to your side. I am torn away now and cannot return."

"But, Jane, I am calling you as my wife. You are the one I intend to marry." I was silent. I thought he was mocking me. "Come, Jane. Come here."

"Your bride stands between us."

He rose and came to me. "My bride is here," he said, again drawing me to him, "because my equal is here and my likeness. Jane, will you marry me?" I did not answer. I pulled myself from his arms because I did not believe what he was saying. "Do you doubt me, Jane?"

"Entirely."

"You have no faith in me?"

"Not a bit."

"Am I a liar in your eyes?" he asked passionately. "You will be convinced. Do I love Miss Ingram? I do not, as you well know. Does she love me? She does not, as I easily have proven. I caused a rumor to reach her that I was not as rich as she supposed. After that I presented myself to see the result. She and her mother were both cold as ice to me. I would not—I could not—marry Miss Ingram. You—you strange, you unearthly thing! I love you as my own flesh. I beg you to accept me as a husband."

"What? Me?" I exclaimed, beginning to believe him. "I have no friend in the world except you—if you are my friend—and not a shilling other than what you have given me."

"You, Jane. I must have you for my own, entirely my own. Will you be mine? Say yes, quickly."

"Mr. Rochester, let me look at your face. Turn to the moonlight."

"Why?"

"I want to read what is in your face. Turn!"

"There! I have turned, but hurry because I am suffering." His face was very disturbed and flushed, and there were strong workings in the features and strange gleams in his eyes. "Oh, Jane, you torture me!" he exclaimed.

"How can I do that? If you are true, and your offer real, my only feelings to you must be gratitude and devotion. Such feelings cannot torture."

"Gratitude!" he exclaimed, and added wildly, "Jane, accept me quickly. Say 'Edward'—use my name, Edward—'I will marry you.'"

"Are you in earnest? Do you truly love me? Do you sincerely wish me to be your wife?"

"I do. I swear it."

"Then, sir, I will marry you."

"Say 'Edward,' my little wife!"

"Dear Edward!"

"Come to me. Come to me entirely now," he said. As he pressed his cheek to mine, he added, "Make my happiness, and let me make yours. God pardon me, and man interfere not with me! I have her and will hold her."

"There is no one to interfere, sir. I have no family."

"No. That is the best of it," he said.

Again and again during the moments that followed, he asked, "Are you happy, Jane?" Again and again I answered, "Yes."

But what had happened to the lovely night? The trees around us writhed and groaned, and the wind roared down upon us. "We must go in," Mr. Rochester said. "A storm is coming. I could have sat with you until morning, Jane." I opened my mouth to speak, but a vivid flash of lightning leaped out of a cloud, and there was a crack, a crash, and a rattling peal of thunder. The rain rushed down. He hurried me up the walk, through the grounds, and into the house, but we were quite wet before we could enter.

Mr. Rochester was taking off my shawl in the hall, and shaking the water out of my loosened hair, when Mrs. Fairfax emerged from her room. I did not see her at first, nor did Mr. Rochester. It was the stroke of twelve. "Hurry and take off your wet things," he said, "and before you go, goodnight. Goodnight, my darling!" He kissed me repeatedly. When I looked up, there stood Mrs. Fairfax, shocked. I only smiled at her and ran upstairs. "I will explain later," I thought. I felt a pang at the idea that she would misunderstand what she had seen. But my joy soon erased every other feeling, and loud as the wind blew, as near as the thunder crashed, I felt no fear. Three times during the storm Mr. Rochester came to my door to ask if I was safe and happy, and that gave me joy and comfort.

Before I left my bed in the morning, little Adele came running in to tell me that the great horse chestnut tree at the bottom of the orchard had been struck by lightning during the night; half of it had split away.

Chapter 24

As I rose and dressed, I thought over what had happened and wondered if it were a dream. I could not be certain it was true until I had seen Mr. Rochester again and heard him renew his words of love and promise.

While arranging my hair, I looked at my face in the mirror. It seemed to me that it was no longer plain. There was color in my face, and my eyes seemed to glow with life and happiness. I often had been unwilling to look at Mr. Rochester because I thought that he could not be pleased with my looks. But I felt sure that now I could lift my face to his and not cool his affections.

As I ran down into the hall, I saw that a brilliant June morning had followed the storm. A fresh, fragrant breeze came in through the open windows. Nature seemed happy for me. A beggar woman and her ragged little boy were coming up the walk, and I ran down and gave them all the money that I had in my purse—some three or four shillings. Everyone must share in my happiness.

Mrs. Fairfax surprised me by looking out of the window with a sad face and saying very seriously, "Miss Eyre, will you come to breakfast?" During the meal she was quiet and cool, but I could not explain to her then. I must wait for my master to speak, and so must she. I ate what I could. Then I rushed upstairs, where I met Adele leaving the schoolroom. "Where are you going? It is time for lessons."

"Mr. Rochester has sent me away to the nursery."

"Where is he?"

"In there," she said, pointing to the schoolroom.

I went in, and there he stood. "Come and tell me good morning," he said. I was glad to do so, not with a cold word or even a handshake but with an embrace and a kiss. It seemed natural—wonderful—to be so loved by him. "Jane, you look blooming and smiling and pretty," he said, "truly pretty this morning. Is this my pale little elf? This sunny-faced girl with dimpled cheeks and rosy lips, satin-smooth hair and radiant hazel eyes?"

"It is Jane Eyre, sir."

"Soon to be Jane Rochester," he added. "In four weeks, Jane, not a day more. Do you hear me?" I did, and I could not quite comprehend it. It made me dizzy. The announcement sent through me something stronger than joy, something that stunned. It was, I think, almost fear. "You blushed, and now you are white, Jane. What is that for?"

"Because you gave me a new name—Jane Rochester—and it seems so strange."

"Yes, Mrs. Rochester," he said. "Young Mrs. Rochester, Edward Rochester's girl bride."

"This can't be, sir. People never can enjoy complete happiness, can they? This is a fairy tale, a daydream."

"It is a dream that I can make come true. I will begin today. This morning I wrote to my banker in London to send me certain jewels that he has in his keeping—heirlooms for the ladies of Thornfield. In a day or two I hope to pour them into your lap. I will give you every privilege and attention that I would give a lord's daughter if I were to marry her."

"Oh, sir, not jewels! Don't speak of them. Jewels for Jane Eyre seem unnatural and strange. I rather would not have them."

"I myself will put the diamond chain around your neck, and I will clasp the bracelets on your fine wrists and load your fingers with rings."

"No, no, sir! Think of other subjects, and speak of other things. Don't speak to me as if I were a beauty. I am your plain governess."

"You are a beauty in my eyes, and a beauty just as my heart desires—delicate and heavenly."

"Puny and insignificant, you mean. You are dreaming, sir, or you are sneering. For God's sake, don't make fun of me!"

"I will make the world, too, see that you are a beauty," he continued. "I will dress my Jane in satin and lace, and she will have roses in her hair, and I will cover the head that I love best with a priceless veil."

"And then you won't know me, sir, and I will

not be your Jane Eyre anymore. I'll be a dressed-up ape, as in a circus."

He went on, however, without noticing my objections. "This very day I will take you in the carriage to Millcote, and you must choose some dresses for yourself. I told you that we will be married in four weeks. The wedding will take place quietly, in the church down there. Then I will take you to London. After a brief stay there, I will take my treasure to regions nearer to the sun—French vineyards and Italian hillsides—and she will taste the life of cities."

"We will travel, sir?"

"We will visit Paris, Rome, and Naples; Florence, Venice, and Vienna. We will revisit all the ground that I have wandered over. Ten years ago I raced through Europe. I was half mad; disgust, hatred, and rage were my companions. Now I will revisit Europe—healed and cleansed, with an angel as my comforter."

I laughed at him as he said this. "I am not an angel," I said, "and I will not be one until I die. I will be myself, Mr. Rochester, and you must not expect anything heavenly because you will not get it any more than I will get it from you."

"What do you expect of me, then? Ask me anything, my dear. I want to please you in all things."

"Indeed, I will, sir. I have my request all ready."

"Speak! But if you look up and smile like that, I will promise before you ask, and that will make a fool of me."

"Not at all, sir. I ask only this: don't send for the jewels."

"Your request is granted, for the time. I will take back the order that I sent to my banker. But you have not yet asked for anything. You have asked only that a gift be taken back. Try again."

"Well then, please satisfy my curiosity on one point."

He looked startled. "What? What?" he said hastily. "Curiosity is very dangerous. It is good that I have not promised to grant this request."

"But there can be no danger in doing this, sir."

"Well, go ahead and ask, then, Jane. But I wish that you would ask for half my possessions instead of wanting to know my secrets."

"Now, what do I want with half your possessions? I would much rather have all your confidence."

"You are welcome to all my confidence that is worth having, Jane. But for God's sake, don't desire a useless burden! Don't ask for poison!"

"My question is harmless enough, surely. It is just this: Why did you make me believe that you wanted to marry Miss Ingram?"

"Is that all? Thank God it is no worse. The answer is simple enough. I pretended to court Miss Ingram because I wanted to make you as madly in love with me as I was with you. I thought that jealousy would be the best weapon available to me."

"Excellent! Now you are small, no bigger than

the end of my little finger. It was a shame and a scandal to act that way. Didn't you think of Miss Ingram's feelings at all?"

"She has only one feeling—pride—and that needed humbling. Were you jealous, Jane?"

"Never mind, Mr. Rochester. You don't need to know that. But truly, don't you think Miss Ingram will suffer? Won't she feel forsaken and deserted?"

"Impossible! I told you, she lost any interest in me the moment she learned that I was, supposedly, a poor man."

"Then, I truly may enjoy my great happiness without fearing that anyone else is suffering as a result of it?"

"That you may, my good little girl. There is not another person in the world who loves me as you do. I take the greatest pleasure in believing in your affection."

I kissed the hand that lay on my shoulder. I loved him very much, more than words had the power to express.

"Ask something more," he said.

I was ready again with my request. "Tell Mrs. Fairfax what has happened," I said. "She saw me with you last night in the hall, and she was shocked. Give her some explanation before I see her again. It hurts me to be misjudged by such a good woman."

"Go to your room, and put on your bonnet," he replied. "I want you to drive to Millcote with me this morning. While you get ready, I will enlighten the old lady. Did she think, Jane, that you had disgraced yourself for love?"

"I believe she thought that I had forgotten my position, and yours, sir."

"Position! Your position is in my heart. I'll go speak with her."

I soon was dressed. When I heard Mr. Rochester leave Mrs. Fairfax's parlor, I hurried down to it. The old lady had been reading the Bible. The book now lay open before her, with her eyeglasses on it. She was staring blankly at the wall before her. Seeing me, she made some effort to smile and started a few words of congratulation. But the smile faded, and her sentence trailed away unfinished. "I feel so astonished," she began. "I hardly know what to say to you, Miss Eyre. I haven't been dreaming, have I? Sometimes I half fall asleep when I am sitting alone, and I imagine things. More than once while I have dozed here, it has seemed to me that my dear husband, who died fifteen years ago, has come in and sat down beside me. Now, is it actually true that Mr. Rochester has asked you to marry him? Don't laugh at me. But I really thought he came in here five minutes ago and said that in a month you will be his wife."

"He has said the same thing to me," I replied.

"He has! Do you believe him? Have you accepted him?"

"Yes."

She looked at me with bewilderment. "I never would have thought it. He is a proud man. All of the Rochesters were proud, and his father, at least, liked money. He means to marry you?"

"He tells me so."

She examined me closely, and it was clear that she saw no charm powerful enough to explain this mystery. "It is beyond me," she went on, "but no doubt it is true since you say so. How it will work out, I really don't know. It is generally a good thing that people are equal in position and fortune. And there are twenty years of difference in your ages. He could be your father."

"No, indeed, Mrs. Fairfax!" I exclaimed, rather annoyed. "No one who saw us together would think that for an instant. Mr. Rochester looks as young, and is as young, as some men of twenty-five."

"Is it really for love that he is going to marry you?" she asked. I was so hurt by her doubt that tears rose to my eyes. "I am sorry to grieve you," she went on, "but you are so young and so little acquainted with men. I only want you to be on your guard. You know the old saying 'All that glitters is not gold.' In this case I do fear that something is not what it seems."

"Why? Am I a monster?" I said. "Is it impossible that Mr. Rochester sincerely loves me?"

"No. You are very good, and I'm sure that Mr. Rochester is fond of you. I always have noticed that you were a sort of pet of his. There have been times when, for your sake, I have been a little uneasy about his affection for you and have wanted to warn you. But I did not want to suggest even the possibility of wrong. I knew such an idea would shock and offend you. And you were so modest and sensible that I hoped nothing would happen. Last night I was so worried when I looked all through the house and couldn't find you, or the master. Then, at midnight, I saw you come in with him."

"Well, never mind that now," I interrupted impatiently. "Everything has turned out all right."

"I hope that all will be right in the end," she said. "But, believe me, you cannot be too careful. Try to keep Mr. Rochester at a distance. Do not fully trust yourself or him. Gentlemen in his position do not usually marry their governesses."

I was growing truly irritated. Luckily, Adele ran in. "Let me go! Let me go to Millcote, too!" she cried. "Mr. Rochester won't, even though there is so much room in the new carriage. Beg him to let me go, Mademoiselle."

"That I will, Adele." And I left with her, glad to get away from gloomy Mrs. Fairfax. The carriage was ready. They were bringing it around to the front, where my master was waiting. "Adele may go with us, may she not, sir?"

"I told her no. I'll have no brats! I'll have only you."

"Do let her go, Mr. Rochester. Please. It would be better."

"Not a chance of it. She will be a restraint." He was quite abrupt, both in look and voice. The chill of Mrs. Fairfax's warnings was upon me. I had lost half my sense of power over him. I was about to obey him, but as he helped me into the carriage, he looked at my face. "What is the matter?" he asked. "All the sunshine is gone. Do you really wish the child to go? Will it annoy you if she is left behind?"

"I would much rather that she come, sir."

"Then, go get your bonnet and come back like a flash of lightning!" he told Adele. She obeyed him as quickly as she could. "After all, a single morning's interruption will not matter much, when I shortly will claim you—your thoughts, conversation, and company—for life," he said.

Once Adele was lifted in, she began kissing me to express her gratitude for my action. Mr. Rochester instantly stowed her into a corner on the other side of him. She then peeped around to where I sat. So stern a neighbor was too restrictive to her, and she looked most distressed. "Let her come to me," I requested. "There is plenty of room on this side." He handed her over as if she had been a lapdog. "I'll send her to school yet," he said, but now he was smiling.

The hour spent at Millcote was somewhat troublesome to me. Mr. Rochester insisted that I go to a certain silk warehouse, where I was ordered to choose half a dozen dresses. I hated the business, and I begged to delay it. I finally did reduce the half-dozen to two, but these two he swore he would select himself. Anxiously I watched his eye move over the bright colors. He settled on a rich silk of the most brilliant amethyst and a superb pink satin. I whispered to him that he might as well buy me a sparkling gold gown and a shiny silver bonnet, too, because I never would wear his choices. With great difficulty I persuaded him to settle for a black satin and a pearl-gray silk. "It will do for the present," he grumbled, "but eventually, I will see you as colorful as a parrot." I was glad to leave the silk warehouse, but then it was on to a jeweler's. The more he bought me, the more my cheeks burned with annoyance and shame.

As we re-entered the carriage and I sat back exhausted, I remembered something that I had entirely forgotten in the rush of recent events: the letter to Mrs. Reed from my uncle, John Eyre, in which he had declared his intention to adopt me and make me his heir. "It would be a relief," I thought, "if I had even a small income of my own. I never will feel comfortable being dressed like a doll by Mr. Rochester. I will write to Madeira the moment I get home and tell my uncle that I am going to be married, and to whom. If I knew that I could bring Mr. Rochester some fortune of my own someday, I could better endure being kept by him now."

Feeling relieved, I was able to tease him on our way home. "I'll wear nothing but my old Lowood dresses for the rest of my life. I'll be married in this cotton dress, and you may make a dressing gown for yourself out of the pearl-gray silk and an endless series of vests out of the black satin. You see, I remember what you said about Celine Varens—about the diamonds and gowns that you gave her. I will not be your English Celine Varens. I will continue to act as Adele's governess; by that I will earn my room and board, and thirty pounds a year. I'll buy my own clothing out of that money, and you will give me nothing but . . ."

"But what?"

"Your respect. And if I give you mine in return, we will be even."

"I never have seen anything equal to your pride," he responded. "You will give up your governessing slavery at once."

"I beg your pardon, sir, but I will not. I will go on with it as usual. I will keep out of your way all day, as I am accustomed to doing. You may send for me in the evening when you want to see me; I'll come then but at no other time."

He threw up his hands in impatience. "It is your time now, you little tyrant, but it will be mine soon. When I have you safely married to me, I will attach you to a chain like this." (He touched his watch chain.) "Yes, I'll carry you in my pocket, for fear of losing you." He said this as he helped me descend from the carriage. While he lifted Adele out, I entered the house and returned to work upstairs.

This conversation set the tone for our next weeks together. I worked as usual during the day, and he called for me promptly at seven every evening. In other people's presence I acted exactly as before, respectful and quiet. It was only during our evenings together that I argued with and challenged him on all points. While he often was cross and crusty about such treatment, I could tell that he was well entertained, his mind as stimulated as his heart was warmed.

When I appeared before him now, he had no honeyed terms such as "love" and "darling" on his lips. Instead he called me "provoking puppet," "malicious elf," "sprite," "changeling," etc. I was more likely to receive a pinch on the arm or a tweak of the ear than a kiss. It was all right; I was determined that he should know exactly what he was getting into in marrying someone like me, and for now I preferred these fierce favors to anything more tender. Mrs. Fairfax, I saw, approved of my behavior. Her anxiety on my behalf vanished; therefore, I was certain that I did well. Yet my task was not easy; often I would rather have pleased Mr. Rochester than teased him. My future husband was becoming my whole world to me. More than the world. He almost was my hope of heaven. He stood between me and every thought of religion. I was making an idol of him.

Chapter 25

The month of courtship was over. All the preparations for the wedding day were complete, and I had nothing left to do. There were my trunks, packed, locked, and standing in a row along the wall of my little room. Tomorrow at this time, they would be on their way to London, and so would I—not I, that is, but Jane Rochester, a person I did not know. The identification cards were not fastened to the trunks yet. They lay, four little squares, in the drawer. Mr. Rochester had written the address on each of them: "Mrs. Rochester, Queen's Hotel, London." I could not persuade myself to fasten them to the trunks yet.

Mrs. Rochester! She did not exist. She would not be born until tomorrow, and I would wait to be sure that she had come into the world alive before I took that final step. It was enough that in the closet opposite me were clothes that were said to be hers. They included a wedding dress, a pearl-colored robe, and a shimmering veil. I shut the closet to hide the strange items that it contained. At this evening hour—nine o'clock—they gave out a ghostly shimmer through the shadows. "I will leave you by yourself, white dream," I said. "I am feverish. I hear the wind blowing; I will go outdoors and feel it."

Why was I feverish? It was not only the hurry of preparation or the anticipation of my new life. There was another reason for my distress. Something had happened that I could not understand. No one knew of the event but me. It had taken place the previous night. Mr. Rochester had been away from home, taking care of business at a small estate he owned, thirty miles away. I waited now for his return, eager to unburden my mind.

I went to the orchard, driven to its shelter by the wind, which had been blowing all day. The wind brought me a certain wild pleasure, helping to drive my troubles from my mind. I found myself facing the wreck of the horse chestnut tree. It stood black and split down the center by lightning. The halves had not been fully separated: the strong roots still held firm. But the tree's life was gone; the sap no longer could flow, and next winter's storms surely would bring one or both halves crashing to earth. But for now they could be said to form one tree—a ruin, but an entire ruin. "You did right to hold tight to each other," I said, as if the monster splinters were living things and could hear me. "You never again will have green leaves or see birds making nests and singing in your boughs. Your time of pleasure is over, but you are not abandoned. Each of you has a comrade to comfort you in your old age."

I wandered into the house to be sure that a fire was burning in the library. Although it was a summer night, the wild windy weather was fierce, and I was sure that Mr. Rochester would like to return to a cheerful blaze. By then the clock was striking ten. "How late it is!" I said to myself. "I will run down to the gates. He may be coming now, and I will meet him and save myself some minutes of suspense."

There was no sign of him, however. My anxiety was such that I could not return to the house. I decided to walk down the road to meet him. Before I had traveled a quarter mile, I heard the tramp of hooves and saw a horseman traveling toward me at full gallop. "There!" he exclaimed as he stretched out his hand and bent from the saddle. "You can't do without me; that is clear. Step on my boot toe and swing up!" I sprang up onto his saddle and received a hearty kiss for a welcome. "But is there anything the matter, Jane, that you come to meet me at such an hour? Is anything wrong?"

"I am well, sir. After you are settled, I will talk to you about something that has troubled me."

We arrived at the house, and John took Mr. Rochester's horse. Mr. Rochester followed me into the hall, telling me to hurry and put something dry on, then meet him in the library. I found him having his supper. "Take a seat and keep me company, Jane. Please God, it is one of the last meals that you will eat at Thornfield Hall for a long time." As the meal ended, I remarked that it was nearly midnight. "Yes. But remember, Jane, you promised to sit up with me the night before my wedding."

"I did. And I will keep my promise, for an hour

or two at least. I don't want to go to bed."

"Are all of your arrangements complete?"

"All, sir."

"Mine as well," he said. "Everything is ready. We will leave Thornfield tomorrow, as soon as we return from church."

"Very well, sir."

"What an extraordinary smile you gave me just now, Jane! What a bright spot of color you have on each cheek! And how strangely your eyes glitter! Are you well?"

"I believe I am."

"Believe? What is the matter? Tell me what you feel."

"I cannot, sir. No words could tell you what I feel. I wish we could sit together like this forever. Who knows what the future may hold?"

"This is not like you, Jane. You are overexcited or overtired."

"Do you feel calm and happy?"

"Calm? No. But happy, to my heart's core. Talk to me, Jane. What has happened to disturb you? Mrs. Fairfax has said something, perhaps? Or you have overheard the servants talk? Has your sensitive self-respect been wounded?"

"No, sir." It struck twelve. I waited until the clock stopped chiming. Then I continued, "All day yesterday I was very busy, and very happy in my preparations. At sunset Sophie called me upstairs to look at my wedding dress, which had just been delivered. Underneath it, in the box, I found your present—the veil that, in your extravagance, you ordered from London. I suppose that because I would not accept jewels, you bought it to force me to accept something as costly. I smiled as I unfolded it; I planned how I would tease you about your aristocratic tastes. I thought how much I loved you. Soon after, I retired for the night. No, sir, don't kiss me now. Let me finish my story. During the night, I was awakened by a light that appeared before me. It was a candle. At first I thought that Sophie had come in. The candle sat on my dressing table, and the door of the closet containing my wedding dress and veil stood open. I heard a rustling there. I said, 'Sophie, what are you doing?' No one answered, but someone came out of the closet. She picked up the candle, held it high, and looked at the garments hanging there. 'Sophie? Sophie?' I cried, but there was no answer. I sat up in bed, and my blood crept cold through my veins. Mr. Rochester, it was not Sophie. It was not Leah. It was not Mrs. Fairfax. It was not—no, I was sure of it and still am—it was not even that strange woman, Grace Poole."

"It must have been one of them," my master interrupted.

"No, sir. I solemnly assure you that it was not. I never had seen the person who was standing there."

"Describe the person, Jane."

"It was a woman, tall and large, with thick, dark hair hanging down her back. She was wearing some sort of loose white garment."

"Did you see her face?"

"Not at first. But then she took my veil from its hanger. She held it up, gazed at it for a long moment, and then threw it over her own head and turned to the mirror. At that moment I saw the face's reflection quite clearly in the glass."

"What was it like?"

"Fearful and ghastly. Oh, sir, I never saw a face like it! It was a discolored, savage face. I wish that I could forget what those red eyes looked like! The lips were swollen and dark, the forehead deeply lined. The heavy black eyebrows rose high over the bloodshot eyes. Should I tell you what the face reminded me of?"

"Do."

"A vampire."

"Ah! What did the woman do?"

"She removed my veil from her head, tore it into two parts, threw them onto the floor, and stepped on them."

"And then?"

"She drew aside the window curtain and looked out. Perhaps she saw dawn approaching because, taking the candle, she retreated to the door. The figure stopped at my bedside. Her fiery eyes glared at me. She thrust her candle close to my face and then blew it out under my eyes. I saw her terrifying face ablaze over me, and I fainted from terror. When I awoke, it was daylight and I was alone. I decided to tell no one except you what had happened. Now, sir, tell me who and what that woman was."

"She was the creation of an overstimulated brain; that is certain. I must be careful of you, my treasure. Nerves like yours were not made for rough handling."

"Believe me, I did not imagine this. When I rose this morning, I found the veil on the carpet, torn in half from top to bottom!"

I felt Mr. Rochester shudder. He threw his arms around me. "If something evil did come near you last night, thank God only the veil was harmed. Oh, to think what might have happened!" He held me so close to him that I barely could breathe.

After some minutes of silence, he continued cheerfully, "Now, Jane, I'll explain it all to you. It was half dream, half reality. No doubt, a woman entered your room. That woman was—must have been—Grace Poole. You have called her a strange person, and you have reason to call her that. You were half awake, and your imagination invented a dreadful appearance for her. It was a kind of waking nightmare. Her awful actions—the spiteful tearing of the veil—were real, and they were like her. You wonder, of course, why I keep such a woman in my house. When we have been married a year and a day, I will tell you, but not now. Are you satisfied, Jane? Do you accept my solution of the mystery?"

I was not satisfied. But to please him, I tried to seem so. Because it was long past one o'clock, I prepared to leave him. "Why don't you sleep with Adele and Sophie in the nursery tonight, Jane? You must be feeling nervous, and I would rather that you weren't alone. Be sure to lock the door before you sleep." He walked to the window and looked out at the peaceful shining moon. There was no more trace of rain. "It is a lovely night," he remarked. "And how is my Jane now?"

"The night is peaceful, sir, and so am I."

"Then go to bed, and dream of happy love and a blissful marriage."

But I didn't sleep at all. Holding little Adele in my arms, I watched her innocent face and waited for the coming day. As soon as the sun rose, I rose too. Adele clung to me as I left her. I remember that I kissed her as I loosened her little hands from my neck, and I cried over her with strange emotion. She seemed to represent my past life, and I was headed toward an unknown future.

Chapter 26

Sophie came at seven to help me dress. She took so long that Mr. Rochester, growing impatient, sent a message asking why I did not come. Sophie fastened my veil to my hair (the veil was the square of sheer, plain fabric that I had wanted in the first place), and I began to hurry away. "Stop!" she cried in French. "Look at yourself in the mirror. You have not taken a single peek." So I turned at the door. I saw a veiled figure so unlike my usual self that it seemed a stranger's image. "Jane!" a voice called. I hurried downstairs to Mr. Rochester.

"Lingerer!" he said, "I am on fire with impatience, and you take so long!" He looked at me and said, "You are as fair as a lily, Jane. You are not only the pride of my life but also the desire of my eyes. You have ten minutes in which to eat some breakfast before we leave for the church!" He made some last-minute arrangements for the carriage and luggage and then returned. "Jane, are you ready?"

I rose. There were no groomsmen, bridesmaids, or relatives to wait for, no one other than Mr. Rochester and me. Mrs. Fairfax stood in the hall as we passed. I would have liked to speak with her, but Mr. Rochester's grip on my hand was like steel, and the look on his face made it clear that he would not endure another moment's delay. I wondered if any other bridegroom ever had looked as he did: so stubbornly purposeful, so grimly determined, with flaming and flashing eyes.

At the churchyard gate he finally paused and realized that I was out of breath. "Am I cruel in my love?" he said. "Rest an instant. Lean on me, Jane."

Now I can remember how the old gray house of God looked, rising calm before me, a crow wheeling around the steeple. I have not forgotten, either, the two strangers reading inscriptions on the tombstones nearby. I noticed them because, as they saw us, they walked around to the church's side door. I assumed that they were going to enter there and witness the ceremony. But Mr. Rochester did not see them.

We entered the quiet church to find Mr. Wood, the minister, waiting at the altar, his clerk beside him. Everything was still. The strangers' shadows moved in a remote corner. We took our places at the communion rails, and the service began. The minister said a few words about the institution of marriage and then came forward a step. Bending slightly toward us, he continued, "I now require you both to answer: if either of you knows any impediment, any reason why you may not lawfully be joined together in matrimony, confess it now, because those who are joined together outside of God's word are not joined by God, nor is their matrimony lawful."

He paused, as is the custom. When is the pause

after that sentence ever broken by a reply? Once in a hundred years? The clergyman already was proceeding. His hand was stretched toward Mr. Rochester as his lips opened to ask, "Will you have this woman for your wedded wife?" Then a voice announced sharply, "The marriage cannot go on. I declare the existence of an impediment."

The startled clergyman looked up at the speaker; the clerk did the same. Mr. Rochester moved slightly, as if an earthquake had rolled under his feet. Steadying himself, but not turning his head or eyes, he said to the minister, "Go on."

Profound silence fell when he had uttered those words. Presently Mr. Wood said, "I cannot go on, sir, not without some investigation into what has been said here."

"The ceremony is broken off," the voice behind us said. "I am able to prove my allegation. An obstacle to this marriage exists."

Mr. Rochester still did not respond. He stood stubborn and rigid; his only movement was to take my hand. How hot and strong his hand felt! How his eyes shone, watchful and wild!

Mr. Wood seemed at a loss. "What is the nature of the impediment?" he asked. "Perhaps it may be overcome or explained away?"

"Hardly," came the answer. The stranger walked forward and leaned onto the rails. He said calmly, steadily, but not loudly, "It is simply this: Mr. Rochester has a wife who is now living."

My nerves vibrated under those words. I

looked at Mr. Rochester; I made him look at me. His whole face was colorless rock. He said nothing; he made no protest. He only put his arm around my waist and pulled me tightly to his side. "Who are you?" he asked the intruder.

"My name is Briggs, sir. I am an attorney at law."

"And you are here to force a wife on me?"

"I am reminding you of her existence, sir, which the law recognizes, even if you do not."

"Tell me about her."

"Certainly." Mr. Briggs calmly took a paper from his pocket and read in an official, nasal voice, "'I affirm that on the twentieth of October, fifteen years ago, Edward Fairfax Rochester, of Thornfield Hall, England, was married to my sister, Bertha Antoinetta Mason, daughter of Jonas Mason, a merchant, and of Antoinetta, his wife, in Spanish Town, Jamaica. The record of the marriage will be found in that church's register, and a copy of it is now in my possession. Signed, Richard Mason.'"

"If that is a genuine document," Mr. Rochester said, "it may prove that I have been married, but it does not prove that the woman mentioned there is still living."

"She was living three months ago," the lawyer replied.

"How do you know?"

"I have a witness to the fact."

"Produce him, or go to hell."

"I will produce him because he is here. Mr.

Mason, please step forward."

Upon hearing that name, Mr. Rochester experienced a spasm that I could feel running through his body. The second stranger, who had been lingering behind the lawyer, now came forward. Yes, it was Mr. Mason himself. Mr. Rochester turned and glared at him. He lifted his strong arm as though he would strike Mason to the floor. Mason shrank away, crying weakly, "Good God!" A look of contempt crossed Mr. Rochester's face. He lowered his arm and asked, "What have you to say?" An inaudible mumble came from Mason's white lips. "To hell with you if you cannot answer directly. I again demand, 'What have you to say?'"

"Sir! Sir!" the clergyman interrupted, "Do not forget that you are in a sacred place." Then he gently asked Mason, "Do you know, sir, whether or not this gentleman's wife is still living?"

"Courage," the lawyer urged. "Speak out."

"She lives at Thornfield Hall," Mason said more clearly. "I saw her there last April. I am her brother."

"At Thornfield Hall!" the clergyman exclaimed. "Impossible! I have lived in this neighborhood for years, sir, and I never heard of a Mrs. Rochester at Thornfield Hall."

A grim smile touched Mr. Rochester's lips, and he muttered, "No, by God! I took care that no one would hear of her." Then he announced loudly, "Enough! Wood, close your book. There will be no wedding today." The man obeyed. Mr. Rochester continued recklessly. "'Bigamy' is an ugly word. I tried to be a bigamist, but fate has out-tricked me. I am little better than a devil, and, as my pastor there would tell me, I no doubt deserve God's sternest punishment. What this lawyer and his client say is true. I have been married, and the woman to whom I was married is still alive. You say that you never heard of a Mrs. Rochester at Thornfield Hall, Wood. But haven't you heard gossip about a mysterious lunatic kept there? Some have whispered that she is my illegitimate half-sister. Some say that she is my cast-off mistress. But she is my wife, whom I married fifteen years ago. Her name is Bertha Mason, and she is the sister of this courageous fellow here. Cheer up, Dick! Don't be afraid! I'd as soon hit a woman as you.

"Bertha Mason is mad. She came from three generations of idiots, maniacs, and drunkards. Her mother was both a lunatic and an alcoholic, as I found out after I had married the daughter. Beforehand the Masons kept those matters secret. Oh, my experience has been heavenly! If you only knew it! But I cannot describe it well enough. Instead I invite all of you to come to the house and visit my wife! You will see what sort of person I was cheated into marrying. You can judge whether or not I had a right to break the contract and seek happiness with a human being. This girl," he continued, looking at me, "knew no more than you did, Wood, of the disgusting secret. She thought our wedding was fair and legal and never dreamed that she was going to be lured into a bigamous union with a wretch. Come, all of you. Follow me!"

Still holding me tightly, he left the church, the three gentlemen following. At the front door of the house, we found the carriage waiting. "Take it back to the coach house, John," Mr. Rochester said coolly. "It will not be wanted today." As we entered, Mrs. Fairfax, Adele, Sophie, and Leah came to greet us. "Away with your congratulations!" Mr. Rochester cried. "They are fifteen years too late!"

He ran up the stairs, still holding my hand, and beckoned the gentlemen to follow. We proceeded to the third story. The low black door admitted us to the tapestried room, with its great bed. "You remember this place, Mason," our guide said. "She bit and stabbed you here." He lifted the hangings from the wall, uncovering the second door, which he also opened. In a windowless room there burned a fire surrounded by a high, strong gate. Grace Poole was there, apparently cooking something in a saucepan. In the deep shadows at the room's far end, a figure ran back and forth. Whether it was a beast or a human being was hard to tell at first. It groveled on all fours; it clawed and growled like some strange wild animal. But it was wearing clothing, and a quantity of dark hair, wild as a mane, hid its head and face. "Good morning, Mrs. Poole," Mr. Rochester said. "How are you? And how is your patient today?"

"We're tolerable, sir, thank you," Grace replied, lifting the boiling pot carefully. "Rather snappish but not outrageous." A fierce cry seemed to contradict her words. The creature rose up and stood tall on its hind feet. "Ah, sir, she sees you!" Grace exclaimed. "You'd better not stay."

"Only a few moments, Grace. You must allow me a few moments."

"Take care, then, sir! For God's sake, take care!"

The maniac bellowed. She lifted her shaggy hair away from her face and gazed wildly at her visitors. I recognized that hideous face.

Mrs. Poole stepped forward. "Keep out of the way," Mr. Rochester said, pushing her aside. "She has no knife now, I suppose, and I'm on my guard."

"One never knows what she has, sir. She is so cunning."

"We'd better leave her," Mason whispered.

"Go to the devil!" his brother-in-law said.

"Watch out!" Grace cried.

The three gentlemen immediately retreated, Mr. Rochester flinging me behind him. The lunatic viciously sprang at his throat and bit into his cheek. They struggled. She was a big woman, nearly as tall as her husband and heavy. She was amazingly strong. More than once she almost strangled him. He could have stopped her with a well-planted blow, but he would not strike her; he only would wrestle. At last he seized her arms; Grace Poole handed him a cord, and he tied them behind her. Then he fastened her to a chair. The entire time, she screamed like a hyena.

Mr. Rochester then turned to the spectators with a smile that was both sarcastic and achingly sad. "That is my wife," he said. "You have seen the only kind of marital embrace that I ever will know. This is what I wished to have," he said, laying his hand on my shoulder. "This young girl, who stands so quietly at the mouth of hell, looking calmly into the demon's face. I wanted her—yes. Wood and Briggs, look at the difference! Compare her clear eyes with those red balls, her face with that mask. Then judge me, minister of the gospel and man of the law! Off with you now. I must shut up my prize."

We all left the room. Mr. Rochester stayed

behind a moment to give some order to Grace Poole. The lawyer spoke to me as he descended the stair. "You, madam," he said, "are cleared of all blame. If your uncle still is living, he will be glad to hear it when Mr. Mason returns to Madeira."

"My uncle! What about him? Do you know him?"

"Mr. Mason does. Mr. Eyre has handled the Masons' family business in Madeira for many years. When your uncle received your letter announcing your intended marriage to Mr. Rochester, Mr. Mason happened to be with him. Mr. Eyre mentioned the news because he knew that Mr. Mason was acquainted with a gentleman named Rochester. Mr. Mason, astonished and distressed, revealed the real state of things. Your uncle, I am sorry to say, is very ill and is unlikely to recover. He could not hurry to England himself to free you from the trap into which you had fallen, but he begged Mr. Mason to rush here to prevent the false marriage. We came here with all possible speed, and I am thankful that we were not too late, as you also must be. If I did not believe that your uncle would be dead before you reached Madeira, I would advise you to accompany Mr. Mason back. As it is, I think you'd better remain in England until you hear further, either from Mr. Eyre or about him. Have we anything else to stay here for?" he asked Mr. Mason.

"No. Let us be gone," Mason anxiously replied. Without waiting to say goodbye to Mr.

Rochester, they left, as did the minister.

I heard them go as I stood at the half-open door of my room. The house having cleared, I shut myself in. I did not weep; I did not mourn. I still was too calm for that. I mechanically took off the wedding dress and replaced it with the cotton dress that I had worn the previous day. I felt weak and tired. I leaned my arms on a table, and my head drooped against them. Until this moment I had only heard, seen, and moved, following up and down wherever I was led or dragged. But now I thought.

All was over. I was in my own room—my usual self, without any obvious change. Yet, where was the Jane Eyre of yesterday? What was her life? What would become of her? Jane Eyre, who had been an eager, expectant woman—almost a bride—was a cold, solitary girl again. A Christmas frost had come at midsummer; a white December storm had whirled over June. My hopes were dead. I looked at my love; it shivered in my heart like a child suffering in a cold cradle.

My eyes closed; darkness seemed to swim around me. I lay faint, weak, wanting to be dead. Only one hopeful thought still throbbed within me: a remembrance of God. I had no energy to whisper the words that wandered up and down in my darkened mind: "Be not far from me because trouble is near and there is no one to help."

Chapter 27

Some time in the afternoon I raised my head. Looking around and seeing the sun beginning to set, I asked myself, "What should I do?" The answer that my mind gave—"Leave Thornfield at once"—was so dreadful that I stopped my ears. I could not bear such words now. "That I am not Edward Rochester's bride is the least part of my sorrow," I thought. "That I have awakened from a glorious dream, and found it empty, is a horror that I can bear. But the idea that I must leave him—instantly, forever—is intolerable. I cannot do it."

With a strange pang I realized that as long as I had been shut up here, no one had come to ask how I was. Not even little Adele or Mrs. Fairfax had tapped at the door. "Friends always forget friends when trouble comes," I murmured as I unlocked the door and left the room. I stumbled over an obstacle; my head still was dizzy, and I was weak with fatigue and hunger. I fell, but not to the ground; an outstretched arm caught me. I was supported by Mr. Rochester, who sat in a chair in front of my door.

"You come out at last," he said. "I have been waiting for you and listening; I have not heard one movement or one sob. Five more minutes of that death-like hush, and I would have forced the lock like a burglar. You shut yourself up to grieve alone. I'd rather you had come and screamed at me. You are passionate; I expected some kind of scene. I was prepared for the hot rain of tears; I wanted them to be shed on my shoulder. Now only the floor or your handkerchief has received them. But I am mistaken: you have not wept at all! I see no trace of tears. Well, Jane!" he continued. "Not a word of reproach? Nothing bitter? Nothing sad? You look at me with such weariness. Jane, I never meant to wound you like this. Imagine a man who had only one little lamb that was as dear to him as a daughter. It ate his bread and drank from his cup, and then by some mistake he had it slaughtered. He would not be sorrier than I am now. Will you ever forgive me?"

Reader, I forgave him on the spot. There was such deep remorse in his eyes and such unchanged love. I forgave him for everything, to my heart's core.

"You know that I am a scoundrel, Jane?" he inquired.

"Yes, sir."

"Then tell me so. Don't spare me."

"I cannot; I am tired and sick. I want some water." He heaved a sort of shuddering sigh and, taking me in his arms, carried me downstairs to the library. He held a glass of wine to my lips. I tasted it and began to feel stronger. Then I ate something that he offered me. I was sitting in his chair, and he was quite near. "If I could just die now, not too painfully, it would be good," I thought. "Then, I would not have to break my heart by separating from Mr. Rochester. I must leave him. I do not want to leave him. I cannot leave him."

"How are you now?"

"Much better, sir. I will be well soon."

"Have some more wine, Jane." I obeyed him.

Suddenly he stooped down as if to kiss me. I turned my face away. "What is this?" he exclaimed. "Oh, I know! You won't kiss Bertha Mason's husband. You think that my arms are filled and my embraces belong to another."

"There is no room for me, sir."

"Why, Jane? I will spare you the trouble of answering. Because I already have a wife, am I right?"

"Yes."

"If you think so, you must have a strange opinion of me. You must believe that I am a plotting monster who has only pretended to love you, in order to trap you and strip you of self-respect. What do you say to that? I see that you can say nothing. You are still faint, and you are not yet ready to accuse and criticize me. You are considering how to act. Talking, you believe, is of no use. You see, I know you; I am on my guard."

"Sir, I do not wish to act against you," I said. My voice was too unsteady for me to say more.

"Not in *your* sense of the word, but in *mine*, you are scheming to destroy me. You have said that

I am a married man, and because of that, you will shun me. Just now you refused to kiss me. You intend to make yourself a complete stranger to me, to live under this roof only as Adele's governess. If I ever say a friendly word to you, or you ever have a friendly feeling for me, you will say to yourself, 'That man tried to make me his mistress. I must be ice and rock to him.' And ice and rock you will become."

I steadied my voice to reply. "Everything around me has changed, sir, and I must change too. There is only one way: Adele must have a new governess."

"Adele will go to school. I have settled that already. And I no longer will torment you with Thornfield Hall's hideous memories. Jane, you will not stay here, and neither will I. I was wrong ever to bring you to this house, knowing as I did that it was haunted. Before I ever saw you, I wanted to conceal the truth about the place because I thought that no governess would stay if she knew who else was living here. But concealing the madwoman from you was, itself, madness. Her neighborhood is poisoned and always was. I'll shut up Thornfield Hall now. I'll nail up the front door and board the lower windows. I'll give Mrs. Poole two hundred pounds a year to live here with my 'wife,' as you call that fearful hag. Grace will do the job for that money, and she will have her son, who lives nearby, to give her a hand when 'my wife' decides to burn people in their beds, stab them, bite their flesh from their bones, and so on."

"Sir," I said, "you are too cruel about that unfortunate lady. You speak of her with hatred. It is wrong to do that. She cannot help being mad."

"Jane, my little darling (I will call you that because you are that), you don't know what you are talking about. You misjudge me again. It is not because she is mad that I hate her. Do you think that I would hate you if you were mad?"

"I do indeed, sir."

"Then, you are mistaken, and you know nothing about me. Every atom of your flesh is as dear to me as my own. If you were sick, it still would be dear. Your mind is my treasure. If it were broken, it still would be my treasure. If you raved, I would quiet you in my arms. If you flew at me as wildly as that woman did this morning, I would receive you in an embrace as loving as it was protective. I would not shrink from you with disgust as I do from her. But why do I say such things? I was talking about taking you away from Thornfield. Everything is ready for a prompt departure. You will leave tomorrow. I ask you to spend only one more night under this roof, Jane. Then farewell forever to its miseries and terrors! I have a place to go to that will be a safe, peaceful place of retirement from hateful memories."

"Take Adele with you, sir," I interrupted. "She will be a companion for you."

"What do you mean, Jane? I told you that I would send Adele to school."

"You spoke of retirement, sir. Retiring alone will be too dull for you."

"Alone? Alone?" he repeated with irritation. "I see that I must be more plain. I will not be alone. You will share my solitude. Do you understand?"

I shook my head.

"Jane! Will you listen to reason?"

I took hold of his clenched hand, loosened the tightened fingers, and soothingly said to him, "Sit down. I'll talk to you as long as you like, and hear all that you have to say, but my answer will not change."

He tried again to pull me to him, but I would not permit it. "Jane! Jane!" he said in a tone of such bitter sadness that it made all of my nerves ache. "You don't love me, then? It was only my station and the rank of my wife that you valued? Now that you think me disqualified to become your husband, you recoil from my touch as if I were some toad or ape."

I probably should have said nothing in response, but it hurt me so deeply to see his pain that I could not control my desire to comfort him. "I do love you," I said, "more than ever. But I must not show my feelings or give in to them. This is the last time that I can tell you that I love you."

"The last time, Jane? How? Do you think that you can live with me, and see me daily, yet always be cold and distant?"

"No, sir, I cannot. That is why I must leave Adele and Thornfield. I must be apart from you for the rest of my life. I must begin a new existence."

"Of course, that's what I told you. I will ignore the madness about being apart from me. What you mean is that you will be a part of me. You will yet be my wife. I am not married. You will be Mrs. Rochester, and I will be faithful to you as long as you and I live. You will go to a place that I have in southern France, a whitewashed villa on the Mediterranean. There you will live a happy and innocent life. I never will make any demands on you, Jane. I will not force you to become my mistress. Why do you shake your head? Jane, you must be reasonable, or I will become frantic."

"Sir, your wife is alive! That is a fact that you have admitted. If I lived with you as you ask, I would be your mistress. To say otherwise is splitting hairs."

"What a fool I am!" Mr. Rochester suddenly cried. "I keep telling you that I am not married and do not explain why. I forget that you know nothing about that woman or of the circumstances surrounding my hellish marriage with her. Oh, I am certain you will agree with me, Jane, when you know all that I know! Can you listen to me, my dear?"

"Yes, sir, for hours if you want."

"I ask only minutes. Jane, did you ever hear that I once had an older brother?"

"I remember Mrs. Fairfax told me that."

"And did you know that my father was a greedy, miserly man?"

"I have heard something of the sort."

"Well, Jane, my father was determined to keep his property together. He could not bear the idea of dividing his estate and leaving me a fair portion. All of it, he decided, must go to my brother, Rowland. Yet he couldn't stand the thought that a son of his would be a poor man. Therefore, I had to make a wealthy marriage. He had an old acquaintance, Mr. Mason, a planter and merchant in the West Indies. He knew that Mason had a son and daughter, and he learned that Mason would give his daughter a fortune of thirty thousand pounds when she married. That was enough for my father.

"So when I finished college, I was sent to Jamaica to marry a bride already chosen for me. My father said nothing about her money. He did tell me that Miss Mason was the toast of Spanish Town for her beauty, and this was no lie. She was a tall, dark, majestic beauty, rather similar to Blanche Ingram. Her family wanted me as a son-in-law because I was of good family. They showed her to me at parties and balls, splendidly dressed. I seldom saw her alone and had very little private conversation with her. She flattered me and lavishly displayed her charms and talents for my pleasure. All the men around her seemed to admire her and envy me. I was dazzled and stimulated. Being ignorant, raw, and inexperienced, I thought that I loved her. We were married almost before I knew where I was. Oh, I have no respect for myself when I think of that act! I never loved her. I never respected her. I did not even know her!

"I never had seen my bride's mother. They had told me that she was dead. After the honeymoon, I learned the truth: she was mad and shut up in a lunatic asylum. There was a younger brother, too: a complete idiot, incapable of speaking. The older one, whom you have seen, probably will be in the same condition someday. My father and my brother knew all of this, but they thought only of the thirty thousand pounds and joined in the plot against me.

"These were terrible discoveries, but I did not blame my wife for them. I did not even blame her when I realized that her mind was low and common, her tastes obnoxious. I realized that we never would have a quiet or happy household because no servant would bear her violent temper or put up with her absurd, contradictory orders. Even then I restrained myself. I hid the deep dislike that was developing within me.

"Jane, I will not trouble you with the horrible details. I lived with that woman for four years, and her evil qualities developed thick and fast. They were so strong that only cruelty could control them, and I would not use cruelty. What a tiny mind she had, and what gigantic, vile desires! She was as immoral as she was stupid. Through her behavior she dragged me through the agonies of hell. At the end of the four years, both my father and my brother were dead. Although I was rich, I was as poor as any man can be because I was tied to the most vicious, impure, disgusting woman imaginable. I could not legally divorce her because the doctors had now discovered that she was mad. Jane, you don't like my story; you look almost sick. Should I tell you the rest some other day?"

"No, sir; finish it now," I said. "I do earnestly pity you. Tell me, what did you do when you found that she was mad?"

"One hot summer night I decided to take my life. I was only twenty-six, and although she was five years older (they had lied to me about her age as well), she was strong and likely to live as long as I. I was hopeless; death seemed the only escape. But then a voice spoke to me. I believed it was the voice of hope. 'Go,' it said, 'and live in Europe again. There, no one knows what a filthy burden you are saddled with. Take the maniac to England, and confine her at Thornfield with a caretaker. Then travel wherever you like. That woman, who has so abused you, so dirtied your name, so outraged your honor, is not your wife in any real sense, nor are you her husband. See that she is cared for kindly, and you will have done all that God and humanity require of you. Place her in safety and comfort, and leave her.' I did exactly that. My father and brother had told no one about my marriage. In the very first letter that I wrote to them after the wedding—already beginning to suspect what sort of bargain I had made—I begged them to keep it a secret. Very soon the outrageous conduct of the wife whom my father had selected for me made him blush to claim her as his daughter-in-law. He became as anxious to hide her as I was.

"We traveled, then, to England. It was a fearful voyage with such a monster in the vessel! I was glad to finally get her to Thornfield, safely lodged in that third-story room. I hired Grace Poole to care for her. She and Dr. Carter (who dressed Mason's wounds the night he was stabbed) are the only two people I ever have confided in. Mrs. Fairfax probably suspected something, but she never asked questions. On the whole, Grace has done an excellent job, although, as you know, the lunatic has fooled her twice. On the first of these occasions, she tried to burn me in my bed; on the second, she paid that ghastly visit to you."

While he paused, I asked, "What, sir, did you do when you had settled her here? Where did you go?"

"What did I do, Jane? I wandered the continent of Europe. My only desire was to find a good and intelligent woman whom I could love: a contrast to the horror I left at Thornfield."

"But you could not marry, sir."

"I was convinced that I could marry and should. It was not my original intention to deceive, as I have deceived you. I meant to tell my tale plainly and make my proposal openly. I believed that some woman would be willing to understand my case and accept me, in spite of the curse with which I was burdened."

"Well, sir? Did you find anyone you liked and ask her to marry you?"

"I can tell you whether I found anyone I liked and whether I asked her to marry me, but her answer isn't known yet. For ten long years I roved. I lived in St. Petersburg, Paris, Rome, Naples, and Florence. Having plenty of money and a respected name, I could go anywhere. No doors were closed to me. I sought my ideal woman among English ladies, French countesses, Italian signoras, and German noblewomen. I could not find her. Sometimes, for a fleeting moment, I would think that I had caught a glimpse of her, but I always was mistaken. I could not live alone, so I tried the companionship of mistresses. The first I chose was Celine Varens. You already know what she was and how my affair with her ended. There were two more: an Italian, Giacinta, and a German, Clara. Both were considered very beautiful. But what was their beauty to me after I came to know them? Giacinta was dishonest and violent; I grew tired of her in three months. Clara was honest and quiet but unimaginative and dull. I was glad to give her money to set her up in a business and decently get rid of her. Jane, I see from your face that you disapprove of me. You think me an unfeeling, loose-living man, don't you?"

"I don't like you as well as I sometimes have, sir. Didn't it seem wrong to you to live in that way, first with one mistress and then another? You talk of it as if it were ordinary."

"It was ordinary with me, and I did not like it. It was a bad way of life, and I never would do it again. I now hate the memory of the time that I passed with Celine, Giacinta, and Clara. Jane, you are looking grave. You still disapprove of me, I see. But let me come to the point.

"Last January, business called me back to England. On a frosty winter afternoon, I rode within sight of Thornfield Hall. That hated place! I expected no peace or pleasure there. On a gate in Hay Lane I saw a quiet little figure sitting by itself. I passed it as carelessly as I did the willow tree opposite it. I had no premonition of what it would be to me, even when my horse slipped and it came up and gravely offered me help. It was a childish little creature! It seemed as if a sparrow had hopped onto my foot and offered to carry me on its tiny wing. I was rude, but the thing would not leave. It stood by me and looked and spoke with a sort of authority. I needed help, and that creature gave it.

"As I returned to the house that night, I realized that something new—something fresh and alive—had stolen into my heart. Now that I knew you were a resident of my own house, I began to watch you from afar. I began to realize how unusual—and, to me, perfect—your character was. I delighted in your company; I yearned to see you every day, every hour. As we spent more time together, I believed I saw you growing to care for me. Your expression became soft and your voice more gentle. I liked to hear you say my name.

When I would give you my hand, light bloomed in your young, wistful face. It was hard for me to resist the desire to take you to my heart then and there."

"Don't talk any more of those days, sir," I interrupted, hastily wiping tears from my eyes. His words tortured me because I knew what I must do, and soon. All these memories only made my work more difficult.

"You are right, Jane," he answered. "Why should we dwell on the past when the future is so much brighter?" I shuddered to hear how he misunderstood me. "You understand now, don't you?" he continued. "After my youth and early manhood passed, first in unspeakable misery and then in dreary solitude, I finally found what I can truly love: I found you. You are my better self, my good angel. I am determined to marry you. For you to tell me that I already have a wife is to mock me. You know now that I had no wife, but a hideous demon. I was wrong to deceive you, but I feared that you would reject my love if you knew all the facts. That was cowardly of me. I should have opened my heart to you completely, at once. Then I should have asked you to accept my pledge of faithful love and to give me yours. Jane, give it to me now. Why are you silent, Jane?" he continued. "Jane, do you understand what I want of you? Just this promise: 'I will be yours.'"

"Mr. Rochester, I will *not* be yours."

Another long silence. "Jane!" he said with

agony. "Jane, do you mean to go one way in the world and to let me go another?"

"I do."

"Jane." He bent down to embrace me. "Do you mean it now?"

"I do."

"And now?" He softly kissed my forehead and cheek.

"I do," I said, pulling myself from him.

"Oh, Jane, this is bitter! This is wicked. It would not be wicked to love me."

"Obeying you would be."

"Jane, think of my horrible life when you are gone. You will be tearing all my happiness away with you. What will be left? The maniac upstairs whom you call my wife? What will I do, Jane? Where will I turn for a companion and for some hope?"

"Do as I do: trust in God and yourself. Believe in heaven. Hope that we may meet again there."

"Then, you will not give in?"

"No."

"You condemn me to live and die wretched?" he asked, his voice rising.

"I hope that you will live sinless and die peaceful."

"Then, you snatch love and innocence from me? You send me back to a life of lust, sin, and vice?"

"Mr. Rochester, I do not send you there any more than I send myself. Like me, you have the ability to do otherwise. You will forget me before I forget you." I walked to the door.

"You are going, Jane?"

"I am going, sir."

"You are leaving me?"

"Yes."

"You will not come? You will not be my comforter, my rescuer? My love, my sorrow, my pleading are nothing to you?"

How pathetic his voice was! How hard it was to repeat firmly, "I am going."

"Jane!"

"Mr. Rochester."

"Go, then. But remember, you leave me here in anguish." He turned away and threw himself face down onto the sofa. "Oh, Jane! My hope, my love, my life!" he said with anguish. Then came a deep, strong sob.

I already had reached the door, but, reader, I walked back. I knelt down by him. I turned his face toward me. I kissed his cheek and smoothed his hair with my hand. "God bless you, my dear master!" I said. "God keep you from harm and wrong. May He direct and comfort you, and reward you for your kindness to me."

"Your love would have been my best reward," he answered. "Without it my heart is broken."

I left the room.

I did not expect to sleep that night, but I slept as soon as I lay down in bed. I dreamed that a face, beautiful and loving, looked down on me. The face was my mother's. "My daughter, flee from temptation," my mother said. "Mother, I will," I answered.

When I awoke, it still was night, but July nights are short. "It is not too early to begin," I thought, and I got up. I already was dressed because I had taken off nothing but my shoes. I gathered together a few articles of clothing. As I went through my drawers, I found the pearl necklace that Mr. Rochester had insisted I accept a few days before. I left that; it was not mine. It belonged to that imaginary bride who had melted into air. I took my purse (which contained twenty shillings), tied on my bonnet, pinned my shawl, took my bundle of clothing, and stole from my room.

"Farewell, kind Mrs. Fairfax!" I whispered as I glided past her door. "Farewell, my darling Adele!" I did not dare to go in for a last embrace because Mr. Rochester might hear me. I paused in front of his door and heard noise within. There was no sleep there. He was pacing restlessly from wall to wall. Again and again he sighed while I listened. My kind master, who could not sleep, was impatiently waiting for daylight. He would look for me in the morning, but I would be gone. He would feel forsaken, his love rejected. He would suffer and perhaps grow desperate. My hand moved toward his door, but I stopped myself and moved on.

I took some bread and water from the kitchen and silently left the house. A mile beyond the field lay a road that led away from Millcote. I never had traveled it but often had wondered where it led. I now walked along that road. I would not allow myself a single backward glance. As I walked along fields and woods, the sun began to rise. I believe it was a lovely summer morning, but I took no joy in it. I thought of Mr. Rochester, now watching the sunrise and hoping that I would come to say that I had changed my mind. I longed to be his; it was not too late. But I could not turn back. God must have led me on.

I wept wildly as I walked along. My self-control quickly was leaving me. A weakness that began with my mind crept through my arms and legs, and I fell. I lay on the ground for some minutes, half fearing and half hoping that I would die. But I rose to my feet again and soon reached the road. When I got there, I sat and rested until I heard wheels and saw a coach driving along. I stopped the driver and asked where he was going. He named a place a long way off, where I was sure Mr. Rochester had no connections. I asked what he would charge to take me there. He said thirty shillings. I answered that I had only twenty, and he said that would be enough. I climbed inside the empty coach, and it rolled on its way.

Reader, I hope you never feel what I felt at that moment. May your eyes never shed such stormy tears, wrung directly from your heart. May you never beg heaven with prayers as hopeless and agonized as mine. May you never dread being the instrument of evil to someone you wholly love.

Chapter 28

Two days had passed. It was evening. The coach-man had set me down at a place called Whitcross; he could take me no farther for the sum I had paid him, and I did not have another shilling in the world. The coach was a mile away by the time I realized that I had forgotten my parcel. Now I was not only penniless but also without a single possession.

Whitcross was not a town or even a village. It was only a stone pillar set up where four roads met and painted white to be more visible in the dark. Four arms sprang from the pillar, pointing to four towns. The nearest one was ten miles away. This was a lonely place, surrounded by meadows and

ringed with mountains. I saw not a single person on the road in any direction. Yet a traveler might pass by, and I didn't want anyone to see me. They might ask questions, and any answer I gave would only make them wonder at me and suspect me. I had no tie to anyone in the world.

Mother Nature was my only friend, so I sought comfort in her. I made my way into a meadow, where I found the grass deep and the earth warm, at least at this hour. The summer sky was clear, and a single star twinkled just above me. Nature seemed kind and good. I had one morsel of bread left, the last part of a roll that I had bought in a town we had passed through at noon. I had paid for it with a stray penny, my last coin. I saw ripe berries gleaming here and there in the meadow, and I gathered a handful and ate them with the bread. This meal didn't satisfy my hunger but slightly dulled its pangs. I said my evening prayers, covered myself with my shawl, and lay down. Gazing up at the stars and planets above me, I took comfort in the thought that the same points of light shone over Mr. Rochester, that he was God's, and that God would care for him. In my sleep I forgot my sorrow for a little while.

But the next day, I felt hunger such as I never had known. It was a still, hot, perfect day. I saw a lizard run over a rock; I saw a bee busy among the sweet berries. At that moment I gladly would have become a lizard or bee, so that I might have found food and permanent shelter here. But I was a human being, with a human being's wants, and I could not stay where there was nothing to satisfy those wants. I set out and returned to Whitcross. There I chose the road that led away from the burning sun.

I walked a long time. When I thought that I could walk no farther, I heard a church bell. Turning toward the sound, I saw a heavy wagon struggling up a hill. Not far beyond were two cows and their drover. These things told me that human life and the possibility of employment were near. I struggled on.

About two o'clock I entered the village. At the bottom of its one street was a little shop with some loaves of bread in the window. I wanted that bread. It could give me a little energy. I did not know how I could go on without it. Didn't I have anything that I could trade for a small loaf? I wore a small silk handkerchief tied around my throat; I had my gloves. I did not know whether the clerk would accept either of these articles, but I had to try. I entered the shop and saw a woman standing behind the counter. She greeted me politely. I imagined how she saw me: a respectable-looking person, a lady. "May I help you, ma'am?" she asked.

Shame gripped me. I could not offer her my worn gloves or creased handkerchief. Stammering, I asked if I could sit down for a moment because I was tired. She frowned but gave me permission to take a seat. Sitting there, I wanted only to cry, but

I forced myself to stay calm. Perhaps I could get some information from her, if no bread. "Are there any dressmakers in the village?" I asked her.

"Yes. Two or three," she answered. "More than there is work for."

"Do you know of anyone in the neighborhood who needs a servant?"

"No, I don't."

"Who are the employers in this area? Where do most people work?"

"Some are farm laborers. Many work at Mr. Oliver's needle factory."

"Does Mr. Oliver employ women?"

"No, it is men's work."

"What do the women do?"

"I don't know," she answered. "Some do one thing and some another. Poor folk must get on as well as they can." She seemed tired of my questions. When a customer came in, I left.

I wandered through the village for an hour or more, looking for some sign of possible employment, but I saw none. I noticed a pretty little house standing at the top of the lane, with a garden before it, neat and brilliantly blooming. I stopped at it and knocked at the door. A cleanly dressed young woman opened the door. I stammered out my request: "Might you be looking for a servant?"

"No," she said. "We do not keep a servant."

"Can you tell me where I could get a job of any kind?" I continued. "I am a stranger, and I know no one in this place. I need some work; it doesn't matter what kind."

But it was not her business to find a place for me. Besides, I must have seemed very odd and suspicious. She shook her head. "I'm sorry; I can't help you," she said, and closed the door. I believe if she had held it open a moment longer, I would have begged her for some food; I had fallen that low.

I could not bear to return to the village, where no prospect of aid was visible. I wanted to head into a nearby forest that I saw and rest there, but hunger kept me on the move. I drew near houses, left them, came back again, and wandered away, always shamed by the thought that I had no right to anyone's help. The afternoon wore on while I wandered about like a lost and starving dog.

Crossing a field, I saw a church steeple and hurried toward it. Near the church stood a small, sturdy house, which I assumed was the parsonage. I remembered that strangers sometimes went to a clergyman for aid when they were alone, in need of help, and seeking employment. It is a pastor's job to help those who try to help themselves. With a renewed sense of courage, I knocked on the kitchen door. An old woman answered.

"Is this the parsonage?"

"Yes."

"Is the clergyman in?"

"No."

"Will he be in soon?"

"No, he is away from home. His father has

died suddenly, and he has gone to Marsh End, where he will stay for at least two weeks."

"I see. Is there a lady of the house?"

"No, there is only me. I am the housekeeper," she said. I could not bear to beg her for aid, so again I wandered away.

Once more I took off my handkerchief. Once more I thought of the loaves of bread in the little shop. Desperate with hunger, I found the shop again, and I went in. Although there were others in the shop, I asked the shopkeeper directly, "Will you give me a loaf of bread for this handkerchief?"

She looked at me with surprise and suspicion. "No," she said. "I don't do business like that."

"Half a loaf, then?" I asked.

"I said no. How do I know where you got that handkerchief?"

"Will you take my gloves?"

"No! What would I do with them?"

Reader, it is not pleasant to dwell on these details. Some say it is rewarding to look back on painful experiences, but to this day I hardly can bear to remember the humiliation that I felt at that moment. I hurriedly left the shop and could only imagine the conversation that followed my departure.

A little before dark I passed a farmhouse. The door was open, and I saw the farmer sitting there, eating his supper of bread and cheese. I stopped and said, "Will you give me a piece of bread? I am very hungry." He glanced at me with surprise, but

without answering, he cut a thick slice from his loaf
and gave it to me. Probably he did not think that I
was a beggar but an odd lady who had liked the
look of his brown bread. As soon as I was out of
sight of his house, I sat down and ate the bread.

I made my bed in the forest, but my night was
wretched. The ground was damp, the air cold; people passed near me more than once, and I had to
move to avoid them. Toward morning it rained,
and it rained the whole next day. As before, I
looked for work; as before, I was refused. I did eat
once. At the door of a cottage I saw a little girl
about to throw a mess of cold porridge into a pig
trough.

"Will you give me that?" I asked.

She stared at me. "Mother!" she exclaimed,
"There is a woman here who wants the porridge."

"Well, girl, give it to the beggar," a voice within replied. "The pig doesn't want it."

I ate it ravenously. It was twilight by then, and
I had strayed far from the village. Where would I
sleep? My strength was failing fast. I believed that I
might be dead by morning. I preferred to die
alone, where the ravens would pick my bones,
rather than to be found in the street by curious
passersby. I turned to the hill, hoping to find a
place where the grass was high and thick and could
offer me a hiding place.

Then a dim light sprang up before my eyes. I
thought that I was imagining things, but it burned
quite steadily. I struggled toward it, falling twice

before reaching some sort of road or track. It led straight up to the light, which shone from the window of a long, low house. Stumbling about in search of the door, I was able to look through a window into a tidy room lit by a fire. A candle stood on a table; beside it sat an elderly woman knitting a stocking. By the fireplace was a sight that interested me more: two young, graceful women sat there. Both showed by their black clothing that they were in mourning. A large, old pointer dog rested its massive head on one girl's knee; a black cat rested in the other's lap. The girls were bent over books, which they seemed to be studying together. As I watched, one of them spoke to the old woman, who seemed to be a servant. She rose and went into the neighboring room and soon reappeared with the preparations for supper. Taking my courage in both hands, I knocked at the door.

The old woman answered. "What do you want?" she inquired in a voice of surprise.

"May I speak to your mistresses?" I asked.

"You'd better tell me your business. Where do you come from?"

"I am a stranger."

"What do you want here at this hour?"

"I want a night's shelter in a garden shed or anywhere else, and a morsel of bread to eat."

Distrust, the very feeling I had dreaded, appeared in her face. "I'll give you a piece of bread," she said after a pause, "but we can't take in a stranger for the night."

"Please let me speak to your mistresses."

"No. What can they do for you? You should not be roving now; it looks very bad."

"But where will I go if you drive me away? What will I do?"

"Oh, I think you know where to go and what to do. Take care that you don't do wrong, that's all. Here is a penny. Now go."

"A penny cannot feed me, and I have no strength to go farther. Don't shut the door. Oh don't, for God's sake!"

"I must. The rain is blowing in."

"Tell the young ladies. Let me see them."

"Indeed, I will not. You're up to no good, or you wouldn't make such a fuss. Move on."

"I will die if I am turned away."

"Not you. You may have some evil plans, coming to the house of decent folks at this time of night. If you have some companions out there with you—robbers, most likely—tell them that we are not alone in the house. We have a gentleman and dogs and guns." The honest but inflexible servant slammed and locked the door.

I sank down onto the wet doorstep, weeping in anguish. "I can only die now," I said, "but I will die believing in God. His will be done."

"Everyone must die," said a voice close to me, "but surely you don't have to die quite yet."

"Who is that?" I asked, terrified at the unexpected sound. Someone was standing near me, knocking loudly at the door.

"Is it you, Mr. Rivers?" the old woman cried.

"Yes, yes. Open quickly."

"How wet and cold you must be on such a wild night! Come in. Your sisters are quite worried about you, and I believe there are bad folks about. A beggar woman has been here. I declare, she is still here! Get up! For shame! Move off, I say!"

"Hush, Hannah! You have done your duty; now let me do mine. Young woman, come into the house."

With difficulty I obeyed him. Presently I stood within that clean, bright kitchen, sick and trembling. The two ladies, Mr. Rivers, and Hannah all stared at me. "St. John, who is it?" I heard one of the ladies ask.

"I don't know. I found her at the door," St. John replied.

"She is as white as death," Hannah said.

"Quickly! She is fainting. Let her sit down," someone said. I sank into a chair, unable to speak.

"Hannah, fetch some water. How thin she is!"

"Is she sick or only hungry?"

"Hungry, I think. Hannah, is that milk? Give it to me, and a piece of bread." Diana (as I later learned was her name) broke some bread, dipped it into milk, and held it to my lips. "Try to eat," she said kindly.

"Yes, try," her sister, Mary, repeated, gently removing my soaked bonnet.

I tasted what they offered me, feebly at first, then eagerly.

"Not too much at first," St. John, their brother, said. "See if she can speak now. Ask her name."

I felt that I could speak, and I answered, "My name is Jane Elliott." Anxious to avoid discovery, I had decided to use a false name.

"Where do you live? Where are your friends?" St. John asked. I was silent. "Can we send for anyone you know?" I shook my head. "What is your story?"

Somehow, now that I had crossed this house's threshold, I no longer felt like an outcast. I dared to begin acting more like myself. "Sir, I can give you no details tonight."

"But what, then, do you expect me to do for you?" he asked.

"Nothing," I replied. I had enough strength for only short answers.

Diana spoke next. "Do you mean," she asked, "that we now have given you enough help? That we should send you back outdoors into the rainy night?"

I looked at her. Her face was filled with goodness. I suddenly felt more courageous, and I managed a smile. "If I were a stray dog, I know that you would not send me out into the night," I said. "Do with me what you think is best, but excuse me from talking tonight. I do not have the strength." All three looked at me in silence.

"Hannah," St. John finally said, "let her sit there awhile. Ask her no questions. In ten minutes, give her the rest of that milk and bread. Mary and

Diana, let's go into the parlor and talk the matter over."

They left. Very soon one of the ladies returned; I could not tell which one. A pleasant stupor was stealing over me as I sat by the fire. She quietly gave some instructions to Hannah, and the servant helped me up a staircase and aided me in removing my dripping clothes. Soon I was wrapped in a warm, dry bed. I thanked God and slept.

Chapter 29

My memory of the next three days and nights is very dim. I can remember some sensations but few thoughts and no actions. I lay in that bed as motionless as a stone; to have forced me from it would have killed me. I did not notice time's passage. I knew when anyone entered or left the room; I could tell who they were, and I understood what they were saying, but I could not answer. To open my lips or move my limbs was impossible.

Diana and Mary appeared in the room several times each day. I could hear them whispering at my bedside. "It is good that we took her in."

"Yes. If she had been left outside all night, she certainly would have been dead at the door in the morning. I wonder what she has gone through."

"Strange hardships, I imagine. The poor wanderer."

"From her way of speaking, I think that she is an educated person. And the clothes she was wearing were of good quality, even though they were wet and dirty."

St. John came in only once. He looked at me and said that I was suffering from only exhaustion, not any real illness, and that there was no need for a doctor. Nature, he was sure, would heal me.

He was correct. On the third day, I was better. On the fourth, I could speak, move, and sit up in bed. Hannah had brought me some porridge and toast. I ate hungrily and felt stronger than I had for many days. On a chair by the bedside were all my own clothes, clean and dry. I found what I needed to wash myself and a brush to smooth my hair. Stopping every five minutes to rest, I finally managed to dress myself. My clothes hung loose on me because I was very thin, but I felt clean and respectable-looking again. Hanging onto the banister, I descended a stone staircase and found my way to the kitchen.

It was full of the fragrance of new bread and the warmth of a generous fire. Hannah was baking. When she saw me come in tidy and well-dressed, she smiled. "What, you have got up?" she said. "You are better, then. You may sit down in my chair, if you will."

"I'll gladly sit, but I'd like to be useful too," I said. "What are you going to do with those gooseberries? Make pies? Let me sort out the bad ones for you."

Hannah evidently was fond of talking. While I picked over the fruit and she made the pie crusts, she gave me an account of her deceased master and mistress and "the children," as she called the young people. Old Mr. Rivers, she said, was a gentleman from an old and respected family. The house, Marsh End, always had belonged to the Rivers family, and it was about two hundred years old. The old man had been very fond of farming and hunting. But the mistress had been different; she had been a great reader and had studied constantly. The three children took after her. It was well that they did because their father had lost most of his money years before, and they all had to earn their own livings. St. John had gone to college to become a pastor, and the girls worked as governesses. The children, therefore, were at Marsh End very little. They had come now for only a few weeks, on account of their father's death. It was a pity, Hannah said; they all loved Marsh End and the nearby town of Morton. "They've been to London and all those grand places," she added, "but they always say there's no place like home. They get along so well, too; they never quarrel. I never saw a family that got along better."

Having finished my task of gooseberry picking, I asked where the two ladies and their brother were now.

"They've walked over to Morton, but they will be back in half an hour for their tea."

They returned as Hannah had predicted. St. John merely nodded at me as he passed through the room, but the girls expressed their pleasure in seeing me up and dressed. Diana took my hand. "You should have waited for me to help you on the stairs," she said. "You still look very pale, and so thin! Poor child!" Diana's voice was like a dove's cooing. That and her friendly, gentle face made me instantly like and trust her. Mary's face was equally intelligent and pretty, but she was more reserved and distant.

"But what are you doing here?" Diana continued. "You are a visitor, and you must go into the parlor. Come, you must be obedient." She took my hand and led me into the other room. "Sit and rest while we take off our things and prepare some tea." She closed the door, leaving me alone with St. John, who sat opposite, a newspaper in his hands. I was able to examine him carefully as he read. He was young (perhaps twenty-eight or thirty), tall, and slender. His face was beautiful. With its straight classic nose and molded mouth and chin, it resembled a Greek statue. His eyes were large and blue. Careless locks of fair hair tumbled over his high forehead. He did not speak to me, or even glance in my direction, until his sisters returned.

Diana brought me a little cake, still warm from the oven. "Eat that now," she said. "You must be hungry. Hannah says that you have had nothing but some porridge since breakfast." I accepted it because my appetite was keen.

St. John now closed his book and sat down at the table with me, looking directly at me with his clear blue eyes. "You are very hungry," he said.

"I am, sir."

"It is good for you that your low fever has kept you from eating much over the last three days," he said. "Otherwise, you might have made yourself ill by eating too much too soon. Now you may eat, although you still should be careful."

"I trust that I will not eat long at your expense,

sir," I answered clumsily.

"No," he said coolly. "When you tell us where your friends are, we can write to them, and you may return home."

"I must plainly tell you that I cannot do that. I have no home or friends."

The three looked at me with curiosity but not suspicion. "Do you mean to say," St. John asked, "that you have absolutely no family or friends?"

"No tie links me to any living being."

"That is a very strange position for someone your age!" I saw him glance at my hands, which rested on the table before me. I wondered what he was looking for, but his words soon explained. "You have never been married?"

Diana laughed. "Why, she can't be more than seventeen or eighteen, St. John," she said.

"I am nearly nineteen, but I am not married. No." I felt myself blush because his question awakened bitter memories.

They all saw my embarrassment, and Diana and Mary relieved me by looking away. But their brother continued to look at me until tears rose to my eyes. "Where did you last live?" he asked.

"You are too inquisitive, St. John," Mary murmured, but he continued to wait for an answer.

"The place where I lived, and the people with whom I lived, are my secret," I replied.

"Which you have, in my opinion, a right to keep, from both St. John and everyone else," Diana remarked.

"If I know nothing about you or your history, I cannot help you," he said. "And you need help, do you not?"

"I hope you will help me get work, sir. Beyond that I ask nothing."

"I will do my best to help you in such an honest cause," he said. "First, tell me what you are accustomed to doing and what other things you can do."

"Mr. Rivers," I said, looking at him as openly as he had looked at me, "you and your sisters have done me a great service. You have rescued me from death. You have my unlimited gratitude. I will tell you as much of my story as I can tell without endangering my peace of mind or that of others. I am an orphan, a clergyman's daughter. My parents died before I could know them. I was educated in a charitable institution, Lowood Orphan Asylum, where I spent six years as a pupil and two as a teacher. I suppose you know the school, Mr. Rivers? The Reverend Robert Brocklehurst is the treasurer."

"I have heard of Mr. Brocklehurst, and I have seen the school."

"I left Lowood nearly a year ago to become a private governess. I obtained a good situation and was happy. Four days before I arrived here, I had to leave that situation. I cannot explain why; it would be dangerous to do so, and it would sound incredible. There is no blame on me; I am as free from wrongdoing as any of you three. I am miserable, and I will be miserable for some time because the catastrophe that drove me from the house where I was happy was strange and awful. I left with the greatest speed and secrecy, and I brought with me only a small parcel, which in my troubled state of mind I left on the coach that brought me to Whitcross. I then came to this neighborhood, penniless. I slept outdoors two nights and wandered about two days. When hunger and exhaustion drove me to your door, you took me in."

"Don't make her talk anymore now, St. John," Diana said as I paused. "This still is too much for her. Come to the sofa and sit down now, Miss Elliott."

I gave an involuntary start at hearing that name. St. John noticed it at once. "You said that your name is Jane Elliott?" he asked.

"I did say so, and it is the name that I think it is best for you to call me, but it is not my real name, and it sounds strange to me."

"You will not tell us your real name?"

"No. Above all, I fear being followed here, so I must avoid my real name being known."

"You are quite right, I am sure," Diana said. "Now, brother, do let her be at peace awhile."

But St. John continued. "You say that you want to be independent of us, do you not?"

"I do, sir. Show me where to work or where to seek work. That is all I ask. Then let me go. But until then, please allow me to stay here. I dread the thought of being homeless again."

"Indeed, you will stay here," Diana said, putting her hand on my shoulder.

"You will," Mary repeated.

"My sisters, you see, want to keep you," St. John said. "I will do my best to help you find employment, but I am not sure what will turn up. It may be very modest."

"She already has said that she is willing to do any honest work that she can," Diana answered for me.

"I will be a dressmaker, servant, or nurse's helper if I can do no better," I answered.

"Very well," St. John said. "I promise to help you, in my own time and way." He then returned to his newspaper.

I soon went back to my room. I had talked and sat up as long as my strength would allow.

Chapter 30

The more I got to know Marsh End's residents, the more I liked them. In a few days I was so much better that I could sit up all day and go for brief walks. I could join Diana and Mary in all their occupations, talk with them as much as they wished, and help them as much as they would allow me. I took great pleasure in their company; our tastes and opinions were similar in many ways. We worked and studied together, drew, and painted. They offered to teach me German; I instructed them in artwork. We were so busy and entertained together that days passed like hours, and weeks like days. I had not gotten to know St. John nearly as well as his sisters. He seldom was home; he spent much of his time visiting the sick and poor among his congregation. His quiet, reserved, and solemn nature was another barrier to our becoming close friends.

A month had passed. Diana and Mary were soon to leave Marsh End and return to work as governesses in a large city in southern England. They worked for wealthy, haughty families who treated them as mere servants. St. John had said nothing yet about finding work for me. One morning, when I found myself alone with him in the parlor, I asked to speak with him.

"You have a question?" he said.

"Yes. I wish to know whether you have heard of any position I might fill."

"I found something for you three weeks ago, but because my sisters had become attached to you, I thought it was wrong to interfere until they left Marsh End."

"They will go in three days?" I asked.

"Yes. And when they go, I will return to the parsonage at Morton. Hannah will go with me, and this old house will be shut up."

I waited a few moments, expecting that he would go on with the subject of my employment. But he seemed to be thinking of something else, and I had to ask, "What is the position you had in mind, Mr. Rivers? I hope this delay will not spoil my chances."

"Oh, no. It is employment that depends on me to give and you to accept. You see, I won't stay at Morton long, now that my father is dead. I probably will leave this place in a year, but while I do stay, I will work for its improvement. When I came to Morton two years ago, it had no school, and the children of the poor had no hope of progress. I managed to establish a school for boys, and I now intend to open a second one for girls. I have rented a building for the purpose, with a two-room cottage attached. That cottage will be the teacher's house, and her salary will be thirty pounds a year. The house already has been furnished, very simply but sufficiently, by a lady named Miss Oliver, who is the daughter of the only rich man in my congregation. You have heard of Mr. Oliver, I think; he runs the needle factory and iron foundry in the valley. Will you accept the position of teacher in this school?"

"I thank you, Mr. Rivers, and I accept it with all my heart."

"But you understand the situation?" he said. "It is only a village school. Your pupils will be poor girls. All you will teach them is sewing, reading, writing, and arithmetic. What will you do with your finer accomplishments—your languages, music, and artwork?"

"Save them until they are wanted. They will keep."

He smiled with genuine pleasure. "When will you begin work?"

"I will go to the cottage tomorrow and, if you like, open the school next week."

"Very well. So be it."

Diana and Mary Rivers became sadder and quieter as the day of leaving their brother and home approached. Diana confided to me that they would be saying goodbye to their brother for years, possibly forever. "He is determined to do something great with his life, Jane," she told me. "St. John looks quiet, but he is greatly determined. In some things he is as stubborn as death. He wants to become a missionary in a foreign land. It is a noble, Christian thing to do, but it breaks my heart!" Tears came to her eyes.

"We are without a father; we soon will be without a brother and home," Mary murmured.

At that moment something occurred that increased their distress. St. John passed the window reading a letter. He entered. "Our Uncle John is dead," he said.

The sisters were startled, but they looked more surprised than sorrowful. "Dead?" Diana repeated. "And . . . ?"

"And nothing. Read it for yourself." He tossed the letter into her lap.

Diana read it, then passed it to Mary. All three looked at one another with dreary, thoughtful smiles. "At any rate, we are no worse off than before," Mary remarked. For some minutes no one spoke.

St. John left. Diana then turned to me. "Jane, you must think that we are hard-hearted not to be sadder about our uncle's death. But we never met him. He was my mother's brother. My father and he quarreled long ago. Years ago my father lost most of his money by following Uncle John's advice. They blamed each other and parted in anger. My uncle was more fortunate in business, and he eventually earned quite a fortune. He never married; he had no near relatives except us and one other person. My father always hoped that he would make up for his error by leaving his money to us, but this letter informs us that he has given every penny to the other relative. He had every right to do so, of course, but it is disappointing news. Mary and I would have considered ourselves rich with a thousand pounds each, and that sum would have enabled St. John to do much good."

After this explanation, the subject was dropped. Neither St. John nor his sisters mentioned it again. The next day, I left Marsh End for the schoolhouse cottage. The day after, Diana and Mary departed for their places of employment. And in a week, St. John and Hannah moved to the parsonage. So the old house was abandoned.

Chapter 31

My home was a cottage: a little room, with whitewashed walls, containing four chairs and a table, a clock, a cupboard, and a set of plates. Above was a room of the same size, furnished with a bed and a chest of drawers.

It was evening. I had sent home, with an orange, the little orphan girl who acted as my maid. That morning the village school had opened. I had twenty pupils. Only three of them could read; none could write or do any arithmetic. Several could knit, and a few sewed a little. They spoke with the strongest country accents imaginable; they and I had trouble understanding one another. Some of them were bad-mannered, rough, and stubborn as well as ignorant, but others were good-tempered and had a genuine desire to learn. I did not expect any great pleasure in my new employment, but I would do my best.

Meanwhile, I asked myself which was better: to have given in to temptation and now be living in luxury in France as Mr. Rochester's mistress (I would have been delirious with love but constantly torn by remorse and shame) or to be a village schoolmistress, free and honest, in a breezy mountain nook in the healthy heart of England? I felt that

I had made the right decision, even though the thought of Mr. Rochester brought hot tears to my eyes. I dried them as I saw St. John's dog, old Carlo, push the gate open with his nose. St. John followed the dog to my door. I asked him to come in.

"No, I cannot stay. I have brought you a gift that my sisters left for you. I think it contains some paints, pencils, and paper." I approached to take the welcome package. He examined my face; the traces of tears doubtless were visible. "Was your first day's work harder than you expected?" he asked.

"Oh, no! To the contrary, I think that in time I will get on very well with my pupils."

"Perhaps your cottage and its furnishings have disappointed you? They are scant enough."

"My cottage is clean and dry, my furniture sufficient and comfortable. Five weeks ago I had nothing. I was an outcast, a beggar. Now I have friends, a home, employment. I wonder at God's goodness."

"But you are lonely? The little house is dark and empty."

"I hardly have had time to be lonely."

"I hope you won't soon become discouraged, but will continue here for at least some months," St. John said. "One never knows where the road may take us; I will count on your good sense to guide you." He hesitated, then seemed to decide to confide in me. "I will tell you that a year ago I was intensely miserable because I thought I had made a mistake in entering the ministry. I was tired to death of its daily demands. I wanted the more active life of the world and thought that I must leave the ministry. But then I heard a call from heaven. I realized that I must be a missionary because a missionary surely needs all the skill, strength, and courage available to him. From that moment my state of mind changed. I knew what I must prepare to do. My father opposed the idea, but since his death I have no real obstacle to deal with. There are some affairs to settle, a new pastor for Morton to engage, and an . . . an entanglement of human feelings to deal with. But I know I will overcome that because I must. And I will leave Europe for India." He said this in a quiet but emphatic voice.

Both he and I had our backs to the path leading to the schoolhouse. We both were startled when a voice, sweet as a silver bell, exclaimed, "Good evening, Mr. Rivers. And good evening, old Carlo. Your dog is quicker to recognize his friends than you are, sir. He pricked up his ears and wagged his tail when I was at the bottom of the field, but you ignored me entirely." A vision, it seemed to me, had risen at St. John's side. It was a young woman dressed in pure white. After bending to pet Carlo, she lifted her head, and there bloomed under St. John's glance a face of perfect beauty. "Perfect beauty" is a strong expression, but she deserved the words. It was as lovely a face as I ever have seen before or since. I stared at this fair creature with amazement, and I wondered what St. John thought of this earthly angel. I looked at him for an answer but found him staring at a tuft of daisies growing in the grass.

"A lovely evening, but it is late for you to be out alone," he said, crushing the flowers' snowy heads with his foot.

"Oh, I came home from town only this afternoon. Papa told me that you had opened your school and that the new teacher was here, so I ran up to see her. This is she?" she asked, pointing to me.

"It is," St. John said.

"Do you think you will like Morton?" she asked me with a pleasant, if childlike, manner.

"I hope I will. I have many reasons to."

"Did you find your pupils as attentive as you had expected?"

"Quite."

"Do you like your house?"

"Very much."

"Have I furnished it nicely?"

"Very nicely, indeed." So this was Miss Oliver, the heiress. What a lucky girl, I thought, to be both so rich and so beautiful! The planets must have been in some happy alignment when she was born.

"I will come up and help sometimes," she added. "It will be a change for me to visit you now and then, and I like change. Mr. Rivers, I have had such fun during my stay in town! Last night, or rather this morning, I was dancing until two o'clock. There was an army regiment stationed there, and the officers were the most delightful men! They put our young knife-grinders and scissor merchants to shame."

It seemed to me that St. John's lower lip protruded, and his upper lip curled a moment as the laughing girl gave him this information. He lifted his gaze from the daisies and turned it on her. It was an unsmiling, searching, meaningful gaze.

Miss Oliver answered it with a second laugh, and laughter went well with her youth, dimples, and bright eyes. As St. John stood quiet and serious, she again began petting Carlo. "Poor Carlo loves me," she said. "He is not stern and distant to his friends; if he could speak, he would not be silent." As she patted the dog's head, I saw a glow rise to St. John's face. His solemn eyes melted with sudden fire and flickered with emotion. Flushed like this, he looked nearly as beautiful for a man as she did for a woman. His chest heaved once, as if his large heart, weary of being so tightly held, had expanded. But he controlled it, I think, as a rider would control a rearing horse. He did not respond to her gentle teasing. "Papa says that you never come to see us anymore," Miss Oliver continued, looking up. "He is alone this evening and not very well. Why don't you come home with me and visit him?"

"It surely is too late to intrude on Mr. Oliver," St. John answered.

"Too late? Not at all. It is just the hour when Papa most wants company, when the factories are closed and he has no business to occupy him. Do come, Mr. Rivers."

"Not tonight, Miss Rosamond. Not tonight." St. John spoke almost like a machine. Only he knew what effort his refusal cost him.

"Well, if you are so obstinate, I will leave you because it is getting chilly. Good evening!" She held out her hand. He barely touched it.

"Good evening!" he replied in a voice as low and hollow as an echo.

She started to go but turned back in a moment. "Are you feeling well, Mr. Rivers?" she asked. She might well ask because his face was as white as her gown.

"Quite well," he said and, with a bow, he left the gate.

She went one way, he another. She turned twice to glance after him as she walked across the field. As he strode firmly along, he did not turn at all. This sight of another's suffering and sacrifice tore me from thinking of my own. Diana Rivers had called her brother "as stubborn as death." She had not exaggerated.

Chapter 32

I worked in the village school as hard and faithfully as I could. It was a while before I began to understand the pupils. Because they never had been taught, at first they all seemed hopelessly dull, but I soon found that I was mistaken. There was as much difference among them as among better-educated people, and I found that many of them actually were sharp-witted. Their natural politeness, innate self-respect, and excellent abilities soon won my admiration; in return, the girls liked me. I passed many pleasant evenings in their homes, where their parents loaded me with attention. Whenever I went out, I received pleasant greetings on all sides and was welcomed with friendly smiles.

Rosamond Oliver kept her word about coming to visit me. Generally she stopped at the school during her morning ride. She would canter up to the door on her pony, followed by a mounted servant. I hardly could imagine anything more exquisite than Rosamond in her purple riding dress, with her black velvet cap atop her long chestnut curls. She usually came at the hour when St. John was giving his daily Bible lesson. I saw how sharply these visits pierced the young pastor's heart. A sort of instinct seemed to warn him of her entrance, even when he did not see it. His cheeks would glow with warm color.

Miss Oliver not only came to the school; she also frequently visited my cottage. I came to know her well. She was flirtatious but not heartless, demanding but not selfish. She had been indulged since her birth but was too good-natured to be badly spoiled. She was vain (she could not help it, when every glance at the mirror showed how lovely she was) but not proud; generous; intelligent enough; gay; lively; and thoughtless. In short, she was charming. I liked her in much the same way that I had liked my pupil Adele.

One evening, while she was rummaging through the cupboard of my little kitchen, she discovered my drawing materials and some sketches, including a sketch of one of my pupils, a pretty little cherub-like girl. She was electrified with delight. "Did you do these pictures? What a miracle you are! You draw better than my old drawing master at school. Will you sketch a portrait of me, to show Papa?"

"With pleasure," I replied, thrilled at the idea of having such a perfect model. She was wearing a dark-blue silk dress; her arms and neck were bare; her only ornament was the chestnut curls that tumbled over her shoulders. I took a sheet of fine paper and drew a careful outline. Because it was getting late, I told her that she must come and sit some other day.

She gave her father such a favorable report of

me that Mr. Oliver himself accompanied her the next evening. He was a silent, proud man but very kind to me. The sketch of Rosamond greatly pleased him; he said that I must make a finished picture of it. He invited me to spend the next evening at his home, Vale Hall.

I went. I found Vale Hall a large, handsome residence, filled with evidence of wealth. Mr. Oliver was full of praise for my work at the school and said he only feared that I soon would leave for a better position. "Indeed!" Rosamond cried. "She is clever enough to be a governess in a high family, Papa." I thought that I would far rather be where I was than with any high family in the land. Mr. Oliver spoke of the Rivers family with great respect. He said that Rivers was a very old name in the neighborhood, that the family's ancestors had been wealthy, and that all of Morton once had belonged to them. He said it was a pity that as fine and talented a young man as St. John should become a missionary. It was clear to me that Rosamond's father would approve of her marriage with St. John. Mr. Oliver clearly believed that the young clergyman's good family and sacred profession made up for his lack of fortune.

It was November fifth, a holiday. My little servant had left after helping me to clean my house. I took out my paint and pencils and began completing my portrait of Rosamond. I was absorbed in my work when there was a tap on my door, and in came St. John. "I came to see how you are spending your holiday," he said. "Not lonely, I hope? No, I see that you are happy with your drawing. I have brought you a new book to keep you company." As I eagerly glanced through the book, St. John stooped to examine my drawing. His tall figure sprang erect again with a start, but he said nothing. I looked up at him. He looked away.

"Is the portrait a good likeness?" I asked.

"Likeness? Likeness of whom? I did not look at it closely," he said.

"You did, Mr. Rivers."

He looked startled by my directness. He glanced again and said, "It is a well-done picture: very soft, clear coloring; very graceful."

"Yes, yes; I know all that. But what of the resemblance? Who is it like?"

With some hesitation, he answered, "Miss Oliver, I presume."

"Of course. Now, sir, to reward you for the accurate guess, I will promise to paint you a careful copy of this very picture if you would like that. I don't wish to throw away my time on a gift you don't want. Would you like to have it?"

"I certainly would like to have it," he replied. "Whether that would be wise is another question."

"As far as I can see," I answered, "it would be wisest for you to take the original at once." He sank into a chair, clearly astonished by my boldness but not objecting. "She likes you; I am sure," I went on. "And her father respects you. Moreover, she is a sweet girl. You should marry her."

"Does she like me?" he asked.

"Certainly. Better than she likes anyone else. She talks of you constantly. There is no subject she enjoys as much."

"It is very pleasant to hear this," he said. "Go on."

"What is the use of going on when you probably are preparing some contradiction or forging a fresh chain to wind around your heart?" I asked.

"Don't imagine such hard things. Right this minute I see myself stretched on a sofa at Vale Hall at my bride Rosamond's side. She is talking to me with her sweet voice, gazing down on me with those eyes you copied so well, smiling at me with those ruby lips. She is mine; I am hers. This present life and passing world are enough for me. Hush! Say nothing. My heart is full of delight; my senses are entranced. Let the time pass in peace."

I did as he asked. He breathed fast and low while I stood silent. After a few minutes he rose to his feet. "Now," he said, "I have given those moments to my imagination. But while I love Rosamond Oliver wildly, I know in my heart that she would not make me a good wife. I would discover this within a year after marriage, and twelve months of happiness would give way to a lifetime of regret. I know this."

"That is strange indeed!" I could not help saying.

"Can you imagine Rosamond as a missionary's wife?" he asked me. "Rosamond as a sufferer, a laborer? No."

"But you don't have to be a missionary. You could give up that idea."

"Give it up? My great work? My foundation laid on earth a mansion in heaven? I cannot give it up. It is dearer than the blood in my veins. It is what I live for."

"And Miss Oliver?" I asked. "Don't you care about her disappointment and sorrow?"

"Miss Oliver is constantly surrounded by sweethearts and admirers. In less than a month my face will vanish from her heart. She will forget me and will marry someone who will make her far happier than I would."

"You speak coolly enough, but you blush whenever Miss Oliver enters the schoolroom."

"That is mere weakness," he said. "I can rise above it, and I will." Bending over my portrait once again, he murmured, "She is lovely, isn't she?"

"May I paint one like it for you?"

"Thank you, no." He covered the portrait with a piece of scrap paper. (While painting, I would rest my hand on this piece of paper, to avoid smudging the picture.) It was impossible for me to tell what he suddenly saw on this piece of paper, but something had caught his eye. He snatched up the scrap paper, then looked hard at me.

"What is the matter?" I asked.

"Nothing," he replied. However, before he put the scrap paper back, he tore a narrow slip from its edge. "Good day," he said hastily, and he vanished out the door.

"What in the world was that about?" I wondered. I examined the paper but saw nothing on it except meaningless doodles and paint stains. I thought about the mystery a minute or two; but, finding it insolvable, I soon forgot it.

Chapter 33

When St. John left, it was snowing, and it continued to snow throughout the night. The next day, a keen wind brought fresh, blinding snowfall. By twilight the drifts made my neighborhood almost impassable. I had laid a mat against my door to prevent the snow from blowing in under the door. After sitting near the fire almost an hour, listening to the blizzard's muffled fury, I lit a candle and took down my new book of poetry. I soon forgot the storm as I read.

Then I heard a noise. I thought it was the wind shaking the door. But no. St. John was coming in from the howling darkness. His cloak was as white as a glacier. I was so surprised to see him that I instantly was worried. "What is wrong?" I demanded. "Has anything happened?"

"No. How easily alarmed you are!" he answered, removing his cloak and hanging it up against the door. He stamped the snow from his boots. "I am ruining your floor, but you must excuse me. It has been hard work to get here!" he said as he warmed his hands over the fire. "I fell into one drift that was as high as my waist. Fortunately, the snow still is quite soft."

"Why are you here?" I could not help saying.

"What an inhospitable question! But since you ask, I am here to have a little talk with you. I got tired of my books and solitude. Besides, since yesterday I have felt the suspense of a person who has heard half of a story and wants to hear the rest." He sat down.

I remembered his odd behavior of yesterday, and I began to wonder if his mind was affected. However, if he were insane, his insanity was of a very cool and collected kind. There was no mad excitement on his face. In fact, he looked rather thin and sorrowful, and I felt an unexpected gush of pity. I said, "I wish Diana or Mary would come and live with you. It is bad that you live alone. I don't think you take good care of your health."

"Not at all," he said. "I care for myself when necessary. I am perfectly well." Then he sat in silence, still looking at the glowing fire. Feeling that someone should say something, I asked if he felt a draft from the door behind him. "No, no!" he responded, sounding somewhat irritated.

"Well," I replied, "if you won't talk, I'll return to my book." So I resumed my reading.

He soon moved, but only to take his wallet out of his pocket. He pulled a letter from the wallet, read it silently, folded it up, and put it away again.

It was impossible to read while he sat there, so I again attempted conversation. "Have you heard from Diana and Mary lately?"

"Not since the letter that I showed you a week ago."

"Has there been any change with regard to your own plans? Will you be leaving England any sooner than you expected?"

"I'm afraid not."

Trying a different tactic, I turned to the subject of the school. "Mary Garrett's mother is better, and Mary came back to school this morning. I am getting four new girls next week. They would have come today if it hadn't been for the snow."

"Indeed!"

"Mr. Oliver is paying for two of them. He is going to give the whole school a party at Christmas."

"I know."

"Was it your suggestion?"

"No."

"Whose, then?"

"His daughter's, I think."

"That is like her. She is so good-natured."

"Yes."

Another long pause followed. The clock struck eight. The sound seemed to awaken him, and he straightened in his chair. "Put down your book a moment, and come a little nearer to the fire," he said. Wondering, I did as he asked. "A few minutes ago," he said, "I mentioned my impatience to hear the end of a story. I think it will be best if I begin the story and perhaps ask your assistance in finishing it.

"Twenty years ago, a poor pastor—never mind his name—fell in love with a rich man's daughter. She fell in love with him and married him against the advice of her family, who consequently disowned her. Before two years passed, the lovers both were dead. They left a daughter, who was raised by an aunt-in-law: Mrs. Reed of Gateshead. You jumped, Jane. Did you hear a noise? It probably was just a mouse behind the wall. To go on, Mrs. Reed kept the orphan for ten years. Whether that was a happy time or not I cannot say, but at the end of that time the child was sent to Lowood School, where you yourself lived for so long. It seems that her career there was very honorable. She was a pupil, then a teacher. Finally she left to be a governess in the house of a certain Mr. Rochester."

"Mr. Rivers!" I interrupted.

"Just listen for a moment," he insisted. "I have nearly finished. I know nothing about this Mr. Rochester's character, but I do know one fact: he pretended to offer this young girl honorable marriage, and at the very altar she discovered that he had a living wife who was a lunatic. I do not know what happened next, but when something happened that required contacting the governess, she was gone. No one could tell when, where, or how. She had left Thornfield Hall during the night. The country was searched far and wide, but not a scrap of information could be found. Advertisements were put in all the papers, and I myself have received a letter from a lawyer, a Mr. Briggs, telling me these details. Isn't it an odd story?"

"Just tell me this," I said. "How is Mr. Rochester? Where is he? Is he well?"

"I know nothing about Mr. Rochester. The letter doesn't mention him except to describe his illegal action toward the governess. Don't you want to know the name of the governess and the event that requires that she be found?"

"Did no one go to Thornfield Hall, then? Did no one see Mr. Rochester?"

"I suppose not."

"But they wrote to him?"

"Of course."

"What did his letters say?"

"Mr. Briggs mentions that the answer to his letter was not from Mr. Rochester but from a lady named Alice Fairfax."

I felt cold and dismayed. My worst fears must be true: he had left England and rushed away in reckless desperation. What had happened to him then? Oh, my poor master! My dear Edward!

"He must have been a bad man," St. John said.

"You don't know him. You have no right to judge him," I said angrily.

"Very well," he answered. "Indeed, he is not my main concern here. Since you won't ask the governess's name, I must tell it to you. See, I have it here. It is always more satisfactory to see important facts written down."

He pulled out his wallet and produced a shabby slip of paper. I recognized it as the edge of my piece of scrap paper, which I had filled with idle scribblings. He got up and held it close to my eyes. I saw the words "Jane Eyre" in my own handwriting. "Mr. Briggs wrote to me about a Jane Eyre," he said. "I

knew a Jane Elliott. I confess I had my suspicions, but it was only yesterday afternoon that I realized I was right. You admit that you are Jane Eyre?"

"Yes, yes. But where is Mr. Briggs? Perhaps he knows more about Mr. Rochester than you do."

"Briggs is in London. I doubt that he knows anything about Mr. Rochester. It is not Mr. Rochester he is interested in. You still haven't asked why Mr. Briggs was looking for you."

"Well, what did he want?"

"To tell you that your uncle, Mr. Eyre of Madeira, is dead, that he has left you all of his property, and that you now are rich. That's all."

"I . . . am rich?"

"Yes, you are rich, quite an heiress." I could not speak. "You must prove your identity, of course," St. John continued. "That will be no problem. Then you can take possession of the money. Briggs has the will and the necessary documents."

Reader, it is a fine thing to be lifted in a moment from poverty to wealth—a very fine thing. But it is not a matter that one can comprehend or enjoy all at once. Besides, the words "will" and "heiress" go side by side with the words "death" and "funeral." My uncle, my only relative, was dead. Ever since I had learned of his existence, I had hoped to see him someday. Now I never would. Still, this was good news: independence would be glorious. Yes, that thought swelled my heart.

"You have come out of your trance at last," St. John said. "I thought that you had turned to stone. Perhaps now you will ask how much you are worth."

"How much am I worth?"

"Oh, a trifle! Nothing to speak of. Twenty thousand pounds, I think they say."

"Twenty thousand pounds?" Here was a new stunner. I had thought that he would say four or five thousand. This news actually took my breath away.

St. John, whom I never had heard laugh, laughed now. "Well," he said, "if you had committed a murder, and I had told you that your crime had been discovered, you scarcely could look more horrified."

"It is a large sum. Don't you think that there is a mistake?"

"No mistake at all."

"Perhaps you have read the figures wrong. It might be two thousand."

"It is written in words, not figures: twenty thousand." I felt like a person sitting down, alone, to dinner and finding the table spread for a hundred people. St. John rose and put his cloak on. "If it were not such a wild night," he said, "I would send Hannah down to keep you company. You look too desperately miserable to be left alone. But Hannah could not break through these drifts, so I must leave you to your sorrows. Goodnight!"

He was lifting the latch when a thought occurred to me. "Stop one minute!" I cried.

"Well?"

"Why did Mr. Briggs write to you about me? What made him think you could help him?"

"Oh! I am a clergyman," he said, "and people ask the clergy for help in all sorts of odd things."

"No, that does not satisfy me!" I exclaimed. Indeed, there was something in his hasty reply that made me more curious than ever. "This is a very strange piece of business," I added. "I must know more about it."

"Another time."

"No, tonight! Tonight!" I cried, putting myself between him and the door. He looked rather embarrassed. "You must not go until you have told me everything," I said.

"I would rather not just now."

"You will! You must!"

"I would rather that Diana or Mary informed you."

Of course, these objections only increased my determination, and I told him so.

"But I have told you that I am a hard man," he said, "difficult to persuade."

"And I am a hard woman, impossible to discourage. You see what you have done: the snow from your cloak has melted, streamed onto my floor, and made it like a trampled street. If you hope to ever be forgiven for the crime of ruining a lady's kitchen, tell me what I wish to know."

He gave in. "Well, you must know someday. Your name is Jane Eyre?"

"Of course. I admitted that before."

"You do not know that we share the name? That my full name is St. John Eyre Rivers?"

"No, indeed! I remember seeing the letter E in your initials, but I never asked what it stood for. Surely, . . ." I stopped, overwhelmed by the thoughts rushing upon me. I knew what St. John would say before he said it.

"My mother's name was Eyre," he explained. "She had two brothers. One was a clergyman, who married Miss Jane Reed of Gateshead. The other was a merchant, John Eyre, who lived in Madeira. Mr. Briggs, being Mr. Eyre's lawyer, wrote to us last August to tell us of our uncle's death. He told us that Uncle John had left his property to the orphan daughter of his brother, the clergyman. A few weeks ago Briggs wrote again to say that the heiress could not be found and to ask if we knew anything about her. A name casually scribbled on a slip of paper has enabled me to find her. You know the rest."

Again he tried to go, but I set my back against the door. "Let me have one moment to think," I said. He waited, and at last I went on. "Your mother was my father's sister?"

"Yes."

"My aunt, consequently?"

He nodded.

"My uncle John was your uncle John? You, Diana, and Mary are his sister's children, as I am his brother's child?"

"Exactly."

"You three, then, are my cousins?"

"We are cousins, yes."

I looked at him. It seemed that I had found a brother—one I could be proud of, one I could love. I had found two sisters who already claimed my deepest affection. What a glorious discovery to a lonely orphan! This was wealth indeed, wealth to the heart! I clapped my hands in sudden joy. "Oh, I am glad! I am glad!" I exclaimed.

St. John smiled. "Your priorities surprise me," he said. "You were calm when I told you that you had a fortune; now you are excited about a matter of no importance."

"No importance? It may be of no importance to you. You have sisters and don't care about having a cousin. But I had no one and now have three relatives—or two, if you don't want to be counted! Nothing could make me happier!"

I walked quickly through the room; I stopped, half suffocated by thoughts that rose faster than I could take them in. A delightful idea had occurred to me: I now could help these people who had saved my life. They were under a burden; I could free them. They were scattered; I could reunite them. Were there not four of us? Twenty thousand pounds shared equally would be five thousand each, more than enough. Now the wealth did not weigh on my conscience. It could become a legacy of life, hope, enjoyment. "Write to Diana and Mary tomorrow," I burst out, "and tell them to come home immediately. Diana said that they both would consider themselves rich with a thousand pounds, so with five thousand they will do very well."

"Let me get you a glass of water," St. John said. "You really must calm yourself."

"Nonsense! And what sort of effect will five thousand have on you? Will it keep you in England and persuade you to marry Miss Oliver and to settle down like an ordinary human being?"

"You are raving. The news has been too much for you."

"Mr. Rivers! You will make me angry. I am rational enough. It is you who misunderstand, or pretend to misunderstand."

"Perhaps if you explained yourself a little more fully, I would comprehend better."

"Explain? What is there to explain? Twenty thousand pounds divided equally among our uncle's nephew and three nieces gives five thousand to each. I want you to write to your sisters and tell them of the money that they have inherited."

"You have inherited, you mean."

"Mr. Rivers, I am not brutally selfish, blindly unjust, or fiendishly ungrateful. Whether or not you like it, I am going to have a home and a family. I like Marsh End, and I will live at Marsh End. I love Diana and Mary, and I will attach myself to them for life. It would please and benefit me to have five thousand pounds, but it would burden me to have twenty thousand. Let there be no more discussion about it, but consider it done."

"This is acting on first impulses. You may regret it. You may marry."

"Nonsense! Marry! I don't want to marry and never will marry. I want a brother and two sisters, and I beg you to say that you will be that brother."

"I gladly will be your brother, but I would do the same without any division of the money."

"Thank you. I know that well enough. You'd better go now because if you stay longer, you may irritate me with some fresh argument."

"And the school, Miss Eyre? It must now be shut up, I suppose?"

"No. I will continue teaching until you find a replacement."

He smiled in relief. We shook hands, and he left.

I will not detail how I had to struggle to get my way. My task was long and hard. But when my cousins finally understood that I was utterly determined, they accepted my decision. The papers were drawn up, and St. John, Diana, Mary, and I received equal shares.

Chapter 34

By the time everything was settled, it was near to Christmas. I closed the Morton school for Christmas vacation. When it reopened, a new teacher would be in place. I felt well pleased with the work that I had done there. I felt that the pupils were fond of me and that they had made far more progress than I had hoped when I began my work.

St. John came up to see the sixty students file out at the end of the day. "Hasn't this been rewarding work for you, Jane?" he said. "Doesn't it give you pleasure to know that you have done so much good? Educating the poor would be an excellent way to spend your life, would it not?"

"It would," I said, "but I want to enjoy my own talents as well as encourage them in other people. Please, let me enjoy my holiday without thinking of work. I have plans of my own."

He looked serious. "What plans? What are you going to do now?"

"My plan," I said, "is to attack Marsh End with all my strength, and I want you to let Hannah assist me. Before Diana and Mary arrive, we will clean the house from top to bottom, rubbing it with beeswax, oil, and innumerable cloths until it glitters. I will arrange every chair, table, bed, and carpet with mathematical precision. Lastly, Hannah and I will devote ourselves to beating eggs, sorting raisins, grating spices, mixing Christmas cakes, chopping ingredients for mince pies, and performing other cooking mysteries that someone like you hardly can begin to understand. I intend to have all things in an absolutely perfect state for Diana and Mary before next Thursday. My plan is to give them an unforgettable homecoming and Christmas."

St. John smiled slightly, but he looked dissatisfied. "That is all very well for the present," he said, "but seriously, I trust that when this first flurry of activity is over, you will look higher than such domestic joys and sisterly pleasures."

I looked at him with surprise. "St. John," I said, "I think you are almost wicked to talk so. I plan to be as happy as a queen, and you try to dissatisfy me. What is your point?"

"My point is that God has a bigger and better plan for you and your talents, Jane. Don't throw your energy away on such trivial pursuits. Do you hear, Jane?"

"Yes, just as if you were speaking Greek. I plan to be happy, and I will be happy. Goodbye!"

And happy I was. Hannah and I went to work with all the energy of which I had warned St. John, and we turned the house topsy-turvy. We not only cleaned; I also purchased handsome new carpets and curtains and some carefully selected antique ornaments. When all was finished, I thought that

Marsh End was a model of bright snugness, a comforting retreat from the winter dreariness outside.

Thursday came at last. They were expected about dark, and the fires were burning brightly in anticipation of their arrival. Hannah and I were dressed, and everything was ready. St. John arrived first. He found me in the kitchen, watching the tea cakes bake.

"Are you at last satisfied with your housecleaning?" he asked. I said that I was and, with difficulty, forced him to tour the house. He glanced around without interest and said only that I had made many changes. His silence dampened my spirits. I thought that perhaps he was unhappy about some of the changes to his old home, but when I asked if that was the case, he shook his head. "Not at all," he said. "You have respected every item that might have sentimental value for my sisters or me. In fact, you've put far more effort into all of this than was at all necessary. By the way, can you tell me where to find the book that I was reading when I was here last?"

I showed him the book, and he took it down and began to read. I did not like this. St. John was a good man, but I began to see that he had told the truth when he had said that he was cold and hard. Humanity and life's ordinary joys had no attraction for him. He lived only to work, and he approved only of work in those around him. As I watched him reading, his face still and stern, I realized that he never would make a good husband. It was best, after all, that he and Miss Oliver had not married. Her happiness would not have been important to him. He was right to have chosen a missionary's career.

"They are coming!" Hannah cried, throwing open the parlor door. At the same moment, old Carlo barked joyfully. In came Diana and Mary, and my thoughts were lost in the joy of laughter, hugs, and kisses of welcome. Their brother came out to welcome them, then retreated to his reading. St. John's lack of enthusiasm over my work was more than made up for by his sisters' delight. They loved everything: their rooms' renovation and decoration, the new drapery and fresh carpets, the colorful china vases. They were immensely pleased with it all, and I was happy to know that what I had done had made their return home even more joyous.

It was a sweet evening. The conversation flew thick and fast. The sisters were so talkative that St. John's silence barely was noticeable. Late in the evening there was a tap on the door; a boy stood there, asking St. John to come see his sick mother. Before the boy was done explaining, St. John had his cloak on and was gone. He did not return until midnight, hungry and exhausted but looking happier than when he had set out.

I am afraid that the next week must have tried his patience very much. It was Christmas week, and we spent it in a sort of merry domestic celebration. He went out a great deal on his visits and church business. One morning at breakfast, Diana sadly asked him if his plans for leaving England were unchanged.

"Unchanged and unchangeable," he replied.

"And Rosamond Oliver?" Mary asked.

"Rosamond Oliver," he said, "is about to be married to Mr. Granby, one of the county's richest and most respected young men. Her father told me yesterday."

His sisters looked at each other and at me. We all three looked at him, but he seemed as serene as the summer sky. "This is very sudden," Diana said. "They cannot have known each other long."

"Only two months," he replied. "They met in October at a ball. But when both families desire and approve a match, there is no need for delay."

The first time that I found St. John alone after this conversation, I was tempted to ask if the news had made him sad. But he showed no sign of distress. Besides, I was out of practice in talking openly with him. His manner toward me was cool and reserved, and my frankness froze under such treatment.

As time went on, Diana, Mary, and I resumed our usual habits and studies. While St. John studied Hindustani, the language that he would need to know for his work in India, Mary and I revived our study of German.

One afternoon, the girls had gone out for a walk, but I had begged off because of a cold. St. John and I shared the parlor and were both engrossed in our studies when he spoke to me. "Jane, what are you doing?"

"Learning German."

"I want you to give up German and learn Hindustani."

"Whatever for?"

He explained that as he progressed in his own study of Hindustani, he was forgetting some of the basics he first had learned. If he had a student—me—he would have to go over those basic points again and again and therefore memorize them firmly. He had thought of asking one of his sisters to be his student, but he had observed that I had the most natural talent for foreign languages, so his choice had settled on me. Would I agree to help him? I did not want to learn Hindustani, but because St. John was leaving in only three months, it seemed selfish of me to refuse him this favor. So I agreed.

I found him to be a patient but demanding teacher. He expected me to do a great deal, and when I fulfilled his expectations, he praised me in his restrained way. I came to notice that he was gaining influence over me, influence that was taking away my sense of liberty. I no longer could talk or laugh freely when he was nearby because a tiresome instinct warned me that such behavior was distasteful to him. I was so aware that only serious moods were acceptable to him that in his presence I fell under a sort of freezing spell. I did not like what was happening to me; I often wished that he had continued to ignore me.

One evening at bedtime, he kissed his sisters goodnight (as was his custom) and shook hands with me. Diana, who happened to be in a playful mood, exclaimed, "St. John! You call Jane your third sister, but you don't treat her that way. You should kiss her, too." She pushed me toward him. I was annoyed and confused. While I was distracted with such feelings, St. John bent down and kissed me. After that, he never let an evening go by without including me in the ceremony.

Reader, perhaps you think that I had forgotten Mr. Rochester. Not for a moment. The craving to know what had become of him followed me everywhere; I brooded over the question alone each night. In my correspondence with Mr. Briggs about my uncle's will, I had asked if he knew where Mr. Rochester now was living and if he was well. But, as St. John had guessed, Mr. Briggs knew nothing about him. I then wrote to Mrs. Fairfax asking the same questions. I had felt sure that she would respond, but two months had passed without a word. I wrote again, in case my letter had been lost. But when half a year had passed, my hope died and I felt sad indeed.

One day I arrived at my language lesson in lower spirits than usual. That morning, Hannah had told me that there was a letter for me. I had rushed to read it, certain that it would be the news that I had waited for, but it had been only an unimportant note from Mr. Briggs about business. My disappointment was so great that I wept. I still was weeping when St. John called me to the parlor for our lesson. He expressed no surprise at my emotion, and he did not ask its cause. He said only, "We will wait a few minutes until you are feeling better." I stifled my sobs, wiped my eyes, and muttered something about not being well that morning. We went about our lesson. As we completed it, St. John put away our books and said, "Now, Jane, you will take a walk with me."

"I will call Diana and Mary."

"No. I want only you with me this morning."

It was a fine May morning, sweet with the scent of blooming heather. We walked along the mossy path for some time, and I noticed an abundance of tiny star-like flowers glittering in the grass. "Let's rest here," St. John said, and we sat on some broad rocks overlooking the hills. He took off his hat and stared over the scene, as if trying to memorize it. "Jane, I am leaving in six weeks. I have booked passage on a ship that sails June twentieth."

"God protect you as you do His work," I answered.

"Yes," he said. "That is my glory and joy. I am the servant of a perfect Master. It seems strange to me that everyone does not burn with the wish to join in the same work."

"Everyone does not have your strength or your faith," I answered.

"But some are worthy to do such work and do not realize it," he said. "It is my duty to stir them up, to show them what their gifts are and why those gifts were given to them, to speak God's message in their ear. Jane, come with me to India. Come as my helpmate and fellow laborer."

"Oh, St. John!" I cried. "Don't ask me such a thing!"

But he continued. "God and nature intended you to be a missionary's wife. They have given you mental gifts, not personal charms. You were created for work, not for love. You must be a missionary's wife. I claim you, not for my pleasure but for my Lord's service."

"But I do not understand the missionary life," I protested. "I never have wanted to be a missionary."

"But you are well suited to it, all the same," he answered. "I have watched you ever since we first met. In the village school I found that you could work hard and cheerfully at difficult tasks. Your calm acceptance of the news that you had become rich told me that wealth has no power over you. At my wish, you gave up a study in which you were interested and adopted another because it interested me. You have all the qualities that I seek, Jane. You are docile, hard-working, selfless, faithful, constant, courageous, gentle, and heroic. As my helper among Indian women, you will provide very valuable assistance."

I sat and thought. St. John's idea was not without good points. In leaving England, I would leave a beloved but empty land. I had to learn to live without Mr. Rochester, wherever he was. I truly needed to find another interest in life to replace the one that I had lost. But to go as St. John asked? Impossible! He was asking me to be his wife, but he had no more of a husband's love for me than the rock on which we sat. He prized me as a soldier would prize a good weapon; that is all. If we were unmarried, that would not bother me. But how could I go through the pretense of marriage with such a man? I turned to him. "I am ready to go to India if I may go as a free person."

"I do not understand what you mean," he replied.

"We have called each other adopted brother and sister. Let's continue to do so. It is best if we do not marry."

He shook his head. "If you were my real sister, it would be different. I would take you and remain unmarried. But I am not yet thirty. How would it look to take a girl of nineteen with me? Your common sense will tell you that is impossible."

"But we do not love each other as a man and wife should," I said plainly. "I repeat: I freely agree to go with you as your fellow missionary but not as your wife. I cannot marry you. If that will not do, seek another who is better suited to you."

"But you are what I want," he said, "just what I want. We must marry. There is no other way. After we were married, enough love might follow to satisfy you."

"I scorn your idea of love." The words burst

from me. I rose and stood before him. "I scorn the false marriage you describe, and yes, St. John, I scorn you when you offer it."

"I did not expect to hear such words from you," he said. "I don't think I have said anything that deserves your scorn."

I was touched by his gentle tone. "Forgive me, St. John, but it is your own fault that I have used such words. You have introduced a topic that we never should discuss. The nature of love is something we never will agree on. My dear cousin, abandon your scheme of marriage; forget it."

"No," he said, "I will not forget it. Tomorrow I will leave for Cambridge, where I have friends whom I wish to see before my departure. I will be gone two weeks. Take that time to consider my offer. And do not forget, Jane, that if you reject it, you are rejecting not only me, but God."

As we walked home, I knew from his iron silence how deeply he disapproved of me. That night, after he had kissed his sisters goodnight, he left the room without so much as shaking my hand. I was so hurt by his behavior that tears came to my eyes.

"I see that you and St. John have quarreled, Jane," Diana said. "Go after him. He is wandering about in the hallway, hoping that you will come after him."

I do not have much pride under such circumstances. I always would rather be happy than dignified. So I ran after him. "Goodnight, St. John," I said.

"Goodnight, Jane," he replied calmly.

"Won't you shake hands?" I asked.

He touched my hand so coldly that it was clear there was no forgiveness for me in his heart. There would be no happy scene of reconciliation. With that, he left me.

Chapter 35

St. John did not leave for Cambridge the next day, as he had said he would. He delayed his departure a whole week. During that time he made me feel the full force of his displeasure. Without one hostile act or one scolding word, he made it plain that he was deeply disappointed in me. It was not that he refused to speak to me; he called me each morning, as usual, for our lesson. But he managed to remove from every sentence that he spoke to me any spark of interest or approval. It was as if he had become marble rather than flesh, and his eyes had turned to cold blue stones.

All this was torture to me. I felt that if I were his wife, this good man soon could kill me without drawing a single drop of blood from my veins or receiving the faintest stain on his own conscience. I especially felt this when I tried to make up with him. No regret met my regret. Unlike me, he was experiencing no suffering from our estrangement. Although my tears, more than once, blistered the page over which we studied, they produced no more effect on him than if his heart really had been made of stone. To his sisters, meanwhile, he was kinder than usual, as if to make me feel worse by comparison.

The night before he left home, I happened to see him walking in the garden about sunset. Remembering that this man once had saved my life, I decided to make a last attempt to regain his friendship. I went out and approached him as he stood leaning over the little gate. "St. John, I am unhappy because you still are angry with me. Let's be friends."

"I hope we are friends," he replied coldly.

"No, St. John, we are not friends. You know that."

"Aren't we? For my part, I wish you no ill and all good."

"Must we part in this way, St. John? When you go to India, will you leave me like this, without a single kind word?"

He now turned to face me. "You will not go to India with me, then?"

"You said that I could not unless I married you."

"And you will not marry me? That is still your decision?" he asked coldly.

"No, St. John, I will not marry you."

"Once more, why this refusal?" he asked.

"At first," I answered, "because you did not love me. Now because you almost hate me. If I were able to go as your assistant, I would go."

"I have told you before what an absurd idea it is for a young single woman to accompany a young single man. A female assistant who is not my wife never would suit me. Apparently, you cannot go with me. However, if you are sincere in your offer, I will speak to a married missionary whose wife needs an assistant. You still may be spared the dishonor of breaking your promise to go."

Having never promised to go, I replied, "I am not under the slightest obligation to go to India, especially with strangers. I would have gone with you because I admire you and love you as a brother. But I am convinced that if I went, I would not live long in that climate."

"Ah! You are afraid," he said, curling his lip.

"I am! God did not give me my life so that I could throw it away. To do what you are asking would be equivalent to committing suicide. Furthermore, before I decide to leave England, I must know for certain that I cannot be of greater use here."

"What do you mean?"

"There is no point in trying to explain. There is a question that I must answer before I think of leaving England."

"I know what you are thinking. You still cherish an illegal and Godless connection that you should blush to think about. You are speaking of Mr. Rochester!" It was true. I confessed it by silence. "Are you going to look for Mr. Rochester?"

"I must find out what has become of him."

"All I can do, then," he said, "is remember you in my prayers." He opened the gate, passed through it, and soon was out of sight.

As I re-entered the house, I found Diana standing at the window, looking very thoughtful. She put her hand on my shoulder and examined my face. "Jane," she said, "you are always worried and pale now. Tell me what is going on between you and St. John. Forgive me for being such a spy, but that brother of mine has some peculiar views about you, I am sure. What does it mean? Does he love you, Jane?"

"No, Di, not one bit."

"Then, why does he watch you constantly and get you alone with him so often? Mary and I had both decided that he wanted you to marry him."

"He does. He has asked me to be his wife."

Diana clapped her hands. "That is just what we hoped! And you will marry him, Jane, won't you? And then he will stay in England?"

"Far from that, Diana. His sole reason for proposing to me is to get an assistant for his work in India."

"No! He wants you to go to India?"

"Yes."

"That is madness!" she exclaimed. "You would not survive three months there, I am certain. Don't go! You have not consented, have you, Jane?"

"I have refused to marry him."

"And this displeased him?" she asked.

"Deeply. He never will forgive me, I fear. I offered to go with him as his sister."

"You must not do so, Jane. Think of the work that you would be undertaking. It kills even the strongest people, and you are not strong. With St. John—you know him—there would be no permission to rest, even during the hottest hours. Unfortunately, I have noticed that whatever he asks, you force yourself to do. I am astonished that you found the courage to refuse him. You do not love him, then, Jane?"

"Not as a husband."

"And what makes you say that he does not love you?"

"He admits it. He has explained again and again that it is not a loving wife he wants but an able assistant. Wouldn't it be strange, Di, to be chained for life to a man who saw one only as a useful tool?"

"It is out of the question!"

"And," I continued, "although I feel only sisterly affection for him now, I can imagine that if I became his wife, I might develop a strange, torturing kind of love for him because he is so talented. In that case, I would be even more miserable. He would not want me to love him, and if I showed the feeling, he would make it clear that it was unwelcome. I know he would."

"Yet St. John is a good man," Diana said.

"He is a good and great man, but he forgets the feelings of little people. It is better, therefore, for us to keep out of his way. Here he comes! I will leave you, Diana." I hurried upstairs.

But I was forced to meet St. John again at supper. I was sure that he would ignore me and that he had given up his idea of marriage, but I was soon proven wrong on both points. He spoke to me in his usual polite manner. After dinner he selected as our evening reading the twenty-first chapter of Revelation. It always was pleasant to listen to his fine voice reading from the Bible, and I was moved to hear him describe the vision of the new heaven and earth: how God would come to live with humans, how He would wipe all tears from their eyes, and how there would be no more death, neither sorrow nor crying, nor any more pain, because all these things would have passed away.

But then St. John continued, looking directly at me. "He that triumphs shall inherit all things, and I will be his God, and he shall be my son," St. John read. "But," he went on slowly and distinctly, "the fearful and the unbelieving shall have their part in the lake which burneth with fire and brimstone, which is the second death." I knew which category St. John feared I belonged to.

When our prayers were over, we said goodbye because he was to leave for Cambridge very early in the morning. Once Diana and Mary had kissed him, they left the room—in obedience, I think, to a whispered request from him. I gave him my hand and wished him a pleasant journey.

"Thank you, Jane. As I said, I will return from Cambridge in two weeks. You still have that time to think about my request. Human pride tells me to say no more to you about marriage, but as my Lord was patient and long-suffering, I will be too. I cannot give you up to damnation. Repent while there is time. God give you the strength to make the right decision!" He laid his hand on my head as he said the last words. He was speaking earnestly and mildly, not as a lover to his sweetheart but as a pastor calling to his lost sheep.

I was moved to great respect for St. John, respect so strong that it brought me to a point I had thought I never would reach: I was tempted to stop struggling against him, to let his strong will overpower mine. I stood motionless under St. John's hand. I was losing my power to resist him. What I had said was impossible—my marriage with St. John—suddenly seemed possible. Strong feelings swept through me. It seemed to me as if angels beckoned and God himself called me, telling me that to live in bliss for all eternity, all I had to do was sacrifice everything in this moment.

"Couldn't you decide now?" St. John asked. His voice was gentle, and he drew me to him as gently.

Oh, gentleness! How much stronger it is than force! I could resist St. John's anger, but I grew weak as water under his kindness. Yet I knew all the time that if I gave in now, I would repent later. His nature had not been changed by one hour of prayer; I only was seeing it in its best light. "If I were convinced that it was God's will that I should marry you, I would promise, and accept whatever happened later," I said.

"My prayers have been heard!" St. John

exclaimed. He pressed his hand more firmly on my head, as if he claimed me. He surrounded me with his arm, almost as if he loved me. (I say almost. I knew the difference; I had felt what it is to be truly loved. But, like him, I had now put love out of the question and thought only of duty.) My mind was cloudy, my vision dim. My thoughts came together in a plea to heaven: "Show me. Show me what to do!"

The whole house was still. I believe that everyone was asleep except for St. John and me. The candle was dying out; the room was full of moonlight. My heart beat so fast that I heard its throb. Suddenly it stood still. An inexplicable feeling had passed through me. It was almost as if an electric shock had flowed through my body, wakening all my senses to abnormal alertness.

"What have you heard? What do you see?" St. John asked.

I saw nothing, but I heard a voice cry, "Jane! Jane! Jane!"

"Oh God, what is it?" I gasped. But I knew what it was. It was a much loved, well remembered voice: that of Edward Rochester. It was calling in wild pain and sorrow. "I am coming!" I cried. "Wait for me! I will come!" I ran to the door and looked into the hallway; it was dark. I ran out into the garden; it was empty. "Where are you?" I shouted. The hills sent the echo faintly back: "Where are you?" I listened. The wind sighed in the trees. All was loneliness and midnight hush.

I broke away from St. John, who had followed me and tried to stop me. But it was my time to take control of my fate. I told him to leave me, that I must be alone. He obeyed at once. I went to my room, locked myself in, fell to my knees, and prayed. I prayed in a different way than St. John but in a way that was effective. I seemed to be speaking directly to a mighty spirit, and my soul rushed out in gratitude at His feet. I rose from my prayer full of determination and resolve. Then I lay down, feeling courageous and enlightened, and eagerly awaited daylight.

Chapter 36

I rose with the dawn and busied myself for an hour or two with putting my things in order. Meanwhile, I heard St. John leave his room. He stopped at my door, and I was afraid he would knock, but instead he slipped a piece of paper under the door. It said, "You left me too suddenly last night. If you had stayed a little longer, you would have picked up your cross to follow your Lord. I will expect your final decision when I return in two weeks. Meanwhile, pray that you will not enter into temptation. Your spirit is willing, I believe, but your flesh is weak. I will pray for you hourly. Yours, St. John."

It was June first, but the morning was chilly. Cold rain beat against my window. I heard the front door open and St. John leave. Looking through the window, I saw him pass through the garden and head for Whitcross, where he would meet the coach. "In a few more hours I will follow you in that track, cousin," I thought. "I, too, have a coach to meet at Whitcross. I, too, have someone to see in England before I decide to depart forever."

At breakfast I told Diana and Mary that I was going on a journey and would be absent at least four days.

"Alone, Jane?" they asked.

"Yes. I want to see, or hear news of, a friend whom I have been worried about for some time."

They could have asked questions because I had told them many times that I had no friends or connections in the world except them. But with their usual consideration, they did not insist on more details than I wished to give them.

I left Marsh End at 3 p.m.; soon after four I stood by the sign post at Whitcross, awaiting the coach that would take me toward distant Thornfield. As I saw the coach appear, I realized it was the same one that I had taken a year ago to arrive at this very spot. Only this time I was not forced to part with my entire fortune to pay for my transportation.

It was a thirty-six-hour journey. I had left Whitcross on a Tuesday afternoon. Early on Thursday morning the coach stopped to water the horses at an inn situated amid scenery that seemed familiar to me. "How far from here is Thornfield Hall?" I asked the man tending the horses.

"Just two miles, ma'am, across the fields."

"My journey is over," I thought. I got out of the coach, stored my box at the inn, and began to walk. My heart leaped as I thought that I already was on my master's lands. It fell as a second thought followed: "Your master may be across the English Channel, for all you know. Even if he is at Thornfield Hall, who else is there? His lunatic wife! You have no business bothering with him. Instead, ask the people at the inn. They can answer your questions. Go up to that man, and inquire if Mr. Rochester is at home." The suggestion was sensible, but I could not force myself to act on it. I dreaded hearing a reply that would crush me. I wanted to hold onto my hope as long as possible.

How quickly I walked toward Thornfield! Sometimes I even ran. How I looked forward to catching the first view of the familiar woods! With what joy I welcomed trees that I knew and familiar glimpses of meadow and hill! I was almost there. Another turn would bring me within sight of the beloved house.

But instead of a stately house, I saw a blackened ruin. Death's silence surrounded what had been Thornfield Hall. Walls and chimneys, windows and doors—all lay in ruins. The blackened stone and timbers made it clear that fire had taken the house's life. But how had it begun? What story was behind this disaster? Had life been lost here as well as brick and wood? These were dreadful questions, and there was no one here to answer. As I wandered around the shattered walls, I gathered evidence that the fire had not been recent. Winter snows had drifted through the ruins because grass and wildflowers were growing among drenched piles of rubbish.

I returned to the inn, and the host himself brought my breakfast into the parlor. I asked him to shut the door and sit down because I had some questions to ask. But when he complied, I scarcely knew how to begin. "You know Thornfield Hall, of course?" I managed to say at last.

"Yes, ma'am. I lived there once."

"Did you?" He was a stranger to me.

"I was the late Mr. Rochester's butler," he replied.

The late Mr. Rochester! I seem to have received, with full force, the blow that I had been trying to avoid. "The late!" I gasped. "Is he dead?"

"I mean the father of the present gentleman, Mr. Edward," he explained.

I breathed again. "The present gentleman," he had said. My Edward was alive! "Is Mr. Rochester living at Thornfield Hall now?" I asked, pretending ignorance of the disaster.

"Oh no, ma'am! You must be a stranger in these parts, or you would have heard that Thornfield Hall burned down last autumn. A terrible thing! Such an immense quantity of property was destroyed! Hardly any of the furniture could be saved. The fire broke out in the dead of night, and before the fire engines arrived from Millcote, the building was a mass of flame. It was a terrible spectacle. I witnessed it myself."

"Does anyone know how it started?" I asked.

"They guessed, ma'am. You probably do not know that there was a lady—a lunatic—kept in the house."

"I have heard something of it."

"She was kept in close confinement, ma'am. No one saw her. They knew only by rumor that such a person was at the Hall. Who or what she was no one knew. They said that Mr. Edward had brought her from a foreign land, and some believed that she had been his mistress. But a queer thing happened a year ago, a very queer thing."

I did not want to hear my own story, so I tried to steer him back to the main fact. "And this lady?"

"This lady, ma'am," he answered, "turned out to be Mr. Rochester's wife! The discovery was brought about in the strangest way. There was a young lady, a governess at the Hall, that Mr. Rochester fell in . . ."

"But the fire," I interrupted.

"I'm coming to that, ma'am—that Mr. Edward fell in love with. The servants say that they never saw anybody as much in love as he was. It was hard to understand because she was a little thing, almost like a child. I never saw her myself, but I've heard Leah, the housemaid, tell of her. Leah liked her well enough. Mr. Rochester was about forty, and this governess wasn't even twenty. And, you see, when gentlemen of his age fall in love with young girls, it is often as if they are bewitched. Well, he wanted to marry her!"

"Tell me this part of the story another time," I said. "Was it suspected that this lunatic, Mrs. Rochester, set the fire?"

"You've hit it, ma'am. It's quite certain that she set it. She had a woman named Mrs. Poole to take care of her. Mrs. Poole was an able woman and very trustworthy, but she had one fault: she kept a bottle of gin by her and now and then took a drop too much. You can understand why because she had a hard life. Still, it was dangerous. When Mrs. Poole would be fast asleep after she'd been drinking, the madwoman, who was as cunning as a witch, would take the keys out of her pocket and go roaming about the house, doing any wild mischief that came into her head. They say that she nearly burned her husband in his bed once, but I don't know about that.

"The governess had run away two months before, and although Mr. Rochester sought her as if she were the most precious thing in the world, he never heard a word about her. He grew savage, quite savage, in his disappointment. He wanted only to be alone. So he sent Mrs. Fairfax, the housekeeper, away. Oh, he did it handsomely, giving her a good pension for life. And Miss Adele, a ward he had, was sent off to school. He broke off acquaintance with all the other fine folk, and he shut himself up like a hermit at the Hall."

"What? He did not leave England?"

"Leave England? Bless you, no! He would not leave the house at all except at night, when he walked about the grounds like a ghost, as if he had lost his senses—which, in my opinion, he had. It was a crying shame, ma'am, because you never saw a finer gentleman before that midge of a governess crossed his path. He was not so handsome, but he had a rare courage and a will of his own. I knew him since he was a boy, you see. For my part, I often have wished that this Miss Eyre had sunk in the sea before she came to Thornfield Hall."

"Then, Mr. Rochester was home when the fire broke out?"

"Indeed he was. He went up to the top floor when all was burning above and below and got the servants out of their beds and helped them downstairs. Then he went back to get his mad wife out of her room. And then they called out to him that she was on the roof. She was standing there, waving her arms and shouting until they could hear her a mile away. I saw her and heard her myself. She was a big woman and had long black hair; we could see it streaming against the flames. I saw Mr. Rochester climb through the skylight onto the roof. We heard him call 'Bertha!' We saw him step toward her. And then, ma'am, she yelled and gave a spring, and the next minute she lay smashed on the pavement."

"Dead?"

"Yes, dead as the stones on which her brains and blood were scattered."

"Good God!"

"You may well say so, ma'am. It was frightful!" He shuddered.

"And afterward?" I urged.

"Well, ma'am, afterward the house burned to the ground. There are only some bits of walls standing now."

"Were any other lives lost?"

"No. Perhaps it would have been better if there

had."

"What do you mean?"

"Poor Mr. Edward!" he exclaimed, "Some say it was a judgment on him for keeping his first marriage secret and wanting to take another wife while he had one living, but I pity him."

"You said he was alive!" I exclaimed.

"Yes, yes. He is alive. But many think he would be better off dead."

"Why? How?" My blood was running cold again. "Where is he?" I demanded. "Is he in England?"

"Oh, yes, he's in England. He can't get out of England, I imagine. He's stone blind, you see."

I summoned enough strength to ask what had caused his injury.

"It was his own courage and his kindness, you might say. He wouldn't leave the house until everyone else was out. As he finally came down the staircase, after Mrs. Rochester had flung herself down, there was a great crash. The whole house fell in. He was taken out from under the ruins, alive but badly hurt. A beam had fallen in a way that had partly protected him, but one eye was knocked out, and one hand was so crushed that Dr. Carter had to amputate it at once. The other eye became infected, and he lost the sight of that also. Now he is helpless: blind and crippled."

"Where is he? Where does he live now?"

"At Ferndean, a house on a farm he has, about thirty miles away. It's a very lonely spot."

"Who is with him?"

"Old John and his wife. He would have no one else. He is quite broken, they say."

"Do you have any sort of vehicle?"

"We have a carriage, ma'am, a very handsome carriage."

"Get it ready at once. If your driver can take me to Ferndean before dark, I'll pay both you and him twice your usual fee."

Chapter 37

Ferndean was an ugly old house buried deep in a forest. I had heard Mr. Rochester speak of it occasionally. His father had bought the estate for the sake of the good hunting there. My master would have rented it out, but no one wanted to live in a gloomy house in such a remote location. So it had remained empty and unfurnished except for two or three rooms fitted up for visits during hunting season.

I came to this house just before dark on this chilly evening. It was threatening rain, and the weather made the neighborhood seem even lonelier and more forbidding. There was not another house in sight, nor any other roads or paths. As I stood gazing at the building, it seemed nearly as lifeless as Thornfield now was. But no, there was life; I heard a movement. The narrow front door was opening, and someone was walking out.

A figure came out into the twilight and stood on the step. It was a man without a hat. He stretched out his hand as if to feel whether it was raining. As dim as the light was, I recognized him. It was my master, Edward Fairfax Rochester. I stopped, holding my breath, and stood still to examine him. He stood as tall and straight as ever.

His hair still was raven black. But in his face I saw a change that made me think of a wild beast, tightly chained but dangerous to approach. A caged eagle whose gold-rimmed eyes had been cruelly extinguished might look like this sightless Samson. Reader, do you think that I feared him in his blind ferocity? If you do, you do not know me. Soft hope rose within me that I soon would kiss that stony face, those lips so sternly set. But I would not approach him yet.

He descended the one step and slowly advanced toward the grass. Then he paused, as if he did not know which way to turn. He lifted his hand and opened his eyes wide, gazing blankly toward the sky. He stretched out his hand (the arm, the mutilated one, he kept tightly at his side). He seemed to hope to touch something, in order to gain some idea of what lay around him, but he met only empty air. He gave up the effort, folded his arms, and stood quietly in the rain, which by now was falling hard on his bare head. At this moment John appeared. "Won't you take my arm, sir?" he said. "There is a heavy shower coming. Perhaps we should go in."

"Leave me alone," Mr. Rochester answered.

John returned to the house without seeing me. Mr. Rochester now tried to walk about, but he was not very successful. He groped his way back to the house and entered, closing the door. I went to that same door and knocked. John's wife opened it for me. "Mary," I said, "how are you?" She started as if she had seen a ghost. "Is it really you, Miss, come so late to this lonely place?" she asked. I took her hand and followed her to the kitchen, where John sat by the fire. I briefly explained to them that I had heard everything that had happened and that I had come to see Mr. Rochester. Just at this moment the parlor bell rang.

"When you go in," I said, "tell Mr. Rochester that someone wishes to speak to him, but do not give my name."

"I don't think he will see you," she answered. "He won't see anybody." She returned after a moment, saying, "You are to send in your name and your business." She then proceeded to fill a glass with water and place it on a tray, together with some candles.

"Is that what he rang for?" I asked.

"Yes. He always has candles brought in at dark, although he is blind."

"Give me the tray. I will carry it in," I said. I took it from her. My hands shook as I held the tray, and I spilled the water. Mary opened the door and shut it behind me.

The parlor was gloomy. A neglected handful of fire burned low in the grate. Leaning over it, his head resting against the high, old-fashioned mantelpiece, was Mr. Rochester. Pilot lay to one side, curled up as if afraid of being stepped on. The dog pricked up his ears when I came in, then jumped up with a yelp and a whine and bounded toward me. He almost knocked the tray from my hands. I set it on the table and patted him.

Mr. Rochester turned. "Give me the water, Mary," he said. I approached him with the glass. Pilot followed me, still excited. "What is the matter?" he inquired.

"Down, Pilot!" I said.

Mr. Rochester had begun to lift the water to his lips. He stopped a moment, listening, then drank and put the glass down. "Mary, is that you?"

"Mary is in the kitchen," I answered.

He put out his hand with a quick gesture, but not seeing where I stood, he did not touch me. "Who is this? Who is this?" he demanded. "Answer me! Speak again!"

"Should I get a little more water, sir? I spilled half of what was in the glass," I said.

"Who is it? What is it? Who speaks?"

"Pilot knows me, and John and Mary know that I am here. I came just this evening," I answered.

"Great God! What hallucination has come over me? What sweet madness has seized me?"

"No madness, sir. Your mind is too strong for that."

"And where is the speaker? Is it only a voice? I cannot see, but I must feel, or my heart will stop and my brain will burst. Whoever—whatever—you are, let me touch you, or I cannot live!" He reached forward again. I took his hand and clasped it between my hands. "Her very fingers!" he cried. "Her small, slight fingers! If so, there must be more of her." The muscular hand broke from mine. My arm was seized, my shoulder, neck, waist; I was entwined and gathered to him. "Is it Jane? Is it? This is her shape. This is her size."

"And this is her voice," I added. "She is all here, her heart too. God bless you, sir! I am glad to be so near you again."

"Jane! Jane Eyre," he said.

"My dear master," I answered, "I have found you. I have come back to you."

"In truth? In the flesh? My living Jane?"

"You are touching me, sir. I am not cold like a corpse or vacant like a spirit, am I?"

"My living darling! But it cannot be true after all my misery. It is a dream. I have had such dreams before. In those dreams I have held her as I do now, and kissed her like this, and felt that she loved me, and trusted that she would not leave me."

"And I never will, sir, from this day on."

"So it is you, Jane? You do not lie dead in some ditch? You are not a lonely outcast among strangers?"

"No, sir! I am an independent woman now."

"Independent! What do you mean, Jane?"

"My uncle in Madeira is dead, and he left me five thousand pounds."

"Ah! This is practical; this is real. And your voice, Jane! It cheers my withered heart; it puts life into it. And you are a rich woman?"

"I am, and if you won't let me live with you, I will build a house of my own beside yours, and you may come and sit in my parlor when you want company in the evening."

"But if you are rich, Jane, no doubt you now have friends who will look after you and not let you devote yourself to a sorry blind thing like me."

"I told you that I am independent, sir, as well as rich. I am my own mistress."

"And you will stay with me?"

"Certainly, unless you object. I will be your neighbor, your nurse, your housekeeper. If you are lonely, I will be your companion—to read to you, walk with you, sit with you, wait on you, be your eyes and hands. Do not look so melancholy, my dear master. You will not be left alone as long as I live."

He did not reply. He half opened his lips to speak, then closed them again. I was a little embarrassed. Perhaps I had been too bold. Perhaps he thought that my proposal was improper. I began to gently withdraw myself from his arms, but he eagerly snatched me closer.

"No, no, Jane. You must not go. No. I have touched you, heard you, felt the comfort of your presence. I cannot give up these joys. The world may laugh, may call me absurd and selfish, but that does not matter."

"Well, sir, I will stay with you. I have said so."

"Yes, but you understand one thing by 'staying with me,' and I understand another. You, perhaps, could decide to wait on me as a kind little nurse, and maybe that should be enough for me! Should I have only fatherly feelings for you? Come, tell me what you think."

"You must feel as you like, sir. I am content to be only your nurse if you think that is best."

"But you cannot always be my nurse, Jane. You are young. You might marry one day."

"I don't care about being married."

"You should care, Jane. If I were what I once was, I would try to make you care. But now . . . I am a sightless block!" He looked very gloomy again.

I, on the contrary, became more cheerful. His last words had helped me to understand what the problem was, and because it was no problem for me, I felt quite relieved. I began a livelier conversation.

"It is time that someone turned you back into a human being," I said, parting his thick, uncut hair. "I see that you have been turning into a lion or something of that sort. Your hair reminds me of eagles' feathers. I haven't yet noticed whether your nails have grown into birds' claws."

"On this I have no hand or nails," he said, showing me his mutilated arm. "It is a mere stump, a ghastly sight! Don't you think so, Jane?"

"It is a pity to see it, and a pity to see your eyes and the scar of fire on your forehead. The worst of it is, all this could make someone love you too much."

"I thought you would be revolted, Jane, when you saw my arm and my scarred face."

"Did you? Don't tell me so. I thought you had better judgment. Now, let me leave you an instant, to make a better fire and have the hearth swept up. Can you tell when there is a good fire?"

"Yes. With my right eye I see a glow, a ruddy haze."

"And you see the candles?"

"Very dimly."

"Can you see me?"

"No, my fairy, but I am only too thankful to hear and feel you."

"When do you have supper?"

"I never have supper."

"You will have some tonight. I am hungry. So are you, I imagine, only you forget." I called Mary, and we busied ourselves making the room more cheerful and comfortable. Then I prepared supper.

As we ate, Mr. Rochester began to ask me many questions about where I had been, what I had been doing, and how I had found him. I gave him only partial replies; it was too late to go into details that night. Besides, I did not want to open any very emotional topic yet, but only to cheer him up. But as we talked, he occasionally would grow dark and gloomy again. "I do not know what I feel, Jane," he said. "Should I give myself over to the joy of having you here? Or will you vanish again tomorrow, like the fairy I always thought you might be?"

"Do you have a comb, sir?"

"What for, Jane?"

"To comb out this shaggy black mane. I find you rather alarming when I examine you close at hand. You talk of my being a fairy, but you look more like a werewolf."

"Am I hideous, Jane?"

"Very, sir. You always were, you know."

"Humph! The wickedness has not been taken out of you, wherever you have been."

"Yet I have been with good people, far better than you. They were quite refined and high-minded."

"Who the devil have you been with?"

"If you twist about in that way, you will make me pull the hair out of your head, and then you will know for sure that I am solid flesh."

"Who have you been with, Jane?"

"You will not get it out of me tonight; you

must wait until tomorrow. By leaving my tale half told, you see, I am giving you insurance that I will appear at your breakfast table to finish it. There, sir, you are combed up and made decent. Now I'll leave you. I have been traveling for three days and I am tired. Good night."

"Just one word, Jane. Were there only ladies in the house where you have been?"

I laughed and left the room, still laughing as I ran upstairs. "A good idea!" I thought with glee. "I see I have a way of teasing him out of the dumps for some time to come."

Very early the next morning, I heard him wandering from one room to another. As soon as Mary came down, I heard the questions: "Is Miss Eyre here? Which room did you put her in? Is it dry? Is she up? Go and ask if she wants anything, and when she will come down."

I came down as soon as I thought breakfast might be ready. Entering the room very softly, I saw him before he discovered my presence. It was sad, indeed, to see how that vigorous spirit was subject to physical weakness. He sat in his chair, still but not at rest. Lines of habitual sadness marked his strong features. His face reminded me of a lantern that has been blown out, waiting to be relit. I had meant to be cheerful and carefree, but the sight of this strong man touched my heart to the quick. Still, I spoke to him as brightly as I could. "It is a bright, sunny morning, sir," I said. "The rain is over and gone, and it is a lovely day.

We should go out for a walk." I had awakened the glow; his face beamed.

We spent most of the morning in the open air. I led him out of the wet woods into some cheerful fields. I described to him how brilliantly green they were, how the flowers and hedges looked refreshed after the rain, how sparkling and blue the sky was. I found a seat for him, a dry tree stump, in a hidden and lovely spot. And I did not object when he pulled me onto his lap. Why should I, when he and I both were happier together than apart? Pilot lay beside us, and all was quiet.

While holding me in his arms, he suddenly broke out, "Cruel, cruel deserter! Oh, Jane, what I felt when I discovered that you were gone and when I could not find you! And, after looking through your room, I found that you had taken no money, nor anything that you could sell! A pearl necklace that I had given you lay untouched in its little box. Your boxes were left tied up as in preparation for the honeymoon. What could my darling do, alone and penniless? And what did she do? Let me hear now."

So I began the story of my experiences during the past year. I considerably softened what had happened during my three days of wandering and starvation because it would have hurt him unnecessarily to hear all that had occurred. The little I did say made his faithful heart bleed. He scolded me. He said that I should not have left with so little to help me. I should have confided in him, he said. He never would have forced me to become his mistress. As great as his despair had been, he loved me too well to do me any harm. He would have given me half his fortune without demanding even a kiss in return, rather than have me throw myself friendless into the world.

"Well, whatever my sufferings were, they were very short," I reassured him. Then I proceeded to tell him how I had been taken in at Marsh End and how I had become the schoolteacher there. The story of my inheritance and how I discovered my cousins followed next. Of course, the name of St. John Rivers came up frequently in the progress of my tale. When I had finished, Mr. Rochester immediately recalled me to that name. "This St. John is your cousin, then?"

"Yes."

"You have spoken of him often. Do you like him?"

"He was a very good man, sir. I could not help liking him."

"A good man. Does that mean a respectable man of fifty? What does it mean?"

"St. John was twenty-nine, sir."

"I see. But he is a dull and inactive sort of person?"

"He is untiringly active. He will perform great deeds in this world."

"But his brain—that is probably rather soft. Am I right? He means well, but it is rather painful to hear him speak?"

"He talks little, sir, but what he does say is always to the point. He has a first-rate intelligence."

"Is he an educated man, then?"

"St. John is a fine scholar."

"His manners, I think you said, are not to your taste? He is prim and preacherly?"

"I never mentioned his manners, but they are, in fact, polished and gentlemanlike."

"His appearance, though. I forget what description you gave of his appearance. Sort of a raw country parson, clumsy and half strangled in his necktie?"

"St. John dresses well. He is a handsome man: tall, fair, with blue eyes and a profile like a Greek statue."

Mr. Rochester turned aside. "Damn him!" he muttered. Then he asked me again, "Did you like him, Jane?"

"Yes, Mr. Rochester, I liked him, but you asked me that before." I saw, of course, what was happening, but I did not hurry to do anything about it. The sting of jealousy was chasing the fang of melancholy from Mr. Rochester's heart.

"Perhaps you would rather not sit on my knee any longer, Miss Eyre," he remarked unexpectedly.

"Why not, Mr. Rochester?"

"The picture you just have drawn suggests an overwhelming contrast. You describe very prettily a tall, fair, blue-eyed Greek god. You are looking at a Vulcan, a real blacksmith: dark, broad-shouldered, and blind and lame in the bargain."

"I never thought of it before, but you certainly are like Vulcan, sir."

"Well, you can leave me, ma'am. But before you go" (he held me more tightly than ever), "you will answer a question or two." He paused.

"What questions, Mr. Rochester?"

A cross-examination followed. "St. John made you Morton's schoolmistress before he knew that you were his cousin?"

"Yes."

"You saw him often? He would visit the school sometimes?"

"Daily."

"You had a little cottage near the school, you say. Did he ever come there to see you?"

"Now and then."

"In the evening?"

"Once or twice."

A pause. "How long did you live with him and his sisters after the cousinship was discovered?"

"Five months."

"Did Rivers spend much time with the ladies of his family?"

"Yes. The back parlor was both his study and ours. He sat near the window and we by the table."

"Did he study much?"

"A good deal."

"What?"

"Hindustani."

"And what did you do in the meantime?"

"I learned German, at first."

"Did he teach you?"

"No, his sister did."

"Did he teach you nothing?"

"A little Hindustani."

"Rivers taught you Hindustani?"

"Yes, sir."

"Did you ask to learn?"

"No."

"He wanted to teach you?"

"Yes."

"Why did he wish it? Of what use could Hindustani be to you?"

"He hoped that I would go to India with him."

"Ah! Here I reach the root of the matter. He wanted you to marry him?"

"He asked me to marry him."

"You are making that up to vex me."

"I beg your pardon; it is the literal truth. He asked me more than once."

"Miss Eyre, I repeat it, you can get up. Why do you remain stubbornly perched on my knee when I have given you permission to leave?"

"Because I am comfortable here."

"No, Jane, you are not comfortable there because your heart is not with me; it is with this cousin, this St. John. Oh, until this moment, I thought my little Jane was all mine! I believed that she loved me even when she left me. That was an atom of sweet in the bitter. While I was weeping hot tears over our separation, she was loving another! But it is useless grieving. Jane, leave me. Go and marry Rivers."

"Shake me off, then, sir, because I won't leave you of my own accord."

"But I am not a fool. Go."

"Where must I go, sir?"

"Your own way, with the husband you have chosen."

"Who is that?"

"You know. This St. John Rivers."

"He is not my husband, nor can he ever be. He does not love me, and I do not love him. He wanted to marry me only because he thought that I would make a suitable missionary's wife. He is good and great but severe and, in my view, cold as an iceberg. He is not like you, sir. I am not happy with him. He has no fondness for me. So must I leave you, sir, to go to him?" I shuddered involuntarily and clung closer to my beloved master.

He smiled. "What, Jane? Is this true? Is this really the state of things between you and Rivers?"

"Absolutely, sir! Oh, you need not be jealous! I only wanted to tease you a little to make you less sad. If you could see how much I love you, you would be proud and content. All my heart is yours, sir; it belongs to you. Even if we were parted forever, it would remain with you."

He kissed and held me, but I could see dark thoughts passing over his poor scarred face. I wanted to speak those thoughts, but I did not dare. I saw a tear slide from under his closed eyelid and trickle down his manly cheek. My heart swelled. "I am no better than the old lightning-struck chestnut tree in Thornfield orchard," he said. "What right would that ruin have to ask a budding vine to cover its decay with freshness?"

"You are no ruin, sir—no lightning-struck tree. You are green and vigorous. Plants will grow about your roots, whether you ask them to or not, because they take delight in your shade. As they grow, they will lean toward you and wind around you because your strength offers them a safe prop."

He smiled again. I gave him comfort. "You are speaking of friends, Jane?" he asked.

"Yes," I answered hesitantly. I meant more than friends, but I did not want to say more.

He helped me. "Ah, Jane. But I want a wife."

"Do you, sir?"

"Yes. Is it news to you?"

"Of course. You said nothing about it before."

"Is it unwelcome news?"

"That depends on circumstances, sir—on your choice."

"Make that choice for me, Jane. I will abide by your decision."

"Sir, I think you should choose the woman who loves you best."

"I will at least choose the woman whom I love best. Jane, will you marry me?"

"Yes, sir."

"A poor blind man, whom you will have to lead about by the hand?"

"Yes, sir."

"A crippled man twenty years older than you, whom you will have to wait on?"

"Yes, sir."

"Truly, Jane?"

"Most truly, sir."

"Oh, my darling! God bless you and reward you!"

"Mr. Rochester, if I ever did a good deed in my life—if I ever thought a good thought—I am rewarded now. To be your wife is the greatest happiness that earth can offer me."

"If that is so, we have nothing in the world to wait for. Only the getting of the license. The third day from this must be our wedding day, Jane. Never mind fine clothes and jewels; all that is not worth a penny."

"The sun has dried up all the raindrops, sir. The breeze is still. It is getting quite hot."

"Do you know, Jane, at this moment I have your little pearl necklace wrapped around my watch chain? I have worn it since the day I lost my only treasure, as a reminder of her."

"Let's go home through the woods; that will be the shadiest way."

He pursued his own thoughts without heeding me. "Jane! You think I am an irreligious dog, but my heart swells now with gratitude to God. Lately, Jane, I began to see the hand of God in my life. I began to experience remorse, repentance, and the wish for reconciliation with my Maker. I began to pray sometimes. They were very brief prayers but very sincere. Then a few days ago—it was last Monday night—a strange mood came over me. Grief replaced the frenzy that I had been feeling. I had come to believe that you must be dead. Late that night, probably between eleven and twelve o'clock, I began to pray. I asked God to let me die soon, so that I could go to that world where I might hope to be with you again. I was in my own room and sitting by the open window. Oh, how I wanted you, Jane! I asked God, in anguish and humility, if I had not been tormented long enough. I admitted that I had deserved my torment, but I scarcely could endure more. I pleaded, I prayed, and my heart's wish broke from my lips. I cried out, 'Jane! Jane! Jane!'"

"This was last Monday night, sir, close to midnight?"

"Yes, but what followed is the strange part. You will think that I am mad, but as I called out your name, I heard a voice. It said, 'I am coming! Wait for me!' Somehow I felt more at peace. I believe that we met, somehow, in spirit. No doubt, you were sleeping at that hour. But perhaps your soul came to comfort mine because I knew the voice that I heard, Jane. It was yours!"

Reader, it had been on Monday night, near midnight, that I had heard the mysterious call. Still, I said nothing; words could not explain what had happened.

"Do not be surprised, then," my master continued, "that when you appeared so unexpectedly last night, I had difficulty believing that you were anything more than a voice. Now I thank God!" He put me off his lap and rose to his feet. Lifting his hat from his head, he bent his sightless eyes to the ground and prayed silently. Only his last words were said aloud: "I thank my Maker that, in the midst of judgment, He has remembered mercy. I humbly ask my Redeemer to give me the strength to lead a purer life than I have before!"

Then he stretched his hand out to me. I took that dear hand, held it a moment to my lips, then put it around my shoulder. We entered the woods and walked home together.

Chapter 38

Reader, I married him. We had a quiet wedding, with only the parson and clerk and ourselves present. When we got back from the church, I went into the kitchen, where Mary was cooking dinner and John was cleaning the knives. I said, "Mary, Mr. Rochester and I were married this morning."

The housekeeper and her husband were decent, quiet people. Mary looked up and stared at me. The ladle with which she was basting a pair of chickens hung suspended in air. When she got over her astonishment, she said only, "Have you, Miss? Well, for sure!" John grinned from ear to ear. "I told Mary how it would be," he said. "I knowed what Mr. Edward would do, and I was certain he wouldn't wait long, neither. He's done right, for all I know. I wish you joy, Miss!"

"Thank you, John. Mr. Rochester told me to give you and Mary this." I put a five-pound note into his hand. Without waiting to hear more, I left the kitchen. In passing the door some time later, I caught these words: "She'll do better for him than any of them grand ladies. If she ain't one of the handsomest, she's got good sense, and she's very good-natured. And to him she's beautiful. Anyone can see that."

I immediately wrote to Marsh End and to Cambridge, to say what I had done. Diana and Mary gave me their instant approval, and Diana announced that after the honeymoon, she would come and see me.

"She'd better not wait until then, Jane," Mr. Rochester said when I read her letter to him. "If she does, she will wait forever because our honeymoon will shine our whole life long."

I don't know how St. John responded to the news. He never answered my letter. But six months later he wrote to me without mentioning Mr. Rochester or my marriage. He has written occasionally ever since. He says he hopes that I am happy and trusts that I am not among those who live without God and who care only for earthly things.

You have not forgotten little Adele, have you, reader? I had not. I soon went to see her at the school in which Edward had placed her. Her frantic joy at seeing me moved me very much. She looked pale, thin, and unhappy. I found that the school was too strict and severe for a child of her age, and I took her home with me. I intended to become her governess again, but I soon found that this was not practical. My husband required all my time and care. So I found a school run by kind and indulgent teachers, near enough that I could visit her often and sometimes bring her home. She became very happy and made good progress in her studies. When she left school, she had become a pleasant and good-tempered companion. By her grateful attention to me and mine, she has well repaid any little kindness that I ever was able to offer her.

My tale draws to its close. I will leave you with a word about my married life and the fortunes of those whom I frequently have mentioned here.

I have now been married ten years. I know what it is to live for and with what I love best on earth. I am supremely blessed—blessed beyond what language can express—because I am my husband's life and he is mine. I never grow tired of my Edward's company, nor he of mine. When we are together, we are as easy as when each of us is alone. The two of us are as cheerful at home together as we are in company.

Mr. Rochester was blind the first two years of our marriage. Perhaps it was his blindness that made us so close because I was his vision and his right hand. He saw nature and books through me. I never wearied of reading to him or guiding him where he wanted to go. And there was a pleasure in my service because he claimed it without shame or humiliation. He knew that I loved him so deeply that to help him was to indulge my sweetest wishes.

One morning at the end of the two years, as I was writing a letter from his dictation, he said, "Jane, do you have something shiny around your neck?"

It was a gold chain. I answered, "Yes."

"And are you wearing a pale blue dress?" I was.

He told me that for some time he had thought that the vision in his remaining eye was becoming clearer, and that now he was sure of it.

He and I went up to London to see a well-known eye doctor, and he eventually recovered much of his sight. He cannot read or write for very long, but he can find his way without being led by the hand. When his firstborn child was put into his arms, he could see that the boy had inherited his own eyes: large, brilliant, and black.

My Edward and I, then, are happy, and our happiness is greatest because those we love best are happy too. Diana and Mary both are married. They often come to see us, and we go to see them. Diana's husband is a navy captain, a gallant officer and a good man. Mary's is a clergyman, a college friend of St. John. Both Captain Fitzjames and Mr. Wharton love their wives and are loved by them.

As for St. John, he left England, went to India, and is still there. There never was a more determined, tireless missionary. St. John is unmarried. He never will marry now because his life is drawing to a close. The last letter that I received from him drew tears to my eyes yet filled my heart with joy. He told me that in his coming death, he anticipated his heavenly reward. I know that a stranger's hand will write to me next, to say that the good and faithful servant has been called home to his Maker. Why should I weep about this? No fear of death will darken St. John's last hour. His hope is sure, his faith steadfast. His own words told me so. "My

Master has forewarned me," he wrote. "Daily He tells me more clearly, 'I am coming soon!' Hourly I more eagerly respond, 'Amen. Come quickly, Lord Jesus!'"

AFTERWORD

ABOUT THE AUTHOR

In the novel *Jane Eyre*, Jane is a woman who hides a proud, passionate nature beneath her plain, childlike exterior. At one point, looking in the mirror, Jane says, "I sometimes felt sorry that I was not better-looking. I wished I had rosy cheeks, a straight nose, and small cherry mouth. It seemed a misfortune to me that I was so little, so pale, and so plain-looking."

Charlotte Bronte herself was only four feet nine inches tall, and as slender as a child. People who knew her always described her as "little," "pale," and "plain." Although *Jane Eyre* is a work of fiction, Jane's physical appearance is only one of many ways in which the novel reflects the real life of its author. People and places that Charlotte knew; events in her life; and, most of all, her fantasies of a happier future are all present in *Jane Eyre*.

First, some background. Charlotte Bronte was born in 1816 in Yorkshire, England. She was the third of six children: Maria, Elizabeth, Charlotte, Branwell, Emily, and Anne. Their father was a pastor. The Bronte family home was a chilly stone parsonage overlooking Mr. Bronte's church, and the local cemetery and its tombstones actually spread across their front yard. The Yorkshire moors (which is rocky, hilly, infertile land) surrounded the parsonage, giving the area a wild, lonely feel. Surely these dreary surroundings influenced the writing Charlotte would do one day.

Life was not very cheerful for the Bronte children. Their mother was always in poor health, and she died when Charlotte was only five. An aunt moved in with the family to help care for the children, but the six were mostly alone together. They spent hours wandering over the moors, and in the evenings Maria, the oldest, would read to the others and teach them as much as she could. Without much else to amuse them, the children began to create detailed imaginary worlds. Sometimes their arguments about these fantasy worlds would become so intense that their father would forbid them to discuss them any more.

Three years after their mother's death, Mr. Bronte sent the four oldest girls away to Cowan Bridge School, a boarding school for the daughters of poor ministers. The food, clothing, and general hygiene at Cowan Bridge were very poor, and after only six months, Maria and Elizabeth became ill and returned home to die of consumption (what we now call tuberculosis). Charlotte and Emily came home as well. Charlotte would later recall the experience in *Jane Eyre* when she wrote about the horrors of Lowood Institution and the death of Helen Burns.

Having lost their mother and two oldest sisters, the four remaining children—Charlotte, Branwell, Emily, and Anne—became extremely close. They plunged back into their imaginary worlds and began to write long stories, plays, and poems about them.

They studied and read on their own, but their father worried that they would not be able to support themselves when he was gone. As a result, he sent Charlotte away to school again when she was 15. Fortunately, this school, called Roe Head, was much different than Cowan Bridge. It had only eight or nine pupils, and the director, Mrs. Wooler, treated the girls more like her own family than like students. Although Charlotte's education so far had been rather hit and miss, Mrs. Wooler recognized her intelligence and quickly helped her catch up to the other students. It isn't hard to imagine that Mrs. Wooler may have been the model for Miss Temple in *Jane Eyre*. Like Jane at Lowood, Charlotte was invited to become a teacher at Roe's Head after she finished her studies. Her little sister Emily joined her there as a student, but she became so homesick that she had to leave. Charlotte wrote later that "my sister Emily loved the moors . . . She found in the bleak solitude many and dear delights. . . . I felt in my heart she would die, if she did not go home."

After a short time at Roe's Head, Mrs. Wooler recommended Charlotte for a job as a governess in a wealthy family's home. From Charlotte's letter to a friend, it is clear that although both she and Jane Eyre worked in fine English homes, the real woman and the fictional one had very different experiences:

> I have striven to be pleased with my new situation. The country, the house and the grounds are, as I have said, divine. But alack-a-day, there is such a thing as seeing all beautiful around you—pleasant woods,

white path, green lawns, and blue sunshiny sky—and
not having a free moment or a free thought left to
enjoy them. The children are constantly with me. As
for correcting them, I quickly found that was out of
the question; they are to do as they like. A complaint
to the mother only brings black looks on myself. . . .
I said in my last letter that Mrs. _____ did not know
me. I now begin to find that she does not intend to
know me; that she cares nothing about me, except to
contrive how the greatest possible quantity of labor
may be got out of me. . . . I see more clearly than I
have ever done before that a private governess has no
existence, is not considered a living rational being,
except as connected with the wearisome duties she
has to fulfill."

Charlotte soon left her unhappy position and
went back home to the parsonage. There, she,
Emily, and Anne—like the Rivers sisters in *Jane
Eyre*—faced the fact that they would soon be forced
to support themselves. Their father was getting elderly, and they could not depend on their brother
Branwell for any help, although he was as brilliant
as any of them. He had begun to drink heavily and
use opium, a highly addictive narcotic. After writing for pleasure for many years, the three sisters
began thinking about trying to earn a living that
way. In fact, Charlotte wrote to a well-known poet
of the time, asking his advice about a writing
career, but his answer was discouraging. He wrote:
"Literature cannot be the business of a woman's
life, and it ought not to be. The more she is

engaged in her proper duties, the less leisure she will have for it, even as an accomplishment and a recreation."

A woman's "proper duties," of course, meant taking care of a husband and children. Charlotte had received several proposals of marriage, but she had turned them down, telling her friends she would rather not marry than marry a man she did not love dearly. She had started her first novel, called *The Professor*, but the poet's advice depressed her, and she stopped work on it to accept another job as a governess. This job was much more pleasant for Charlotte—in fact, perhaps a little too pleasant. She wrote to a friend, "I like Mr. _____ (the master of the house) extremely." Not long after that, her mistress asked her to leave. Nothing like the Jane-Mr. Rochester romance had occurred, but a spark had been lit in Charlotte's heart—a spark that would later grow into a great, if fictional, love story.

As being a governess didn't seem to suit Charlotte, she and Emily enrolled in a school in Brussels, Belgium, to improve their French. Charlotte returned home in January 1844 intending to open a school, but she found that her father was losing his sight. She decided to devote herself to writing while she cared for him. She and her sisters put together a book of their poetry, which they successfully published under three men's names: Currer, Ellis, and Acton Bell. The book didn't sell very well, but the good reviews it received encouraged them, and Charlotte soon began work on her most famous novel. *Jane Eyre* was a combination of her own experience and a bit of gossip she had heard in Brussels, about a writer who kept his insane wife locked in the attic. In 1847, *Jane Eyre* was published under the name Currer Bell. The following year, little sister Emily published *Wuthering Heights*, a novel set in the moors she had been so homesick for when she went away to school. And in a few months, Anne Bronte published a third novel, *Agnes Grey*. Emily and Anne, like Charlotte, published their books under men's names.

All three books were well received, but *Jane Eyre* was the most successful of them all. Rumors began flying that "Currer, Ellis, and Acton Bell" were really just one man. Charlotte decided to set the record straight, and she and her two sisters traveled to London to meet her publisher (who, like everyone else, believed she was a man). He was astonished to meet the women, and the news soon spread that the Bronte sisters were the real authors of the popular new novels.

Charlotte stayed on for a while in London, where she was something of a celebrity. She enjoyed herself, but this happy time of life was brief. Back at the parsonage, Branwell was breaking down as the result of his alcoholism and drug addiction, and Emily, too, was ill. Charlotte returned home to be with her siblings, and in September, Branwell died. The following December, Emily died as well. Almost unbelievably, Anne fell ill a few weeks later, and her death came in May.

Devastated by the deaths of her siblings, Charlotte stayed on in the parsonage with her blind father for five more years, writing and making occasional trips to London to enjoy the company of other writers. In 1854 she married her father's assistant, Arthur Nicholls, although it is clear she did not love him. She died of complications of pregnancy the following year. She was only 39.

There is more than a little sad irony in reading the end of *Jane Eyre*, the story of the governess whose life parallels Charlotte Bronte's in so many ways. At the novel's close, Jane is well-off, independent, and blissfully happy in her marriage. She says:

> "I have now been married ten years. I know what it is to live for and with what I love best on earth. I am supremely blessed—blessed beyond what language can express—because I am my husband's life and he is mine. . . . My Edward and I, then, are happy, and our happiness is greatest because those we love best are happy too."

It was not Charlotte's fate, or the fate of those she loved best, to be "supremely blessed" with happiness here on earth. We can only hope that it made Charlotte happy to create Jane—a heroine who was so much like herself, who did achieve such joy, and who has brought so much pleasure to millions of readers.

ABOUT THE BOOK

Jane Eyre was published in 1847 and was an immediate success. Sometimes books that are very popular when they are new don't age well, and they are soon forgotten. But this is not the case with *Jane Eyre*. Many modern readers list it among their favorite novels, and there have been at least eleven film versions made of the story. The two leading characters in the novel—a poor, plain, but courageous young woman, and a brooding, mysterious, passionate older man—capture the reader's imagination today as much as they did in the mid-19th century.

After so many years of being read, loved, and discussed, *Jane Eyre* has been analyzed in dozens of different ways. People have studied it as a feminist novel, looking at the ways in which independent Jane defies a society that says women should be quiet, passive, and obedient. Other critics have considered the character of Mr. Rochester's first wife, Bertha, locked up like an animal in her third-story room. What was Charlotte Bronte saying, they ask, about how society treats rebellious women? Still more readers have enjoyed looking for important symbols in *Jane Eyre*. They ask questions like these: What did it mean when the horse-chestnut tree was struck by lightning after Mr. Rochester's first proposal to Jane? Why are there so many references to fire and warmth, and an equal number to their opposite: cold, snow, ice, and frost? What does the red room symbolize to Jane?

Charlotte Bronte provided one very convenient way to analyze *Jane Eyre* when she made the book take place in five different locations. You might almost think of the novel as a five-act play. As Jane moves from Gateshead on to Lowood, later to Thornfield and Marsh End, and finally to Ferndean, she is passing through five important stages of development. It's as though each location holds a lesson she must learn before she can move into the next stage of her life.

At Gateshead, where the novel opens, young Jane learns to think of herself as an outsider, but a proud one. Her Aunt Reed and her cousin John are horrible to her. They frequently remind her that because she is a poor, dependent orphan, she is inferior to them. But Jane does not accept the Reeds' opinion of her. Deep down, she knows that she is morally and intellectually better than they are. In the memorable scene where she turns on Mrs. Reed, she tells her, "People think you a good woman, but you are bad, hard-hearted. You are the liar here!" Jane goes on to comment, "As I spoke these words, I suddenly felt the strongest sense of freedom and triumph that I had ever experienced. It was as if invisible chains around me had broken." Jane may be poor and powerless, but her experience at Gateshead has taught her that she has great inner worth. All the "upper-class" people in the world cannot take that away

Jane spends the next eight years of her life at Lowood Institution. There she begins to develop her own view of religion, after she is exposed to two very different types of Christianity. One type is demonstrated by Mr. Brocklehurst, the director of the school. Mr. Brocklehurst constantly talks about the Bible, makes the girls listen to long sermons, and frightens everyone with stories about bad children going to hell. He thinks of himself as a very religious man. But Jane sees that there is no love or kindness in Mr. Brocklehurst. In fact, he is a hypocrite. While he preaches to the girls about modesty and simplicity, his own family lives in luxury. When an epidemic hits the school, he stays far away instead of trying to help the students. But Jane also meets Helen Burns at Lowood. Helen believes in a God of kindness and love. Her faith is so strong that it enables her to forgive the wrongdoers around her. Although Jane is too headstrong and lively to ever suffer quietly as Helen does, she admires her friend very much. Helen's example makes Jane want to be a better person. Among other things, it makes her able to forgive Aunt Reed later in her life.

At Thornfield, Jane finds what feels like her first real home. Mrs. Fairfax and Adele love and value her, and the rest of the household staff respect her. Her sense of contentment and self-respect blooms. As she and Mr. Rochester fall in love, however, she is hit with a whirlwind of troubling thoughts and feelings. Their social inequality

is a real problem for Jane. She makes this clear when she says to Rochester, "If God had given me beauty and wealth, I would make it as hard for you to leave me, as it is now for me to leave you. . . . It is my spirit that speaks to your spirit, just as if we had both passed through the grave, and stood at God's feet as equals—as we are equal!" In the heat of passion, Rochester agrees that he and Jane are equals. But as they both know, society does not see them that way. Jane worries about what will happen after their marriage. Will Rochester regret marrying his governess? Will he be embarrassed by her? After the honeymoon, will he suggest (as gossipy neighbors certainly will) that she married him for his money? Jane cannot bear any of these thoughts. So she spends the weeks of their engagement making sure that he understands her independent, argumentative nature. She refuses to give up her duties with Adele; she rejects his offers of jewels and fine clothes; she argues with him and challenges him on every point. She forces Rochester to see her as she sees herself: a warm, loving, but strong-willed and opinionated woman. After their disastrous interrupted wedding, Rochester asks her to be his mistress. Jane desperately wants to stay with the man she loves, but her principles won't allow her to say yes. Instead of risking giving in to temptation, she runs away from Thornfield, the place where she has learned the value of her own self-respect.

When Jane arrives at Marsh End, she finds a temptation that is, in a sense, the opposite of the

one she resisted at Thornfield. Rochester had offered her romantic love, but without principle. St. John Rivers offers her a cold, passionless marriage, but one in which she could satisfy her principles by serving God and her fellow man. Although Jane seriously considers St. John's proposal, she realizes that her lively, passionate nature would make marriage with him a terrible mistake. As she says "I felt how if I were his wife, this good man could soon kill me, without drawing from my veins a single drop of blood or receiving the faintest stain on his own conscience." By rejecting St. John, Jane chooses life, even if it must be a life without Mr. Rochester.

At Ferndean, the lessons of Jane's life come together and bear fruit. By being true to her principles, retaining her religious faith, not betraying her self-respect, and honoring her inner nature, she is finally able to join Mr. Rochester in a genuine, loving marriage of equals. She describes their marriage in ideal terms:

I am supremely blessed—blessed beyond what language can express—because I am my husband's life and he is mine. I never grow tired of my Edward's company, nor he of mine. When we are together, we are as easy as when each of us is alone. The two of us are as cheerful at home together as we are in company.

And after all Jane and Rochester have gone through to be together, what reader *isn't* happy for them?